Silence In Numbers: FILE ONE

By Jake Taylor

This is a work of fiction. Names, characters, places and incidents are either the product of the author's imagination or are used fictitiously, and any resemblance to actual persons, living or dead, business establishments, events or locales, is entirely coincidental.

Silence In Numbers: File One

Copyright 2013 by Jake Taylor

This book is dedicated to my sister, Kelsey, without whom I wouldn't have the love of fiction that pushed me to write in the first place; to my parents, Randy and Susan, whose support and encouragement of my writing has always been above and beyond anything that could be expected of normal human beings; to my friends Jon and Daniel, who helped turn my love of writing into an obsession; and to that one kid in the 6th grade who said I'd never be good at anything (suck it, Jason).

A Note to the Reader

You might see some things in this book that are familiar to you. You might say this isn't the Great American Novel or an astounding work of literary genius that changes the way you think or a brilliant example of an esoteric form of writing.

I never wanted to write any of those things. What I have always wanted to write about are characters - people. If, after you finish this, you remember any of the characters in years afterwards, if one of them becomes a favorite, if one feels like a friend, or if you're sad to see one go, then I've accomplished what I set out to do. I put everything into making these characters real, giving them their own personalities, and letting them tell their own stories - it doesn't really feel like I've written this book, to be honest. I just watched them; the book is only here so I can tell you what they did.

So, focus on the people, as I do. I hope you enjoy reading it half as much as I enjoyed writing it. You can visit my blog at www.theseventhshadow.com for info on other works.

Oh, yeah, and buy the sequel when it's out, too. What? Honest emotion doesn't pay my rent, man.

Table of Contents

Prologue

Date: March 20, 2068
Time: 11:37 PM
Location: Sapporo, Japan
Operation: Ghostcrawler

"Get away! Get away!"

"What is that thing?!"

"Unit 42 is gone! They're just gone!"

"Pull back! We can't – aaagh!"

Police officers and civilians both scattered in the wake of an attack by a huge beast the likes of which they'd never seen. The thing had black skin that seemed impervious to their bullets, four long clawed reptilian arms that were tearing people and buildings apart, and a long neck ending in an eyeless head with huge jaws. It was five stories tall and carving a swath of destruction through the city block.

They'd set up a blockade on a suspension bridge hoping to stop the demon's path of destruction, but they weren't going to hold out long. The police had no idea what they were dealing with. Anyone close was torn apart while those out of reach of the arms found themselves scrambling for cover from the acid-like saliva the monster spit out at them, melting metal and bone alike.

A captain stood nearby calling for an evacuation and assistance in a panic. "Nothing we do phases this thing! What the hell is it?! Get a military group out here, we need better hardware! We're getting slaughtered!" He watched in fear as the beast came closer. Monsters didn't exist, but how could he deny what was in front of his eyes? His radio hung loosely from his hand as he gave up calling in. He couldn't imagine any assistance that could come help them with this.

~ ~ ~ ~ ~

"SIN 2, you're clear to enter Zone 1."

"About time!" A man with ragged brown hair, shades rather than goggles and an inappropriately casual Hawaiian shirt pulled on the throttle of the hyper-advanced black helicopter he was piloting, soaring between skyscrapers towards the location on his Heads-Up Display. "You hear that, Captain? We're going in!"

Behind him sat a woman looking out the open side of the helicopter. Cigarette smoke surrounded her, lit faintly by the embers on the end of the small white cylinder. Purple-painted lips held the object carelessly as, a few inches higher, lavender colored eyes scanned the city calmly. Delicate fingers lifted to brush violet curls of hair from one of her eyes as she turned to regard the man. "Understood, Reno. Take us in high and give me a good spot."

Reno gave her a thumbs-up and her attention went to the rifle at her side, longer than the average human was tall. Her hand re-checked it out of practice, loading the chamber and switching off the safety in instinctual movements. She lifted one hand to her ear. "Sano, we're heading for a rooftop view. Take the low road and get the civvies out of there."

"Yes, sir. On it already."

~ ~ ~ ~ ~

"Get away from the bank, it's collapsing!" The police captain was shouting orders into his radio as if it would help, but truth be told he didn't know what else do to. The creature picked up one of his men and tore the man in half, flinging the pieces at others. It was chaos, violent chaos.

He blinked in surprise as black-clad soldiers rushed past him, setting up a line and lifting strange rifles. The captain jumped as a hand fell on his shoulder, turning to see a younger man with spiked back crimson hair, brown eyes and handsome features. The man was wearing a suit as casually as one could be worn, with the jacket open, no tie and the top couple buttons of his white shirt undone.

"We'll take it from here." He walked past the officer, moving towards the black-armored soldiers. "Fire!"

"Who are you people?!" The officer yelled. "You don't have jurisdiction here! I can't just let anyone-"

He was cut off by the high-pitched whine that emitted from all the soldiers' rifles as they unleashed what looked like blue tracer rounds. The monster roared, turning its attention to them. The red-haired man looked back and pointed behind the officer. "Get your men and the civilians out of the area! You can't do anything more here!" He turned back and drew a large pistol with blue-lit lines on it, firing at the creature.

The officer decided to take the advice, calling on his radio for his men to pull out and evacuate the block.

Kurasano made sure the officer was following his directions before putting a hand to his ear. "Captain? I've got a little issue here," he said as he watched the beast roar in pain and make its way towards them.

A woman's voice replied in his ear after a few seconds, "What's the problem, Sano? You can't take a Class-C by yourself?"

Sano ordered his men to back up, walking backwards himself. "Well I mean, I could, but then you'd feel left out."

"You're so sweet."

Sano grinned. "What are friends for?"

~ ~ ~ ~ ~

Up above the city, Katsumi Samakura stretched out, having been sitting in the same position for far too long. She slung her rifle over her shoulder and stepped up to the edge, looking down on the fires and chaos caused by the creature in the center. She stepped out and dropped through the air; wind rushed past her and whipped her shoulder-length violet curls across her face and neck.

She flipped at the last second and hit the roof of a building with a crack, landing on her feet in a run to the edge of the rooftop. She dropped to a prone position and set her rifle on the edge, getting a view on the chaos below. A small whine emitted from her left eye as a targeting reticule appeared only to her in front of her iris, scanning the street below and giving her angles and distance estimations.

Her vision zoomed in on the beast before she switched it off and put her eye to the scope of her rifle, taking aim as her finger rested on the trigger. She fired and the shot rang out over the city, the rifle kicking back viciously as a blue shot streaked down through the air and through the creature. It roared in pain as the bullet went clear through, putting a hole at the base of its neck on both sides.

Katsumi began reloading as the creature turned its attention to her, leaping onto the side of the skyscraper she was on and climbing quickly. Sano's voice flared up in her ear. "Looks like you've got a guest, Captain Sama."

"Yes, but I can take a demon myself."

"Fine, so you're better than me."

"Don't forget it." Katsumi stood and stepped up to the edge, firing straight down. This shot went through the demon's head and its entire body, eliciting another roar, but it kept climbing, shaking the building as it did. Katsumi growled and steadied her footing. "Reno, I'm gonna need a pick-up in twenty-four seconds."

"I'll be there."

"Hurry."

"Patience is a virtue, Captain Sama."

"Spare me the platitudes and get over here Reno."

"Fine, fine. On my way."

Katsumi fired again and this time the demon responded by unleashing acidic spit in her direction. She dodged to the side but the demon was doing more than that, shaking the building and smashing his head inside to spit on the supports. The building's integrity was rapidly dropping, and it wouldn't be standing for much longer. "Reno…"

"Almost there."

The demon was closer now, only a couple stories below the roof, and the groaning of the building's metal supports was louder.

"Reno!"

"Can't make it go faster by yelling!"

The creature reached the roof and opened its jaws, forming a warped ball of acid and flame in its mouth that increased in size before it shot towards her. She sprinted a few steps and dived out of the way of the explosion, cursing as her cigarettes fell from her pocket during her roll. She wisely decided to leave them to the expanding wave of fire and leapt from the roof of the building, spinning in midair and firing a final shot that caught the creature in the middle of the chest.

The special round burned through its center and the demon gave an odd sound, staggering back and forth before falling and crashing through the roof into the floor below. The impact was enough to start the building's collapse.

Katsumi slung her rifle onto her back and turned to face down, falling faster every second. The chopper suddenly caught up to her mid-fall and she spun, catching the edge of the open doorway and pulling herself in as the chopper pulled out of the dive. Reno looked back and waved at her. "Told you I'd pick you up. You worry too much."

Samakura pushed herself up and turned to sit with her legs out the side. "I hate you, Reno."

"I just saved your ass. You should be kissing my feet! Or just kissing me."

Captain Sama tilted her head. "You know, maybe it's time to throw you out the side of this thing and invest in an AI to pilot this for me…"

Reno waved his hand. "Shutting up now."

"You sure? We're high up enough you probably wouldn't even feel anything on impact."

"You don't know that."

"I don't care either, as long as hitting the pavement shuts you up."

"So violent…"

~ ~ ~ ~ ~

"Hey, Captain?" Sano was looking upwards, staring at the building that was starting to collapse. "It wasn't very nice of you to drop a building on me…"

Samakura's reply came back promptly, which he was glad to hear since she'd been on top of that building. "It's not my fault you couldn't bring it down yourself."

"I'm going to blame you anyway." Sano backed up, looking around. He was the only one left on the bridge. "You could at least give me an exit strategy. Do you have a lock on my location?"

"Don't I always? Why don't you just jump off the bridge?"

"If you want me dead just say it, Captain," Sano grinned, looking back to the building as metal snapped and collapsed in on itself.

"Just trust me. Leap of Faith."

"Indiana Jones style?"

"You have a choice?"

Sano dodged as a huge piece of concrete slammed into the ground near him. "Nope." He turned and dashed for the edge of the bridge, dodging debris and leaping over the edge as the building collapsed onto the area behind him. There were a few seconds of weightlessness before gravity took over to drag him towards the coast below. Fortunately, he only fell a few meters before a strong grip caught his wrist.

He looked up to see Samakura hanging out the edge of their chopper, smiling at him. "Nice exit. Next time try not to be so clumsy."

"Conversations are better inside helicopters than hanging from them, Captain!"

She laughed and pulled him up as Reno looked back at them. "Careful, she's threatening to throw people out of this thing."

"Again?" Sano brushed some bits of debris from his hair before sitting down with a relieved sigh.

"Yep, she must be PM-"

"If you finish that sentence I'll feed you feet first through the rotor blades, Reno."

"Yes, ma'am, sorry, ma'am."

Sano shook his head. "Learn to keep your mouth shut, man."

Captain Samakura glanced at Sano as she pulled the chopper's door closed. "You don't look too bad in a suit, Sano. Maybe you should wear them more often."

"Huh?" He glanced down at himself and then nodded in agreement. "Yeah, it's not too shabby. Thanks." He looked back up, automatically returning the compliment. "And your outfit looks…" He paused because, while his commander's attractive features - especially her curly light-violet back-length hair and lavender eyes - were easy to compliment, the skin-tight gray-and-black combat outfit currently wrapped around her form was probably not the most appropriate thing to comment on. "Uh…"

Reno snickered. "Now who's the one with his foot in his mouth?"

Samakura rolled her eyes, taking one of the seats. "Focus on flying us back to headquarters."

"Right, victory flight commencing."

Chapter 1: Silence

From: H.
To: R.
Subject: Monthly Global Status Update
Date: March 21, 2068
Current Global Status:

NATIONAL: Nations continue to merge and combine, losing individual definition but gaining stability (stagnation?). African Unification Project moving forward but slowed by terrorist activities.

MILITARY: National militaries continuing to be dissolved. Private Corporation Militaries continue to grow in demand, size and power. Forces including Police, Security, Military, Special Task Force, Intelligence, and Counter-Terrorism are now 83% privately owned corporations. Remaining 17% national forces expected to decline to less than 1% in the next decade.

TOP SECRET: Supernatural Invasion Null Units that were created to combat increasing number of paranormal entities have proven highly successful. Recommend continuation.

TECHNOLOGY: "Cyberization" proving increasingly popular and profitable. The average citizen is estimated to have a Cyber Percentage (CP) of 4%, with military members having an average of 15%. Average Human Lifespan due to Cybernetics and Medicinal advances is now 120 years; youth continues to be extended, with age 30 bearing little difference to age 20 and age 40 now what age 30 was in the early 2000's. Immortality remains out of reach, but our private researchers estimate it being attainable within 20 years. Artificial Intelligence is moving towards "perfection" ever since creativity and "thought" were achieved three years ago.

Hello, R. The information for this month is, as usual, mostly redundant, but I find it helps me focus on our company's best interests. To that end I've a question I'd like to pose to you.

You see, I've spoken to some of the other board members and while we're happy with the direction the company is currently heading in, we aren't quite sure about the future. A crew doesn't trust their captain simply because the ship's heading the right way at the moment, right? You have to consider the skill of the captain in more than direction. There are storms to consider, which must be weathered. Rocky shores that must be avoided. Pirates that must be fought off.

I'll get to the point as we're both busy men. I want to test this company with a storm. It's not that I distrust G and the way he runs things, but we haven't seen how he handles the real waves. Let me know your thoughts and if you're in. Our providers and clients would be much more comfortable if they had proof that this company won't sink.

H.

~~~~~

```
Date: March 21, 2068
Time: 3:08 AM
Location: Aegis Corporation Japan
Division Headquarters, Tokyo
Operation: Ghostcrawler (Debriefing)
```

As the hangar doors closed, Katsumi Samakura stepped out of the helicopter and waved over her shoulder to her two team members as she headed into the main building. The Aegis Corporation building was massive but she knew her way around, which allowed her to think as she walked through the clinical white hallways. Intel had dropped the ball; that much was obvious, or at least it was her conclusion. They'd been expecting Class-E or D at most, which slowed their response time when it became clear it was a Class-B demon. Hopefully answers would be available. Or someone to blame and kick through a window. Katsumi wasn't picky, she'd take either at the moment.

She reached a large office several floors up, ignoring the secretary that stood to greet her and entering the office beyond. It was a large room, the kind of office you could enter and instantly know how successful the owner of it was. The walls had a warm beige color instead of the sterile white of the building's hallways. More color was added by a couple ferns and an attractive red lamp on the large desk in the center. Katsumi didn't notice these details anymore, having been in the room many times. Instead she closed the door behind her to shut out the protests of the secretary and looked at the only other person in the room.

It was a man standing with his back to her and his gaze out the window, with his hands clasped behind his back. He wore a long black trench coat with a matching hat that was similar to the old fedora hats often seen in black-and-white movies. The hair beneath was a stark white, though the man only seemed to be in his thirties or forties. His eyes were obscured by small circular sunglasses that glinted in the office's warm lights as he looked over his shoulder with a highly amused smile, speaking in a voice that held a strange quality, like he was simply an observer of the world with nothing to fear from anything within it.

"You really should stop avoiding the secretary; it's her job to question and announce you."

Samakura folded her arms and leaned back against the door. "It's not my job to be delayed and annoyed. Or to get torn apart."

The man's smile widened as he shifted his stance so he could look at her. "Yes, I recall reading something about a little collateral damage during your mission."

"A little collateral damage? I had to dive off an eighty-story building while avoiding giant claws and acid."

"Hardly anything new."

"Not new, but not expected either, M. You wanna tell me why Intel mentioned nothing about the giant Class-B Kilk'tal that nearly killed me and a member of my team?"

M chuckled. "Don't be dramatic."

Katsumi sighed. "Fine, but it was still a nasty surprise."

He shrugged. "We didn't have all the information. It's unfortunate, but you can't always expect to know everything."

"You're saying no one's to blame?"

His smile returned. "Looking for someone to hurt? I'd appreciate if you let it go. Our Intelligence division isn't up to your unit's level yet and sometimes they miss things."

"You giving me an order?" Samakura grumbled.

"No, Captain Samakura, I'm not. Speak to them if you wish. However, we have more important things to focus on."

She perked up, pulling out the disc Sano had recovered on the mission he'd been on before they'd been forced to respond to the demon's attack. "Right, this." She turned it in her hand. "Looks a lot more important than I'd expect from something in the hands of petty business criminals."

M took it as she handed it to him. "People like moving up in the world. Petty criminals never remain petty; either they have the skill to move up or they're used by those that do."

"What you're saying is," Katsumi continued, folding her arms, "this isn't theirs."

"Of course not. They aren't fit for the big game but they don't know that. What they do have is money to fund a big player."

"So which big player does this belong to, and what exactly is it?"

"Those are questions we hope this little artifact will answer." M set it on his desk. "I appreciate your reliability once again, Samakura. You and your team get a few days off as our people look this over. I'll let you know what we decide to do with it."

"Great…" She sighed. "At least Reno will be happy. I'll let him know he can spend some time with his family."

"Yes, personal time is important to take every so often. Perhaps you should think about that yourself."

Katsumi waved her hand dismissively as she opened the door. "Not interested." She left the office, receiving a dirty look from the secretary and heading back down the hallway towards the building exit nearest the train station. With her eyes on the ground she nearly ran into a large form in her path, which startled her for a second before she recognized the 7'1'' muscular form in her way and smiled. "Hello, Law."

The dark-skinned member of her team that stood before her was unbothered, as it was hard to bother a 285-pound giant by bumping into him. He ran a hand over his bald head, looking at his leader through his dark shades. "Captain Sama. I heard you were back, and about what happened. Uninjured?"

Samakura smiled at his concern. "I'm fine. Dodging acid and leaping from buildings is in the job description. Only real loss is that I dropped my cigs before I jumped."

Samuel Lawrence chuckled, reaching into a pocket of the open tan military jacket he wore (the sleeves were ripped off for mercenary flavor and worn over a dark green shirt to complete the Vietnam War-style look). He pulled out a pack of cigarettes, offering one to her.

"Wanna replacement? Only one now, I'm not careless enough to lose all mine."

Katsumi snagged one before he could change his mind. "Sorry if I preferred to leave them behind instead of lighting them with a shrapnel-spewing nuclear fireball."

"Pussy."

"Watch your language in front of a lady."

"I don't think the secretary back there can hear us."

"You're just asking for me to break some bones, aren't you?"

Samuel laughed and shook his head, offering her a light. "I'm always honest, ma'am. So what's next on the team agenda? Hopefully I'm on the next assignment."

Katsumi drew in a slow breath, blowing out smoke with her eyes closed. When they opened they were looking at him as she nodded her head down the hallway. "Walk with me, Law." As he fell into step beside her she held her cigarette between two fingers, speaking around it. "Can't say I know what the next mission'll be, or who'll be on it. Sano got what we were sent for before we were called to respond to the demon, but M's people need to look it over before they know what to do with it so we get time off."

Law had to hide a smile at the near-disgust in Samakura's voice and on her face at the last two words. "Might not be too bad, Captain."

"I'm only happy when I'm doing something, you know that."

"Then think of something to do for yourself."

"If a third person suggests that I'm shooting them right in the head. I have no desire to take time for myself or sit around in my apartment doing nothing."

"So you'll check for an individual job to do in the meantime? You know I'd go with you."

She smiled. "Yeah, I know. Maybe I will see a two-person job. We'll see. Might just need a personal challenge."

"Understandable. I'll be around either way."

"No plans yourself?"

The large man shook his head. "Nothing exciting as a job."

"Nothing requiring explosions, you mean," she corrected dryly.

"Excitement and explosions are interchangeable, ma'am."

"Demo guys are so one-dimensional. Anyway, I'd better go catch the train. I'll see you, Law."

Samuel nodded. "Take care Captain Sama."

"Of what?" she added under her breath, exiting the building and heading towards the train station. Apparently it'd started raining while she'd been inside. It looked like it'd be a gray, dreary and overcast morning, which she found acceptable as it seemed to fit her mood. With a glance down she realized she'd forgotten to change, but she couldn't summon the effort to go back inside. It was something like five AM but she had somewhere important to be in a few hours. She acted like she hated time off, and she truly did, but there was a part of it she loved that she never spoke about.

The train station was mostly empty, as was the train that was already there, since it was too early for most people to be heading to work. The only people on the train were night owls like her who hadn't yet been to sleep, and the kind of people she automatically assumed were creeps and avoided. The train was soon rushing along the tracks, allowing her to lean back in her seat and look to the side out the window at the buildings rushing by. The pistol on her hip aided her by making others leave her alone, so she was left to her thoughts once again.

Last night was a small job. She leaned her head back against the glass, closing her eyes and drawing deeply from the cigarette. *It'll probably lead to bigger ones, but I don't know what kind. That's exciting... but waiting isn't.* She sighed, running a hand through her hair. *How long is this gonna take, a few days, a week? A week to sit around and think. I don't do well when I'm not moving. Focusing on the future is all that keeps me from drifting back to the past.*

Katsumi let out a breath of smoke, looking to the side as the train slowed down. Apparently the half-hour had passed already. She headed for the doors and went through the second they opened enough, taking the stairs to street level and walking down the street ignoring the looks she got mostly due to her clothing; skin-tight combat suits tended to stand out. She reached the South Ashfield hospital around six, about an hour too early, but she could wait. One of the nurses smiled at her as she entered the third floor. "Good morning, Miss Samakura. You're here a little early aren't you?"

"Well, I came when I got off work," Katsumi smiled a bit shyly. "I don't mind waiting until she's awake."

"Of course," the woman smiled kindly. "You can take a seat in her room if you like."

"Thank you." Katsumi nodded gratefully. She entered Room 302 quietly, smiling at the woman asleep in the bed. She took a seat in the chair beside the bed and studied her, trying to see if there were any changes in her condition.

The woman in the bed shared many similarities in appearance with Katsumi, most notably the non-standard hair color; hers was a very pale blue that was longer than Katsumi's violet, falling to her waist. She was three years younger than Katsumi but looked far younger than her due to the fact that she had a soft, youthful appearance as opposed to Katsumi's harder and sharper one. Katsumi reached over to gently take her hand and she blinked awake, her intense blue eyes focusing on Katsumi. She smiled brightly and sat up. "Katsumi! Shouldn't you be chasing a ghost or something right now?"

"I'd appreciate you keeping your voice down seeing as how that's supposed to be extremely top-secret."

"Oh please, it's not like anyone would believe I was serious if they heard."

Katsumi grinned at her. "They might move you to the psych ward."

The younger woman pouted. "Big sisters are supposed to be protective, not condemning! Did you come here and wake me up just to be mean?"

"Of course not." Katsumi reached up to brush some hair from her sister's eyes. "Speaking of waking you up, I didn't intend to. You should go back to sleep, Ayane. You need rest."

"All I get is rest." Ayane smiled. "Besides, you know I wake up with too much energy to go back to sleep."

"You never try."

"That can't be proven. Anyway, you're rarely here at this hour. You have the day off?"

Katsumi's smile faded into a frown. "A few days off until they figure out what we're needed for."

Ayane grinned. "You must be going crazy."

"Not yet, but I might," Katsumi said with a smirk. "Ask me again in a couple days. Can I just stay with you until the next job?"

"I would *love* that," Ayane laughed, "but you'd go even crazier here; you know how you are about hospitals. Hey, maybe a big demon will attack and give you something to do!"

"Already happened," Katsumi sighed. "Few hours ago. Short distraction."

"Maybe there'll be a bigger one."

"Maybe there'll be a whole swarm of them."

"Or a swarm of them joining together into a giant one!" Ayane smiled at her older sister's laugh. "Either way, I'll annoy you more through the cyber link for the next few days. That should keep you sane."

"Or drive me insane more quickly," Katsumi said dryly.

Ayane gave her a petulant smile. "Depending on my mood, yes."

Cyber links were expensive and dangerous implants available for anyone with a high enough CP and endurance to handle the implanting process. They allowed for one to contact someone else they shared a link with by transmitting directed thought. Normally they were reserved for special military operatives or covert spies, but Katsumi and Ayane had had them and shared a link for almost twenty years; they were far more used to using them than most people that had one, and they used it far more often. In recent years they'd come to appreciate it even more with Ayane stuck in the hospital and Katsumi in a demanding and dangerous job.

"How have you been feeling?" Katsumi looked over her sister, trying to gauge her condition.

"I've been alright. Fighting it as always." Ayane eyed Katsumi. "What about you, Sumi?"

The elder sister looked away. "You know the answer to that as well as I do."

Ayane's eyes saddened. "I worry about you a lot. You know how dangerous it is, doing what you do. I always worry it will hit while you're in the middle of something insane."

Katsumi smiled softly at her. "I'll be fine. I have a great team, they can cover for me if it does happen."

"But none of them would expect it. They have no idea."

"Just… Let me do things my way, okay?"

Ayane sighed. "Alright, Sumi. Just remember, since I can't kill you if you die on me, I'll speak at your funeral and tell everyone every story I have about you."

"You know I'll haunt you."

"I enjoy your visits."

"You're a pain, Aya, you know that?"

"We both know I'm immune and an exception to your whole 'RRRGH I'm tough and cold FEAR ME' thing, so don't even try it!"

Katsumi chuckled. "Fine. I *will* be careful, but only for you. I'll get out of the situation if I feel it coming on, okay?"

"Thank you. You have no idea how much better that makes me feel."

"It better."

"You act like taking care of yourself is such a big problem."

"There are more important things to take care of." Katsumi smiled at her.

After another two hours of talking the nurse seemed to get a bit impatient with them, obviously wanting her patient to get back to sleep. Katsumi stood and kissed her sister's forehead. "I'll visit you again tomorrow, since I have the day off."

"Wow, more than your usual twice a week? You're really spoiling me, Katsumi." Ayane smiled.

Katsumi returned the smile and squeezed her hand. "I'm trying to."

Katsumi left the hospital and bought cigarettes on her way back to the train station, figuring she'd need them if she was going to survive the next few days. She lit one and stepped onto the train, leaning her head back and closing her eyes for the return trip. As she grew closer to home she let out a breath of smoke, opening her eyes and staring at the ceiling of the train car. The grating of the wheels, the churning of the engines and the rush of air outside all seemed to get louder in her ears as she sat there. She could feel a headache coming on and at the moment she was just grateful no one was there who saw her as a leader. Random people on the train, that was all.

She forced herself up as the train finally came to a stop, focusing on balance as she walked through the car, exiting and heading away from the station and down the street. The edges of her vision were already starting to swim a bit, and by the time she got to her building she'd already lost the cigarette, though she couldn't remember the specific instance of dropping it. Pain was now rising through her body and drawing her focus inward, preventing her noticing outside details like that.

She pushed through the doors of the Culsor Apartment Building, ignoring the greeting of the attendant at the front desk and moving directly to the elevator. Grateful that the elevator she entered was empty she hit the button for the 67th floor, dropping to sit and not of her own volition. Putting a hand to her forehead Katsumi tried to focus, listening for the ding signifying the elevator's arrival at her floor. When it came and the doors opened she sat there for a full minute with both vision and sound swimming. *Almost there… C'mon Katsumi, stand the hell up.* After a few seconds she gripped the metal bar inside the elevator, pulling herself up and focusing on moving each foot alternately.

Reaching room 6711, she put her hand on the door and it unlocked, allowing her to stumble in and fall to the floor. She heard the door click shut behind her and decided that making it into the room was good enough. The bed, sitting a few feet away in the very small, shabby and currently unlit apartment, seemed like too far a goal to her at the moment. She couldn't even be sure which way was up so lying on the floor would have to do. Finally vision and hearing faded completely and she felt lucky as she fell into the darkness, leaving conscious thought behind.

Chapter 2: Innocence

```
Date: Forgotten
Time: Unknown
Location: Apartment... Home... Room
Status: Lost confu- pain dark... da-pain-rk...
c-c-can... nt...
```

"Stop what you're..." "D-don't, y... at you're doing..."
"...acceptable."

Katsumi wasn't sure if she was breathing. She certainly couldn't move. It took all her will just to curl up on her side, her fingers gripping at the carpet as her mouth remained open in a silent gasp, her eyes clenched tight in agony. Pain wracked her body as something else assaulted her mind, images and sounds rushing through her brain. A distant voice said they might be memories but it was impossible to tell. They didn't come one at a time but all at once, joining and mashing together in a maelstrom of confusion and a storm of rapidly shifting emotions. She never got a chance to recognize one, or even understand. Her mind couldn't focus on any one thought.

This is... wasting the remains... would you please consider... think about our future... when is it time... see her face... unarmed... this is against... won't be a part anymore... LISTEN TO ME... LISTEN...

Sweat made her hair stick to her cheeks and forehead and the lone thought she was able to bring up was a hope that it would end as long as she could hold on. Her nerves were on fire and her body shook under the pressure. Time had long been gone; she assumed she'd been lying there for days, but it could have been hours or maybe minutes. Ideas such as time were beyond her grasp for the moment, leaving her stuck in the tormenting darkness. She reached out for the one source of understanding she knew existed, the one comfort possible in this situation: *Ayane...*

Katsumi? Her sister's voice replied quickly. *You sound horrible...*

Lots of... pain... Katsumi fought to organize her thoughts enough to speak over the link.

It's hitting you now, isn't it? Ayane's voice was sad. *Where are you?*

I got to... home... my place... thankfully... It hit me... this morning? Whenever I got back... I passed out... through the door... inside. Home...

You've been out for twelve hours?!

I... guess so? I can't figure out the time... It's hard to think because... Now it's doing that... voices thing... Memories? I can't... remember... Think I hear...

Oh no... Okay, focus on my voice, Sumi. Only on mine. Focus on my words and ignore all the others. Katsumi shut her eyes, blocking out all but her sister's words. *Follow me back to reality...*

Eventually, very eventually, it began to subside. Katsumi felt herself take a breath for what must've been the first time in hours, a ragged gasp. Every joint and muscle burned as she started by moving a finger, slowly releasing her death grip on the carpet. Her thoughts began to sort themselves out. *Thank you, Aya... I don't know what I'd do without you.*

I'm just glad you come to me, Sumi. Take care of yourself... Don't go anywhere tonight, okay?

Even in her current state Katsumi smiled. *I won't.*

A knock came on her apartment door, but it was still distant, her vision and hearing returning but still swimming as she opened her eyes. She pressed her hand to the ground, pushing with all her willpower just to sit up, but it felt like a boulder sat on her back. Another knock came but she ignored it, sitting on her knees and crawling to the bathroom, vomiting into the toilet.

"Boss? C'mon, it says you're home, can't fool me."

Katsumi recognized Kurasano's voice but the best she could do right now was rest her forehead on her arm on the edge of the toilet, close her eyes and silently curse his timing.

"Alright, fine, I'm coming in. If you aren't decent that's just your own fault!"

She tried to tell him to leave and not come in but speaking was still beyond her ability. In her mind's eye she willed the bathroom door to shut, but to her disappointment she didn't spontaneously gain psychic powers right at that moment. Sano lived in the same building on the same floor as she did and they'd exchanged key codes for simple convenience, such as getting something the other person forgot. At this moment, though, Katsumi was regretting the decision.

The door slid open and Sano stepped through. He was surprised by the darkness of the apartment; it was 10 PM, Katsumi had obviously been home for over twelve hours, surely she'd had plenty of time for a nap. He noticed the bathroom door was open and saw her sitting inside, her head on the toilet seat, and suddenly things made more sense. "You sick, Captain? Stomach virus seems a little odd for you. Survive an explosion and get brought down by the flu?"

He expected a sharp retort and possibly a death threat, but instead Katsumi just turned her head slowly to glare over at him. Her eyes were red-ringed and bloodshot, and the color of her skin certainly wasn't normal either. On top of that he noticed she was still in her combat suit, meaning she apparently hadn't changed since the night before. "Whoa… Sama what the hell happened to you?"

"Captain… Sama," she managed to croak out, her voice not completely answering her will. She sat back against the wall, closing her eyes as a dull pounding rang through her head.

"Right, sorry… Still, it looks-"

"Shut up, Sano…"

"Should I call some-"

"I'm fine."

Samakura's lavender eyes locked on him and Sano got a very unwelcome feeling, as if he was right on the verge of going from friend to hated enemy somehow. It felt like he was very close to losing Katsumi's friendship forever if he did just one thing wrong. He didn't understand it at all, didn't have any answers, but he knew enough to shut up and not push the issue. Instead he shrugged and sat down against the wall across from her, watching her but looking down at the floor when she shot him another glare. They sat in silence like that for ten minutes. Sano kept stealing glances but Sama didn't give him another look. She continued to stare at the floor, unmoving. If he didn't know better he'd swear she'd forgotten he was there.

He wanted to ask what the problem was, or what was with her reactions to him, or why she was suddenly so distant and serious. Something told him he wouldn't get an answer but a dismissal, and it wouldn't be something he'd easily recover from. There were sensitive issues, sure, everyone had them, but what was so bad that even acknowledging it could cause hatred towards him? He'd come to ask if she wanted to get something to eat, assuming she'd be bored, but it didn't seem like an understanding thing to do at the moment.

Then again… Samakura didn't seem to want to talk about things right now, if ever. He shifted his thoughts away from how he'd handle normal people and adapted them to fit his unique Captain. Pretending like he hadn't noticed anything different would probably be a good idea, after all acknowledging weakness or any problems had never been Sami's strong suit. Sano looked up, running a hand through the short crimson spikes of his hair. "So yeah, I'm surprised you didn't shoot me for barging in uninvited, but I figured you'd be bored. Wanna let me make it up to you by ordering some food or something?"

Katsumi seemed to drift out of her thoughts and back to reality, running through his words. She gave him a look that he swore was grateful, though of course there was no way she'd ever say it. "You do owe me."

Sano grinned. "What, for me barging in here or for you keeping me from hitting the pavement last night?"

Katsumi scoffed softly, looking back at the floor. "Barging in. It'll take a lot more than food to pay back saving your life." Her voice was still distant and distracted, but at least it wasn't angry.

"You also told me to jump." He stood up and was about to offer her a hand up before he thought better of it and pulled out his phone, leaving the room to call for food.

Katsumi sighed, psyching herself up for a few moments before managing to pull herself to her feet, focusing on balance and slowly making the way to her closet to finally change out of her mission outfit. Fortunately Sano hadn't made any comment on that, and she trusted that he probably wouldn't bring the situation up with anyone else, but she dreaded him asking about it in the future. It was almost guaranteed that he would eventually. Still she wished that, somehow, he'd forget about it. Maybe- if she was lucky- he'd at least think it was a one-time thing.

~ ~ ~ ~ ~

"Yee-ha!" Reno leapt out of the company helicopter that had delivered him to the small Tesoro Village, unable to wipe the grin from his face as he waved to the pilot before jogging off down the street. It was already late but he had wanted to make sure he'd have the week off guaranteed, uninterrupted. His grin widened once he reached the house he felt he never spent enough time at. Entering the door he spotted his beautiful wife Lenora, catching her in surprise and pulling her into a kiss.

The brunette woman laughed at the end of it, resting her arms on his shoulders. "You should greet me like that more often. What's with the excitement?"

"I'm just an exciting person. And aren't you lucky? You get me for an entire week!"

Lenora flashed him a smile. "A week? They're actually letting you go for more than a day?"

"Better believe it. Where's my other angel?"

"She went to bed, reluctantly, but you should wake her."

"I was planning to either way." Reno grinned and kissed his wife again before heading to his five-year-old daughter's bedroom, opening the door. "Liaaaaanne…"

The little girl stirred, sitting up and rubbing her eyes before they opened fully as she suddenly raised her arms. "Daddy!"

Reno swept her up, kissing her blonde head and spinning in a circle before lowering her to look at her face, pulling off his shades and sticking them on her. "Why're you sleeping, huh?"

Lenora stood in the doorway, shaking her head with a smile as their daughter pointed at her. "Mommy made me!"

"Mean old Mommy, huh?" He grinned, catching his wife's look. "Uh, I mean, good girl for obeying her. But we have more important things to do right now, I'm here for a week and we're taking advantage with some family time!"

"Yay! Do we get to play games?"

"Pff, what's more important than games?"

Lenora raised an eyebrow. "School? Learning? Life experience?"

"Laaaaaaaaaaaame," Reno rolled his eyes as Lianne nodded in agreement. "Games are the most important life experience. School can be done when I'm at work and not here spreading large amounts of awesome around."

Lenora knew better than to argue and agreed with him anyway as she took a seat on the couch, soon joined by her husband and daughter. Reno set the little girl down between them as she asked about his work. "Were you a hero Daddy?"

"Ha! Was I?! I won the night! I even saved Captain Sama's life! Lemme tell you about my skill…"

~ ~ ~ ~ ~

M watched with his trademark ever-present smile as his window shimmered, becoming a view screen upon which an older man with salt-and-pepper hair appeared. The man had a strong bearing that commanded respect, but that didn't seem to affect M. He didn't even take off his hat or glasses to greet the Chairman of his company; he just kept that same damn smile on his face. "Chairman Hackett, I've been waiting for you to contact me."

"Are you dissatisfied with my punctuality, M?"

M's smile widened. "I didn't say anything."

Joseph Hackett sighed. He hated dealing with this man, but it was necessary. "I understand you acquired the disc we asked for."

"My team did, yes. I've sent it in for processing, research and analysis. Our next move will be determined based on its contents."

"Your next move will be determined by me, Director."

M responded with a grin. "Of course."

Hackett waited for further confirmation but all he received was a continual smile. He shook his head. "Just be sure to forward all findings to me before making any decisions. Understood?"

"I wouldn't think of undermining you, Chairman."

"I didn't say anything about…" Hackett grimaced. "I'm done dealing with you, Director. Get back to work and bother me when you have results."

The screen cut off and M chuckled to himself, looking out the window. "You aren't nearly finished dealing with me, Chairman Hackett. You'll know when you're finished, and you'll be far more than annoyed when it happens."

~ ~ ~ ~ ~

Katsumi's apartment was small, a lot smaller than she could probably afford with her pay, but she never seemed to mind. At the moment it was as trashy as always with clothing and junk spread over the little space there was on the floor and counters. The apartment really only had two rooms, a kitchen and a bedroom/living room, plus the small bathroom, so the only seating was a couch with a table in front of it and a TV on the other side of the table. Katsumi and Kurasano were both sprawled back on the couch with their feet on the table next to the remnants of their ordered food, watching the flickering screen in the dark.

Katsumi had changed into simple shorts and a half-shirt, getting as comfortable as possible while Kurasano had remained in his suit, though the whole suit was ruffled and uncared for now. Katsumi picked a piece of popcorn from the far-too-large bowl between them, popping it into her mouth as she pointed at the screen, watching a man in a terrible-quality horror movie running from the camera. "That guy's so dead. That camera's killed four people so far."

Kurasano grabbed a handful of popcorn, shaking his head. "No one can outrun that thing. You think it's really the camera or the cameraman?"

Katsumi shook her head. "No, it's the camera; did you see when it was, like, slithering on the ground? A guy can't do that."

"So how's it killing them without hands then? It just keeps zooming in and fades out."

"I dunno, maybe it beats them with the lens like in that one zombie movie."

The camera spun upside-down for the fifth time in what the director must have thought was artistic and Sano sighed in exasperation. "The hell man, you can't even see when it does that! Fine," he spun around, putting his legs over the back of the couch and leaning his head back to watch the TV upside-down, "I'll just watch it like this from now on."

Sama nodded. "Tell me what I'm missing from this viewpoint."

"Uhh… Okay, those two people you see are just talking."

"Ah. I can see why that needed to be upside-down."

"Yeah, it really adds a new angle to the conversation."

"That was just a bad joke."

"Don't blame me; this movie's flipped its lid."

Katsumi groaned.

"Seriously, I can't make heads or tails of it."

"That one didn't even make sense."

"Bite me. It's hard to think with blood rushing to your head."

"Then maybe you should sit right." Katsumi grabbed his foot, flipping him forward off the couch to the floor.

"…Ow…."

"Baby." Katsumi smirked, looking back to the TV. That lasted about five seconds before the bowl of popcorn was dumped on her head from behind.

Sano laughed as Samakura turned to look at him, but stopped at the glint in her eye. "Uh-oh…" He took off running and dived behind the bed as the bowl spun through the air and slammed into the wall where he'd just been, leaving a clear dent. "Truce, truce!"

Like he was getting off that easily.

~ ~ ~ ~ ~

Ayane lay in her hospital bed, her room dark and silent aside from the low background noise of the air conditioner. She was on her side, curled up a bit with her eyes closed and her head pressed into the pillow, her arm around the stuffed plushy – a "moogle" from the Final Fantasy video game series - that Katsumi had gotten her a long time ago. She was smiling, unable to prevent the expression from widening as she listened to the humming in her head. It was a soft song – even a sad song – but one that she had heard thousands of times before, one that she just couldn't feel sad during.

Hmm, hmm, hmm, hmm, hm hm hmhmm... Hmm, hmm, hmm, hmm, hm hm hmhmm-mmm... Ahh, ahh, ahh, ah, ah, ah ah-ah-ahhhh...

Ayane sighed softly, continuing to smile as she hugged her stuffed moogle tighter. *Your voice is prettier now...*

Mmm. So it wasn't pretty when we were younger? Katsumi responded in an amused tone.

It was... It's just prettier now. I bet if you actually sang it'd be beautiful.

I can try, next time I see you. But I only do it for you – you know that.

Ayane smiled. *I know. My lullaby is enough.*

Do you know you're thirty-one? Katsumi's chuckle reached Ayane. *Are you ever going to grow out of wanting me to sing you to sleep?*

Never, Ayane answered with conviction. *It's your job.*

I'm not complaining. I love anything I get to do for my baby sister, Katsumi responded in an overly-adoring tone that made Ayane's face nearly split in a grin.

Sumi...

Yes?

I wish you were here.

There was a pause for a few moments.

...So do I. Nights apart still haven't gotten any easier.

Ayane could hear the regret in Katsumi's voice, and she saddened. *Sorry... I didn't mean to make you sad, I just... I wish I was with you right now. It doesn't feel right.*

Good.

Huh?

It shouldn't feel right. It's not right. And it's not normal, either – or permanent. Once you're better we'll go back to normal, and right. Before too long I'll be back to singing you to sleep in person.

Ayane opened her eyes. *Promise?*

I promise. I hate... You know I hate this. I only get to see you twice a week usually, that's not... Katsumi's frustration was evident, and it helped Ayane as she listened. *That's not good, or... Twice! Once every three days, it should be every day! In a perfect world I'd never even leave...*

Ayane smiled – only her sister would say things like that and mean every word. *Then I hope we get a perfect world. But… Until then… I'll take as much time with you as I can get.*

Right now I'm lying in my bed staring at the ceiling, listening to Sano snoring on my couch, Katsumi said in a tone that made Ayane giggle. *How much do you think I'd rather be over there?*

I know how much. But like you said, it will happen. She smiled, closing her eyes again and getting comfortable. *Until then… Sing me to sleep.*

As you wish, Katsumi responded with the soft chuckle that Ayane recognized as the one her older sister often did when she found her cute. Katsumi always managed to make her feel special… valued… even needed. It was something that made lonely nights in the hospital a thousand times easier, because she knew that, while she was lonely, her sister was lonely without her as well. She was lonely, but she never felt alone, and that was the difference; that was the thing that made her smile at night.

Well… That and other things.

Mmm, mmm, hmm, hmm, hm hm hmhmm…

Chapter 3: Ghost

Date: March 22, 2068
Time: 3:58 AM
Location: Guuren International HQ

A man stumbled slowly down the street, paying no attention to passers-by. His hair was brown, dirty and unkempt, and he wore a tattered brown coat which was only slightly less ragged than the rest of his clothing. His face was unshaven but not old, somewhere in the thirties or forties. The man's eyes were unnaturally wide as if he was in shock or something similar, but he muttered to himself as he stumbled down the sidewalk. Others avoided him, casting glances and whispering, but the man appeared to notice none of it.

He finally stopped in front of the Headquarters building for Guuren International, a large banking firm. The building was incredibly nice as the company was well-off. All the men and women visible inside were in nice suits, even the ones at the doors or desks. The man's dirty hand rested on one of the windows as he pushed in through the door, walking forward but tripping and falling to the floor of the lobby.

Several people looked over, concerned, and one of the doormen headed over towards him to help him up. "Excuse me, sir, but this is a private business-"

The dirty man stood with his help, waving a hand to push him back so he wouldn't be forced out. The doorman sighed, waving over someone else to help him, but his attention was drawn to the strange look on the man's face. His eyes were still wide and his gaze seemed to be boring into him. As the doorman watched, a vein stood out on the man's forehead, and then another slowly swelled into view. "Whoa…" the doorman stepped back, calling a coworker to come help.

The dirty man started shaking as more veins stood out, his eyes bulging as his forehead seemed to swell. More and more veins began appearing as his face was contorted into something more like a mockery of a human to the horror of everyone watching.

Then he exploded.

~ ~ ~ ~ ~

Date: March 22, 2068
Time: 4:03 AM
Location: Culsor Apartment Building,
Apartment 6711

Katsumi Samakura was awakened by a loud buzz in her ears. She'd only gone to sleep about an hour earlier (due to spending a bit more time than she should have talking to Ayane), so this was a rather unpleasant experience. Sitting up and letting her eyes adjust to the darkness of her apartment, she put a hand to her head, as the buzzing wouldn't stop. After another few seconds she suddenly realized it was an emergency call and opened the channel in her mind, speaking out loud in answer. "Captain Katsumi Samakura."

"Rise and shine, Samakura," M's voice greeted her in her ears. "There's been a rather large incident several blocks from your current location and I need you to meet me there."

Katsumi slid out of bed, moving to her closet and pulling her shirt off on the way. "Care to fill me in, Director?"

As she listened she pulled on a black military outfit that was more formal than her normal attire and made for street duty. "The specifics are unknown at the moment, but there was a large explosion at the Guuren International Headquarters building. The bottom three floors are on fire with dire structural damage on floors one and two and lesser damage on floor three."

Katsumi straightened her uniform, moving back to her bed. "No cause identified?"

"Not until you get here and tell me, Captain. Fire control teams are already here so your main worries are civilians and investigation."

"I'll be there in ten minutes." Katsumi drew the pistol from under her pillow and tucked it into the holster at her side, walking

towards the door and kicking the couch on the way, stirring
Kurasano. "Get up, Sano; we've got work to do."

~ ~ ~ ~ ~

Sano sat in the car with his head in his hands, groaning. "Why
did we have to do something now? I only went to sleep like three
hours ago, you know." He glanced at Katsumi, who sat beside him
with her arms folded and one leg crossed over the other, looking
fully professional. He had no idea how she did it seeing as she
should be as messed up as he was.

"Must be the cyber thing…"

"What cyber thing?"

"You know, the fact that your Cyber Percentage is 83%."

"I fail to see what relevance that has to anything currently
going on."

"C'mon, you're only like 17% human. The vast majority of
people, even military, aren't even 17% *cyber*."

Katsumi looked out the window. "That isn't important now,
nor do I wish to discuss it."

"Right," Sano sighed, running a hand through his crimson
hair. *Stupid idiot, you aren't supposed to talk about that, especially
not so lightly. Why'd you call her seventeen percent human?
You're an asshole. What next, you wanna ask about her bad
childhood? See if there are any dead pets you can bring up? Talk
about her parents?* He sat back, looking out the window at the
smoke on the street ahead. He looked over at Samakura, but she
said nothing to him as he got out of the car.

Katsumi saw M standing in front of the building and moved to
join him. Smoke still poured from the building, though the fire had
been put out already. Civilians were huddled all around, some with
blankets or medical personnel tending to them. Some were on
phones talking to loved ones. Many were injured and dirty, bloody
or burned. The dead had yet to be recovered as the living were top
priority.

But the living weren't Katsumi's job this morning. M looked
at her as she walked over, wearing his dark circular glasses even
though it was four in the morning. "You're always prompt, Captain

Samakura; very good. As you can see, the scene is chaos right now, but I was fortunately able to keep them from messing with evidence."

Katsumi nodded, looking over the scene as Sano stood behind her with his hands in his pockets, surveying the damage. Katsumi looked back to M. "This looks like high-grade damage. Where does it start?"

M nodded towards the building and she followed him in, stepping over rubble and around a couple charred or torn corpses. "It's a messy scene; not only is there the damage to the lobby, but it's littered with everything – and everyone – that fell from the two floors above."

Katsumi looked up, noticing the gaping hole above them that went up to the bottom of the fourth floor.

M stopped her at a point in the lobby where there was a large, dark scorch mark in the middle of a small crater. "This is where the blast originated, as you can tell by the rings and the dome shape of the destruction extending from here."

She nodded, kneeling to inspect the crater. Sano whistled behind them, turning in a circle. "Jesus, look at this stuff... Not your normal bombing."

Captain Sama nodded her agreement as she looked around. "Too small to be an attack from a competitor, too large to be a disgruntled individual. Any witnesses or security footage left?"

M nodded. "Fortunately some civilians from the street were able to give a description of the bomber. Mid-to-late thirties, dirty, basically a bum with ratty clothing. No business here and no one recognized him; they said he just walked in and a few seconds later there was an explosion."

"No visible weapons on him?"

"None, but he had a heavy coat so anything could've been hidden under it."

Katsumi nodded. "It wouldn't be hard to get something strong enough to do this damage in here without it being seen, but my problem is with how a broke street urchin managed to get his hands on such a thing in the first place. And besides that, there's no clear motive."

Sano shrugged. "Maybe he was a former employee who was fired and wanted revenge?"

"Maybe…" Katsumi looked over the destruction. "Let's hope it's more than that, or this was even more of a waste than it is now."

"People like that don't usually think that rationally, Captain."

Katsumi looked down, running a finger over the scorched ground. Something didn't quite feel right about this. Somehow, she knew this wasn't that simple. She stood up as she rubbed human dust between her fingers, looking around. "Point me to one of the witnesses." M led her to the closest, a young man still in his early twenties. She knelt before the shaken witness. "You saw the bomber?"

The man looked at her, taking in her black-and-silver military uniform before looking into her lavender eyes. "Yes. I mean I think so. I didn't see him… do this, just go into the building."

"Tell me what you can about him."

"There's nothing to tell except what I told the others. Dirty, looked like a street rat, ragged old clothing with a big brown coat."

"You left out his hair."

The man frowned, having no idea why that was important. "It was just hair, brown and messy. Why does that matter?"

Katsumi grabbed his shirt to get his attention, her eyes narrowing slightly in a dangerous manner – she had never worked on her ability to deal with civilians. "You let me worry about what matters. If you miss one detail you might miss another. Is there anything else you remember?"

He shook his head. "N-nothing."

"Are you sure? You better think. I won't be happy if you leave something out."

He shut his eyes, scavenging his memory for any other detail. "Um… His eyes…"

"What about his eyes?"

"They were wide… like he'd seen something horrible or shocking, or maybe he was on drugs. I don't know, but they were creepy."

Katsumi let him go, looking at the floor in thought. "Could he have seen something…?"

The man shrugged. "All I know is it was weird. He was stumbling and muttering like he was drunk or drugged though, so maybe he was on something that caused hallucinations?"

"It could be." Katsumi looked back at the man, patting his shoulder as she stood up. "Thanks for your help. I'm sorry I was rough. You're free to go."

He thanked her, leaving the area. Sano stepped up beside Katsumi, who looked to be deep in thought. "What are you thinking?"

"It's an unusual case…" She looked over her shoulder at the wreckage. "I have more questions than answers. Why was this man who 'seemed mindless' coming to attack this building? If he was just an insane bomber, why did he pick here instead of running into the nearest crowded area? If he was a sane bomber looking for a real attack, why pick four AM, when no one's working and far fewer people are here?" Kasumi folded her arms, looking back at the ground. "Every fact contradicts another fact. It makes no sense. And that's just motive."

"What else is there?"

"How, where and why did he get the explosive? What was the explosive? Why didn't he throw it in here and save himself instead of dying with it? Why blow it up in the lobby? If it wasn't this man's idea to do it but that of someone more powerful, why blow it up in the lobby? Is it because his chosen tool couldn't get past security to get to more vital areas? But then, if he knew that, why not use another tool, someone with business here who could get further? Did he just have no other options? None of the people killed had much to do with this company besides making this building run, so what was the point? Is he just trying to scare them or was it a personal attack against one of the workers in here? And if it was personal, why such a large explosive when assassinating him would be so simple?"

Sano shook his head. "Okay, geez, I get it, lots of questions and no answers."

"Even the possible answers add more questions. I'm at a loss here, but something tells me I have a short time limit to find the answers in."

"You think this will happen again," M clarified.

Katsumi nodded.

Sano looked between them. "What? Why? How do you know that?"

"I don't know it, I just…"

"Feel it," M smiled.

Sano raised an eyebrow. "You're basing your expectations of further bombings on a random feeling?"

"The feelings of an experienced officer are more than simple emotions, Mr. Lionel, and Captain Samakura has a great deal of experience in violent matters such as this. The main reason we have her on investigation in addition to her other duties is her ability to get into the head of criminals and terrorists, as well as her rather unnatural 'sixth sense'."

"But she hasn't even seen this guy. And we don't even know if there is a guy!"

"It's a hunch, Sano, that's all," Katsumi looked at him. "But if I'm right, we'd better learn what we can as fast as we can." Katsumi moved away from the group, sighing and opening the main cyber link in her mind. *Ayane? I'm sorry to wake you so early again, but I don't think I'll be coming today. We had something big happen.*

Something big...? It was obvious Ayane had been awakened by Katsumi's voice, but she still had her full attention. *What is it? Are you okay?*

I'm fine, it had nothing to do with me, Katsumi reassured her younger sister. *Someone bombed GI's HQ. Lobby and a couple floors above it.*

Lobby? That doesn't make a lot of sense.

That's the problem. We're looking at a mystery terrorist attack here. I don't know how long it will take to figure this out, but I can't leave right now, not while more people could be hurt.

No, no, of course not. You do what you have to, just be careful. You have a tendency to be in the middle of explosions.

I'm hoping I can prevent there being another explosion. I'll let you know if something happens. Katsumi closed the link and headed back, her mind already working through what she needed to do.

~ ~ ~ ~ ~

Samuel Lawrence stepped out of the car, barely fitting through the opening. The dark-skinned, 7'1'' and 285-lb man stood out instantly among the people gathered at the destructed site of the morning's bombing. He found himself reminded of how fast the world moved these days as he watched the final civilians leaving the area. Fire control teams were already switching to structural integrity analysis and the area was full of soldiers and peacekeepers from the Aegis Corporation, which held jurisdiction over this area. And all of this was only twenty minutes after the bomb went off.

Samuel flashed his own Aegis badge and walked in, whistling at the destruction inside the building. "Must've been pretty heavy ordinance."

He smiled as he spotted Katsumi Samakura inspecting the area. There was something special about the way she focused on a job. Even in the midst of this chaos, he couldn't help but notice he wasn't the only one watching. The woman was only thirty-four, after all, barely halfway to middle-aged, in her prime in every definition of the word. She worked with an efficiency and dedication beyond what most were willing to put into anything. Above all else Sam noticed that; he figured the others were more focused on the soft curls of her violet hair, the intense gaze of her lavender eyes or the shape of her body. He shook his head, realizing that by listing those things he was acknowledging that he, too, had noticed them.

Which wasn't a problem, it was just that he appreciated his boss's other qualities more. Still, he thought as those lavender eyes focused on him, they aren't bad qualities. "Law," Katsumi's voice brought him out of his thoughts. "I'm glad you're here. I need to know anything you can tell me about the explosive used to do this."

"I'm hoping I can tell you a lot, Captain. Wouldn't be much of an explosives expert if I couldn't."

Katsumi nodded, looking back to data screens only she could see. He wasn't surprised by her distraction considering the state of the area. Sano stepped up beside him, raising a hand. "Yo, Law! Man, I haven't seen you in like three days!"

Law turned to him, meeting the high-five in greeting. "How's it goin', Sano?"

"Man, I'm on like three hours of sleep and dealing with this at four in the morning, how do you think it's going?"

"That's how the job goes some days."

"Yeah, unfortunately." Sano glanced back at Katsumi, who wasn't noticing either of them at the moment. He'd been watching her since they got up, but she'd shown no signs of the horrible condition he'd found her in the previous night. He wasn't sure if something had happened yesterday to put her in that condition or if it was something she'd been dealing with. It wasn't likely he'd get any answers and looking for them would probably just end badly anyway.

Law tapped his shoulder. "Somethin' up?"

"Huh?" Sano looked back at him. "Nah, man, I'm just out of it. Not a great morning person, y'know. C'mon, lemme show you the origin point."

Sam followed him. "I'm guessing it's the small crater in the middle."

"Yeah, kinda hard to miss, ain't it?"

Law stopped in the center, kneeling down to inspect the ground. "Definitely an unfocused blast."

Sano folded his arms. "Unfocused?" He was good at using weapons, but when it came to the technical side of explosions he usually just let Law handle it, so he liked things to be clarified in situations like this.

The big man nodded, his deep voice making his explanation seem more serious than the simple lesson it was. "Focused blasts are like det charges opening doors, or modern-day missiles. The explosion is basically aimed to deal precise damage."

"As precise as an explosion can get."

"Point. Anyway, unfocused blasts are what you get from most grenades or bombs – the force is unleashed in all directions."

"So since this is unfocused, you're saying it's not professional?"

"I wouldn't say that. Could've just wanted to make it messy. But to me it looks a lot more like a terror thing than attempting to deal physical damage."

"Any idea what the weapon was?" Katsumi's voice cut off Sano as he was about to reply. Neither had noticed her coming up behind them, or knew when she'd done so.

Samuel looked over his shoulder at her. "Can't say for sure, but there are a couple strange things about this."

"Enlighten me."

Law pointed around. "Number one is kinda hard to notice due to all this rubble, but there's no shrapnel from the explosive. Whatever it was didn't leave a trace of itself."

"And number two?"

Law looked back at the ground, tracing a finger over it. "Number two is the weird one. Based on the burn patterns, I'm almost positive the explosive was inside the guy's body when it went off."

They all paused to take that in and Sano broke the silence as he ran a hand through his hair. "Dude, that goes way beyond weird. That goes straight past the 'weird' line and sails right into 'fucked up' territory."

Katsumi shook her head. "Not the first time."

Sano stared at her. "You've seen this kinda thing before?"

"I've seen a lot before." She looked at the small crater for a few seconds longer before sighing. "Alright, that's probably all we're gonna get from here. Sano, I want you compiling a list of places in the area that might be hit next."

"Can do, Boss."

"Law, take some samples from here and see if you can figure out anything more about what did this."

"Thinking some sort of chemical residue?"

"It's worth a shot, we're flying blind here at the moment." She looked up, using a cyber link to call Reno.

It took a minute, but he finally answered, groggily. "Ugghhh… Hello?"

"Reno, I need you out here soon, ready for a fast response."

"What? Captain, it's my time off."

"I'm sorry, I wasn't aware playing in the amusement park was more important than public protection. Maybe I can send some soldiers out there to join you, give you enough to make a baseball team. It's obviously more important than duty."

"Alright, alright, I'll be out there. Just promise you'll give me time off later to make up for this."

"Don't try to force me into bargaining, Corporal, or you'll get some permanent time off along with a dishonorable discharge."

Reno hung up cursing, but Katsumi wasn't paying his attitude any attention. Her focus was on the destruction around her, and the potential for this to happen in a more crowded area. She nodded to M as she left, heading to find the final member of her team. There was an itch at the back of her neck that told her this was only the beginning.

~ ~ ~ ~ ~

The train station was beginning to grow crowded as all the early-morning commuters left their houses at 5 AM and headed to their jobs. One man there just stood, waited and watched. His hair was light blond, about 4-5 inches long and slicked back, slightly spiky. He wore an expensive pair of shades with a lot of technology in them, and a white-and-silver duster over a fine white suit with a silver tie. He stood out mainly because he was alternately balancing a knife on his finger and throwing it into the air to catch it. To him it was idly passing the time; to those around him it seemed slightly unbalanced.

He tossed the knife again, but this time before he could catch it another hand shot out over his and snatched it from the air. He turned to face the woman, taking the proffered knife. "About time, Captain, I was getting bored."

"You're a danger to the people around you, Rufus," Katsumi reprimanded him.

"Only if I do my job right." He slid the knife back into its hidden sheathe in his sleeve and slipped his hands into his suit pockets. "So, did I hear right? Large explosion with no details known?"

"Some details known, but not many."

"So we're working off a hunch here." Rufus smirked. "I have to say, if it wasn't you with the hunch I'd just laugh this off, Captain."

Katsumi looked at him. "I appreciate the trust."

He shook his head. "Not trust, respect. Trust is given while respect is earned, so it's worth more."

"Both are earned unless you're stupid."

"Maybe." Rufus smiled. "But I don't completely trust anyone."

"*That* is because you aren't a fool."

Rufus laughed. "These are just cynical thoughts on humanity, not mission details, Captain."

Katsumi sighed. "Unfortunately there aren't a lot of mission details to go over yet. You and I will have to trace this back to the source and we can't do that until we get more evidence."

"I can tell you're disappointed."

"Of course I am. I want to catch this terrorist."

Rufus smirked. "Sure, that's part of it. The part you tell people, anyway. Truth is, you were partially glad this happened so you'd have something to do, and now you're stuck waiting until you can do something again."

Katsumi gave him a sidelong glance. "You notice entirely too much for your own good."

"Probably. The only part I don't get is the guilt."

Katsumi looked away again, watching the people waiting for the train. "No part of someone should be happy about innocent deaths."

"Don't kid yourself. Part of you enjoys killing, too. So do I. We need to have those parts, Captain Sama. That's what keeps us from going insane while doing this depressing job. It's why we're the ones able to do it."

"I suppose you're right."

"That doesn't make any difference to you, does it?"

"Not in the least."

Rufus shook his head. "Ah, well. We can head back to headquarters and start looking through what information we have, planning things out. I'm sure catching the people responsible and preventing further death will soothe your guilty conscience."

"I can hope." Katsumi turned and headed up the stairs with Rufus following, her mental state of determination and efficiency returning. Now was not the time for small worries and distracting emotions, now was the time to avoid mistakes. If she did everything right, she could prevent the next bombing entirely.

All of her actions now were based off of a simple suspicion, a feeling… But her team was behind her. If she was wrong, then nothing would happen and it would be a little wasted time. But, if she was right and did nothing, it would mean a lot of civilian deaths.

To her, it wasn't even a choice.

~ ~ ~ ~ ~

Date: March 22, 2068
Time: 7:14 AM
Location: South Ashfield Hospital, Room 302

"Ayane, you look terrible!"

Ayane smiled wryly, looking at her friends as three of them entered the room. "Thanks, Yuri. I really needed that uplifting comment this morning!"

Her pink-haired friend put a hand to her lips. "Oops! I'm sorry, I didn't mean it!"

A more mature-looking woman with softly curled brown hair and intelligent green eyes passed by the younger girl. "Not even two steps into the room and your foot is in your mouth already. I've seen better starts, Yuri."

"It's not my fault, Mikoto!" Yuri huffed, her magenta eyes glaring at the thirty-year-old. "I was just making an observation."

"No one's surprised," Kyo said, uselessly brushing his black bangs out of his eyes as he, too, stepped past Yuri and moved to lean against the wall.

Yuri sighed. "Am I the only one here who's concerned for Ayane?!"

Ayane grinned. "Use your inside voice, Yuri. You don't want to get thrown out again."

Mikoto chuckled as she took a seat beside the bed. "Are you sure you want to warn her against that? I know it'd improve my mood."

Ayane looked at her. "Why does your mood need improvement?"

"Well as it turns out, representing your company in court becomes a bit harder when they lie to you."

"Oh, I can imagine. Does this mean you're switching companies again?"

Mikoto sighed. "I'm not sure yet. Although it'd be nice to be with one that was relatively sane for once," she said in a dry tone.

"Still, it isn't like there's a shortage of companies looking for lawyers these days."

"Especially good ones!" Yuri put in, hugging Mikoto from behind. "You should relax and stop worrying for once."

Mikoto smiled and patted Yuri's hand. "Thanks, I'll try."

Kyo put his hands in his pockets. "Maybe you could represent the company I work for."

Mikoto narrowed her eyes suspiciously at him. "Why, what'd you do?"

"Hey, why do you automatically assume I did something?"

Ayane looked at Mikoto. "It's alright, we'll just watch the news and find out."

"*One* time I get on the new - two, *two* times I get on the news – and no one ever lets it go."

"Two?" Yuri began counting on her fingers.

"Okay! Not important!" Kyo waved his hand. "Minor details, we don't need to focus on them. Besides, it's not like I'm causing things like that attack this morning."

Mikoto sighed. "Ah, yes. That was a depressing start to the day."

Ayane looked between them. "You guys saw that?"

"On the news, yes." Mikoto looked at her. "You learned about it another way?"

Ayane nodded. "Katsumi's leading the investigation."

"Oh," Mikoto sighed and squeezed her hand. "I'm sure she'll be fine."

"Yeah, they're saying it looked kinda amateur," Kyo added. "And I've never heard about your sis having trouble with amateurs."

Ayane smiled. "Thanks. I hope you're right, although from what I hear a lot of things about it don't make sense. Not that I can say any more about it."

"Conspiracy stuff?" Yuri tilted her head. "Is the government censoring you, Ayane? Ooh, can I do a story about it?!"

Mikoto rolled her eyes. "Put the reporter instincts away, Yu. Try to remember what 'no' means."

"Oh, right… Sorry!"

Ayane smiled at her. "Yeah, I don't think Sumi would appreciate my being an information leak."

"Still," Kyo put in, "it'd be pretty cool to know this stuff. You're lucky for that."

"Most of the time it doesn't feel lucky."

"You don't care about the details?"

"It's not that…"

"It probably makes it harder to deal with sometimes," Mikoto explained for her, receiving a grateful look from Ayane. "Knowing exactly what kind of danger your sister is in might just make you worry more."

"Huh. I didn't think about that," Kyo nodded.

"I think… that's the wrong way to think about it." Yuri tilted her head. "At least you know. The imagination can be a lot scarier than actual facts sometimes. If you were in the dark you'd worry all the time about what you didn't know."

"That's… true," Ayane smiled. "I'll try to think about that more."

Mikoto looked at Ayane. "Maybe we could help more if we really met her."

Ayane laughed. "Very subtle, Miko. I told you before that's up to her, and she's really busy."

"Not too busy to visit you twice a week. That means she must not be too busy to meet us."

Ayane sighed. "Fine, I'll bring it up again, but she's gonna worry about bringing you into danger."

"It'll bring us into danger?" Kyo straightened. "Really? Awesome."

Ayane rolled her eyes. "You are not normal. Anyway, let's move on to another topic, I like to be distracted."

Her friends obliged and Ayane only half paid attention as they talked, responding to things directed at her but lost in her own thoughts. Katsumi had never met her friends besides Mikoto, who she'd known for several years, and that had only been a very short greeting. She wasn't really the socializing type, Ayane knew, but it did sound nice to have her friends know the person she so often talked about. After all, she'd already been guaranteed she'd meet Katsumi's team at some point, so it made sense.

Ayane sighed; now she just had to hope they'd both survive long enough to do so.

Chapter 4: Memories

Date: March 24, 2068
Time: 8:57 PM
Location: On the Move
Operation: Safety Net

Cold wind blew Katsumi's violet hair around her face as she stood in the open doorway of the helicopter looking down on the lights of the city below. The sound of the blades spinning above her head drowned out all other sound, which she found made it easier to think. For the past two days they'd been moving around the city; inside the chopper, Reno was piloting, but she was the only passenger. Sano, Rufus and Law were all on the ground in different areas around the huge city.

They'd compiled a list of the most likely targets and Katsumi had put her best plan into motion; unfortunately, even her best wasn't much this time. They'd been able to divide the likely locations into three quadrants and Katsumi sent Sano, Rufus and Law each to one of the three. They'd stay ready in a car in the most central location between their possible targets while Reno and Katsumi flew a circle in the center, ready to respond to any calls in. In addition each specific location had two or three Aegis Corp soldiers in disguise staking it out for suspicious figures.

This "safety net" was their best option for stopping the next attack. Of course, there was no guarantee there would be a next attack, but Katsumi was grateful to have a Director like M who would act on her feelings and was willing to devote as many resources to this as he had. Now it was simply a waiting game, but for how long they couldn't know. Still, none of the soldiers complained, or if they did it wasn't in front of her, except for Reno's muttering of course.

Katsumi's cyber implants expanded a window of data before her eyes, listing the names of all operatives involved. As the clock hit 9 PM each name lit up green as they checked in, which she had them doing every half hour. If there was an explosion it'd be hard to miss, of course, but she couldn't be sure that was the only method this unknown – and unproven – criminal used. She gave a sigh as the last name lit up green, responding to all at once with her own signal. Everything was calm and everyone was fine... so far.

Katsumi leaned back into the helicopter, looking into the cockpit. "Take us around the Kitsuine Tower again." Reno nodded and Katsumi looked back outside as the chopper turned at an angle, heading towards the city's tallest building.

The Kitsuine Tower was the most expensive building in Tokyo. It had been constructed after the Tokyo Tower had been brought down during one of the country's worst terrorist attacks. Built partially from materials sent from seventeen other countries, it was one of the symbols of the new world, a sign that the borders between countries were being blurred and ignored more than ever before. As such it was considered a prime target for terrorist attacks and thus had impressive defenses, but those with a strong national pride such as Katsumi, who had been but a child watching it on TV as the Tokyo Tower fell, were very protective of the Kitsuine Tower.

Katsumi didn't know if what they were after was really a terrorist or not, but it never hurt to be careful.

~ ~ ~ ~ ~

Law sat back in his car, lighting a cigarette as he looked out the window. The giant black man had a way of standing out in Tokyo crowds so sitting out of sight was always his preference on missions like this where you were meant to notice someone else rather than being noticed. Besides, he liked being able to listen to music as he waited for something to happen, he found it helped prevent anxiety. Not that he really had an anxiety problem, not after his life, but he wasn't a big fan of the calm before the storm and always preferred the storm's arrival to the silence prior.

Breathing out a puff of smoke he let his mind wander a bit after making sure his music wasn't loud enough to prevent him noticing a call. As it usually did in these situations his mind chose a similar event to take him back to, delving into memories he rarely indulged in on purpose.

2054, Central America, Amazon Rainforest:

The Amazon had once been deadly only due to its natural predators and exotic diseases, but that was before one of the biggest terrorist coalitions in the world had moved in. Private militaries had made a huge push into the region, all vying to take down the threat for varying reasons, the most prominent being the renown that would come from such a victory.

Samuel Lawrence, he remembered that was all he was known by, no nicknames. Just as large a man then, he had a big advantage in close combat so frontline fighting had always been his forte, and it was no different in this conflict. But rules had no place in those jungles. His unit lost several commanders and many men to the mines, traps, ambushes, guerilla tactics, and straight-out attacks. Military drills dissolved in the face of the true chaos that ruled that forsaken battlefield.

Still, Command refused to give up; the company he'd worked for back then had no trouble with throwing people away. After all, each death was a face they'd never seen and a name they wouldn't remember. They'd simply hire another person to take the place of the deceased and repeat the process when necessary.

Sam remembered the last commander they had die. The men who had survived the longest, including Sam, just looked at each other and shook their heads after that little skirmish. The officers they were sent were usually the staunch military type with starched uniforms, shiny boots and stern faces. By the end of the month their posture would be slumped, uniforms torn, boots bloody and faces afraid. The ones that still had faces after a month, at least. Eventually they'd either leave or die.

Sam read the latest letter explaining their next officer and how this one was "different", a promise they'd heard many times. However, the information they were given only succeeded in making the men even more skeptical than usual, rather than infusing them with hope.

It was a woman this time, though that wasn't unheard of obviously. According to Command she was top in her class - every class. Not much was given about her personality, but one attribute was the main focus of the group's discussion over the next few days: "Age: 20."

At first they'd been shocked, then they moved on to laughter, then back to shock, and finally anger and indignation. "They're desperate," some offered as an explanation.

"Finally gave up on us, I say."

"It's ridiculous! Sending a kid to order us around? She'll get us all killed!"

Sam had remained silent. It wasn't that he had any more faith in their new unknown commander than the others; he didn't. Not in the least. He was sure she'd be dead within the month, if not the week.

It was that fact right there. He didn't find himself agreeing with sending someone so young into such a brutal conflict unprepared. It wasn't right, but that didn't really matter here he supposed. It would happen either way.

She arrived three days after they'd been told of her appointment. She was young and beautiful, which only added to her being out-of-place in this hell. Her curly violet hair and pale complexion seemed too gentle for the harsh reality of the jungle, and every man there was ready to disobey her orders, most not out of resentment but to stay alive. She'd stepped off the helicopter with a younger girl with bright blue hair, but they were given no explanation at the time; the younger girl (only seventeen) had simply moved away and taken a seat in front of a tent to watch while the new commander stood in front of the group of men that had absolutely no faith in her abilities.

But Sam had noticed something different. The young woman folded her arms behind her back and looked over her new charges as the transport helicopter lifted behind her, not staying in the area any longer than to drop off the girls and their supplies. She took in the hard men wearing torn and bloodstained clothes and numerous scars and moved in front of them, examining without any shown emotion. When she spoke it was far more even than they expected to come from those lips. "My name is Katsumi Samakura. You're mine now. Things are about to change."

One of the men shrugged. The lack of respect wasn't really a personal insult to her; they'd heard this sort of thing before, several times. She'd break soon. "We've got it handled."

Her eyes turned to the speaker. The deep lavender gaze seemed to hold some strange power within it that silenced him. "If that were true you'd have won by now."

Anger was the response. They'd been facing death for months, fighting like mad. This new girl with no experience here had no right to talk about it like she had, insulting their sacrifices and those of their fallen allies. One of the men stepped out of the line they'd reluctantly formed, moving to strike her. Sam didn't blame him; it was like she'd spat on the graves of their fallen allies and on the shreds of their own dignity. She hadn't done one thing to earn their respect or the ability to speak as she had.

But she wasn't the type to take that sort of thing. She ducked the swipe and slammed her fist into the man's stomach, doubling him over. Her knee came up and he snapped back with a spray of blood emitting from his now-broken nose. After he hit the ground she stomped her foot onto his throat, holding him there as her lavender eyes flared to life with hidden emotion. "I don't need your respect, but I demand your obedience." The others were startled, but after a second rage took over, and Sam knew it was going to get ugly; out of the corner of his eye he noticed the blue-haired girl watching carefully, her fingers playing over a pistol on her belt.

Their new commander drew her own pistol, pointing it at the downed man and ignoring the others, who stopped to watch as she continued. "This company's death count is ridiculous and its progress is nil. You're thinking yourselves heroes? What have you done to earn that distinction? All you've done is survive. That's not victory, that's just stalling. I'm here to change that." She removed her foot to allow the soldier up, but she kept her pistol drawn even if it was hanging at her side. "I'm not here to earn your respect. I'm just here to win battles and keep you alive, prioritized in that order."

But despite her statement, she had gone on to earn their respect. To their surprise she not only directed them with amazing precision and insight, but she did it with an extremely cool head and even tone, even during the fiercest and bloodiest skirmishes.

The most amazing thing, though, was that not once after her arrival did they ever fall into a trap. She had an almost supernatural sixth sense; she was never able to divine specifics out of thin air, of course, but she always guided them around ambushes with nothing more than a mutter about a "bad feeling".

Progress had been made after that as they began to form into a real team, but of course that was before –

Law was snapped out of his memories by a loud beeping informing him that it was time to check in again. He sighed, making contact as he looked out the window once more. It was times like this that made him almost long for open warfare. Silence was worse than the sound of any weapon.

~ ~ ~ ~ ~

Sano leaned against the side of his car, running a hand through his crimson hair with a sigh. "So boring…"

He was ready to move at any moment, but there was nothing to move towards yet. All he could do was wait, just like everyone else. He slid his hands into his pockets. He'd decided there were worse things than wearing suits, especially as he caught his own reflection in the car window and winked at it, grinning as he imagined his Captain rolling her eyes at the gesture. Reno would probably throw an insult his way, too. Still, as he looked up into the night sky, he couldn't help wishing he was in the helicopter with them rather than standing around on his own bored out of his mind.

He pulled out his phone, flipping it open and starting to look around on their network. Nothing was happening anyway, he might as well see what everyone else was doing. According to it, they were all still in their usual positions. Law was on a street corner miles away, Rufus was on a rooftop somewhere, and Reno and Katsumi were apparently circling the Kitsuine Tower again. That thought made him hope that wouldn't be the target. Unlike the others on their team, Sano was like Katsumi, a native of Japan. He had similar feelings towards the tower.

Terrorism was always a heavy subject for him. He still remembered his first real experience actually fighting it as a rookie cop eleven years prior:

2057 was a year without wars but with enough crime to make up for it. Kurasano, 22 years old and fresh out of Academy, had been in his first year of active duty as part of a firm specializing in Public Security, basically what would've been the police force in the early years of the century. Sano had strong feelings about his job, strong reasons for doing it, but those were things he didn't like to dwell on.

He was on a simple patrol the day a real terrorist group attacked. He, along with most of the men in the area, were used to criminals, even the vicious kinds that could bring dozens of deaths, but they weren't used to what real terrorists could do.

It started with an explosion; Sano found he hated how many things had exploded during his lifetime. They'd been after government officials who weren't important enough to bring in the real Special Forces so Public Security had been sent in. It wasn't a fair fight.

Sano ran with familiar men into the front of the building only to be greeted by a hail of gunfire from weapons a lot more powerful than the handguns they held. Men three times his age fell around him, shredded and pouring blood, viscera and other things he still couldn't cleanse the images of from his mind despite trying. He dived into cover, watching his partner's head explode near him, covering him with blood and brain matter. His eyes were wide in horror and shock. Training hadn't taught him about this, about what real weapons did to a human's body, about the sheer violence and brutality of a real conflict.

The smell was as bad as the sights, things he'd never wanted to recognize the scent of assailing his senses. It was all he could do to keep from curling up and crying right there, forgetting the people around him and trying to ignore the horrific reality.

But that was before he heard the laughing.

The cops who were on the ground around him were good people, mostly. Sure, there was the odd bad egg, but they had all chosen to make protection their profession. Most had families, children, wives, husbands, homes they wouldn't be going home to at the end of the day. And Sano could accept that, he could; he already knew from personal experience that life was unforgiving and harsh. Not cruel, but harsh. People died, he knew that.

But he couldn't accept that the people who were killing them were laughing about it. Those lives meant so little to them that the brutality was humorous. That was when something new triggered. That was when Sano stood up.

It wasn't like his fear and horror disappeared; they just didn't matter anymore. Anger rushed through him, a tidal wave of rage that made thinking about little details like personal danger or fear impossible. At that moment all he wanted was to stop the laughter and the slaughter, he wasn't thinking about the future at all.

They fired of course but he moved as they did, returning fire with his handgun as he swooped down to pick up another from a fallen officer. He remembered screaming though he didn't remember starting to. He moved from cover to cover, always moving forward, bringing down target after target. They couldn't get a real shot at him, he moved too much and they were too confident to do the same. Their confidence faded once they realized just how many of them he'd brought down, but by that point fear and anger clouded their judgment instead.

It was strange, Sano thought, how his anger enabled him to cut through their numbers while their anger prevented them from winning. The few surviving officers moved forward behind Sano, working with him towards victory, and soon enough the entrance was clear. Sano didn't stop there, though the killing mostly did. He pushed forward into the building towards the government officials, working with his allies to bring the rest down, and it got easier as it went. Many gave up without even firing, knowing the majority had been taken care of downstairs.

Sano had walked into the official's office without hesitation, the end of the road. A terrorist stood with a gun to the official's head, demanding he drop his weapon. Sano had complied; he knew it was the best course of action even as the terrorist took the opportunity to shoot him in the chest.

As Sano had stumbled back another officer had swung around the edge of the doorway, shooting the now-open terrorist dead. Sano remembered hitting the wall and slumping down, others coming to his aid and calling for medical attention. Sano had just smiled. He'd never expected to get out of there alive; he'd forgotten about that back in the lobby.

Later, as he recovered after surgery, another officer had told him that was the point when he became a real protector, when he'd forgotten about his own safety. Sano never forgot that, and ever since he'd never put his own safety before another's.

Sano smirked as he was snapped out of his reverie by a loud beeping. "Yeah, I'm a hero alright." He checked in and dropped his phone back in his pocket, looking up at the sky once more. "A big damn hero…"

~ ~ ~ ~ ~

Wind howled over a rooftop as it picked up for a moment before settling down again. The weather seemed to be reacting a bit oddly, but maybe that was just his mind reading too much into things. Nature didn't care what was going on with humans; it never had.

Rufus adjusted his shades, appreciating the protection they offered his eyes from the wind at this altitude. It was night so his shades were on a light night vision setting, bathing the world in a faint green glow. He could pick out any detail of the street below, but right now all of those details were boring. A few people walking, some cars, a bus every now and then. Rufus shook his head as he thought about how few people he was seeing. It wasn't normal, but that was no reason to assume it was because they were somehow "sensing" possible trouble in the air.

He blamed Captain Samakura for these stray thoughts. He could tell he was trying to have the same "sixth sense" she seemed to have. Ridiculous. He'd seen too much to ignore hers, of course - that was why he was on this rooftop - but no one else had the same ability as far as he knew, even himself.

His thoughts logically went to his Captain as he sat against a raised vent on the rooftop with his sniper rifle resting on a tripod beside him. He'd always preferred lone work before her, but she was the first person he'd worked for that he was truly able to respect. He respected M of course, but he rarely dealt with M, and he didn't trust that man enough to work to change that fact. Samakura was different; she'd been in enough different situations to understand how things worked in different walks of life. She'd even understood his own. After another glance at the street below Rufus sat back, allowing himself to follow that line of thought to an examination of his past:

It was seven years ago. Rufus, thirty years old at the time, knocked on a door, smiling before kicking it in. A knife slipped from each sleeve into his hands as he stepped inside and ducked. A shotgun blasted apart the wall over his head and he turned to the right, one hand knocking the barrel upwards and the other gutting the offending criminal. He yanked the shotgun from the dying man's hands, tossing it behind him and stalking further into the hallway.

Criminal organizations were always going after each other; after all, they had to compete just as much as any legitimate company, they just sometimes did it a little more brutally (or at least they were more forthcoming about their brutality). For those times when his own organization decided a more violent solution was required, Rufus was often the answer.

A door in the hallway burst open as an attacker rushed out but Rufus just stepped past him, jamming a knife into his eye socket as he did and leaving it there as he continued on, knowing the man's screaming was making his targets nervous. He found a doorway at the end of the hall and entered, finding himself face to face with a veritable armory of guns. The criminal he was after stood against the room's windows; between them were eight armed guards who immediately opened fire.

Rufus stepped out and pulled the door shut behind him, letting it take the hail of fire. He kept hold of the doorknob and kicked the door off the hinges, rushing into the room with the door as a shield. He slammed it into two men, pushing them further until they smashed through the window, falling with a scream to the streets far below. Rufus shot his left hand out to catch one of the bars that had held the windowpanes together and shot his right hand out to grab one of the falling guns.

He swung around to the left, narrowly dodging more fire, and opened up on the others who all dived for cover. It was risky, but it worked. Then things got a lot more chaotic.

Rufus ducked as he heard fire behind him and looked back to see, surprisingly, a woman swinging towards the room on a rappelling wire. He dived to the side as she swung in, landing between him and his target. She had violet hair, strong lavender eyes and a skintight black military combat suit, which to him meant she was quite out of place in this fight between criminals. He aimed the gun but she moved faster, her pistol shooting it out of his grip. He flung his remaining knife and charged as he drew another.

She sidestepped and slapped the thrown knife away with the flat of her free hand, bringing up her pistol to block his stab attempt. In the next few seconds their limbs were a blur as she avoided stabs, he avoided shots and they both tried to get the upper hand, punches, kicks and grapples being countered. They wouldn't know who'd come out on top, though, as the other criminals in the room had recovered and both opened fire. Rufus and the woman instantly dropped below the table, but noticed as Rufus' target took off out of the room.

The woman vaulted over the table, gunning down two guards and chasing the man into the hallway. Rufus flipped the table, kicking it into the remaining guards, picking up another gun and following. He fired on both people in the hallway; the woman rolled into a side door, the man wasn't that lucky. His legs were caught by a few bullets and he went down heavily with a loud cry. Rufus tossed the empty gun aside and readied his knife for the kill but the woman came out firing to stop him. Fortunately for him, he managed to avoid both shots, and that must have been the last in the weapon since she flipped it around in her hand and came at him with melee strikes once more.

Rufus did his best, and after several hard strikes it seemed he was the stronger, but she was faster. He stabbed at her stomach and she jerked to the side, catching his wrist. She ejected the magazine from her pistol and, as it fell to the floor, kicked it back up into his face, which only stunned him for a second, but in that second she jammed the empty pistol on top of the knife so the blade went inside the magazine chamber, twisted hard and ripped the *knife out of his grip, struck him hard in the stomach with the hilt and kneed him in the chin sending him to the ground.*

She dropped her knee into his stomach and pulled the knife from the gun, holding it to his neck and speaking in an even voice touched by a hint of breathlessness. "Don't move. I need him alive, but not you."

Rufus sighed, following her directions as he heard someone else coming from further down the hall, probably more of her unit. "I can tell when I'm beaten."

"You're still planning a way out of this." He was surprised at her intuition, and more so when she knocked off his shades, looking into his eyes. "What's a professional like you doing with these thugs?"

Rufus smiled. "I was trying to kill them, obviously."

"Not the answer I was looking for."

He shrugged. "This is what I'm talented at, and what I enjoy."

After watching him for a long moment, the woman nodded and stood up, sliding her pistol into her belt. "We could put your talent to a much better use. If nothing else it's a free out."

Rufus still remembered the swirl of thoughts in his mind as he watched his knife thud into the ground next to his head followed by her last three words. "Think about it."

The beeping reminding him to check in brought Rufus from his ruminations. He sent his in, looking back at the street below. It'd turned out to be a good choice, he couldn't deny that.

~ ~ ~ ~ ~

Reno casually guided his helicopter around the Kitsuine Tower. He was probably one of the only pilots who casually flew a multi-million dollar war machine around between skyscrapers, not to mention thought of it as his. Then again he might be the only one with the talent to do so.

With non-action flight like this, he was always able to sort of half-focus on it, knowing he wouldn't make a mistake. He glanced back at Katsumi but she seemed distracted herself, paying him no attention, her eyes raking the ground below. He felt for her, knowing how much she wished she knew what would happen, where and when. He hated to admit it but he himself didn't have much faith that they'd be able to catch the guy before more damage was done. He'd never say it out loud, but he already knew everyone else felt the same way. That was certainly what was eating Katsumi so much.

None of them wanted a bunch more civilian deaths, and if the next attack was anything like he'd heard the last one was, it'd be bad. He'd complained at being called in, but really he had no regrets being out here. He wished he was with his family but he knew there were more families than his and he had a job to protect them if possible. After all, if his own family died…

He shook his head, knowing that was a bad line of thought to go down. He'd go insane if he thought about that happening. Instead he backtracked, smiling to himself as he thought not of his family dying, but simply of his family:

"I'm getting fat."

"Oh come on, you are not fat."

"I'm fat," Lenora pouted, frowning.

Reno laughed, turning to look at her. Her frown turned into a glare aimed in his direction. "Are you laughing at me?"

"No, at what you said. That's ridiculous. It's like you don't even realize you're still more beautiful than anyone else in the world." He shrugged. "Maybe pregnancy messes with memory, too."

Lenora was unable to prevent a smile, patting the seat beside her on the couch. "Okay, that was a good line."

Reno grinned and sat on the couch beside her, dropping his arm around her shoulders as she leaned against him. "That wasn't a line. You know my lines. You want a line?"

"Oh, good gracious, no."

"Hey baby, did they just take you out of the oven? Because you are hot."

Lenora groaned, resting her head on Reno's shoulder.

"Falling for you would be a very short trip."

"What does that even mean?"

"If I could rearrange the alphabet, I'd put U and I together."

"We are together."

"You're ruining my lines, dear."

"They were ruined before you even said them, honey."

Reno chuckled, kissing her head. "Fine. How about 'I love you'?"

Lenora smiled. "Stick with that one. I like it."

Reno snapped out of his thoughts once he saw the flashing red light telling him to check in. He hit the button to reply and then sat back with a sigh. He couldn't wait to be back home. With a grin, he thought it might be fun to try out some new lines he'd come up with on the beautiful woman waiting for him; she'd roll her eyes and groan, but he knew she enjoyed it.

"Head down closer to street level. Take a route between buildings starting with the Levicorp building."

Reno nodded at Katsumi's new instructions, guiding the chopper lower and through the area. He looked back and suddenly straightened, noticing Katsumi's face was hard. He could tell by the look on her face she was talking with someone, maybe someone had seen something suspicious. He put his focus fully back into flying, keeping his eyes open and following what his Captain said. If things were finally happening, there was no telling what could –

The sudden explosion rocked the helicopter, jerking Reno violently. He fought to get it under control, taking a quick glance and noting with relief that Katsumi had managed to stay in the chopper. Several floors of the building beside them had just exploded; red lights were flashing along with a warning siren inside the aircraft, and Reno knew why; that much sudden, intensely heated air erupting right beside them was wreaking havoc and making it impossible to fly with any sort of control. As a result the chopper went into a spin and the tail slammed into a building, smashing off with sparks, flame and shredded glass and metal. They were going down and there was nothing Reno could do about it. Unlike his Captain he only had a Cyber Percentage of 5%. In other words, he was dead.

In the wild rush of air, metal and flame, he managed to focus his thoughts on his family one last time as regret washed through him.

Then he felt Katsumi's strong hand on his shoulder, saw her rip through his restraints and felt her hug him to her. There was a sudden feeling of weightlessness and a mad rush of wind as she leapt from the chopper with him in her arms. The spinning aircraft's tail slammed her before they were away from it but somehow she kept hold; Reno wasn't even able to breathe, only watch with wide-open eyes. Katsumi hit a building and slammed her hand into it as they fell. The shriek of tearing metal was intense and blood sprayed above them as he watched her hand shred, but it did slow them down some. She spun and slammed into the street hard, cracking it beneath her feet and knees.

Reno was in shock as she dropped him; the two feet to the ground was the only impact he felt. Katsumi knelt in front of him, panting and sweating with obvious effort, her right hand leaking blood and fluid. He was about to say something when his eyes widened again, looking at the helicopter that was falling right on top of them. There was nowhere to go and nothing to do, but once again Katsumi's hand gripped him, the front of his shirt this time. He gasped as he was lifted and flung from the street, landing and tumbling in the nearby alley. Reno only managed to sit up and look in time to see Katsumi's lavender eyes staring at him for half a second before the burning aircraft slammed down on top of her, sending a wave of heat and shrapnel over him. For the third time in under a minute, all he could do was stare.

~ ~ ~ ~ ~

Ayane…
The girl jerked upright in her bed, her sheets falling around her. *Katsumi?* Something about the way her sister had said her name bothered her. It wasn't a normal call; it was more similar to the way Katsumi had said it the first time the sickness had hit her and she wasn't sure she'd wake up from it – there was something in her tone that had tried to convey her feelings for Ayane just by saying her name. Ayane watched the number on the dark hospital room's clock change, still with no response. She hesitated for a few seconds before trying again. *Katsumi? Are you there?*

Her cyber link assured her the message had been received. Ayane slowly went from nervous to terrified, trying again a few more times and still getting nothing. It wasn't what she'd hoped for, not after hearing Katsumi say her name in that emotional manner. Ayane threw off her sheets, slipping out of bed and moving towards the door, but falling as she did so. Her weakness was bad tonight, but she growled and pushed herself up, grabbing the door handle and pulling it open.

Then she leaned against the wall, staring out into the dark hallway helplessly. She knew she had no idea where to go or what to do. Katsumi had always told her to try to let logic control her actions rather than emotions, so she backed up and slammed the door shut, tears beginning to run down her cheeks as she ran her hands through her hair. She dropped back onto the bed, reaching behind her pillow and pulling out her stuffed moogle. While she had a lot of stuffed animals, it had always been her favorite – the moogle had been a gift from Katsumi when they'd first been forced to separate due to her job and Ayane being hospitalized.

It'd been meant for exactly this sort of situation, when Ayane had no idea if her sister was still alive or not, or where she was. She hugged the moogle to her as she cried, remembering many nights spent just like this when she was younger. Unfortunately, all those times when she'd cried as a child, she'd had Katsumi to hug onto, and right now she had no way of knowing if that'd ever happen again.

Chapter 5: Absolution

Screams. Fire. Metal. Blood.
Screams from people on the street and from his own lips.
Fire spreading due to the fuel from the helicopter's wreckage.
Metal, the helicopter's wreckage itself and the pieces taken from the building above.
Blood visible everywhere.
He couldn't see anything under the wreckage, couldn't even get close enough due to the heat of the burning fuel. Others were arriving but he couldn't shake the feeling of "too late" that settled onto his shoulders like a physical weight, dropping him to his knees in the alley and leaving him to simply stare.
"Honey…"

Reno slid his hands down his face, looking over them at the opposite wall. He was sitting on a bench in a sterile hallway on the 43rd floor of the Tokyo Tech and Healing Center. His elbows rested on his knees and his face had been in his hands on and off for the past few minutes until his wife's voice snapped him out of his thoughts for the seventh time. He looked to his right and saw her, eyes red, watching him with concern. He thought he should say something but he couldn't. It was one of those times where you felt removed, as if you were just watching your own life without the ability or inclination to actually influence it.

His eyes drifted left. Law sat on a bench against the other wall to their right, arms on his knees and gaze on the floor. Reno couldn't read him at all; he still had sunglasses on and his face was a mask as usual anyway. He'd been almost as quiet as Reno had. Looking further left, Reno noted the last two members of their team.

Rufus was leaning against the wall with his arms folded, one leg crossed in front of the other. He looked relaxed, or maybe just distant. Reno would never be able to tell what he was actually thinking. Kurasano, however, was much easier to read, as the man was pacing back and forth in the hallway as he'd been doing restlessly for the past hour. Silence reigned in the hallway except for his muttering every so often.

Reno shook his head, lowering it and running both hands through his ragged brown hair. He took a moment to gather himself before leaning back and taking his wife's hand, knowing the night wasn't much easier for her. She knew how close he'd come to dying, but in reality all he had were a few small cuts and a couple light bruises. Meanwhile, he was distracted by the knowledge that what was left of his Captain was on the same floor, maybe alive, maybe not. He'd thought about losing his family earlier that night, but as he looked around the hallway he found that he'd thought a little too exclusively. After all, there was a lot more to family than blood.

Sano kicked the wall, then backed up from it and ran a hand through his hair before spinning to look at Reno. "Seriously, what kind of condition was she in?"

It wasn't the first time he'd asked and Reno could only answer as he had the first time, with a shrug and a shake of his head. "Like I said, I didn't see."

"Bullshit!" The others in the hall turned as Sano yelled. The Lieutenant bent down in front of Reno. "How could you just sit there and not try to get to her?"

"There was too much fire, and the wreckage-"

"Wreckage?!" Sano laughed, but it was completely devoid of humor. He straightened, backing up a step as he threw his arms wide. "Wreckage stopped you? It sure as hell wouldn't have stopped her if your positions had been reversed, would it?"

Lenora stood up. "You listen to me, my husband-"

Sano pointed at her. "Your husband crashed the fucking helicopter."

"It wasn't his fault!"

"Right, yeah, the explosion. That still doesn't change the fact that he somehow got out with barely a few scratches while she's-"

Lenora put her face directly in front of Sano's, her eyes narrowing. "You need to back the hell off. He did everything right but things got out of control. He couldn't do anything more than you could. He's unharmed because Captain Samakura decided to make his life a priority, and as his friend you should be grateful he's okay instead of blaming him. Reno doesn't need guilt on top of everything else." She looked around at everyone in the hallway. "Do any of you need that guilt?! Or is this situation bad enough without making it worse?"

Sano stepped back, his eyes wide for a moment before he shook his head, running a hand through his hair once more. "You're right… Sorry, Reno, I just… There's nothing to do."

Lenora placed her hand on his shoulder. "There's nothing any of us can do. Trust me; every person in this hallway is going crazy wishing they could do something besides waiting."

Reno smiled at his wife, squeezing her hand in gratitude that she was here to help with the situation, getting a smile in return.

"I can't believe you three are surprised." They all turned to look at Rufus, who only moved enough to tilt his head towards them. "This job is always surrounded by death and pain, either ours or someone else's. You sign up, you know someone's going to die. Our retirement plans might as well be gravestones."

Sano folded his arms. "So what, you're saying we should just accept that she might be dead?"

"Of course you should. Didn't you already?"

"What? No!"

Rufus smiled at him. "Come on now. This isn't the first time one of us has been nearly killed. This definitely isn't the first time she's been nearly killed. I'm not surprised and you shouldn't be." He nodded past them. "Sam isn't."

They turned to look at Law, who'd more or less remained in the same place the whole time. Sano studied him. "You aren't surprised?"

Law shrugged, not bothering to look at them. "Not happy but not surprised. This job is basically being a soldier in a never-ending war. Never know when someone will die but the chances are high. I'm not giving up on her until we're told, but none of this surprises me."

They looked back to Rufus as Lenora voiced their thoughts. "But what about Captain Samakura?"

Rufus tilted his head to look at Reno. "Did she look surprised?" Reno shook his head and Rufus shrugged. "There you go. At first she didn't accept either of you dying, but obviously she accepted her own death at the end there. The only thing she didn't accept was Reno dying, which is why she got him out of the way. After the fall she could only save herself or Reno so it's a logical move."

"Logical?" Sano shook his head. "What about that move is logical?"

"Logical to her, I mean. She accepted her death years ago. Also…" He looked pointedly at Lenora. "She doesn't have a family. Any family."

Law grunted at that, grimacing – though it wasn't noticed by the others. Unbeknownst to them, half his thoughts were currently on Katsumi's family – as far as he knew, Ayane had no idea anything was going on, which was the entire reason he hadn't called her; he knew the effect it would have on her to be unsure like they were. Unfortunately, he had no way of knowing that she did know something was happening – and was even more in the dark than the rest of them.

Lenora sat down, gripping Reno's hand tightly as she thought about what Rufus had said. Sano looked at them and back to Rufus, sighing. "Just 'cause it makes sense doesn't mean we can be emotionless about it like you."

"I'm not emotionless." Rufus looked at him over his shades. "Just calm."

"Ah…" Sano nodded, leaving it at that. He now realized that Rufus wasn't any less affected by the events than the rest of them; he was just more prepared. Sano kind of wished he had the same emotional walls Rufus, Law and Katsumi seemed to have, but at the same time he didn't. It definitely seemed like a double-edged sword.

Lenora snapped them all out of their thoughts with her own question. "How is it… I mean, knowing what happened… How is it possible she could be alive?"

"Her Cyber Percentage." Sano turned towards her, folding his arms as he transitioned into what Katsumi often jokingly called his 'Serious Teacher Time Mode'. It was usually at these points when people would see the brilliance underlying his attitude, or at least that's what Katsumi had said once during a moment of rare honest praise. "Captain Samakura isn't like most people. The average citizen has a CP of 4%, meaning four percent of them is cybernetic parts - tech. As you probably know your husband has 5% CP, which is really low for a member of the military."

She nodded. "I'm a nurse, so I know most of this... I wasn't aware Reno's was relatively low, though."

Sano continued, "Well, he can mostly get away with that because he's a crazy-good pilot and isn't on the field itself. The average solder has 15% CP. I myself have a much higher CP, 32%."

"So... 32% of your body is cybernetic?"

"Yep."

"Why so high?"

Sano shrugged. "Generally not a good question to ask someone. You'd be surprised how often it has bad memories attached."

"Sorry. So what does this have to do with Samakura, her CP is higher, too?"

"83%."

Lenora blinked. "Eighty... three? But that's-"

"A lot, yeah. Most actually. She's almost full-body. Of course, tech is so advanced these days you'd never be able to tell unless you were told, at least until you saw her put her fist through a concrete wall. Her body still works as much as anyone else's but it's mostly synthetic."

"And we can't ask why..."

"I wouldn't."

Reno shook his head. "I wouldn't either, ever. There's no guarantee what response you'll get from her and none of the ones I can think of are good. I mean, I can only imagine the story behind a CP of eighty-three."

Lenora looked between them. "So she can survive a lot more than the ordinary person."

Sano nodded. "Yeah, but... obviously she's not invincible."

"Obviously..."

The fell silent again after that. Time passed with them all in their own thoughts until the click of boots on the floor drew their attention.

M walked up to them with his trademark smile on his face, shining glasses hiding his eyes beneath the brim of his hat. In short he looked the same as always so none of them could read him at all. "Hello gentlemen, lady. I am assuming you aren't doing as well as you could be."

They all stood and Sano nodded at him. "Good eyes Director. You got any news for us?"

"Of course, First Lieutenant Lionel, I didn't come simply to tease you. And to prevent doing so, I will first state that you may put aside your fears, Captain Samakura will recover in time." There was a collective sigh and a heavy feeling of relief. M paused to allow the rest of them to process the good news before continuing. "Tonight did not go well for us, but it could have gone worse. It has been a rather expensive night, however, and the others on the board tend to forget their gratefulness for your survival rather quickly and focus more on the bill."

"Which means?"

"Captain Samakura is in a bit of trouble with the company leaders." M held up a hand to stop Reno speaking even as he opened his mouth. "It was not your fault Corporal Hillford, the mission was the Captain's idea and responsibility, and we both know she won't argue that. And no, the fact that she saved your life doesn't mean anything to the board, sad but true. They only appreciate hard facts, and those facts are that we lost a very expensive aircraft and nearly lost a very important asset."

Reno blinked. "Asset?"

Sano growled. "Captain Sama's more than-"

"Yes, yes, I know, do calm down, Lieutenant. But you must understand, they are businessmen, and to them an asset is all any of you are. The fact remains that this was a failed mission on all counts."

"So what do we do?!"

M smiled. "I'm glad you asked. We fix things."

"How the hell do we do that?!"

"Patience. Let's wait until the team is back together, shall we?" M pointed down the hall. "If you take the elevator up one floor you'll find I've secured rooms for the night for anyone who wishes to stay. If all goes well you might be able to visit the Captain tomorrow if you wish." His glasses seemed to flash as he grinned. "Though I am almost certain she will not wish it and you will get a less-than-friendly greeting." He turned to head back down the hallway. "But then, this team is nothing if not stubborn…"

Law bid them goodnight before heading after M towards the building's exit. Rufus gave a wave and followed them, leaving Sano, Reno and Lenora behind looking at each other. Sano shrugged, turning to head towards the rooms. "Guess they're not willing to risk her wrath. Cowards."

Lenora smiled as she and Reno followed him. "Maybe they'd just prefer not to see her in such a position."

"Nah. Cowards."

"You say that," Reno countered, "but they aren't the ones who ran scared out of the building two weeks ago after trying to sneak in to her locker room while she was changing."

"She had a gun!"

"Coward."

"She was firing the gun! At my head! I like my head! Preferably in one piece!"

"Coooooooowaaaaaard."

"Bah! I'd like to see you stand your ground against bullets."

"I wasn't stupid enough to bring it on myself in the first place."

"I wasn't trying to sneak in, I just wasn't thinking!"

Lenora intruded with a smile. "So you're not stupid, just ignorant?"

"Yes! I mean, no! Rrrrrgh, don't make me shoot you two." Sano stepped into the elevator, hitting the button to the floor above after the other two stepped in.

They laughed softly and Lenora grabbed his sleeve as the elevator doors opened back up. "Come to our room before going to yours, we can have a drink and talk for a bit before retiring for the night."

Sano looked at her, appreciating the gesture and the genuinely caring look in her and Reno's eyes. It sounded a lot better than just heading off to his room alone immediately. He smiled, shrugging. "Yeah, sure. So long as there's a limit on how much you two can talk about your kid. Don't get me wrong, I love the kid, but you people have no concept of limits."

Lenora laughed, pulling him and Reno along. "No promises!"

~ ~ ~ ~ ~

"Hahahahahahahaha…"

Katsumi jerked, her head leaning back as it felt as though her spine were being stretched and snapped. When the pain subsided a bit she was able to notice the stranger part of her situation: she couldn't feel anything besides her own body, and even that felt distant. It was as if she was merely floating with nothing else around her.

"It's not polite to sleep when you have guests."

Katsumi forced her eyes open as she heard the male voice again. It was just as she'd felt, there was nothing around her but darkness. Thin blue lines of light that reminded her of electronic wiring spread in front of her, filling miles and miles like lines of code in an infinite darkness. It was indescribable, and she floated in the center of this strange world, arms and legs as weightless and useless as the rest of her.

There was a rush of wind and, before her, a figure floated down from above, feet coming first into view. His clothing was a strange mix of electronics and old styles. His entire body was encased in something very similar to the look of the world: black light body armor with similar glowing blue lines of electronics, code, energy, whatever it was. A long black trench coat was added to this, the kind they used to wear in the 1940's well over a century ago. On his chest was a symbol: Σ. Altogether it gave him a look that screamed he was something different than anything anyone had dealt with in this age, something new.

She couldn't see his face; all she could see was a smiling mouth. The rest was hidden in the shadows of his black hood, though she could see a shock of white hair that reached his shoulders. His arms were spread out to either side, one foot in front of the other as he floated down into view, wind from nowhere blowing his coat around him.

Katsumi remembered what had happened and at first took this for a strange dream, but it seemed far too "real" for that. He "stood" on nothingness in front of her as she felt her body tilt upright to face him. He seemed to be waiting for something, so she decided to start by asking one of the many questions she had: "What's going on?"

"Complicated." He waved his hand causing images of fractions to float past her head.

"Simplify." His voice seemed filled with subdued amusement that she didn't like. There was something else about it she disliked that she couldn't quite put her finger on, but it was smooth.

"Who are you?"

"Good question," he smiled. "Still complicated. My name," he touched the symbol on his chest, "is Sigma."

"That's an enigmatic name."

He spun in the air once, grinning. "I am an enigmatic person!"

"You're certainly trying to be," Katsumi deadpanned.

"I feel effort is important," he retorted, seeming not at all put off by the insult. "Next question."

"Where am I?"

"In a hospital. Or did you mean where is your consciousness?"

"I'm sorry?"

"You aren't feeling your physical body at the moment. Lucky you! It would be causing you quite a large amount of pain!" He seemed a little too happy about that for her tastes.

Katsumi sighed. "Fine then, where is my consciousness?"

"It's in your head as usual… sort of." He floated over beside her, gesturing to the endless space before them. "I'm visiting, and of course I thought I should say hello as I did, perhaps a 'get well soon'. No card or flowers, sorry. I did do a bit of redecorating though. Like it?"

Katsumi shook her head, shutting her eyes as she felt she was somehow getting a headache while inside her own head. "It's a little too cyber for me."

Sigma waved a hand. "Nonsense, you like everything cyber."

"How did you get inside my head?"

"Please, hacking people is just as easy for me as hacking computers."

"Hacking… people?"

He laughed and she grimaced, though at first she didn't know why. After a moment she realized it was because of how much he enjoyed the statement. "Nearly everyone has at least a small CP. Even that can be a window into some truly nasty things."

"So you're hacking into my brain."

"Yours is easy. I'd find a defense for that if I were you."

"What are you after? How do you know me? What is this even about?"

Sigma spun around to face her, floating back a few feet. "I've answered enough questions for now. I won't give everything away. I hate spoilers."

Katsumi glared at him, not amused. "Listen to me, you're going to answer my questions or-" Sigma snapped his fingers and her head jerked back as she screamed at the incredible pain now shooting through her spine. She felt her consciousness fading with Sigma's voice trailing after her before she was out again.

"Mind your manners next time and you'll get further! But as a token of our newfound friendship I'll give you one hint for the next round: the answer's in the heart!"

There was laughter… then darkness… then nothingness.

~ ~ ~ ~ ~

Samuel Lawrence stepped out into the cool night, grateful for both the cool air and the fact that he was finally outside. He pulled the pack of smokes from his tan army jacket and removed one, lighting it and taking a long draw followed by a sigh. He needed to clear his head and that wasn't gonna happen inside that building. The door swung open behind him and he glanced back to see Rufus exit the building as well. He turned around to face him. "Not staying either, huh?"

Rufus put his hands up and shrugged. "Why would I stay? I'm a little surprised you aren't, though."

"Why's that?"

Rufus removed his shades to let his silver eyes give Sam an obvious look. "You've been dead silent all night and I know it's not because you don't care."

Law shrugged. "I've seen her in this position before."

"Seen it once, seen it every time? I don't buy that."

Law smirked around his cigarette. "I know better than to see her at any point before she's up, walking and able to pretend nothing's wrong."

"Sano and Reno know that too, don't they? We all do."

Law nodded, taking a moment to let out a breath of smoke before replying. "Sano never worries about her reaction; he'll go in anyway and take whatever she throws at him just for the sake of seeing her condition for himself."

Rufus folded his arms. "I guess it makes sense, though I have sense enough to trust the doctors' word. What about Reno?"

"He's feeling guilty. He's weighed the risk, but he'll take it just to be sure she doesn't blame him."

"Do you think she does?"

Law chuckled. "Of course not."

"Mmm. I would." Rufus understood the look Sam directed at him despite the bigger man still wearing his shades. He shrugged in reply. "It was his fault."

"There was an explosion right beside the chopper. No pilot could save that."

"Not that. I can't blame him for the chopper crashing, that would be ridiculous."

"What, then?"

Rufus lifted his hand up to shoulder level, gesturing with an open hand as if the answer was obvious. "The man is weak. Relative to the rest of this team he's a borderline cripple. It's his fault Captain Samakura had to focus on and worry about him during the crash; if she'd only thought of herself she would've been fine."

Law turned to him. "She would've done the same for any of us."

Rufus' eyes hardened. "She wouldn't have to. If I was the one up there with her we would've gotten out fine."

"So you think she should've just let him die."

"No." Rufus shook his head. "I don't want Reno dead. I don't even want him off the team, really. I just want everyone to accept his responsibility in this matter." Rufus spread his arms. "Every one of us has weaknesses. This tragedy was caused by Reno's."

"I'm surprised you aren't blaming the Captain's need to protect him."

"That isn't a weakness. If she were working alone it would very much be, but as it is she survived and kept a team member alive, one whom we will not now need to replace. We still have his skill thanks to her actions."

"Good."

Rufus smiled. "Defensive of our Captain, aren't you?" Sam ignored him, but he didn't take the hint. "You've known her longer than any of us, that's to be sure. Could it be you've developed feelings stronger than friendship for her in those years?" Law only grunted which made Rufus chuckle. "Well, her birthday is in- let's see, as of right now it's 2 AM on March 25th- two days, isn't it? At thirty-four is when most women are entering their prime. She's probably starting to look for a husband!"

Sam looked at him with a raised eyebrow which lasted a few seconds before both broke into laughter. Law flicked his finished cigarette away. "Yeah, she's definitely in the market for that."

"A wife, then?"

"Don't ask me."

Rufus chuckled. "I bet she wants a white-picket fence with a daisy garden and two pleasant children."

"It's 2068. When's the last time you saw a white-picket fence?"

"Good point. More realistically she'd probably have an underground bunker with laser turret defenses and an AI security net."

"This is a dangerous conversation. If she heard we'd be risking our health."

"That's why we're having it while she's unconscious." Rufus folded his arms again. "In all honesty though-"

"Rufus, what does she do when none of us are with her?"

"I have no idea."

"Right. She won't let anyone into her personal life; she'll hardly even let them into her apartment. The chances of her letting someone in enough for anything more than a 'war buddy' relationship are basically non-existent."

"Hmm. Sad. Dreadful waste of an attractive woman."

"You go ahead and go tell her she's a waste of an attractive woman. I'll wait out here."

"One team member in hospital is enough for now, I think. Anyway, I think it will be bad if she wakes up and learns we've all wasted the whole night sitting around waiting for her to do so, so I'm heading back to the scene to see what I can figure out."

Law nodded. "I'll come and see what I can tell about this explosion. Maybe it will be different from the other one."

"We can only hope," Rufus sighed as he started walking. "Otherwise we're dealing with a serial mass-murderer with an uncomfortable talent for nearly killing our Captain…"

~ ~ ~ ~ ~

The first thing Katsumi felt when she woke up was pain; the second thing she felt was guilt. The emotion hit her for various reasons, but the most pressing one was that she remembered her last thought before blacking out, the one she'd sent across the city, and she knew how her sister would be feeling.

The room around her was silent for the moment; she could tell she'd been left alone for now. She began moving one muscle at a time, trying to check her damage. She found it harder to move her left arm, wondering why that was until she felt for it with her other arm and realized it was missing. She groaned, dropping her remaining hand and returning to her thoughts. She couldn't wait another moment without fixing the problem she'd caused hours ago…

~ ~ ~ ~ ~

Ayane sat in her bed, looking at anything and everything in the room trying to distract herself. She'd been going a little crazy for the past five hours; since she'd heard her older sister say her name, and then nothing. Since then she hadn't been able to reach her at all; it wasn't the first time, but it took all her willpower not to stomp right out of her room and go find her sister. As it was she'd just sat in bed and cried more or less nonstop, watching the clock and hoping for any response.

Ayane… I'm alright.

Katsumi's voice startled and relieved her. *Katsumi!* Her own voice was full of anger and worry; she knew the first one wasn't fair but she couldn't help it. *What happened?! The last thing I heard was you say my name and then...*

Our helicopter was blown out of the sky. I managed to save Reno but I couldn't get myself out from under it when it came down.

Ayane put her hands over her mouth and closed her eyes, taking a deep breath. She normally had incredible composure, but this was her weakness. *And you're okay?*

I'll be fine. Apparently it was... a little close, but they said I'll make a full recovery. I should be fine by tomorrow.

Ayane let out a sigh, leaning her head back and staring at the ceiling. *You scared the hell out of me. All I heard was my name, and... then I couldn't reach you.*

I'm sorry... I honestly... I didn't know if I'd make it. It was a reaction. I didn't want to hurt you, I just... I couldn't stop myself from trying to reach you a last time...

Katsumi's voice sounded weak and apologetic to her; guilty. Ayane knew her sister was biting her lip at that moment, a rare sign of worry. *I appreciate your call to me, really, I do, Katsumi... I just...*

M would contact you if I was really gone. Unless that happens, always believe I'm alive.

I know, I just worry. Was there no way to save yourself?

It was either me or Reno.

Well I guess you made the obvious choice, then. Ayane smiled. *I didn't expect anything less from you, Sumi.*

Don't pretend like you're any different.

Ayane laughed softly. *You sound so accusatory when you say it like that.*

I'm pretty sure it's your fault.

I will gladly take that blame. A lot of things are my fault because you're wrapped around my finger.

What?!

Ayane laughed again. *Now who's pretending? You just try to say no to me. Just try.*

She grinned as she heard her older sister's grumbling, followed by *Oh, look, a doctor just happened to come by and tell me to get more sleep. Looks like I have to go!*

Uh-huh. I'll let you off the hook this time, Sumi.

I love you, Aya. Katsumi's voice returned a final time, softer and more serious. *Try to sleep...*

I love you too. Ayane looked up at the ceiling, silently thanking God as she started to cry again, but for an entirely different reason this time: relief.

~ ~ ~ ~ ~

Kurasano stepped into the room after clearing it with the doctor. Katsumi lay on the bed in the center surrounded by various instruments and hardware, but she was conscious. It was eleven in the morning, later than Sano would've liked, but it'd taken that long for Captain Samakura to wake up and another hour for the doctors to clear entry to others.

The glare her lavender eyes sent his way as the door clicked shut behind him would've sent almost anyone else back out the door but Sano just ignored it, standing before her bed and shaking his head disappointedly. "Oh, Captain, the things you get yourself into. What're we gonna do with you if you can't take care of yourself, huh?"

The woman's eyes narrowed and Sano's widened a bit as she pushed herself up on one arm even though the other one seemed to be missing and her condition was bad enough that she shouldn't have even been awake. "Even in this state I can still kick your ass, Kurasano. Don't make me get out of this bed and show you."

Sano held up his hands. "Hey, I didn't mean anything by it, I was just joking! Honestly you don't look weak or anything, I promise!"

Katsumi nodded and leaned back, looking out the window instead. She was obviously unhappy and Sano realized now probably wasn't the time to be making jokes so he switched gears. "Your birthday's in two days, right?"

"Don't remind me."

"Still, kinda bad timing."

Katsumi gave him a look. "Tell me, when is a good time to have a helicopter land on you?"

Sano scratched his head. "Ahhh... Point taken. Look, I'm just trying to lighten the mood."

"Doing a bang-up job, Sano," Katsumi muttered as she looked away again.

He sighed. "Fine, I give up. I'll leave, but first, Reno wants to come visit."

She spoke without looking at him. "Fine, let's parade the whole department through the room, take pictures or video even."

"Don't be like that; he just wants to make sure you don't blame him."

Katsumi finally looked back at him. "Why would I blame him?"

"Don't have the conversation with me, talk to him."

She grimaced. "Fine. Tell him to come in."

"Right," Sano smiled and exited the room, looking at the nervous man waiting outside with his wife. He pointed his thumb over his shoulder. "She says you can go in."

Reno nodded, unsure whether or not he was relieved about that. "What about Lenora?"

Sano shrugged. "Your choice and risk, not mine."

Lenora smiled at her husband. "Go in alone, no need to make her angry." She didn't understand the Captain's feelings about it, but she'd heard enough to know that their visits weren't exactly welcomed.

Reno nodded, opening the door and carefully stepping inside, shutting it behind him and staring unblinking at the hard look he was receiving from Katsumi. After a few moments of him not moving at all she sighed and looked out the window again. "Talk, Reno."

"Right…" He cleared his throat, tried to start, cleared his throat again, and then spoke. "I'm sorry-"

"Seriously?" Katsumi interrupted, looking back at him in irritation. "Are we really going to do this?"

Reno blinked. "I…"

"You're honestly going to try apologizing to me. Are you trying to make me angry? Are you feeling left out without an injury and looking for me to fix that for you?"

"No! I just-"

"You're just being an idiot. We take blame for mistakes and bad decisions, not any negative occurrence that happens involving a team member. The blame for this one is mine," she pointed at him as he opened his mouth, "and if you try to argue I swear to God I'll break just enough bones that you only almost die." His mouth snapped shut again and she lowered her hand, satisfied. "I'm the one who said to take the helicopter lower, between the buildings. That was a stupid decision to make. You followed orders and you couldn't save it after the explosion; that was just beyond your power to control. Fortunately I was the only one hurt so I don't have to deal with having injured or killed a member of my team this time."

"Yeah, but, during the crash-"

"I can survive more than you can."

"I saw your eyes, Captain. You didn't think you were going to survive."

Katsumi was silent for a few seconds before she gave him a genuine, soft smile, a sight that nearly knocked him off his feet. "I didn't. But at that point in time it was more important to me that you were going to."

"Why...?"

"Don't act ignorant, Reno. You have a wife and a child; your death would destroy three people. I live alone... and I haven't nearly as much to protect." Katsumi bit her lip at the lie, but at the moment her goal was getting rid of Reno's guilt, not being honest. "You have a future you're always talking and thinking about."

"And you don't have a future?"

Katsumi shrugged, her voice lower than normal so that he had to listen carefully to hear. "I don't know. I know I don't think about it. I have hopes, but... it's possible those hopes could be lost and... I'd rather not think about it." She really wouldn't have a future if Ayane... But she couldn't deal with thinking along those lines, so she moved past the thoughts quickly. Reno shook his head and Katsumi looked back up, speaking louder. "We've talked. You've realized how stupid it is to blame yourself or feel guilty, and moreover, how angry I'll get if you do it, at least until you do screw up. Now get out, I'm tired of people being in my room. You can talk to me when I get out of this damn place."

Reno nodded, opening the door but pausing to look back at her. "Thanks, Captain."

"Better be the last time you bring it up, Corporal."

Reno smiled. "No worries." He stepped outside, pulling the door closed.

Sano clapped him on the shoulder. "Hey, you're alive! And you have all your parts!" He raised an eyebrow. "Unless she ripped off something I can't see."

"Nope, I got lucky." Reno grinned. "Though she did threaten me."

"Noooooooo, really? That's so out of character!"

Lenora caught Reno's chin to turn his gaze to her. "Feel better?" He nodded and she returned his smile. "Good."

Reno grabbed her hand. "C'mon, let's all go get some lunch or something. I wanna get back to my daughter soon."

Lenora smiled. "You two go ahead for a moment, I'll catch up; I just want to question the doctors a bit."

Reno nodded; since his wife was a nurse, it made sense she would have a few questions. "Lemme know what you learn."

Sano patted his back as they started walking. "C'mon, let's decide where we're gonna celebrate your surviving that meeting with Captain Sama!"

"I'm starting to wish you were the one stuck in bed, Sano."

"Aw, come on, don't say that, you'll hurt my feelings!"

Lenora watched them go until they turned a corner. She then turned to the room and entered it, catching Katsumi's gaze as soon as she was inside. The older woman's eyes narrowed in a glare aimed at her. "I'm not going to ask why you decided to bother me as well. I assume you have a damn good reason."

Lenora had only met Katsumi Samakura a few times in the past, less than ten to be sure. She'd always gotten the impression of a harsh but caring person, but for some reason the woman currently in front of her seemed a lot more of the former and a lot less of the latter. Lenora was smart enough to know that wasn't always the case, though. Something about this situation made her husband's boss very angry, but without a real knowledge of the woman she couldn't truly understand how she felt. Still, she needed to be here. She stepped away from the door, meeting Katsumi's gaze steadily. "My reason is good for me; it may not be for you. I need to thank you."

Katsumi didn't seem surprised, though her glare did fade into a simple hard look. "For your husband."

"Yes," Lenora nodded, stopping in front of her bed. "You saved his life and you didn't have to."

"Of course I did."

Lenora blinked. "I'm sorry…?"

Katsumi sighed. "Maybe someone else could just let someone die in that situation, but I couldn't. Especially since I actually care about Reno."

"Still, I want to thank you."

"Mmm." Katsumi pulled her legs up to rest her remaining arm on her knees. "He's lucky to have you. I'm glad you're thanking me, but not for me."

Lenora tilted her head. "I don't follow…"

"I'm glad to see how grateful you are that he survived. It proves to me that I made the right choice."

She smiled at Katsumi. "I'm also grateful he has you for a boss."

"So he's lucky on both fronts." Katsumi smirked at Lenora. "Works for me. Look, as long as I have any say in the matter, Reno won't die. You can be sure I'll always do whatever I can to keep my team alive. According to Rufus that's how I'm going to die, which is probably true. It almost happened last night. Still it isn't going to change."

Lenora smiled gratefully at her, leaning down to hug her. "I really can't thank you enough."

Katsumi looked off to the side as she was hugged, not hugging her back but making an uncomfortable sound. "You really don't know me at all, do you…?"

Lenora laughed and backed off. "I decided to take the risk. Listen, I'm not going to try to pay you back; nothing I could ever do would be enough and you probably wouldn't accept it anyway. But I hope you'll think about simply having dinner at our house sometime. If nothing else I want you to realize your importance to our family."

Katsumi sighed. "If you'll stop talking like that, I'll accept whatever invites you give me."

Lenora blinked in surprise and then beamed. "Great!"

"Didn't expect me to accept?" Katsumi looked at her as she shook her head. "I can understand why. But trust me, your invitation means more to me than you know. Now, please, leave the room and lock the door behind you so no one else comes barging in."

Lenora smiled as she opened the door. "Of course, sorry. Thank you again." She pulled the door shut behind her, hearing a long sigh from inside as she did. The whole thing had gone far better than she'd expected, though. She could hardly believe the closed-off woman had not only accepted her invitation but had seemed grateful for it. It really made her feel as if she'd managed to pay her back just a little.

With a satisfied sigh Lenora turned around to see both Sano and Reno standing in front of her, wide-eyed.

"You went in…"

"And survived?!"

"She should've killed you for even opening the door a third time!"

"And thrown your body out the window!"

Lenora rolled her eyes, turning both men around and pushing them down the hall. "I'm smarter than the two of you put together and she appreciates my conversation."

Sano looked over at Reno. "Must be a female thing."

"Are you denying my intelligence, Sano? Don't make me hurt you."

"Aww, dude, the boss is rubbing off on your wife! You're doomed."

Reno laughed at Sano's overdramatic expression as Lenora pushed them both out of the building and into the sunlight.

~ ~ ~ ~ ~

Katsumi sat on the edge of her bed, readying herself to get out of it. The doctors had told her she shouldn't even be awake this much and she knew there was no way she should even be trying to stand considering her condition, but she felt as if she was going mad sitting in the bed all day. The stream of people coming into her room had been bad enough.

She hated looking weak. Despised it. The fact that people were coming in to see her while she was stuck in bed unable to do anything drove her crazy. If she had her way, not only would they not see her in such a state, they wouldn't even know she'd ever been in said state. She wanted to be thought invincible and their worried looks shattered her illusions. It was obvious that Samuel was her oldest friend, the one who knew her best; she hadn't seen him at all since before the crash and she was sure he wouldn't say anything about this. The only person she ever wanted to see her like this was Ayane, and like hell was anyone else getting the kind of complete openness they had between them.

She slowly rested her weight on her foot, edging off the bed gingerly, wincing and hissing at the pain but forcing herself forward. Soon she was standing on both legs beside her bed waiting for the pain to subside, which it eventually did. She stepped away from the bed and moved towards the window, leaning against it with a sigh. The whole investigation was on pause while she was in here. She wanted to get back out there and do her job!

Katsumi looked out the window but she wasn't seeing the view anymore; she was seeing dozens of possible explosions, hundreds or thousands of deaths. Whoever was behind these attacks wasn't sitting in a room doing nothing, she was sure of that. They were probably planning their next attack. There was nothing Katsumi could do from in here. She looked back at her bed, glaring at it. She admired her sister's strength for being able to stay in-hospital as much as she did. As far as Katsumi was concerned there was nothing worse than being stuck in bed all day.

As if taking her thoughts as a challenge her head suddenly pulsed with pain, sending her off balance and forcing her to catch the windowsill to remain standing. Katsumi cursed as pain began to flood through her body, her vision blurring as sound faded into the background, every sense feeling like it had to come down a tunnel before getting to her. "Not now... Can't I just get a break now...?"

She stumbled towards the bed but she could only handle the sickness for a short period in the best of times; the added heavy injuries she was suffering combined to make it hit faster than usual and she only managed to get her hand on the bed before she fell against it, unable to pull herself up. Another curse escaped her lips as she slipped back, hand gripping and dragging the blankets down with her, knocking over a couple instruments on her way to the floor. She heard the door open, saw the blurry outlines of several doctors who rushed in to pick her up and was, at least for now, grateful she was already in the hospital at this time.

The pain stopped swelling and subsided as they attached some unseen things to her, sending her back into a mindless darkness she welcomed with open arms.

Chapter 6: Whitewash

Date: March 25, 2068
Time: 6:09 PM
Location: Tokyo Tech and Healing Center,
43rd Floor

A nurse literally flew out of a room near the end of the hallway, landing in what had to be a painful manner on the hard floor. Those present were just happy the door had been open or he'd have gone through it. A hard smack came from the room next, followed by a doctor who stumbled backwards out of the room and fell at its entrance. A female hand slammed onto the doorframe, gripping it hard enough to dent the metal.

Katsumi stepped slowly into the hallway. She was bent over a bit and breathing deeply but she flexed her newly replaced left arm and used it to grab the other side of the doorframe, standing up straight and glaring down at the doctor through violet hair. "Thank you for treating me, doctor, but I'm ready to leave and I'm leaving."

The man sat up, rubbing his jaw. "M-miss Samakura, you aren't fully healed, especially after your episode this morning. You haven't even been here for twenty-four hours and considering your condition we have to keep you here another…" He trailed off as the woman's look changed subtly.

Katsumi tightened the last tie on her vest. She silently thanked M for leaving the black vest, pants and boots in her room; he most likely knew she'd be leaving as soon as she could walk, clothing or not. "Don't make me switch from grateful to angry, doctor." She tightened her fists, forcing her body to move without showing any of the pain or weakness she felt. No one else tried to stop her as she made her way down the hallway to the elevator. Once she was inside it and the doors were closed she leaned against one of the walls, watching the numbers change and returning to the straight-edge posture before the doors opened on the ground floor.

A few of the receptionists and security personnel eyed her but she ignored them and went right for the door. Finally outside she let out a sigh of relief, breathing in the fresh air thankfully. She turned and headed down the sidewalk towards the subway. She could call a car but she'd have to wait for their arrival, and at the moment she was really looking forward to getting back to headquarters and jumping back into work. As far as she was concerned, the wait had been long enough already.

She descended the stairs with a care she resented having to take. Still, it was better than slipping and ending up on the ground in the middle of a crowd of people. As she reached the bottom step her vision went black, flashing green for a split instant before everything was back. She looked around in confusion but no one else seemed to have noticed anything, meaning it was a problem with her. She waited in dread for some new phase of her sickness to strike but nothing ever came. Her eyes narrowed a bit in suspicion as she examined the subway terminal, fingers reaching back to touch the gun stuck in her belt. It almost felt like something was off about the area, but not enough to draw the gun and panic everyone around. Not yet, anyway.

She always followed her gut instincts, but this time they were so vague she didn't even know how to follow them. The only hint she really had was "be wary". As far as she knew, it could mean anything was about to happen, from a woman dropping her purse nearby to a demon exploding out through the ground. She pushed away the feeling as unhelpful paranoia; after all, seeking out danger at all times would only lead to seeing danger where there was none. She resolved to watch everything around her but still continued forward, waiting for the next train and boarding it once it arrived.

Katsumi took a seat as far away from the majority of passengers as possible, in the back of the last car. It was a crowded time of day with people leaving work and catching a ride home, so even this car had a good number of passengers, from obvious businessmen to shoppers to the homeless. Katsumi watched the dirty men in rags and the ones in fine suits equally; stereotyping led to assumptions that led to deadly mistakes. She was probably just being paranoid… The stress of the past few days, of trying…

and failing… to catch a serial terrorist was getting to her, that much she knew.

She lifted a hand to rub her eyes, suddenly tired as her mind began to work against her. The vibrations of the car as it moved quickly along the tunnel's tracks lulled her into deeper thoughts she wanted no part of. Failure weighed heavily on her and, what was worse, she was no closer to finding and stopping the culprit than she'd been before. She didn't want to admit it, but she didn't know where to go from here.

In the background, several people in the car talked quietly to each other. A business man spoke firmly on his phone about some deal he should have left at work but couldn't let go of. A homeless-looking man slipped away from the handle he was holding, moving down the car seeking handouts from all the passengers.

The first two didn't bother her, but the homeless man eventually reached Katsumi, moving to hold his hand out in front of her for a handout when he tripped and fell towards her. There was a glint and a flash of movement as Katsumi shot out of her seat, one hand swiping down as the other slammed palm-first into the man's chest, sending him flying back the other direction. He slammed into one of the poles in the center of the car, bouncing off of it with a cry and hitting the floor. Everyone's attention shot to the short altercation with a collective gasp.

A knife hit the ground between Katsumi and the man and he scrambled to recover it, lunging at her again. In the few seconds she had, she noticed several things very wrong with what had at first appeared to be a normal beggar: for one, his eyes were wide as if in shock, though he showed no other signs of shock. Two, his veins were visible through his skin, bulging as if every muscle in his body was flexing or as if he was on some crazy drug. And three, his entire body was subtly shaking.

Katsumi dodged the knife a second time, reaching back to pull the pistol from her belt. She ducked a third swipe, slamming her elbow into the man's side and sliding past him, turning gracefully to take aim at his head as her finger slipped onto the trigger.

The answer's in the heart!

Katsumi's breath caught as the words and voice from her dream shot through her mind with astounding clarity. As the beggar turned back to face her with the knife she moved her aim lower, unsure why but following her instincts as she always did. The sound of the shot filled the small subway car as the bullet exploded from her gun and ripped through the beggar's chest. He jerked back and fell with a spray of blood as the other passengers in the cart erupted in screams. Katsumi was still eyeing the body, though, and an instant later she slid one foot back and turned to face the passengers, raising her voice. "Everyone get out of the car, run to the front of the train! NOW!"

The absolute authority in her voice made even these total strangers in the car jump out of their seats and rush through the door, yelling and pulling other confused passengers with them. Katsumi wasted no time as she fired again, shooting out a window. She bent down and grabbed part of the dead beggar's clothing, lifting him up and hurling his body through the window in one smooth move.

Three seconds later an explosion rocked the train and tore off the back half of the subway car. The sound of rending metal, erupting flame and shattering cement deafened Katsumi for the second time in as many days. A blast of hot wind washed over her and she felt herself fly into the air as the subway shrieked, the back car flying off the rails and pulling the rest of the train with it in a domino effect.

Katsumi dropped her gun as she flew through the air, twisting mid-fall and catching the last metal pole in the center of the car. She looked down and saw the rails rushing quickly beneath her. Around her were the shorn edges of the train car, sparks flying as the metal grinded against the tunnel's walls. Katsumi hit the floor as momentum left her, pulling herself quickly into what remained of the car. She looked back and saw the flames dying down further back in the tunnel as the subway train slowly screeched to a stop. She jumped up to check on the passengers and immediately fell again, gasping as pain shot through her. She wasn't nearly healed from the injuries she'd received less than twenty-four hours earlier, and this kind of thing was the last thing her body needed.

Unfortunately for her body, Katsumi didn't care. She growled angrily and slammed a fist into the floor, pushing herself up onto her feet once more and stumbling to the door between cars, forcing it open and looking at the people inside. "Is everyone okay? Who's hurt?"

The people in front of her looked shaken, but apart from a few bruises and a small cut here and there, there didn't seem to be any injuries. Katsumi allowed herself a moment of relief and pulled out her badge, a sight that visibly relaxed the passengers. She moved through to the next car to check on the passengers in there, but they were even better than those in the previous car. She continued all the way through to the front car, informing the conductor and answering the few questions he had mind enough to ask. He called in for help as Katsumi headed back through the train until she reached the back car again, where she dropped down onto the rails.

Katsumi could scarcely believe it as she walked down the dark tunnel. Not only were there no casualties but the only real injury was one mildly broken arm, and that wouldn't even be labeled "serious" by any report. Her actions had apparently saved everyone on the train. She should've been ecstatic.

And yet, as she walked towards the smoking wreckage down the tunnel, all she could think was that saving them wouldn't even be necessary if she had been able to catch this criminal in the first place.

~ ~ ~ ~ ~

Samuel Lawrence whistled as he looked at the rubble in the collapsed portion of the tunnel. "Twice in two days; you sure know how to attract 'em, boss."

Katsumi Samakura stood behind him with her arms folded, watching him inspect the edge of the collapse. She was waiting for him to determine the structural integrity of the remaining tunnel so they could get to work clearing the debris and get to what she hoped would be something left of a body somewhere in the middle of it. "You're going to attract the back of my hand if you don't shut up and get to work."

Law shrugged, focusing on the mess in front of him. The Captain obviously wasn't in the mood for jokes so he wasn't going to push it. Kurasano came up behind them, tucking his phone into his suit jacket's pocket and running a hand over his crimson hair. "Crew's ready as soon as we get the clearance from you, Law." He glanced at Katsumi. "Hey, boss... Should you even be outta the hospital yet?" Law cringed without even having to look. Sano took a step back at the dangerous look Katsumi directed at him, giving a sheepish shrug. "Just sayin'…"

Katsumi kept the glare on him as she spoke slowly. "I am, *Lieutenant*," Sano and Law both winced at the venom in her tone, "perfectly capable of walking, and I don't need to be babysat any longer."

"I wasn't saying-"

"I need to get back to my job. Is that okay with you, or should I have asked permission?"

Sano held up his hands in a placating gesture. "Sorry I even brought it up."

Katsumi gave a low sound he swore was a growl and turned back to watch Law impatiently. The large man finally stood up, nodding back to her. "Structure's good, the blast mostly caused surface damage."

Samakura immediately waved to the crew they had standing by. "Alright, get over here and get to work! I want this cleared quickly and efficiently!"

The team jumped to work, expertly removing slabs of concrete and iron. Several minutes in one of the workers shouted over to them and Katsumi headed in his direction with Sano and Law on her heels. The man moved out of their way and Katsumi stepped into his place to see his find. Sano looked over her shoulder and winced at the sight as she kneeled to inspect it. "Yeesh, there go my dinner plans… For the next three weeks…"

It was a bloody sight, to be sure. Katsumi recognized the top half of her attacker's head, but everything below part of the jaw was gone, leaving half the jaw hanging loose along with some stuff Sano would rather not identify. The bottom half of the pelvis and legs lay nearby, along with some random pieces she couldn't identify at first glance. Sano stuck his hands in his pockets and looked up at the ceiling. "So I'm guessing he had the bomb on him."

"Not on," Law corrected as he kneeled beside Katsumi once she made room for him, "in."

"In," Sano repeated. "Inside him. Well that's even *better*," he remarked with more than a hint of sarcasm.

Katsumi nodded. "His body seemed to be under a great deal of stress. His veins grew more visible over time, muscles and skin seemed to stretch, eyes bulged more."

"Taking that into account, along with the appearance of these remains... See the small tears in the skin of the areas still intact?" Law shook his head. "Doesn't look like a bomb was just implanted into him."

Katsumi looked at her Demolitions expert. "What, then?"

"He *was* the bomb."

Sano looked back down with a frown. "Biological?"

"Maybe."

Katsumi shook her head. "So this criminal turns people into bombs."

"That's what it looks like to me. We'll take these remains in and I'll look into it a little more, but I'm almost sure."

Katsumi stood up, moving past the two and brushing herself off. "I don't like this."

"Well yeah," Sano said as he turned to follow her, "Making people into living bombs is all kinds of sick."

"It's also new and requires some sort of genius." She looked back at Kurasano. "I don't like my criminals to be geniuses with new ideas. We don't have a counter for this."

"We won't have to. If we catch him, we can stop this just like that."

"Just like that..." Katsumi sighed, looking in his eyes. "Why do I not believe it will be 'just like that'?"

Sano shrugged, offering a humorless smile. "Because nothing's ever easy for us."

~ ~ ~ ~ ~

Date: March 26, 2068
Time: 10:28 AM
Location: South Ashfield Hospital, 3rd
Floor, Room 302

"So... You were told how to stop these attacks... in a dream?"

"Not a… dream, exactly… I mean, he said he was hacking into my mind."

Ayane sighed. "I didn't know that was possible. This sounds insane."

"That's why I've only told you," Katsumi said as she sat back and folded her arms.

"I've never heard of this 'Sigma'. I've never heard of this mind-hacking stuff, either." Ayane hugged her moogle. "I don't like this, Katsumi… I don't like any of this. Someone breaking into your mind? Assassination attempts on you? I don't like anything about this case."

Katsumi sat forward. "We don't know for sure this was targeted at me-"

"You just got out of the hospital, Sumi!" Ayane glared at her. "You've almost died two times in as many days – no, within twenty-four hours! What about that sounds like a coincidence?!"

"Okay, okay," Katsumi said calmingly as she moved to sit on the side of the bed, putting her arm around Ayane and pulling her against her. "It's okay, really. You don't have to worry."

Ayane sniffed and hugged her back. "Of course I do. Everything's trying to kill you."

"Not everything," Katsumi looked down at her. "This 'Sigma' warned me, so at least for now he's trying to keep me alive. As for the attacks, well, they keep failing."

"They keep getting close."

Katsumi sighed. "I don't know what you want me to say, Aya. I don't have a choice in this."

"I know you don't… I just…" Ayane huffed. "Why couldn't you be, like, a librarian?"

Katsumi smiled, leaning back on the bed so they were more comfortable. Ayane laid her head on her shoulder and Katsumi watched her as she spoke. "I'd be a horrible librarian."

Ayane frowned. "So? It'd be a whole lot safer."

"You know my own safety isn't my highest priority."

"I wish it was higher." Ayane leaned up enough to look at her sister's face, laying a hand on her cheek. "Try to stay alive, okay? I don't… I really can't…"

Katsumi reached up and took her hand, squeezing it reassuringly. "I know. You'll just have to trust me, okay?"

Katsumi smiled at her. "I promise I won't leave you alone as long as you promise the same thing."

Ayane returned the smile and nodded. "I promise. But you better catch this criminal as soon as you can. I hate these ongoing cases."

"You and me both."

~ ~ ~ ~ ~

Date: March 26, 2068
Time: 11:57 PM
Location: Aegis Corporation Japan Division Headquarters, Tokyo – Captain Katsumi Samakura's Office

Katsumi leaned her elbows on her desk and rubbed her eyes, releasing a sigh for what seemed like the four-hundredth time that day. She was tired; exhausted, even. She hadn't slept since two days earlier when she'd been unconscious for a few hours, and that could hardly be considered sleeping. Before that... Well, she guessed the last time she'd actually slept was four days earlier, before the first bombing. She'd had about one or two hours of sleep that night. Was that what she considered "actual sleep" now? She couldn't remember the last time she'd had a solid six hours, which was probably a problem.

She wasn't planning on doing anything to fix it, though. What she was doing was staring at a computer screen as she had been on and off over the past twenty-eight hours. She'd also gone to each previous crime scene and a few other places she'd hoped to find clues, not to mention meeting with each member of her team for various tasks. Law had confirmed his earlier estimations; the victims were turned into bombs.

According to the evidence they had, something was introduced to the victim's bloodstream that converted the oxygen in their blood into a highly volatile explosive. It gained pressure as it spread through the body, which was what led to spasms and the expansion of blood vessels. Eventually the pressure would become too great and the victim would explode. Law's theory was that each victim had some degree of CP as most people did, and electrical sparks would be triggered in the cyber parts as the body was torn apart and exposed to open air, setting the now-explosive blood aflame. The explosion would rip through the air, feeding on the oxygen in the air and spreading even further until it burned out.

According to Law the original catalyst for this grim series of events was almost certainly always placed in the victim's heart so that, when triggered, whatever it introduced to the bloodstream would be pumped throughout the body as quickly as possible. Apparently, Katsumi's heart-shot on the most recent victim most likely destroyed the implant before it could spread its toxin throughout the entirety of the victim's body, causing the explosion to be less than the previous ones.

The answer's in the heart!

Katsumi didn't tell anyone that her so-called "lucky shot" had been determined based on a dream she'd had while unconscious. Well, she hadn't told anyone other than her sister, but Ayane was as lost as she was as to what it meant.

A knock on the door drew her attention to her open doorway where Sano stood outlined by the light from the hallway, a contrast to her currently dark office. "Hey, Captain." Sano leaned against the doorframe. "Happy birthday."

Katsumi glanced at her computer screen. 12:01. Just now March 27th. Apparently, she was thirty-four now. She sighed, running a hand through her soft violet curls. "Thanks."

Sano smirked. "You forgot."

"Why would I remember?"

"It's a big deal to some people."

Katsumi leaned back in her chair, looking at him. "I don't see the point in marking the day I was born. I didn't do anything worth celebrating on that day."

Sano shrugged. "It's the one day of the year when things are supposed to focus on you."

"You know how much I hate people focusing on me."

Sano chuckled. "True. Don't worry; nobody's been stupid enough to try throwing a surprise party since Reno's first year on the team."

Katsumi was unable to prevent a smile forming on her lips at the memories that brought up. "You could've warned the rookie, you know."

Sano blinked. "I see… And how would that have been fun to watch?"

Katsumi laughed, shaking her head. "I've never seen someone so crestfallen by a reaction to a party. I had to pretend to enjoy it just for his benefit."

"That was pretending to enjoy it?"

"Hey, give me a break. At least I tried."

"Not very hard."

"You're asking a lot from me."

"Yeah, yeah." Sano pushed off the doorframe and gestured towards the computer. "Anything new?"

Katsumi sobered with a sigh and shook her head. "I haven't found anything, not even a suspect." She glanced at him. "Did you get Law's report?"

Sano grimaced. "Yeah, pretty disturbing stuff."

"Needlessly so. What's the point of going to such trouble? Why not just use normal explosives or something similar?"

Sano shrugged. "It's an act of terror, right? I guess living bombs spread more terror."

"Mmm." Katsumi clasped her hands and leaned her chin on them. "I still don't know what he's trying to terrorize."

"At this point I'd say you. The last attack was on you directly, wasn't it?"

"And maybe the one before that as well."

"Right. So I guess the only question is why."

"If you're going to come up with a list of people who may want to kill me, you're going to need a lot of data space."

"Yeah, that's not exactly helpful." Sano tapped his chin. "Maybe trying to kill you is just a reaction? The guy got worried we were gonna catch him."

"Or he wants to take out the leading counter-terrorist in the city."

"World."

"City."

"Country?"

"Fine," Katsumi sighed. "The point is, if he wants to conduct terrorism here, our team is the main obstacle."

"Oh, so he's after the whole team now, is he?"

Katsumi raised an eyebrow. "You think it's personal?"

Sano shrugged. "Honestly, I don't know. This guy's unpredictable as hell. Basically all I can tell you is that he'll blow something up. It's just that the last two times he did so he came kinda close to killing you, so either it's a really bad coincidence or you're his current target."

Katsumi leaned back in her chair. "At least that's better."

"Yeah, who doesn't love having their own personal terrorist? I know *I'm* jealous. Can't wait until I'm popular enough to get one of my own."

"You know what I mean, Sano."

"Yeah. Less danger for innocents, more on you. Most people wouldn't consider that a good thing, you know."

"You would."

"Yeah but I'm crazy. What's your excuse?"

"I have an obsession with danger?"

Sano snorted. "Can't argue with that one."

Katsumi waved towards the door. "If I'm going to be a target for a madman, I need to learn more. Get out, you're distracting me."

"Fine, fine." Sano backed towards the door, pointing at her. "You better get some rest soon, though."

"I'll sleep when I'm dead."

"If you don't sleep that might be sooner than you think."

"Lecture me some other time, Mother. Don't you have work to do? And close the door on your way out."

Sano grinned at her as he pulled the door closed. "Kids are so rude these days."

Katsumi rolled her eyes as she looked back at her computer. She had pulled up every bit of data they had on the bombings and the victims, which wasn't much. She had hoped that staring at the entire picture would make something come together for her or reveal some little detail they'd missed, but so far she'd learned nothing new.

In all honesty it was driving her crazy. While actively out in the field she was able to slip into an attitude fueled by determination and duty, and while with others she could put on a mask of slight distraction or focus so that they knew something was up but were able to assume it wasn't that big a deal.

But when alone, when sitting in a dark room staring at a screen of the pitiful amount of clues she'd managed to collect, willing something, *anything* to appear and lead her towards her quarry, she could feel herself becoming less sane with every passing hour. She stared at the words until they blurred so much she couldn't read them anymore, then wracked her brain for answers that simply weren't there. There wasn't enough to go on, to lead her anywhere. She knew she needed more information, but she wouldn't get that until there was another bombing, and the fact that she had to wait for people to die before she could figure out how to protect them was practically taking a sledgehammer to her sanity.

Thirty-four... My big sister is getting so old!

The words drew Katsumi out of her self-hating reverie and brought a smile to her face. *Why does everyone remember my birthday but me?*

Because you're really, really bad at focusing on yourself. Really, Sumi, you should try to be a little more selfish.

So what, I should just abandon my job for the day and spend it all with you?

Yes! Exactly! Now you're thinking straight!

Katsumi laughed softly. *That's exactly what I want to do, Aya, but I can't. I'm already going crazy here, I need a lead or something. I'd barely be able to enjoy myself.*

She could hear Ayane sigh. *Fine, work yourself to an early grave instead of spending all day with your shining star of a sister.*

Maybe I should take lessons from you on focusing on myself more. You seem to be good at it.

Hey, I'm worth it!

Katsumi smiled. *I won't disagree.*

In all seriousness, happy birthday, sister. I'm truly happy to celebrate your surviving your crazy death wishes and mad terrorists and evil spirits and giant demons for another year. I love you, Sumi.

I love you too, Aya. Thank you for keeping me strong and keeping yourself stronger. You know I'll be up there at some point today, as I always am.

I look forward to it! We're totally staying outside!

Katsumi smiled softly. *Of course we are. Even if it's raining. Now go back to sleep, it's midnight. I don't want you falling asleep on me when I'm there.*

Ugh, you're such a slave driver! You and your 'caring about my health' nonsense, I swear...

Katsumi laughed at her sister. *Sleeping now, try to get some yourself, see you when I get there!*

Katsumi sat back with a sigh, feeling better than she had earlier. She counted herself lucky that she and her sister had each other, and friends like Sano and the ones Ayane had that Katsumi had only met a couple times. Doing things alone made them a thousand times harder.

A small beep from her computer caught her attention. She'd received a message from an online chat program she never used, and the name on it was one she didn't recognize, what appeared to be a random series of letters: *ASDF*. Frowning, she clicked on the window to read the message.

`You're still alive. I guess you think you're smart, beating my attack.`

Katsumi sat up ramrod-straight, her entire body tensing. She immediately began typing furiously, setting up a back-trace protocol that would follow the message back to the computer it had originated at. She also started a scan over her system to ensure nothing was breaking in or would be able to break in, and activated a program that would record all activity on her computer. It only took her a few seconds to start most of this, and in-between she typed a response to the message.

`I've taken down terrorists and criminals worse and more brilliant than you could even imagine. Working in my jurisdiction was your last mistake.`

She pressed enter and finished her set-ups before watching the message window anxiously until another beep announced the reply.

I don't think so. You see, you don't know
who I am, but I know enough about you.
You've got some real big weaknesses and
they're going to be easy to use to get you.

Katsumi typed back, trying not to let her emotions direct her responses.

It doesn't matter what you know, you
don't stand a chance. Sooner or later I'll
find you and you'll spend the rest of your
life in a prison cell. All you're doing is
stalling the inevitable.

I disagree. I don't lose.

Seems to me you lost in the subway.

A minor set-back. You're the one stalling
the inevitable now by staying alive. You'll
die soon enough. Trust me; you won't be able
to stop the next one.

He disconnected before she was able to respond to his last statement. She rapidly checked her back-trace and discovered with immense relief that it had gotten a location locked down before the disconnection. Katsumi shot up from her desk and threw the door open, shouting down the hall. "SANO! Get down to the car; we need to get going, NOW!"

~ ~ ~ ~ ~

In a dark room lit only by the glow of six bright monitors sat a man who was still unknown to the world at large. He was shrouded in shadow both physically and figuratively, a status that suited him well for the moment but was destined to change soon enough. One of his monitors had recently shown a surge of activity on a computer belonging to one Katsumi Samakura, and a little investigation had led him to learn she'd just been contacted by the person who'd been giving her so much grief over the past few days.

A strange smile lifted his lips as he rested his cheek against the fist of one hand, browsing through tons of data on several of the screens with the other. "Looks like Round One is finally kicking off... Let's review the players." He lifted his hand and tapped a part of the screen, bringing up a large information page with pictures along the side, reading over the information displayed there.

```
Name: Samuel Lawrence
Nicknames: Law
Gender: Male
Age: 39
Birth Date: January 3rd 2029
Birth Place: Chicago, Illinois
Citizenry: United States American
Current Residence: Araton Apartment
Building, Apartment 112
Surviving Family: None Known
Cyber Percentage: 43%
Company: Aegis Corporation
Division: SIN
Rank: Sergeant First Class
Currently Serving Under: Captain Katsumi
Samakura
Expertise: Demolitions and Heavy Weapons
```

"The old war buddy…" The man smiled. "Dangerous to any opponent using explosives, such as their current target. Blindly loyal to his Captain but he won't be involved as much directly." He closed the tab and opened the next page.

```
Name: Reno Hillford
Nicknames: Ace
Gender: Male
Age: 31
Birth Date: October 5th 2037
Birth Place: Phoenix, Arizona
Citizenry: United States American
Current Residence: Tusori Village
Surviving Family: Wife (Lenora, 29),
Daughter (Lianne, 5), Parents, Two Sisters
Cyber Percentage: 5%
Company: Aegis Corporation
```

Division: SIN
Rank: Corporal
Currently Serving Under: Captain Katsumi
Samakura
Expertise: Piloting / Transportation

"The family man. That could be a problem for him at some point." The man tapped another screen, bringing up a report. "His low CP and relative weakness nearly caused his Captain's death. Perhaps a weak spot on the team, perhaps not." He moved to the next page.

Name: Rufus Ivanov
Nicknames: Ice
Gender: Male
Age: 37
Birth Date: July 18th 2031
Birth Place: Volgograd, Russia
Citizenry: Russian
Current Residence: Turin High-Rise Apartment
Building, Loft Apartment 82
Surviving Family: Brother (Location Unknown,
see File 487)
Cyber Percentage: 67%
Company: Aegis Corporation
Division: SIN
Rank: Specialist
Currently Serving Under: Captain Katsumi
Samakura
Expertise: Assassination and High-Profile
Infiltration

"Ah, yes, the expert." The man smiled at the cold picture on the page. "Calculating and without the compunctions his current officer is restrained by. Possibly a weak link psychologically. I believe I have him marked as the most likely candidate in the event of a team betrayal." He closed the page and opened the next one.

Name: Kurasano Lionel

```
Nicknames: Sano, Lion, Red
Gender: Male
Age: 33
Birth Date: September 17th 2034
Birth Place: Itami, Japan
Citizenry: Japanese
Current Residence: Culsor Apartment
Building, Apartment 6732
Surviving Family: Mother, Sister (Both
living normally in Japan)
Cyber Percentage: 32%
Company: Aegis Corporation
Division: SIN
Rank: First Lieutenant
Currently Serving Under: Captain Katsumi
Samakura
Expertise: Combat and Low-Profile
Infiltration
```

"The second-in-command." The man tilted his head and studied the page. "He doesn't have quite as much experience as some of the others, so more thought must have gone into his placement. According to my other files his position was requested by Captain Samakura based on his history and psych evaluation reports… How very interesting. I don't believe he is a weak link in any way. He will factor strongly in this round." He switched over to the final page in this file. "And here we have our champion…"

```
Name: Katsumi Samakura
Nicknames: Sama, Boss
Gender: Female
Age: 34
Birth Date: March 27th 2034
Birth Place: Osaka, Japan
Citizenry: Japanese
Current Residence: Culsor Apartment
Building, Apartment 6711
Surviving Family: None Known (Father went
MIA, presumed KIA, see File 683)
```

```
Cyber Percentage: 83%
Company: Aegis Corporation
Division: SIN
Rank: Captain
Current Handler: M.
Expertise: Leadership, Investigation, Combat
```

"Hmm, I didn't send any birthday regards. How rude of me. Let's see… How will she do in this round? What do we know of her opponent…?" He tapped a window on another monitor, expanding it.

```
Name: Jerne Kintashi
Gender: Male
Age: 26
Citizenry: Japanese
Current Residence: Temporary Apartment in
Tokyo
Cyber Percentage: 13%
Occupation: Data Translator for Goliath
National Bank
```

The man inspected the page for a minute as his smile widened. "I give you… Three weeks. You'll fit right into the schedule, I'm sure." He was interrupted by a call on a phone which he drew out of a pocket and answered calmly. "Sigma." He listened for a moment, smiling. "And no congratulations or well-wishes? Such terrible manners."

He chuckled a few seconds later, tapping his fingers on the arm of his chair. "Really? Are you sure about making contact that soon?" Another pause. "Well, I don't plan to argue. The timing is good. You should try in… Two days. Mmm, yes, but it shouldn't take long… Correct." He waited for a few seconds, listening, before smiling. "Go ahead, then. Just remember not to bring me into it; I would be terribly disappointed if you ruined my introductions."

He closed the phone, an eerie smile on his face as he watched new data scroll onto one of the monitors.

~ ~ ~ ~ ~

Sano shook his head as he and Katsumi got out of the car, happy to be alive. On the way Katsumi had driven like a madwoman. He was, in fact, pretty sure there wasn't a single road safety law in existence that she hadn't broken in the short ride there. That alone was telling about her current state as she was usually a reliable, if a bit reckless, driver.

He silently thanked God that they hadn't taken any flying vehicle as he looked up at the sign of the internet café they were heading for the entrance of. "So he was contacting you from here, huh?"

"Unfortunately," Katsumi replied as she pushed through the doors. She and Sano showed their badges to the people inside. "Everyone remain calm and stay where you are. We're in the middle of an investigation and have reason to believe our suspect was here recently." Katsumi didn't believe the terrorist would still be here. In fact, she'd half expected to find a smoking crater once she got here. Even now she and Sano were watching everyone in the place, worried that one of them would explode at any moment. They both drew their guns and moved around inspecting the café for anyone trying to hide, and then Katsumi managed to find the computer she'd been contacted from.

Before touching anything she and Sano did a sweep of the entire area for explosives. Katsumi then accessed the computer to learn every recent log-in had simply been "ASDF". She looked up at the corner of the ceiling, pointing to the camera there and speaking to the owner of the internet café. "We'll need the feed from that camera, and any others you might have." The owner agreed, eager to help.

An hour later Katsumi and Sano had every bit of data they could get from the place. They'd reviewed the tape, which of course didn't show the face of their suspect, but they'd been able to determine none of the people in the café were their target and had released them. Outside the establishment Sano leaned against the smooth black car, hands in his pockets, watching Katsumi as she slowly paced, deep in thought. "What's bothering you, boss?"

Katsumi shook her head, not responding. About a minute later he was about to ask again when she spoke and interrupted him. "Why wasn't this a trap?"

Sano blinked, then raised an eyebrow. "Did you want it to be a trap?"

"No... No, of course not, I just..." She shook her head. "Why wasn't it? Why didn't he have a victim there waiting to explode on us, to erase evidence of himself and possibly erase us?"

Sano shrugged. "Too obvious?"

"It's only obvious because it's the smart course of action to take. Even if he knew we'd suspect a trap he'd still succeed in destroying evidence and killing more people."

"Not everything has to be a trap."

"This did." Katsumi looked at him wearily. "Don't you get it? This simply doesn't make sense. Some of his moves have been very smart, brilliant even, but some are downright amateur or simplistic. He was able to set a trap for our chopper along a specific flight path between buildings and nearly kill us. Then he knew what subway train I'd be on and when, even what car, but instead of safely blowing it up he had his attacker try to stab me first instead. I could let that go because perhaps he wanted to be sure I wouldn't survive that encounter. But now, after already trying to kill me once, he misses an opportunity to do so tonight? Why would he contact me if it wasn't to set up a trap for me? He knew I'd have no choice but to come and investigate even if I suspected a trap."

"Maybe he didn't have time to prepare one?"

"Then why did he contact me in the first place?! He had all the time in the world to prepare, he chose the time I would come here!"

Sano ran a hand through his hair. "I guess it doesn't make sense. Maybe we're missing something."

"That's what's bothering me." Katsumi sighed. "Let's get what we have back to HQ. We'll see what our agents can do with this, maybe they can find him with this new information." Katsumi looked back at the café, biting her lip quietly before moving to get into the car. She didn't know what she was missing or what, exactly, was going on, and she didn't like that at all. She really hoped that whatever she was missing wouldn't result in more deaths that should have been prevented.

Chapter 7: Ardent

Date: March 27, 2068
Time: 11:30 AM
Location: South Ashfield Hospital, Gardens

Katsumi laughed as Ayane lifted her hand as if she was holding something, talking through her own laughter. "And you were like 'look, Aya, see, I totally caught this thing myself, we can do this!' And what happened?"

Katsumi rolled her eyes. "It jumped out of my hands."

"That's right, it jumped out of your hands. And how many other fish did you catch that day?"

"None."

"So I was totally right and you were wrong."

"Fine, so you've proved it," Katsumi smirked at her sister. "You're right every once in a while."

"Hey! I said always! Do I have to give more examples?!"

"No, no, five is fine," Katsumi chuckled, leaning back.

The two were sitting in the impressive gardens behind South Ashfield Hospital. To the delight of both of them Ayane was feeling great and thus able to sit outside on the grass for lunch. Katsumi had brought all kinds of food for them to gorge on which Ayane, obviously sick of hospital food by now, greatly appreciated and dove into. She was also dressed in more normal clothes which Katsumi had brought, wanting the day to be as lighthearted as possible.

Katsumi leaned back on her hands and looked over at her sister. "I hope the day comes when we can do this all the time," she spoke softly. Ayane had the same mysterious affliction Katsumi had, but there was a difference: for Katsumi it tended to manifest in bursts of extreme pain, weakness, and loss of senses; at all other times, it was like nothing was wrong. For Ayane it was a more general, constant drain, a weakness that prevented her leaving the hospital for long, along with occasional bouts of pain.

Ayane looked over and smiled, tilting her head. "I know it will. We just have to hold on until then. We'll both get fixed and then I can move back in with you instead of living in this stupid place."

"I look forward to that." Katsumi looked up at the sky. "I live in a small, cheap place right now. I'm saving everything I can so that I can get a larger place for us once you're able to live with me. We're going to have a lot of money to spend."

Ayane studied her for a moment before moving to hug her. "Sumi… That means so much to me. I know how much you think about me and I… I appreciate it."

Katsumi smiled and returned the hug. "It's been you and me for decades. This hasn't changed anything, just made it a bit more difficult for a while."

Ayane shoved her down and lay against her, eliciting a laugh from her older sister. They both looked at the sky as she spoke. "It's not so difficult. Still… I can't wait until I'm back to living with you. I look forward to meeting the people you talk about. It's weird that none of them besides Law know I exist."

"The more people that know you exist, the more danger you're in. Neither of us wants that."

"I know, I know." Ayane sighed. "And I agree. That's why I look forward to being fixed." She turned her head to look at Katsumi's face. "You could tell one more of them, couldn't you?"

Katsumi raised an eyebrow. "…Maybe. I'll think about it."

"Sano, right?"

Katsumi rolled her eyes. "I'll think about it."

Ayane smiled. "Thought so. He doesn't sound like anyone would learn it from him."

"I trust him, it's just…"

"You have to be absolutely sure," Ayane finished for her. "I know. Well I hope someone earns that level of trust from you because I've got all these great stories and no one new that knows you to share them with. Law's already heard most of them!"

"On second thought, maybe it really is best no one else knows."

"Sumi!"

~ ~ ~ ~ ~

Date: March 27, 2068
Time: 5:45 PM
Location: Tusori Village

"HERE?!"

"Mmm."

Reno grabbed the sides of his hair. "She's coming here?!"

Lenora continued calmly stirring something in a pot, tasting it before adding more seasoning to it. "Mmm."

Reno waved his hands wildly. "Why on earth is she coming here?! When?! How?! Who?!"

"You already know who."

"I know, but it only sounds good if you include all the questions."

"You forgot where."

"Damn."

Lenora looked back at her husband. "Where? Here. Who? Captain Samakura. When? In about…" She glanced at the clock. "Half an hour. Why? Well, several reasons. I want to get to know her, I want to thank her, and most importantly for today, it's her birthday."

"Yeah, I know, but she hates things having to do with her birthday. Trust me on that."

"Everyone deserves something on their birthday. We're not giving her anything, all we're doing is inviting her for dinner. She can pretend it's not for any occasion if she wants, but I don't think she will."

Reno raised an eyebrow. "Need I remind you of the party…"

"That was different. She doesn't like to be the focus of people, right? You made her the focus of everyone she knew."

Reno sheepishly looked away. "Yeah, that was dumb."

"We aren't making her the focus and there are only three of us. Besides, she needs this."

"You don't even know her."

Lenora smiled. "Trust me, I can tell. I'm guessing she'd just disappear for today if someone didn't make her come to something."

Reno stared at her. "You *made* her?!"

"No, that's the thing. I called her this morning and only asked once. She agreed." Reno blinked and Lenora pointed at him. "Think about that."

"I just don't want to get shot in my own house."

Lenora rolled her eyes. "Honestly, you can be such a baby sometimes."

Reno put both hands on his head. "I can't help it I'm SCARED!"

Their five-year-old, Lianne, looked up at her father before putting both hands on her own head. "I'm SCARED!"

Reno pointed down at her. "Are you mocking me?!"

The little girl pointed back at him. "Are you mocking me?"

Lenora chuckled as Reno swept up the laughing little girl. "Oh, you're gonna pay for that,

sister!"

~ ~ ~ ~ ~

Katsumi sighed as she turned off the car, remaining in the seat for a little longer, enjoying the silence. Outside the window it was dark already, but the houses in this village were all pleasantly lit. It had a strong family feel to it, something Katsumi had never really understood. It didn't suit her at all, but for some reason there was something about it that was a little comforting anyway. She glanced down at herself, hoping she was dressed alright; earlier, while getting ready, she'd realized the only "nice" clothing she had was military, so at the moment she had on a light formal version of her military uniform comprised of black pants with a silver stripe down the side and a long-sleeved black military jacket with silver buttons, a short collar, the Aegis Corp shield logo on one shoulder and the two silver bars denoting her rank of Captain on the other. It wasn't as formal as the uniform she wore for specific situations, and it looked good with the jacket undone and a black shirt underneath. The smooth black color of the uniform made the violet of her hair stand out even further and she usually got compliments so it couldn't be too bad.

She opened the door and climbed out of the car, shutting and locking it as she appraised the house in front of her. It was a nice two-story, neither small nor large, with yellow siding, white trim and white columns. There was a small front porch in front of the doorway, as well. Katsumi could almost imagine a white picket fence in front of it, if Lenora had that type of taste.

She approached the front door, finding and ringing the doorbell. This was the first time she'd been to this house but it had been easy to agree to coming. Lenora felt like a good friend to have, and besides that she was still waiting for their agents to get more information on her target anyway so she had nothing to do tonight. A home-cooked meal and unobtrusive company was a pretty hard deal to pass up, and a good enough distraction.

The door opened and Lenora smiled at her. "Captain Samakura! Welcome, I'm so glad you could come. Happy birthday! Please, come in."

Katsumi stepped through the doorway. "Thanks. You don't have to call me 'Captain'."

Lenora closed the door behind her. "Just Katsumi, then?"

"That's fine."

Reno waved at her with a grin. "Hey, Katsumi!"

She turned a glare on him. "*You're* still part of my team."

"Er, right, uh, hey, Boss."

"You can use my name. I'm just saying don't get used to it. On duty you use the proper terms."

Reno smiled. "Right, got it."

"Forget about duty for tonight," Lenora interrupted. "This is a friendly family dinner, not a business meeting."

Family dinner. Katsumi couldn't help but wish at that moment that she could bring her sister here. She looked at Lenora, nodding. "Of course. I'll try to relax."

"Excellent! Reno, show her to the table and I'll get everything out. By the way, Katsumi, you look really nice."

Katsumi blushed a bit, glancing over at her. "Thank you. Not as nice as you, obviously." It was true, though Lenora was dressed in a far more feminine manner with a white blouse and skirt that worked well with her brown hair, which was currently curled over her shoulders. Katsumi didn't think she even owned a blouse.

Lenora beamed at the compliment, figuring one probably meant more coming from Katsumi than from someone else.

Reno led Katsumi into the dining room, smiling at his five-year-old who was setting the table.

"C'mere Lianne, someone I want you to meet." He picked up the girl, turning around. "This is Katsumi. She's my boss."

Lianne cocked her head and held out her hand. "Hi Kasmi!"

Katsumi smiled and shook the girl's hand. "Katsumi. Like a 'cot'."

"What's a cot?"

"It's a bed. See…" She held up one finger. "Cot." She held up a second finger. "Soo." She held up a third. "Me."

"Cot-soo-me?"

Katsumi smiled. "Right. Then you push it all together and say it as one word: Katsumi."

"Katsumi!"

"There you go."

The little girl held up a finger. "Lee." Katsumi bit her lip and Reno snickered as she held up a second finger. "Ann."

Katsumi nodded. "Lianne?"

"Uh-huh!"

"You have a very pretty name."

"It's from my grandmother."

"You should be proud to carry a family name."

Lianne beamed and Reno put her in her seat on the side of the table. He himself took one end and gestured to Katsumi to take the other as Lenora brought out the food, starting to set things on the table, though it took several trips. Katsumi raised an eyebrow at the food. "You didn't have to go to so much trouble…"

Lenora smiled as she set down the last thing. "It isn't trouble, honestly."

Reno nodded. "She's not kidding. Seriously. She loves making tons of food."

"Really, I do." Lenora took her seat beside her daughter on Reno's end of the table. "Now, no more waiting, eat!"

They began putting food on their plates as Katsumi continued the conversation. "You have a very nice house." She felt that if silence fell her mind wouldn't be distracted anymore and would wander back to things that would make her a terrible guest. Tonight was, for her, about distractions.

Lenora smiled. "Thank you, I did most of it myself."

"I think it shows. It practically screams family."

Lenora laughed. "That's the idea. What about you, does your home say anything?"

Reno became curious to see if he'd actually learn anything about his boss as she answered with a smirk. "I think calling it a 'home' is a bit of an overstatement. It's just the place I sleep. If anything it says 'this person doesn't care'."

"No, you didn't strike me as the type of person to design or decorate. If you don't care and you don't care what others think, then it doesn't matter, right? I'm guessing you're more about practicality."

Katsumi smiled. "Good guess. I keep the place intact and that's about it; it's barely even clean, although it's… relatively alright. Until Sano comes by, at least."

Reno blinked. "Sano gets to go in your home?!"

Katsumi looked at him. "He lives in the same building on the same floor. Like… Ten meters away."

"Yeah, but I don't recall ever being invited."

"I don't invite Sano, either. He shows up and lets himself in."

"He has the code?!"

Katsumi shrugged. "It's convenient… Most of the time."

"How?!"

Lenora looked at her husband. "They live and work at the same places, dear. If one needs something the other can get it. Besides, they're friends."

Reno pouted. "So I'm not a friend?"

Katsumi rolled her eyes. "Fine, you can go in my apartment sometime, I don't care."

Reno grinned. "Awesome. Wonder what I'll find?"

"I take it back."

"Hey!"

Lenora smiled. "That's probably why you aren't invited, Reno."

Katsumi took a sip of her drink. "Nail on the head."

"What if I behave?"

"You don't behave."

"But what if I behave?"

"Then I'll be too busy ice-skating in Hell to invite you over."

"That's just mean."

"Reno will have to give up flying due to all the pigs clogging the airspace," Lenora pointed out.

"Oh, not you too!"

Lenora smiled. "I'm sorry, dear, but you're very easy to make fun of."

Katsumi chuckled. "It's true. You're an easy target."

Reno looked at her. "Oh yeah? Well I can make fun of you, too, you know."

Katsumi raised an eyebrow at him as she took another drink. She remained silent as he tried to think of something he could say that would work without getting him killed.

"Uhh…"

"Go ahead," Katsumi smiled. "Let's see what you have to say to the person that saved your life."

Lenora laughed as Reno gaped. "Now that's just unfair!"

Lenora shook her head. "I don't know, Reno, I think she earned it."

Lianne looked up at her mother. "Katsumi saved Daddy?"

Katsumi looked down at her drink as Lenora smiled. "Yes, she's the one who did."

"So she paid Daddy back for saving her all those times?"

Katsumi raised an eyebrow at Reno. "I did what now?"

Reno rubbed the back of his neck and laughed. "Ahaha, Lianne, you don't have to share *everything* Daddy says!"

Katsumi leaned forward. "No, no, this is good. What else did you do for me, my *hero*?"

Reno adjusted his glasses so the glint hid his eyes. "No no, I mean, maybe I exaggerate a little, sometimes, rarely, barely ever really…"

"Uh-huh." Katsumi suddenly blinked and looked down.

Lianne had slipped out of her seat and was, at the moment, hugging her leg. "Thanks for helping Daddy!"

Reno's eyes widened. *My daughter just hugged Captain Sama. My daughter's gonna die!* He started to stand. *Hang on, Daddy will save you, baby!*

He froze as Katsumi smiled softly, laying a hand on the little girl's head. "It was nothing. Your father has saved me plenty of times."

Lianne looked up at her. "Is he really a hero?"

"Oh, yes. His whole job involves doing heroic things. You're very lucky to be his daughter."

Reno just stared at them in shock. He certainly hadn't expected that reaction. At the very best he'd imagined an awkward "No problem" and a look demanding he remove his daughter from her leg. Instead Katsumi was picking his daughter up and setting her on her leg, telling her a story about him being a big hero. He looked at Lenora who just smiled and shrugged at him before looking back at the two.

Maybe, Reno thought, he'd overestimated the hardness of his boss just a little.

~ ~ ~ ~ ~

"No! No, no, no! Damn them, DAMN THEM!" Objects flew off the desk as a man swatted them aside in anger. He was 26, just getting started in his criminal career of terror, and already he could feel the net of the law slowly closing around him. He gripped his hair. "It's not fair!"

The man on his computer screen sat calmly and watched, a slight smile that never left the only detail of his face that could be seen in the shadows.

Jerne Kintashi turned and pointed at the screen, still yelling. "Tell me what to do! Tell me how to get out of this!"

The man on the screen lifted his hands in a shrug. "What am I supposed to tell you? All criminals get caught eventually."

"NO!" The younger man slammed his hands down on the desk, yelling into the screen. "Not me! I'm different! I'm BETTER! They won't catch me... I'll kill them before then!"

"You should think of something soon, then," Sigma smiled. "Your mistakes are catching up with you quickly."

"I DON'T MAKE MISTAKES!" Jerne stabbed his finger into the screen as if he could push the man back just with the force of his mind. "You're the one getting me caught!"

"You aren't caught yet. All you need is to show what you're capable of and they'll be too afraid to come after you."

The man finally slowed down, panting heavily and speaking in a more normal tone. "What I'm capable of?"

"Something that will elevate you from an ordinary criminal to someone worthy of actual terror. If you can do something that strikes fear into and horrifies them, they'll never try to catch you."

"Right…"

"They'll be too afraid of you."

"Right, right… That makes sense…" Jerne straightened, turning around and thinking. "Something to show them the horror I'm capable of…"

Behind him, Sigma smiled.

~ ~ ~ ~ ~

The rest of the night had gone even better than the beginning. They'd finished dinner and moved to the living room where Katsumi and Reno had begun sharing stories, ones they could tell Lianne anyway. The little girl was enthralled by them all, but eventually it grew too late for her to remain awake. Reno picked her up, carrying her to her room. "C'mon, little girl, time for bed. I'll read you a story."

Lianne laid her head on her father's shoulder, waving. "Night Mommy, night Katsumi."

"Goodnight, honey," Lenora smiled as Katsumi gave her own with a wave.

Lenora looked at Katsumi once her husband and daughter were out of the room. Now seemed like the perfect time to bring up what she'd been thinking all night, but now that it was time to talk she found it a little difficult. The night had been going well and she didn't want to ruin it, but the longer she watched the older woman staring at the floor ignoring the drink in her hand, the more she felt the need. "Something's wrong."

After a moment, Katsumi registered her words and looked up. "Hmm?"

"With you," Lenora continued softly. "Something's wrong."

"What makes you say that?"

Lenora smiled. "I can tell."

Katsumi tilted her head, studying her. "You know, you don't know me."

"Maybe not, but I know what I see. You've been enjoying yourself, but only part of you. There's a constant distraction like something's eating away at you, and more than that... You look tired."

Katsumi smirked. "Thanks. I thought I looked nice."

Lenora smiled. "You do. But also tired."

"I am tired. That's probably why I look it. It is getting kind of late."

"You looked just as tired when you arrived."

Katsumi sighed. "I can't bluff you, can I?"

Lenora smiled at her. "You could, but you're too tired to do it successfully. If you don't want to talk I'll understand, but we are alone, I'm a good listener, and I'm not about to judge."

Katsumi nodded, staring into her drink. She was quiet for another few minutes before she sighed. "This week hasn't been easy."

"Of course not. I don't know all of what's going on but I know enough to know that."

"It's wearing on me."

"Well you need a break-"

"No," Katsumi interrupted her, giving her a hard look. "Things are going slowly enough as it is. Everything's grinding at a snail's pace. Nothing's getting done."

"Haven't you been learning things, gathering evidence?"

"So what?" Katsumi shook her head. "None of it's enough to lead me to the killer. I'm not any closer to finding him."

"You will find him."

"When?" Katsumi looked up and Lenora leaned back a little at the sudden intensity in her voice. "After he's killed another dozen people? I'm supposed to be protecting them, not cleaning up after they're dead. I'm supposed to prevent these things from happening in the first place and yet, right now, all I can do is wait for another *fucking* attack and then look through the rubble hoping for another *small* clue to bring me a step closer to him." Her voice lowered from angry to almost silent. "Right now I'm just... helpless. Reacting."

"You saved those people on the subway," Lenora pointed out quietly. "You saved my husband."

"I shouldn't have to. I should've caught the man on the subway before he even attacked. I should've known not to tell Reno to fly where he did, where we were attacked."

"You couldn't have known."

"How do you know that? How do you know I didn't miss something?"

"I don't…"

"And neither do I." Katsumi shook her head. "Those people on the subway should hate me for letting that happen. You should hate me for nearly getting your husband killed."

Lenora remained quiet for a moment. Simple denial was useless at times like these; telling someone they shouldn't feel like they did never helped, she found. "Do *you* hate you?"

Katsumi sighed, looking up at the ceiling. "Sometimes. Right now I do. I'm disappointed in myself for failing. All these people rely on me, I've been letting them all down this past week. Sometimes I wonder, why am I the leader? Why am I being followed, obeyed by people?" She shook her head. "They're stupid thoughts, I know that. I've done well in the past. I'm a good choice for this position. It's just times like this, when I fail, that I question if I'm slipping, or if I'm really the person to do this."

"You are." Both of them looked up as Reno entered the room. "I don't regret following your orders, Captain. I'd fly straight into an explosion on purpose if you told me to."

Katsumi studied him for a moment before asking the question she needed to ask. "Why?"

Reno shrugged. "Because I trust you enough to believe we'd be flying out the other side. Hasn't let me down yet. I followed your orders this week and we crashed, but I didn't die because you were determined not to break that trust. It doesn't matter if you fail sometimes, Boss. What makes Lenora, what makes me, what makes the whole team trust and follow you isn't some belief that you'll never fail or that you're perfect. It's the fact that we know you won't give up even if you do fail, and that you'll always try to get us through."

Katsumi looked away from him, staring at nothing as she thought in the silence that followed his statement. Reno sat down beside his wife, who gave him a smile before they both looked back to Katsumi. She finally looked back at him. "You remind me why I started doing this in the first place."

"Why's that, Captain?"

"I hated when protectors gave up and was determined to be one that didn't." She took a sip of her drink, letting out a sigh afterwards. "Thank you. Both of you."

They both smiled and Reno saluted. "Anytime, Captain."

~ ~ ~ ~ ~

Katsumi arrived back in her building later than she'd expected. It was sometime past three in the morning; she'd stayed at the Hillford's house until two. It had been a good day, one she'd needed. She checked her phone for any messages as the elevator opened onto her floor, but there were none. Apparently there hadn't been any advances in the case yet, news she met with disappointment. She stepped around the corner, spotting Kurasano leaning against the door to her room.

Sano smiled, holding up a bottle and shaking it a bit, without even a word. Katsumi smiled at him and shook her head at his being here, a motion that made him chuckle silently. She opened the door and entered, with him following.

Inside, Katsumi tossed her things on a table and Sano dropped onto the couch. "How was your night in Pleasantville?" he asked.

Katsumi chuckled, taking a seat as Sano opened the bottle. "Good; very good. We talked a lot, had a great meal."

"Sounds cool. Thanks for inviting me, by the way."

Katsumi laughed. "It wasn't my house or my invitation. Talk to Lenora."

Sano passed her the bottle and she took a drink. Rarely did the two bother using glasses. "I'll do that. Let her know she hurt my feelings."

"Poor baby," Katsumi grinned as she passed the bottle back.

"I know, right?" Sano winked and took a drink. "So c'mon, gimme details, don't leave me in the dark here."

"Why are you acting like a girl whose friend just went on a date?"

"You don't have to tell me what base you got to." Sano laughed as he ducked a thrown pillow.

She did end up telling him all that happened, receiving mostly jokes for her trouble, but that was something she appreciated. When everything in life was getting darker and more serious, it was nice having someone who could turn that around and show you how to laugh at it.

~ ~ ~ ~ ~

The next morning at about 9 AM Sano awoke, groaning as he was immediately subjected to a headache. He groggily lifted his head off the table, thankful that Katsumi's apartment was kept dark and only a bit of dim light was streaming in. He rubbed his eyes a bit, standing up to look around the apartment and noticing he was alone. Apparently Katsumi had left a while ago, which didn't surprise him, and he wondered if she'd even slept at all. While looking for her he did notice some woman's clothes lying on her bed that were too small to fit her, but he decided it was probably best to ignore that.

After checking his phone and making sure he had no messages he left the apartment, making his way to his own to change before he went out for some breakfast. If Katsumi hadn't gotten him up then there wasn't any emergency, so there was no rush.

An hour later, washed, refreshed and fed, Sano arrived at Aegis Corp HQ. The place was busy and noisy, but thankfully he'd had enough time to get past the worst of his hangover so it wasn't too bad. He found Katsumi in a preparation room with some others, and she smiled at him as he entered. "Sano, I'm glad you're here, I was going to call soon."

"No need, I'm up, just not as ungodly early as you. What's up?" he asked as he took a drink of his coffee.

"We're compiling a list of possible suspects. We're going to visit them today."

"No kidding? Look at that, one night of drinking with me and progress is made."

Rufus passed by him, handing a paper to Katsumi. "I don't think the two are related."

"Pff, what do you know. You're Russian; drinking to you just involves vodka and singing."

"That's a racist stereotype."

"*You're* a racist stereotype." Sano returned Rufus' grin before looking back to Katsumi. "So when are we going?"

"As soon as the list is complete." Katsumi's phone rang and she answered. "Katsumi Samakura." Sano watched with concern as her face became stony and she stepped away from the group, heading quickly out of the office and gesturing to him to follow her, which he did immediately. "If you're calling now, you must be desperate." She slid into her office and shut the door after Sano, setting her phone to speaker so he could hear as well. A male voice was talking in a harsh manner.

"…esperate, Captain, *you're* the one who's *desperate*. I'm calling to warn you to stop coming after me, you'll only regret it."

Sano immediately assumed this was the bomber, their suspect, and he pulled out his own phone and tapped into hers, starting to trace the call as Katsumi answered. "Nothing is ever going to stop me from catching you."

"I warned you, Captain. I'm going to take you down a few pegs. Find me in Risuji Square and we'll see how long your arrogance lasts!"

The call cut off and Katsumi looked at Sano, who shook his head. "Too well protected to trace."

"That's strange, he was easy to trace on the computer. Let's transfer the data to company servers and let them deal with it."

"Are we going to Risuji Square like he said?"

"Of course we're going."

"You know it's a trap."

"Of course it's a trap."

"I'm guessing we don't care at this point."

Katsumi flung the door open. "I stopped caring the last time he tried to blow me up."

~ ~ ~ ~ ~

Katsumi, Sano and Rufus, the three team members who had been at HQ at the time of the call, arrived at Risuji Square, a large market-like area, only a few minutes later. Upon arrival they noticed a large gathering of people on one end and Katsumi immediately began sprinting towards it with the other two in tow; she was getting a very, very bad feeling.

The building the crowd was near had a giant screen and, on it, was the image of a man with one of those old theater masks on, the smiling one. Katsumi pushed her way through the crowd to the front and she froze as she came out the other side. Several people in the crowd were holding back a screaming woman who was struggling to get to a child that was tied up in the middle, a young boy.

The man on the giant screen spread his hands. "Welcome, Katsumi Samakura, so good of you to come!" Katsumi stepped out of the crowd and started towards the boy, but the man on the screen shook his finger. "Ah-ah-ah! I wouldn't do that! You see, this boy wasn't just *kidnapped* yesterday, he was taken by me, the magnificent Director! He's got one of my special treats inside him and if you take another step towards him… Boom!" The man laughed. "I even invited his mother to the show. She wouldn't want to miss her son's big part!"

Katsumi's blood was cold but her eyes were on fire, her entire body tense. She gritted her teeth, her jaw clenched as she practically seethed. She pointed at the screen. "What the fuck is *wrong* with you?! Why would you do something like this?!"

"Because you won't let things lie like you should. I told you you shouldn't mess with me!" He suddenly sounded a little whiny, stressed, not nearly as cool and collected as he was trying to be, but he tried to return to it. "Do you know what I'm going to do, Miss Samakura?"

Katsumi shook her head. "Don't…"

"I'm going to give a little show."

"Don't… please…" Katsumi looked up at the screen. "I'll let you kill me instead. *I'm* the danger to you. I'm the one you want to get rid of."

"Tempting… Very tempting." The man pretended to rub his chin. "But… No."

Everything slowed down.

The boy suddenly fell over and convulsed. The crowd erupted in screams and began to run. Katsumi yelled at the man to put a stop to it but he just laughed. Behind her, Sano turned away, sick. Rufus shook his head, looking at the ground. And Katsumi watched as the boy's mother, now free, ran to him and fell on him in a hug, trying to help him.

The explosion destroyed part of the front of the building. It created a crater before her and sent cement, dust and ash in all directions. It knocked most of the people off their feet and peppered a few with debris. It incinerated the two in the middle.

As the explosion faded and things returned to normal speed with falling dust and rising screams, Katsumi stood with her eyes hardening and her body trembling… no… shaking, violently. Sano felt like he would vomit, but he looked at Katsumi and grew scared.

The woman was literally, visibly shaking, her entire body tensing as her gaze bore a hole into the screen before her. Her fingers curled together and clenched in fists so tight blood began leaking through her fingers.

And in the background, what was this "Director's" reaction? Could he not believe what he did?

Was he as horrified as she? Did he regret such an… inhuman action?

No… All he was doing, his only reaction to what he'd just done, was laughing. His laughter cut through her just as much as the sorrow, regret, hate, helplessness, and rage did.

Katsumi dropped to her knees, a scream of pure fury erupting from her throat as she smashed her fist into the ground.

And above it all, the man just… kept… *laughing*.

Chapter 8: Search

Kurasano sighed for what felt like the thousandth time that morning, sending yet another witness away with no new information and looking across the square. Cleanup crews were halfway through cleaning the debris; medical crews were helping the few with small injuries. M was even there, surveying the scene, with Law examining the destruction to confirm it was the same type of explosion as before.

The only thing missing from the scene was Katsumi.

She'd disappeared soon after the explosion, and given the look on her face none of them had wanted to risk stopping her. Sano had no idea where she was at this point; no one did. She wasn't answering any call, and Sano finally had to give up and deal with what was happening around him. Rufus stepped up beside him, handing him a picture someone had snapped of the man on the screen. "This 'Director'... I've never heard of him."

Sano rubbed his forehead, taking the picture and looking at the masked face. "I think he just made it up. He didn't really seem like any sort of professional, he wasn't at all in control of his emotions."

"So he's an amateur? How has he managed to do what he's done so far, then?"

Sano shrugged. "I don't know, maybe there's more than one."

"Someone's helping him? This 'Director' could just be the front man, then."

"Nah, he took it too personally."

"So he's just had help."

"Probably."

M strolled over with Law behind him, his familiar smile the only one in the group. "Law says it's the same as the others. It seems we've found our culprit, but not his identity."

Sano shrugged. "One step closer, anyway. We'll see if we can trace anything from the hack into that screen."

"Yes, that is the next logical step." M seemed to glance around a bit. "Where is Captain Samakura?"

"I… uh…" Sano's shoulders sagged. "I don't know, sir."

"You don't know? I do hope *someone* knows." He watched both Rufus and Law shake their heads. "It isn't like her to abandon such a situation…"

Rufus adjusted his shades. "She seemed a bit more… affected… by this incident than usual, sir."

"Indeed?"

"We're thinking, sir, that she's past the point of waiting and pursuing the criminal on her own," Sano put forward.

Rufus nodded. "She has connections throughout the city that she's most likely going for as we speak."

M nodded. "That does make the most sense. With anyone else I would be angry with them for doing something this seemingly rash, but Miss Samakura does know what she's doing." He looked between the two. "I would ask that either of you let me know if you hear from her. Until then, both she and I are trusting you to keep this investigation running topside. Send the Captain any information you find and be ready to assist her at any moment should she call for it."

Both men saluted and M turned away, intending to head back to the HQ. His familiar smile returned like it had never left. Never once had he regretted the team he'd help build, and days like this reminded him why. At a point when other teams may give up or fall into depression, his got angry and fought even harder. He was always amused when other board members in the company asked if SIN Unit Alpha was capable of taking on all they intended to take on.

Honestly, it wasn't even a contest.

~ ~ ~ ~ ~

Reno shut his phone, reaching for his jacket without a thought. Lenora watched him worriedly, as she had been since soon after he'd answered the call. "What is it, what's wrong?"

"There was another bombing; this time involving a child." Reno couldn't tell his wife the details of it; as it was he himself ground out the words between gritted teeth. His wife looked as sick as he felt, but at the moment those facts weren't something anyone could do anything about. "Captain Sama went missing soon after."

"Missing?" Lenora's face grew darker. "You mean after the attack-"

"Yeah." Reno laid a hand on his wife's shoulder to calm her. "She wasn't hurt, she just took off. No one knows for sure why or where she is, and she isn't answering any calls. This isn't like her at all, so everyone's a little... confused."

Lenora nodded, though she believed she understood the reasoning behind the woman's actions.

"So you're going out there."

"I have to help, and the team could stand to be together at the moment, what with our leader missing and all."

"Don't blame her... This is harder on her than anyone else, it makes sense she might need some time alone."

"Time alone?" Reno looked at his wife. "I don't think she's taking time alone. If that were true we wouldn't be in a rush to find her, we'd leave her alone."

Lenora blinked, not understanding. "Then why...?"

"We think she's making it personal."

"It was already pretty personal..."

"No, I mean... She's probably going after the guy already. Alone. And angry." He sighed.

"Really angry."

"Oh..." Now she understood.

~ ~ ~ ~ ~

The door not only slammed open, it flew off its hinges, flipping through the dank room to collide with the opposite wall, sending up a cloud of dust. The force knocked over the man hiding behind it, and before he could bring his pistol to bear an iron-hard hand clamped down on his own, twisting and forcing him to drop it. Another hand caught his throat and whirled him around, lifting him into the air and slamming him into the wall hard enough to knock all breath out of him.

Katsumi leaned in, glaring into the criminal's eyes from only inches away. "Are you done running yet? Ready to talk a bit?"

The man squirmed, fighting pointlessly against the forceful hold and choking out his words. "Ready… Jus' let go…"

"Talk, then I'll let go."

"I d-don' remember th' ques-"

Katsumi slammed her fist into his face before throwing him to the floor and placing her foot on his neck. "I'm in no mood for games. The man I'm looking for uses the name of 'the Director'. He's responsible for the recent bombings. With your connections I'm sure you've heard something, and you better hope you've heard something, or you'll be useless to me." She pressed her heel into his throat and finished in a low voice, *"You don't want to be useless to me."*

"G-Gamlen…" He man coughed, scratching at her boot as he struggled to breathe. "Gamlen Ordo… got some guys fer 'im…"

Katsumi released the man, stomping off down the hallway. "I'm sure you know better than to lie. Don't tell anyone I'm coming."

The man pushed himself up on his elbow, rubbing his neck as he glared after her. "No problem…"

~ ~ ~ ~ ~

Samuel knocked on the hospital room's door and opened it to see Ayane smile weakly at him.

"Hi Big L."

"How's it goin', blue-hair?" Law shut the door behind him and walked over. "Feelin' alright?"

"More or less." Ayane watched him sit down and then looked at her hands. "I think I can guess why you're here."

"Yep." Law settled as much as he could in the small seat. "We're tryin' to figure out where she is, and if I know you two at all, you know where she is. She wouldn't do this without telling you."

"No, I know." Ayane sighed. "I know where she is, where she's going."

"But you're not gonna tell us."

"No, I'm not. She doesn't want you to know where she is or she'd have told you herself."

"I figured that, but she could be in trouble."

"My sister can take care of herself, Sam, you know that. She has to do this herself or it might be worse for her than physical injury."

Law sighed, running a hand over his bald head. "You know her best. Just let her know we're tryin' to help, alright? She's not talking to any of us."

"That has nothing to do with you." Ayane looked at him sadly. "Any of you. This is her thing."

"Why is she doing it?"

Ayane sighed and lay back, looking at the ceiling. "Sumi is… angry. She's past her limit of control right now. She can't stand back and not do anything anymore, not after this morning. She can't sit and wait for clues or reports. She doesn't have a choice but to do this, for her own sanity." Ayane looked at Samuel. "And she can't bring anyone with her because if she doesn't do this herself, she's failed… again."

"That doesn't make any sense."

Ayane smiled sadly. "It doesn't need to make sense to anyone else. It makes sense to me and her and we're the only people it needs to make sense to."

Law shook his head. "I'll never understand you two."

Ayane smiled genuinely this time. "No one will, and believe it or not, that's something of a comfort in a way."

Law raised an eyebrow. "I guess no one but you two would understand why that's a comfort, either."

She laughed softly. "Now you're getting it. I'll be a little nicer and explain just a bit for you, Law. When you only have one person for most of your life, the more exclusive things you have with each other the better it is."

"'Cause your relationship is more special?"

Ayane smiled. "Exactly!"

"Still seems twisted."

Ayane shrugged with another small smile. "In lives like ours you take what you can get."

~ ~ ~ ~ ~

Date: March 29, 2068
Time: 9:37 PM
Location: Aegis Corp HQ, Kurasano Lionel's Office

Sano ran a hand through his hair, staring at his computer screen as if it'd suddenly show new information. He was currently, temporarily, leading this investigation, plus he was trying to find Katsu- Captain Samakura – and he wasn't having any luck with either of those endeavors. Reno had been flying patrols across the city, Law was asking around any of Katsumi's contacts he knew, and Rufus was working his way through the criminal underground for any information on either pursuit.

Sano had no idea what he was doing. He was trying to coordinate things, but really he was just hoping; hoping for a resolution to either problem to present itself. So when his phone suddenly gave a tone signaling he'd received a message he immediately grabbed it, hoping it was from Katsumi. He frowned as he saw it was from an unknown number.

I can help you. Meet me in Room 3.5 in the tunnel beneath the Takagawa Building at 11.

So much about the message seemed odd. Who was this mysterious person who not only knew his problems, but could help with them? And why were they meeting in an underground tunnel? What kind of weird address was "Room 3.5"?

It could be a trap by the bomber or any number of other things but Sano was beyond caring by that point. He grabbed his gun and took off, informing the rest of his team of the message and where he was going. When going off alone, you never went without telling others – not unless you were Katsumi, anyway.

"Want me to come with you? Sounds suspicious."

Sano smirked at Rufus' tone. "Just a little suspicious. Keep doing what you're doing; if whoever this is can help us, I don't want to scare him away. And if not, I can put a bullet in his head myself."

"Your call. I'll stay within the area anyway; we'll know if your phone goes offline."

"Probably smart," Sano replied before ending the call as he pulled up to the building in question, inspecting the entrance. It was apparently closed so he searched a bit and found what appeared to be a cellar door, completely unlocked. "Convenient." He opened it to reveal a ladder descending into darkness.

At the bottom was a long maintenance tunnel with dim white lighting and doors lining the walls. He counted as he walked past, stopping at Room 4 and looking back at 3. "No 3.5... Obviously." He took a few steps to a point between them, his eyes flickering and scanning the wall there, finding a slim line and a small spot of energy. Upon pressing his hand to the spot a section of the wall slid up revealing another, thinner hallway. He stepped in and the door shut behind him, but he continued forward.

He ended up in a small square room with a glass wall on one side, very similar to an interrogation room. "You came alone. I'm glad you're sensible." A light on the other side of the glass turned on, revealing an older man with graying hair in a short ponytail and a well-groomed short beard. He also wore glasses which, like M's, hid his eyes. He had a harsh, experienced look to him and his build was strong. He stood at least six feet tall with a solid frame, clothed in a large brown trench coat over a black sweater and pants.

Sano turned towards the glass, studying him as he ran a hand through his hair. "Yeah, well, the sense behind coming to a mysterious meeting in a secret underground room alone is debatable."

"It was a wise move this time. I'm sure you're wondering who I am."

"That'd be one of my questions, yeah."

"One I can't answer at this time. However, do know that I am going to help you."

"Great. So what should I call you, Mysterious Messenger? The Night Man?"

"John Briggs is my name; one you won't find in any database."

"So it's a fake name."

"It's as real as any name. You won't need to know any more of that."

"Fine. Let's get to the part where you help me."

"Very well." The man pressed a button and a panel on the wall slid open to reveal a piece of paper. "On that is information that will aid you in discovering one of the paths your 'bomber' took through computer systems. It will take you one step closer to him."

Sano picked it up. "Why didn't you just send this in the message?"

"I prefer to do business face to face. Besides, there is something I need in return."

"Of course there is. There's always a catch."

"It will be worth it for you, though. I will aid you more over the following days."

"And in return?"

"In return, once your Captain Samakura has finished with this case, I want you to bring her here to meet me."

"Ah…" Sano peered through the glass as if he hoped to see the man's intentions just by looking hard enough. "So what you really want is to kill Katsumi."

"Were that the case I would be aiding her target, not you. I only desire a face-to-face meeting with her."

"Why?"

"I have information she will be interested in learning. About her condition."

Sano frowned. "She doesn't have any condition. Besides, why don't you just give the information to me, and I'll pass it to her?"

"I told you, I do business face to face."

"Well, I'll let her decide on that. We'll see just how helpful you are before then. Thanks for the mysterious visit, Mr. Briggs."

Sano headed for the exit, contacting Rufus. "It wasn't a trap, but it was strange anyway. John Briggs - fake name - wants to help us in exchange for meeting the boss."

"Hmm. Assassination?"

"Doesn't sound like it. If nothing else this seems like a strange way to go about it."

"Well, it's not how I would do it, but maybe it's personal. Captain Samakura has made a lot of enemies in her time. I should know, I was one of them. Briefly."

"He did say he had information she'd want to know. I'm not sure if he even knows what he's talking about."

"I suppose that's her decision. What about helping us, did he actually give you anything useful?"

Sano dropped the paper in the passenger seat of his car as he started it. "Maybe. I'll have to check it out once I get back. Supposedly a lead on the target, a possible trace on one of his hacks."

"Could be a false lead."

"I considered that, but then, if he doesn't lead us to the target, he won't meet Kat – Captain Sama."

"Good point. Well we'll consider more based on whether or not this checks out, but I can't imagine he'd set this up just to give us useless information."

"It does seem pointless. I'll let you know what I find; you keep working on your job. With luck we'll have our boss back within the week."

Sano worked on the data the moment he got back in his office and was unsurprised to find it actually helped. He managed to find the hacking method their target had used to hack the screen the day before. How the mysterious Briggs got a hold of such he had no idea, but he copied it and sent it to Katsumi's phone right away with a short explanation of what it was.

He didn't expect a reply and he didn't get one. He hoped she'd received it, at least, as he turned in his chair to look out the window at the dark city beyond. "It's gonna be a long week…"

~ ~ ~ ~ ~

Date: March 30, 2068
Time: 3:22 AM
Location: New Tokyo Slums, Apartment Block F

Katsumi ducked into a doorway and pressed her back against the wall as bullets flew in after her. She'd expected troubles of this sort. As a well-known officer there were certain dangers one could expect in the less reputable areas of a city, and running into criminals with personal problems against you was one of them. There were eight of them outside, spread in different rooms down the hallway. Katsumi was fairly certain she could take them down easily.

She leaned out the door and fired twice, catching another one in the head before ducking back into the room to avoid the return fire. Pick them off one by one, use a little skill and intelligence, and they'd either leave or die eventually. All she had to do was take her time.

Unfortunately for Katsumi, fate decided that time was not something she'd have today. It started with a headache; at first she ignored it, but soon dread filled her. She'd worried about this before but so far she'd been lucky. Apparently, today was the day her luck ran out. She clenched her jaw as the pain began to spread through her body, leaning out again and firing more rapidly, suddenly aware that if she didn't take these guys down fast, her chances were zero.

She managed to get another two but that still left five; five that would now be much harder to kill now that her vision was blurring. "No, no, no, no, no... Please, no... *Not now...*" Panic tore at Katsumi as she leaned against the wall, weakness draining her ability to fight. She resisted as long as she could but willpower could only do so much. The world swam before her eyes. Balance disappeared and she fell to the floor, the gun slipping from her hands. *Ayane... I'm about to be hard to reach again...*

What? What's going on?!

It's hitting and... people are after me... They're here to capture though, not kill. Try not to worry... Katsumi grunted in pain, her eyes closing.

How... how can I not worry about that?!

Trust me... That's how. I'll let you know when I'm back.
Just... keep calm...

Sumi...?

She heard footsteps cautiously nearing her room, but her hearing was dimming at the same time, giving her that familiar 'through a tunnel' effect.

Katsumi cursed fate, God and herself, but regardless of where the blame truly lied, one fact remained: she was done.

"Did we hit her?"

Sumi!

The words were distant; she barely registered them.

"I don't think so, there's no blood... Something's wrong with her."

"Good. That's saved us a shitload of trouble. Grab her and let's go."

Please stay alive...

Katsumi half-noticed large hands gripping her arms before she finally fainted.

~ ~ ~ ~ ~

"So Captain Samakura was down here," Rufus repeated his question.

"Yeah, like I already told ya."

The man sitting a few feet from where Rufus and Law were standing was a wholly unpleasant man in Rufus' opinion. His house reflected that; Rufus wouldn't dare sit on anything in the dingy place in his pristine white suit. The man himself was even worse; a dirty, odorous, loathsome rat of a man. The left side of his face sported some nasty bruising and he rubbed at his neck as he continued, "Bitch gave me a lotta trouble. Broke my door down, attacked me. That 'ow you guys do things now?"

Rufus moved his foot as a roach crawled past, looking from it to the man, Lou Phelps, as if he considered him and the vermin equals. Which he did. "It depends on who we're dealing with, Mr. Phelps. Can you tell me what she asked?"

"She was lookin' fer some guy named 'Director'."

"And did you give her anything to help with that?"

"A name."

"What was the name?"

"Gamlen Ordo. Sort've a merc boss who got some guys for 'im."

"Excellent. Anything else?"

"No, 'cause it doesn't matter." The man grinned, revealing a clear lack of dental hygiene.

"Why not?" Rufus asked curiously.

"You guys got no right t'be down 'ere, so I tipped Gamlen off she was comin'." He snickered.

"You'll prob'ly find nothin' but a corpse."

Law looked at Rufus, who tapped his chin. "...I see."

"An' you can't do anythin' t'me, that ain't the law."

"Mhmm." Rufus drew his pistol, shooting the man square in the forehead. "You saw that, right, Law?"

"You mean how he tried to attack you?" Law shrugged. "Damn tragedy."

"Indeed." Rufus holstered his pistol. "Let's go pay Ordo a visit, and fast. I really doubt he'll get Captain Samakura, but I'm not willing to leave it to chance."

"Right behind you."

~ ~ ~ ~ ~

Katsumi woke with a scream, jerking and unable to breathe. Only after it stopped did she recognize the effects of electrocution. *An old friend...* She opened her eyes to see that she was inside some basement, which was not surprising in the least. A few thugs stood before her, including one undoubtedly more important man who was looking at her like a dog with a bone. Unlike some of his men he wore a suit and looked far cleaner.

"Welcome back to the world of the living, Ms. Samakura. I hear you're looking for me. It appears you've been successful."

Katsumi tried to stand only to realize her wrists were manacled to the wooden chair she'd been placed in. Wiring connected to the manacles showed her where the shock came from.

"Yes, I'm quite aware rope would be useless on you. I wanted a conversation, though, with one of the people who have made our enterprises so difficult over the last few years."

Katsumi shot him a glare that could melt metal. "You're just asking for a painful death, aren't you?"

The man shook his head and pressed a button on the remote he held. Katsumi screamed again as electricity ran through her, setting her nerves on fire. It lasted long enough for her to smell burning before he turned it off. "We can have as many of these lessons as you like. Sooner or later you'll learn to be my pet, and then you'll get to leave the chair and get a collar. Won't that be fun?"

Katsumi seethed, grinding her teeth together and testing the manacles with a few pulls.

The man gleefully electrocuted her for another ten seconds, enjoying the screams. "Those are reinforced, my dear, you won't be breaking them. Calm down and chat with me." He grinned, obviously trying to get under her skin. "Why don't you tell me the kind of outfits you'd like to wear for me? I do try to be kind; I'll let you wear your preference, so long as it's suitably… entertaining." He was enjoying having such a powerful enemy in this position far too much.

Katsumi wrenched her hands down, setting her feet firmly on the floor. She looked down for a few seconds before realization hit her and she smiled. "Alright then… You've hit the jackpot because, let me tell you, you have no idea what I can do." She looked up at him through her hair, her voice lowering to a sultry tone. "I can do things for you…" She smiled playfully. "To you… in exchange for letting me go. All I want is to get out of here."

She obviously had the man's attention now, as well as the attention of the other men in the room. She tilted her head, letting her violet hair fall to hide one eye. "I can't fight my way out of this and I have more important things to get to, so I'll do whatever you want in return for a quick release."

"This is a pathetic escape attempt."

Katsumi shook her head. "I can't do an escape attempt. There's only one way out of here and even if I somehow took you out while we were alone – while in this chair where you can shock me at any time – I don't have any weapons and your men would be guarding the only exit."

The man raised an eyebrow. "You're really trying to barter for your escape?"

"Really. I'll do anything to catch the man I'm after. I just want you to promise you'll release me."

The man grinned. "Very well." He waved to his men to exit the room and guard right outside the doorway. Once they were alone he walked towards her. "I still think you're bluffing, but that will make it more entertaining. I'm not letting you out of that chair and I'm keeping this," he held up the remote, "in my hand." He gripped Katsumi's chin roughly, enjoying the disgusted look she got, and pressed his lips to hers in the worst excuse for a kiss she'd ever imagined was possible. He even had the gall to shove his tongue down her throat. It took everything she had not to retch right then.

At least until she snapped the chair arm free with her right hand and stood, spinning around him and wrapping her free arm around his neck from behind. She set her left foot on the chair and shoved, tearing the other arm free just in time as the man jammed on the button. Fortunately, with the wires torn, the button now did nothing. "You're an idiot," she hissed into his ear as she choked him, ignoring his nails tearing at her arm. "Reinforced manacles don't mean anything on a wooden chair. I would love to take my time killing you, but the screams would alert your men. You have no idea how much this disappoints me."

Katsumi jerked her arm and snapped the man's neck, releasing him and letting his lifeless body crumple to the ground. She immediately spat on the ground several times, coughing and rubbing her mouth with her arm. "Fuck… Fucking pig… I will never be able to rinse enough." She shuddered, suppressing the urge to vomit by kicking his corpse. She then picked him up and headed for the door, opening it and flinging the body out. All she needed was for the eyes of the men on either side of the door to follow the body, which they did, curses of surprise forming on their lips. They would be simple; it was the two men further down the hall, outside of melee range, that would be trouble.

Katsumi went for the guard immediately to her right, shoving her arm into his neck and slamming him back into the wall, crushing his windpipe. She ripped the gun out of his hand and ducked as the man directly behind her fired, turning and kicking upwards with her left foot, disarming the second guard. She set her left foot down, stood and spun, her right foot kicking the man into the wall. As he bounced off of it from the impact she slid behind him and caught his shirt, holding him in front of her as the guards down the hallway opened fire. The man's body took most of the bullets as she put her right arm over his shoulder, returning fire and taking out one of the guards.

She felt a bullet hit her stomach and grunted, focusing and shooting down the last guy. She threw the body away from her, leaning back against the wall and feeling her stomach. The bullet was still in her, she could tell, but she'd be alright. Her abnormally high CP meant it wouldn't get infected, so as long as she could stand the pain – and didn't bleed out – fixing it could wait. Right now Katsumi had more important things to do. *I'm back, Ayane.*

Oh, thank God... The relief in Ayane's voice was palpable. *What happened?*

Captured, some electrocution, had to kiss the most disgusting mouth I've ever touched, got shot but it's not bad.

Oh my God... You're supposed to be being careful!

I am being careful.

Well you're terrible at it! Katsumi heard a sob through the link and it pained her. She stopped and leaned against the wall for a moment.

Ayane, listen to me. I'm fine. If I was in real trouble I'd go back, but I'm not. And you know I can't go back, not now.

After that boy...

Yes. I can't let someone like this get away.

No, of course not, I just...

I'll stay in contact with you now. I need you to focus me and you need reassurance. Besides... it'll be like old times.

Really? I'd appreciate that... Okay, but if you black out on me again I'm coming down there myself.

Katsumi smiled. *I expected no less.* She picked up a new gun and readied it, intent on finding hers, as well as information on her target, before leaving this place.

~ ~ ~ ~ ~

"Jesus." Rufus stepped over another corpse, avoiding the blood pooled around it. "I guess I was worried for nothing."

Law shook his head as they entered the last room. There was a dead man in a nice suit in the middle near the wreckage of a chair which he pointed at. "Not for nothing. Torture chair right there." He walked over and held up the torn wires. "Electrocution."

Rufus sighed, rubbing his eyes. "Lucky for these guys they're dead already. Looks like we were slow on this one, Law."

"I agree. If she hadn't been able to escape on her own, by now we'd find barely anything left."

"We have to do better, then." Rufus turned and headed for the door.

Law nodded and followed him. "We can't leave her alone on this. We're a team, it's not right."

"Maybe you should've told her that."

"She wouldn't have listened. She's just going on instinct right now."

"Trust me, I understand. I just wish she wasn't. This bastard she's after isn't worth losing her, it's simple math; she's worth more than his death is. If I'd known this was what she was going to do I'd have gone with her." Rufus looked back at Sam. "I'm not trying to retrieve her, Law. I'm just trying to catch up to her so our kill counts remain competitive."

Law smiled. "Now that is a thought she'd appreciate."

"She and I are more similar than most people realize." Rufus stopped outside the door of the room, looking down. "Hold up."

"See a sign of her?"

"Unfortunately…" Rufus knelt, gesturing for Law to investigate with him. He pointed to a small patch of blood and fluid on the wall and floor. "Unless one of these guys has a CP over fifty."

"Doubtful." Law shook his head. "Looks like she got hit."

"Think it was bad?"

"I only know it's not bad enough to drop her or we'd have found her, and it's not bad enough for her to call this off."

"That's something, then. Still… Feels like we should speed up a bit."

"I'm with you." Law stood and started down the hallway. "None of us ever did know when to back off."

"At least we're dealing with humans for this. If she was going after a Class A supernatural target or something alone, we'd be in a lot more trouble."

"Don't give her ideas."

~ ~ ~ ~ ~

Date: April 1, 2068
Time: 1:18 PM
Location: Aegis Corp HQ, Hangar

Reno set the chopper down with a sigh, turning everything off and exiting it with no joviality. Everything was grey right now; even the skies reflected that, overcast and dreary as a light drizzle cast a depressing pall over the city. Weather was fascinating in the way it sometimes matched the mood, Reno thought. It was April 1st – April Fool's Day – usually one of Reno's favorite days of the year, but not this year. No one was joking, no one felt like joking and no one had anything to joke about.

Captain Sama had been missing for four days. Rufus had reported his and Law's trail had gone cold, though they were still out looking. Reno himself was getting in a car to go home because he had nowhere else to look and nothing else to do. He'd been needed when the team was together, but now they were all split apart and he knew going his own separate way wouldn't make anything worse. Sano was stressed out but being there wasn't helping him at all. The problem wasn't too many things to deal with; it was having nothing to do. Ironically, the one thing that always drove Captain Sama crazy was now being inflicted on all of them by her actions.

The drive home was as dreary as the rest of the day had been, and Reno was glad to finally get home. Lenora was waiting for him at the door and questioned him as he wiped the rain from his glasses. "Still no word about her?"

"None," Reno shook his head. "No more leads or anything."

Lenora's expression saddened. "I'm sure she's fine."

"Probably. Everyone's just unhappy with the 'unsure' part."

Lenora sighed and closed the door. "I'm worried about her myself."

"Didn't you just say you're sure she's fine?"

"Well... It sounds like she took what happened really hard, right?"

"Yeah."

"If she was doing fine emotionally she wouldn't have run off on her own." Lenora folded her arms. "This was obviously the last straw for her. You saw her when she was over here – this whole thing has been pushing her, and four days ago was the breaking point. I'm worried about her emotionally and physically, though I'm starting to understand how much she'd hate knowing that." Lenora looked at Reno. "I had started to believe she and I could be friends. I'm hoping I'll still get that chance."

Reno hugged her. "You will. We'll find her or she'll finish her job and come back, one or the other."

"I hope for her sake it's the latter."

~ ~ ~ ~ ~

Date: April 3, 2068
Time: 5:01 AM
Location: Takagawa Building Basement Level

"Your Captain has been causing quite a stir in the Underworld."

"She's on a warpath," Sano sighed. He was leaning against a wall in 'Room 3.5' again, hands in his pockets and eyes on the mysterious man in the next room.

"She's caused enough casualties." Briggs hit a button and a panel slid open in Sano's side of the room. "I've got something you'll appreciate much more this time... a location."

Sano stood up quickly. "What? The Director's location?!"

"Jerne Kintashi's location," The man corrected. "Trying to be known by the alias 'The Director', which he's hardly worthy of. I suggest you send that to Captain Samakura quickly so she finds him before he finds her."

Sano ripped the paper out of the alcove. He once again wished Katsumi had her cyber link open but it'd been off since she'd disappeared, so he quickly entered everything he saw into his phone and sent it to Katsumi's. He looked through the window at Briggs. "I need to go now, then. I guess now we'll see if you're really telling the truth."

"I do suggest you hurry. And don't forget our deal."

"If you really just helped us catch this guy, I'll do what I can to make it happen," Sano nodded before rushing out of the room and contacting the rest of the team over the cyber link. "Guys? Get ready and get moving, we have a possible location for our target. I've already sent it to the Captain."

Rufus' voice jumped in. "That contact, Briggs, really came through, didn't he?"

"I guess we're about to see if he did," commented Law.

"Hey, how about we all rush out there and see for ourselves instead of debating?" Reno interjected.

"Get the chopper and let's go, then. I think we're on a time crunch because, if I know anything about her at all, Captain Sama's already on her way."

Chapter 9: Tears

Jerne Kintashi was scared.

More than that, he was terrified.

His door shuddered again under another powerful impact and he recognized the voice of the person on the other side... the voice of someone he'd only imagined meeting in his moment of victory, standing over her bleeding form as he explained to her his brilliance and how he had beaten her. He'd imagined telling her all her mistakes and relishing the fear and awe in her eyes as she realized how outmatched she was. He'd imagined her begging for her life as he held it in his hands like a god.

He'd never imagined her tearing his apartment door from its hinges as she was doing now. He'd never imagined her walking into his room with a fury that made his blood run cold and robbed him of the ability to do anything but scramble backwards. He'd certainly never imagined the whimpers that escaped his own lips as her powerful hand gripped his shirt, lifted him bodily off the ground and hurled him across the room into one of his bookcases, shattering the furniture and scattering books onto the floor around him.

Katsumi Samakura was in his home, and he could do nothing about it. Suddenly he felt the same hopelessness he'd wished on his enemies. She leapt over his couch and landed beside him, picking him up again and slamming him into a wall, causing him to cry out in pain. She leaned in, growling out her words like a feral beast who was struggling to prevent herself from tearing him apart. "Why, Kintashi? I want to know why. I want to know the reasons for your actions."

"F-fear..." Answering her questions was completely involuntary by that point. Jerne, despite his previous beliefs, wasn't a hardened criminal. He'd thought himself invincible. "I wanted you... everyone... to fear me."

Katsumi stopped breathing, staring at him. "...That's it...?"

Anger rose through Kintashi finally, anger at his failure, at the way this woman broke in and acted like he wasn't a threat of any kind, wasn't someone worthy of respect. He yelled back in her face, "I am no simple criminal! I am greater than ordinary men! They are nothing but tools! I will reign-" He was cut off by a vicious punch to his stomach that robbed him of all ability to breathe.

Katsumi threw him to the ground, rage overwhelming every other emotion. "That's it? THAT'S IT?! All of that... all those deaths... for nothing?!" She kicked him hard enough to send him into the wall, cracking it. He coughed up blood but she didn't care, stalking after him. "This was all just some stupid little game to you?! What about those people you killed?! What about the lives you ruined?!" He tried to sit up and the back of her hand caught his face so hard his head hit the floor. "What about that mother and son?!"

She fell to her knees and slammed her fist into his face, tears now running down her cheeks. "All of that and you DARE tell me you don't care?! You fucking..." She slammed her fist into his face again. "Piece of..." Another punch. Blood spattered her face and clothes. "SHIT!"

After that the blows rained down, harder and faster with every punch. Blood coated the floor, the wall, and her, and still she didn't stop. By the time she finally finished her violet bangs were spotted with red, as were her arms, face and the front of her clothing. She wiped her eyes on her arm, looking down. There was no longer any head; Katsumi's full-strength blows were able to shatter concrete - a human skull had no chance. And what was worse – what made a little part of Katsumi wonder what her life had turned her into – was that she couldn't find any part of her that cared.

Katsumi stood and screamed, slamming her fist into the wall and punching a hole in it. She smashed another one before stumbling back and running her fingers through her hair, realizing she was shaking again. All her rage had boiled over to the point where she'd beaten a man to death and still she was filled with it. The job was over, the attacks were over, and still rage flowed through her body and mind unchecked. With no one to unleash it on it turned on the only target available: herself.

Katsumi Samakura stalked out of the apartment and headed for the roof.

~ ~ ~ ~ ~

I got him...

Ayane breathed a deep sigh of relief at the words. *Thank God... What about you?*

I'm... not alright. Still angry... Still enraged. I beat him to death and it still isn't enough.

You're losing yourself, Sumi, Ayane said in a worried tone. Her sister sounded odd and it was something she'd heard before; something she didn't like. *I love my sister and I don't want to lose her to that rage, that other person, again. Remember that!*

I'm trying, but I... I failed so many things on this case...

Hey, no one is better at doing what you do than you are. No one. The city needs you to be its protector.

There are others who would be better.

Not for your friends, Ayane argued. *Not for me. If it wasn't for you I'd be dead. And if it wasn't for your actions today more people would be dead later on. Don't hate yourself, Sumi, there's too much to like.*

I know... You're right... I just feel so worn down right now... so beaten. I won but it feels like I lost.

That's what it means to care. Come see me later, okay? Promise you'll come see me.

I promise, Ayane.

Then hold on until then. Talk to someone if you can... being alone is the worst thing for you right now.

Katsumi went silent and Ayane looked out the window worriedly, thinking about the things her sister was going through and wishing she could be there herself.

~ ~ ~ ~ ~

Date: April 3, 2068

Sano, Rufus and Law moved slowly down the hallway towards the room they suspected was home to Jerne Kintashi, the terrorist they'd all been hunting for the past two weeks. Reno was in the chopper outside, watching for anyone trying to escape. They still didn't know where Katsumi was but all of them hoped they'd meet her here.

Sano edged up to the doorway, looking back. "Door's gone."

"Guess she's been here already," Law said in an even tone.

"One way to find out." Rufus stepped around Sano and spun to face into the room, pistol ready. He lowered the weapon immediately and looked at the other two. "Looks like you're right, Law."

Sano stood straight and looked around the doorjamb into the room. The apartment was an utter mess; furniture was broken, books and other items were scattered everywhere, and there were some spots of heavy damage on the walls. He stepped further into the room and noticed the body. "Either Captain Sama was here or Kintashi decided to use his own methods on his own head…"

Rufus and Law entered to look around as well. Rufus moved towards the body, looking it over. "Lots of blood… On the floor, walls, little bit on the ceiling… couple of bloody footprints I think are her size…"

"Wasn't an explosive, though," Law said as he tapped the wall beside one of the holes. "A fist did this." He pointed at the headless body. "And that."

"Guess we never intended to take him alive," Sano muttered.

"I think that went out the window about a week ago," replied Rufus. "You can't tell me you're surprised by this scene."

"Not surprised." He looked around, speaking to Reno over their cyber link, "Reno, we found Kintashi… or what's left of him. Captain Sama's not in here though. Do a sweep of the area for her."

"Got it."

Rufus turned on the computer to see if he could find any useful information while Law began searching the room for evidence of what Jerne had used for his explosions. Not a minute later Reno contacted Kurasano again. "Sano, you're not gonna believe this, but I found her."

"Already? Where?" Rufus and Law looked at him, waiting for answers.

"Above you. On the roof."

"You're kidding... Alright, I'm heading up there." Sano looked at the other two. "She's on the roof. I'm gonna go up there while you guys finish up in here."

After they nodded Sano headed for the stairs, taking them two at a time until he came out on the roof. The sky was tinted a light purple as the sunrise began, allowing him to see Katsumi sitting on the edge of the roof. Wind bit through him given how high up they were, and Sano wondered just how long she'd been up here. He walked forward cautiously, having no idea what kind of reaction he'd get.

"Captain Sama?"

She looked back at him. Whatever he'd been expecting, it wasn't tear-stained cheeks. He was shocked into silence, able only to stare. To his even greater surprise she didn't even seem ashamed of it or angry that he saw her that way. She just looked back at the sunrise. Sano's hands dropped to his sides as he tried to think of something to say. He took a few steps forward. "Katsumi...?"

"The city's still intact..." Katsumi's voice was quiet.

"Yeah... Nothing's happened since you disappeared. Why are you up here?"

"I just... needed to think."

"Alright." Sano moved up, carefully sitting on the edge of the roof beside her, watching for any sign he needed to back off. She didn't react to him at all so he assumed it was okay. "What are you thinking about?"

"I don't have the best record..." Katsumi looked down at the street below. "I was a lot better at killing people than I am at protecting them."

"Killing people?" Sano looked at her, curious at her choice of words.

"That's what I used to do," Katsumi answered quietly. "That was all I did. I was never asked to protect. Lately..." She sighed. "Lately I've been wondering if I should've just stuck with that..."

"That's ridiculous. You're meant to be a protector."

"I'm no good at it, Sano." She looked at him sadly. His immediate argument died on his lips as he saw it wasn't just self-hate; Katsumi truly believed what she was saying. "I'm not a protector. I try to be one but really I'm more of an… avenger. I can't stop people dying; I can only kill the person that did it after they're already dead."

"That's just bullshit," Sano shook his head, "You've protected plenty of people. You saved Reno's life."

"Saved him from my own mistake," Katsumi muttered.

"You saved those people on the train," Sano said louder, trying to argue her down. "You saved anyone this guy was going after next. You've saved all our lives at some point or another. Hell, your simple existence protects so many people in this city."

"I want to believe you," Katsumi said softly as she looked down. "I don't know how much longer I can do this, though."

"You're the toughest person I've ever met. Since when did you become weak?"

He'd expected an angry reaction, which was why he'd said it. He didn't expect her to simply smile. "I've always been weak. I just don't show it. And I've been doing this for longer than a few years, Sano."

"Doing what?"

"All of this." Katsumi looked up. "All the killing and death and loss. I've been doing it since I was twelve."

Sano blinked. "Twelve? You… what?"

Katsumi shook her head. "Maybe another time… My point is… I feel worn down. I feel old even though I'm only thirty-four. I lost my control, what kind of sign is that?"

"You were angry…"

"I abandoned my position and duties because of personal emotions. I almost abandoned them entirely."

"You were going to quit?!"

Katsumi smiled sadly at him. "I thought about it." She looked back down at the street. "For a moment…" Katsumi shook her head. "I didn't know what to do… I don't know… Everything's suddenly harder and I don't…"

Kurasano looked down and sighed. This was so different from the Katsumi he knew that he felt lost himself. Suddenly she wasn't his boss or the Captain or the tough commander everyone feared to anger; she was just a woman. He was suddenly angry at himself for having thought her invincible all this time, even though he knew that's how she wanted it. What was worse was that he knew she'd look back on this moment and hate it even though she needed it.

She really was self-defeating; it was surprising he hadn't seen her break before now, and he was starting to wonder when she would again. Katsumi was quiet now. She cleared her throat once and Sano could tell she was a little more normal by the blush on her cheeks; he could tell she was embarrassed so he decided to cut it off quickly before it led to anger at herself. "We're friends, Katsumi." He met her gaze. "I couldn't admire you more for this."

"Admire?" She cocked her head to the side a bit, curious. "For childish-"

"Bullshit," he cut her off. "After all you've dealt with you're still doing it and you still care. Most people either have to stop caring at some point, or stop doing it because they're not strong enough. That's why you're the strongest. You're still able to care about every death and yet you keep going despite every death weighing on you. This city's lucky it has you as a protector because no one else would be able to do it the same way."

Katsumi smiled at him. "You have a way with words, Sano..."

"I try, Captain," Sano smiled.

"I appreciate it. I..." Katsumi looked away. "I'm sorry... for running off, and leaving you to deal with everything. I shouldn't have..."

"Hey, it's fine. You got angry and I understand. It's over now though, and I was able to take care of stuff."

"Good." Katsumi smiled at him again. "I'm proud of you. It sounds like you handled the team as well as I expected you to. I... appreciate it."

"Thanks, Katsumi." Sano smiled back. "I appreciate your appreciation." He looked around. "You wanna get down off this roof now? I'm freezing and other people are waiting to hear you're alright."

"I suppose I should talk to them, then... But..." She looked at Sano. "Right now..."

"Right," he said, looking at her tear-stained cheeks and reddened eyes. It made sense she wouldn't want others to see her this way. "Hey, weren't you hit?"

"That's why I'm sitting down," Katsumi said with a smile, pointing to her bloodstained midsection.

"That's gotta be bad by now…" Sano shook his head. "Anyway, we'll have Reno pick us up on this roof and take us back now so you can get fixed up. Rufus and Law can meet you later."

Katsumi sighed in relief. "That's perfect. Thank you, Sano."

"Eh, they have jobs to do anyway." He called Reno and put Katsumi's arm over his shoulders, helping her stand. He looked at her as he helped her towards the landing helicopter. "You really hate this, don't you?"

Katsumi smirked at him. "I really do."

"Well don't worry, soon you'll get fixed up and you'll be back to not needing anyone again."

Katsumi sighed sadly. "I always need someone." She climbed into the chopper, leaving Sano standing there trying to figure out the meaning behind her words and the sadness lacing them.

Reno looked back as she got in, grinning. "Captain! I was beginning to think you'd left us all for a younger, hotter team."

Katsumi sat down heavily in a chair, glad to finally relax a bit. "Don't be silly, Reno. You know very well I like being the hottest person on a team."

"Well thank God you're back, then. We've got, like, no hotness rating without you. Drops like a rock."

Sano climbed in and headed for the back, nodding towards the front. Katsumi sighed as she understood his meeting, standing slowly and moving to take a seat in the co-pilot's chair. Reno smiled at her. "Hey boss. Making sure I don't run into a building?"

"Reno…" Katsumi looked away from him, out the window, so he wouldn't see her face.

Reno blinked. "You sound serious."

"You can take off. Just… listen."

He nodded, taking the chopper into the air and heading back towards HQ as he looked at her.

"I'm… sorry," Katsumi began in a soft voice as she looked out the window. "I should never have left like I did."

Reno glanced over at her. It was now that he noticed the signs of tears on her face, which made it the first time he'd ever seen such on his boss. He was shocked speechless for a few moments before he was able to stutter out a response. "Captain, I…"

"There isn't an excuse, Reno. I have a responsibility as this team's leader and I failed it." Her voice grew quieter. "I failed all of you."

"I don't think you failed, boss, you just…"

"I let my emotions get the better of me. It was… wrong. And I need to apologize for that."

Reno nodded. "Alright. I understand your reasons, then. I accept your apology. Honestly though, boss, I'm just glad you're okay."

Katsumi smiled a little. "I know, Reno."

"Lenora will be relieved, too."

Katsumi looked at him curiously. "Lenora?"

"Yeah. She said she was really hoping you two could be friends. She's been worried all week, like she gets with me when I'm not back on time."

"Oh…" Katsumi looked out the window thoughtfully. "I should probably talk to her, too, then…"

Reno smiled. "I'd appreciate that, as would she."

"I am… very thankful to have her care about me. I'll let her know that."

"It would mean a lot. Maybe you two should have lunch or something."

"Lunch?" She looked back to him. "What are you trying to do?"

"I'm not trying to do anything, it's just that Lenora isn't the type of woman to have a lot of real friends. I know I can't be everything to her, there are just some things she needs a friend for."

Reno glanced at her. "And no offense, boss, but I think you'd benefit a lot from having her as a friend, too. Besides, she likes you."

"Mmm." Katsumi looked away again, smiling. "I like her too. Tell you what, Reno, when you talk to her tonight tell her to come up with a time to meet me tomorrow. Her choice. Tell her to call me and I'll be there."

Reno smiled. "Thanks, boss. I really appreciate you giving it a chance. I know you're not really fond of getting to know random people."

"Lenora isn't a random person, Reno, she's your wife. She's as close to family as any of you are."

"She'd be ecstatic to hear that."

"Yes, she does seem to be a very caring person… I agree with your belief that she'd be good for me. Even if she is a little too good at seeing through me for my liking."

Reno grinned. "Yeah, she has a habit of doing that. She doesn't like to let painful things lie, she prefers trying to fix them."

"So I've seen. I hope she's willing to let some things lie, though. There are some things I don't talk about, friend or not."

"Hey, she'll learn like the rest of us did, right? Just, uh, don't hit her like you did the rest of us, please."

"Honestly I'm not sure who would come out on top if I did," Katsumi responded dryly, eliciting a laugh from Reno. Katsumi was grateful that the conversation ended there, allowing her to go back to thinking. She was starting to believe she'd have to give up a little of her "acting strong" in order to gain some more actual strength, otherwise she wasn't sure how much longer she could take everything.

That meant opening up a little, a thought that both angered and scared her. In the end, though, if it helped keep her sane, it would be worth it.

~ ~ ~ ~ ~

It didn't take Katsumi too long to be fixed up, which she was thankful for. For once she was actually feeling like lying down for a while. It'd been two weeks since she'd really slept; she'd only had about eight hours total since then and it was really wearing on her by this point. On top of that she was on the verge of breaking down more than she'd done in front of Sano, barely keeping control of her emotions – and she needed to keep that locked down until she could get to Ayane. She stood in the OR of Aegis HQ, staring out the window as she flexed a recently-repaired wrist, deep in thought as she often found herself these days.

She felt a presence behind her and turned to see Law standing in the doorway. She'd known this conversation was coming… She'd been dreading it since she left, but she wasn't going to avoid it. Law walked into the room until he stood right in front of her, staring down at her. "We're a team."

"I know," Katsumi responded quietly. "I'm sorry."

"You're sorry?" he asked a little incredulously. "You just ran off. You didn't ask me to come, didn't take anyone else with you or even tell us what you were doing. Is that how a leader acts?" Katsumi looked at the floor and Law sighed, running a hand over his bald head. "You messed up."

"Again," Katsumi said softly. She didn't even look back up at him. Law was her oldest friend; she'd known the man for well over a decade. He knew her, knew why she did what she did, but still… "You deserved better," she voiced her thoughts. "You're right, about everything you just said." Law watched her as she sat on the windowsill. "I've spent the last two weeks wondering if I'm the right person for this job… Hating myself for mistakes and failures… Even now, none of my questions are answered and none of my emotions are solved." She looked up at him. "I lost control, Law… I abandoned my responsibilities, my duty and my team because of my emotions. It was wrong… childish, even… but I feel like I'm beginning to break down bit by bit."

Law set a large hand on her shoulder. "I didn't mean to be so harsh…"

"Yes you did," Katsumi smiled sadly. "Don't start making excuses for me just because I feel like this. Just…" She looked away. "Tell me… if you think I'm unfit to be leader now. I'll listen to you. Be honest…"

Law took a step back, shaking his head. This really wasn't what he'd been looking for at all. He'd just been angry. "No one's perfect. You're just going through a rough patch right now. Everyone's got a rough patch. I don't think you're going downhill or unfit to lead us."

"You'd tell me if I were, wouldn't you?" she asked quietly as she looked at him.

"I wouldn't risk your life and our lives by lying if I really thought you should step down. You just need to relax a bit, take a little break and get some actual sleep. When was the last time you slept?"

Katsumi smiled softly. "I've been trying to remember."

"Then go home and do so. That's my honest opinion. That's the repayment I want for this little stunt of yours."

Katsumi smiled at him. "Thank you, Law." She stood up and looked into his eyes. "I'm sorry, again... I'm disappointed in myself and... I hope you'll forgive me and let me re-earn your trust."

"You've had my trust for years. You can't lose it that easily. As for forgiveness, you had it when you apologized the first time. I was just angry and needed to hear you say it."

"I understand. Thank you... Do me a favor? I'm going to visit Ayane, and then crashing... Tell the team they have the week off. Let Reno stay home with his family and you do whatever you want. It'll give us all a week to rest up, and it'll give me some time to get myself back together."

"Will do, Captain." Law smiled and waved her off. "Have a good night."

Katsumi nodded and left the building, not planning to stop - until she ran into Rufus outside. Both of them stopped for a second, staring at each other until Rufus spoke. "You went emotional."

"I did."

"Try not to do it again. That was not a valuable sacrifice."

"Value wasn't in my head." Katsumi smiled slightly. "Are you including underworld clean-up in your calculations?"

"I can factor it in." Rufus smirked. "Although I wouldn't call anything you did 'clean-up' considering the amount of cleaning that is now required in your wake."

"You're just upset at the kill-count difference."

"Perhaps." Rufus paused, tilting his head.

Katsumi was silent as well, meeting his gaze. He understood why she'd done what she'd done, so that didn't need to be said – and 'I'm sorry' wasn't something she had to say to Rufus. She knew that all he was looking for was an acknowledgement – and that she was willing to do. "I made a mistake," she stated, watching him nod. "I'm looking into the reasons."

"We both know it wasn't the kid."

Katsumi smiled sadly. "Of course it wasn't... Not entirely, anyway. We've both seen things like that many times before." She looked off to the side. "Unfortunately I'm not sure about anything… A combination of stress, fatigue, frustration and pride is looking possible."

"Maybe." Rufus walked closer, stopping beside her and adjusting his shades. "Keep an eye on it. We can't always afford weakness."

"Understood."

Rufus moved past her but stopped after a few steps, looking back. "Glad you've returned… But I won't forgive you the next time you decide to ignore the law and go on a killing spree and don't allow me to join in the fun."

Katsumi smirked over her shoulder. "I'll keep that in mind."

~ ~ ~ ~ ~

Reno arrived home and got out of the car in a far better mood than he'd been in for the past two weeks. The terrorist was gone, Katsumi was back and he'd just been told he had the week off again, this time without interruption. He walked up to the door and smiled as his wife greeted him at it again. "Any news?"

Reno nodded and took off his coat. "We found her, and she's more or less alright."

Lenora sighed. "Thank God. What does 'more or less' mean?"

"Well she wasn't really injured, but… she's definitely not back to normal. I don't know if I should really talk about this, but I know you won't tell anyone." Reno folded his arms, looking troubled. "When we picked her up it looked like she'd been… crying. Which is ridiculous, she doesn't do that."

"Everyone does that."

"Not Katsumi," Reno corrected. "Not Captain Sama. She didn't seem like herself. She apologized to me for leaving and she was all soft-spoken while she was doing it."

"All of this has affected her, Reno, even though she tried not to show it. I hope you were understanding."

"Of course I was. Oh, by the way, she wants to know if you'd like to have lunch with her tomorrow."

Lenora blinked. "Lunch?"

"Yeah. Just you two, I'd be watchin' my little girl."

"Well, yes, of course!"

"Good, I think she could really use a friend right now. She said to call her at some point and tell her whatever time you'd like to meet tomorrow."

"I'll do that!" Lenora smiled. "I'm surprised… You said something, didn't you?"

"Well," Reno rubbed his neck, "I may have suggested it a little after she said she wanted to apologize to you, too."

"Me?"

"Yeah. She seemed happy about my idea, though. Believe it or not she said you're as close to being her family as any of us are."

Lenora blinked. "Wow… She really said that? That's a lot of pressure… And she deserves actual family. Everyone needs family."

"Well you're the best family anyone could ask for, so if anyone can help her with that, it's you."

"I hope so. At least I know she's open; I don't imagine she'd force herself to do this if she didn't want to. I'll come up with a time and give her a call. Why don't you go ask Lianne where she'd like to go with you tomorrow?"

Reno grinned. "Great idea!"

Lenora watched him walk off before her thoughts went back to the following day. People like Katsumi Samakura rarely opened up, if ever. Lenora was excited knowing she had a chance to actually get to know the woman, but she was also a little nervous. She knew Katsumi needed someone close more than she did; after all, Lenora had Reno, while Katsumi had no one. Messing this up would be worse for Katsumi than anyone else and Lenora hated being unable to help people more than anything. She didn't plan to lose this chance.

~ ~ ~ ~ ~

Ayane looked up as Katsumi came in. She immediately read the emotions in her older sister and moved over on her bed, opening her arms. Katsumi dropped onto the bed, curling up against Ayane as the younger woman wrapped her arms around her. "Oh, Sumi… I haven't seen you like this in a long, long time."

Katsumi laid her head on her sister's chest, closing her eyes as tears ran from them. "I haven't felt like this in a long, long time…" she said softly. "I feel like I failed everything. I wanted to give up today."

Ayane hugged Katsumi tightly. "I know. It's impossible not to feel that at some point when you do what you do."

"I feel like I did right after mother…"

"Hey, this is nothing like that," Ayane said as she looked down at her sister.

"It's similar," Katsumi said with a distant look in her eyes. "I failed… every part of this. I didn't even find him. I abandoned my team, my duties, you… all for nothing. I didn't even find him myself, only when they sent me his location. Everything would have been the same without me."

"You didn't fail anything, Sumi. And this is coming from someone who knows every detail of your last two weeks. I'm proud of you. Do you hear me?"

Katsumi looked up at her. In reality, while Katsumi had almost always been 'the older one', the adult, the one that usually took care of her… in truth, she was only three years older than Ayane, and times like this really reminded the younger girl of that. Even Katsumi couldn't always be the adult. "Really?"

Ayane met her look with a gentle smile. "Yes. You should know that. You know how highly I think of you; doesn't it mean something that I'm not disappointed?"

"Yes… Of course it does."

"You tell that stupid self-deprecating mind of yours that, then. You should trust me more than it."

Katsumi gave a small smile. "I do. Your opinion's more important to me than anyone's."

"Well I've known you almost thirty-one years now. I know everything there is to know about you." Ayane smiled. "I know you deserve a lot better than to be hating yourself for not saving 'enough' people. I guarantee you that none of the people you saved hate you. Be proud of what you did, Katsumi, because no one else could've done it. You've always been amazing like that."

Katsumi sighed, burying her head in her sister's chest, surrounded by pale blue hair. "You always know exactly what to say. It's almost not fair…"

"That I won't let you stay in a depression?" Ayane smiled. "Come on, you're better than 'poor me', Sumi. I like when you're happy. Plus when you're happy you don't think about making stupid decisions like quitting."

"Stupid?"

"Of course it was stupid. We both know you'd go crazy without that job. What would you do, sit around and knit?"

Katsumi laughed softly. "You have a point…"

"And more than one, too. What about the money for our house, huh? I'm not exactly making millions sitting in here."

"You're right… as always." Katsumi lifted her head to look at her. "Still… I think I did pretty well at… being selfish, for a second there."

"You could use practice," Ayane smiled.

"I might get it… Now that this is happening again."

"Your emotions, you mean?" Katsumi nodded and Ayane sighed, running her fingers through her older sister's hair.

"We still don't know why…"

"I know. But this time wasn't as bad as last time."

"What if it becomes that bad? What if they get even more uncontrolled? I could-"

"That won't happen," Ayane assured her. "I won't let it. We'll work at it together."

"I feel like they're tearing their way out of me," Katsumi said in a quiet voice, not lifting her head from her sister's chest. "Everything's in chaos…"

"Then let's focus the good ones," Ayane said comfortingly. "And you can let everything out with me – it's keeping them in that causes so much stress."

Katsumi sighed, closing her eyes. "I guess you're right…"

"You need to relax, and to rest, and to take care of yourself… or for me to take care of you." Ayane smiled. "Will you stay here tonight?"

"You just don't want to send me home where I'll be alone."

"Maybe… Is that a no?"

"Of course not." Katsumi smiled. "I'm surprised you don't mind sharing the bed again, though, having had it to yourself all this time."

"It's overrated. I prefer a sleeping arrangement that gets me breakfast made in the morning."

Katsumi chuckled. "After the life we've had you still ended up spoiled."

Ayane smiled brightly. "It's a talent!"

~ ~ ~ ~ ~

Katsumi grunted, rolling over as her phone rang. Having been asleep for the first time in nearly two weeks it was a little hard to wake herself up enough to answer. She checked the time: 8:00 PM. Ayane grumbled beside her, snuggling closer in an obvious 'I'm not getting up' move. "Whoever's calling, kill them so they can't call again…"

Katsumi chuckled. "You're violent when you wake up…" She pulled the phone to her ear. "Hello?" she answered groggily. Hardly her professional manner, but she wasn't exactly feeling professional at the moment.

"Oh! I'm so sorry, you were sleeping, weren't you? Of course you were sleeping, I should have realized-"

"Calm down, Lenora," Katsumi said through a yawn, "any time you called me I'd be asleep. I'm not getting up until tomorrow morning. I expected to be woken up by your call."

"Oh, okay. I'm glad you're catching up on sleep."

"That makes two of us," Katsumi chuckled. "I'm taking this whole week to play catch-up. Catch up with sleep, catch up with rest, catch up with friends, catch up with work. In that order."

"You're actually putting work last for once?"

"For this week only." Katsumi smirked. "Don't expect me to change. I just don't want to lose all my sanity. But yes, I figured the whole team needs a rest week at this point. I don't think it's been easy for anyone."

"No, I don't think it has. I really appreciate that decision myself; the time off you give Reno is always important to our family."

"Mmm. People with families should spend time with them." She looked at Ayane who opened an eye to stare back at her through her now-messy blue hair.

"I know you give him more time off than anyone else. The rest of you need it, too, though."

"Sano has friends he visits and places he goes during time off, so he enjoys it. I don't ask what the other two do, but they seem not to care one way or the other on vacation days."

"And you?"

"I tend to hate extended time off. I need to take it this week though." Katsumi's voice grew a little quieter. "I'm starting to take more notice of my limitations," she continued as Ayane continued to watch and listen.

"If you work yourself too hard, you burn out. You'll be a lot more effective if you take a rest every so often. It's pure logic."

"That's how I'm trying to think about it. I'm still going to go crazy on days off."

"Well maybe I can help you stay sane a little. Reno told me you wanted to go to lunch tomorrow?"

"If you're available." Katsumi rubbed her eyes. "I need to talk to you as much as I do the members of my team."

"Well, we can get into that tomorrow. How does one in the afternoon sound? It will give you plenty of time to be awake, but later than that I think you'd be starving."

Katsumi smiled. "Sounds good. I'll talk to you tomorrow, then."

"Great! I'll text you directions to the place to meet me tomorrow. Sleep well!"

"Thanks. Tell your daughter hi for me." Katsumi ended the call and programmed an alarm for ten the next morning before setting the phone back on her nightstand.

Ayane closed her eye again. "I'm glad you're thinking about your limitations now."

"Some things are more important than pushing myself." Katsumi yawned again.

"Good. Nice emotional breakthrough. Now go back to sleep, you're keeping me awake," Ayane huffed.

Katsumi smiled, closing her eyes. "So sorry."

~ ~ ~ ~ ~

Ayane woke up in the middle of the night, blinking and stretching. It was probably around two in the morning; she always woke up around two in the morning. She smiled as she realized she was still curled against her sister, snuggling closer and tightening her arms around her. She couldn't deny that she'd missed this.

Ayane was a strong-willed woman, but the loneliness of living in a hospital bed was difficult even for her. Even though Katsumi visited her twice every week and she had friends that visited on other days, it was still hard. She'd long ago grown tired of waking up alone, spending the day alone, and going to sleep alone. The nights were the worst; she'd wake up around two and have no one around, and the feelings of loneliness would be amplified as many fears were by the night. More than just a general loneliness, the amount to which she missed Katsumi – and felt her absence – was sometimes enough to even make her cry, although whenever it got that bad she always contacted her sister and talked to her for a few hours.

She felt much better as she laid her head on her sister's shoulder, looking up at her serene face. Katsumi was the only one who'd been there for her from birth until now, and she was the only one who'd been there for Katsumi. The two sisters had really had only each other for the longest time. Even now, when they had others in their lives that cared, there was still no one as important or as close. There would never be. It was simply impossible, really; no one else could ever truly understand what they'd been through. No one else had been through it. But she and Katsumi, they'd both been through the same things, and each of them had only survived because of the other. And of all the days they had lived, the only time a single day had ever passed without them talking to each other for at least an hour had been when one of them was unconscious.

Ayane sighed. Because Katsumi was the older and stronger-willed one, she'd always tried to take care of Ayane even though she was only three years older. Fortunately Ayane herself wasn't useless. She was strong, fast, skilled, smart – just like her sister. But Katsumi was something she wasn't, and that was a leader. She had a strong desire to protect and take care of others, especially Ayane. Her sister was stubborn that way. It was part of the reason she always acted hard and invincible, a rock that could support anyone.

But Ayane knew differently. Katsumi wasn't invincible – she could be hurt just like others, physically and emotionally. Ayane had seen her sister in the absolute worst conditions imaginable. She'd seen her break in ways her friends would never know were even possible. It had been so bad at some points that Ayane remembered being told by her sister that she was the only reason Katsumi wasn't giving up life entirely. She'd been there for those times and all the others, and she knew she was a guiding strength behind her sister.

That was why she knew no one would ever replace either one of them for the other. For Katsumi specifically, she was past the point of letting anyone in completely. Ayane knew her sister would never again fully open up to someone; parts of her were forever closed off. But Ayane had been let in long before that ever happened; she knew every part of her sister's mind and personality. It was impossible for anyone else to reach such a state. It made her sad for her sister, but Ayane couldn't help feeling happy to be so important and needed by the person she cared for most.

It was something entirely special knowing you would forever be the closest person to someone, the only one who could be totally close to them. Ayane took this position very seriously and did her best to support Katsumi like only she could, and she knew how appreciated it was since Katsumi told her fairly often. And it was times like this when she realized how necessary it was.

Ayane yawned, looking at her sleeping sister through half-lidded eyes and smiling softly. Sometimes Katsumi seemed like the younger one, the one who needed looking after. Katsumi often said they were "equal in age" and it made sense at times like these. She was looking forward to living with Katsumi again for more than herself; she also knew how much it would help her sister.

Of course, the fact that I won't be spending entire days and nights without her anymore is pretty nice, too, she thought with a smile as she closed her eyes and hugged her sister more tightly.

~ ~ ~ ~ ~

Date: April 4, 2068
Time: 1:07 PM
Location: East Wind Restaurant, Chiba, Japan

Katsumi yawned as she stepped out of her car, tucking her hands in her jacket pockets as she headed towards the restaurant. She was wearing casual clothes this time, something that helped her a little in changing her mindset for the day from "Captain Samakura" to "Katsumi". She entered the place and gave them the name Hillford, smiling as she saw Lenora wave at her. "I'm glad you chose somewhere casual," Katsumi said as she sat in the booth across from the woman. "I wasn't feeling like getting dressed up today."

Lenora smiled at her. "I didn't think you would be. This isn't anything formal though, just lunch."

"Yeah, it always starts with lunch. Next time it'll be dinner, and then back to your place."

"Don't be ridiculous – I won't ask you back until the third date. I'm a classy woman."

Katsumi chuckled. "Good, I'm no slut. Despite whatever Reno might suggest."

Lenora laughed. "You think he's brave enough to say that about you?"

"Behind my back, maybe, so long as he doesn't think I'll find out. You'd be surprised what I've heard him say."

Lenora raised an eyebrow. "Oh, really? Anything he should be sleeping on the couch for?"

"Probably." Katsumi smirked. "I'll let you know. It could make a good punishment, although I usually like dealing out my own."

"So I've heard. He's shown me a few bruises he got that way. Half the time he says it's worth it."

"He would. I'm glad he's stubborn enough to keep going, though. Reno's one of the major factors in keeping the team together."

Lenora smiled softly. "He does have a talent for lightening moods."

"That he does." Katsumi looked out the window. "Speaking of… Reno… You're the last person I owe an apology to."

Lenora tilted her head. "Me?"

Katsumi nodded, looking at her. "I talked with Sano when he found me. I talked with Reno on the ride back. Sam yelled at me after I got fixed up. Rufus…" Katsumi gave a sad smile. "Rufus doesn't need, or want, an apology, because I only did what he and I both used to do long before we met each other. He has no problems with my actions, though I still spoke with him. Even though I knew exactly how it would go." Katsumi set her hands in her lap. "You, however…"

"I'm not part of your team."

"You don't go on missions with us, no." Katsumi looked down. "Still, I feel I let you down just as much. I abandoned my team, Reno included, even though I promised you I'd look after him. Of course I don't need to watch him all the time, he's just as capable as the rest of us, but I endangered my entire team with my actions and I think you deserve an apology for that." Katsumi looked away and her voice dropped. "I truly am sorry… Not only for that… I know you care about me and consider me your friend. You… have no idea what that means to me. So you deserve an apology as much as anyone else on the team does, and I'm sorry for worrying you."

Lenora smiled gently at her. "I think you already know how I feel. I'm honored you appreciate my friendship like you do. I was relieved to learn you were okay, and I *was* worried about you. However, I will always worry about you. Just like I'll worry about Reno, just like I'll worry about Sano, and Sam, and yes, even Rufus. I know how dangerous your daily lives are. I will always worry about it. The only way you're different is that I'm closer to you than the others, or at least I think I could be."

Katsumi smiled. "You could. You have a… unique personality," she chuckled, receiving a grin from Lenora. "It's hard to describe. You're pushy, which I usually hate… and I do hate it when you push, don't get me wrong… but I still end up talking. You win, that's the problem. You're very hard to resist."

Lenora laughed. "I can back off if you like, hard as it would be."

Katsumi shook her head. "So long as I can trust you, you can push. You'll learn, with time, what you can and can't press me on."

Lenora nodded. "Don't worry, I'm not trying to be your psychiatrist. I want you to be my friend, too."

"That won't be a problem," Katsumi said with a smile. "Believe it or not I can be a pretty good friend. Sano would probably vouch for me."

"You and he are pretty close, aren't you?"

Katsumi nodded. "I guess you could say he's one of my better friends."

"Why is that?" Lenora tilted her head curiously.

Katsumi shrugged. "I guess his personality just works with mine. It always seems like he has a respect for me that I can't lose because he accepts the things I do. Even though I haven't known him as long as I have Law, he and I fit in a different way. We don't agree on everything like Rufus and I do, and sometimes we argue or fight, but even then there's an acceptance beyond that which isn't jeopardized by disagreement. He's one of the easiest people to be around I've ever known."

Lenora smiled. "That explains why you can relax around him."

"I suppose it does. You know, sometimes it seems like he's at my place more than his own." Lenora raised an eyebrow and Katsumi shook her head. "Not like that."

"I see. I had suspicions though."

Katsumi looked away. "No, we're just friends…"

Lenora nodded, watching her quietly for a few moments. "You wish it were like that?"

Katsumi smiled a little. "No. It can't be. Maybe someday I'll say why, but for now let's just leave it at that."

"Fair enough." Lenora sat back and offered a smile. "Well! I hope someday you'll relax like that around me, too."

Katsumi returned the smile. "So do I."

~ ~ ~ ~ ~

"I'm home," Lenora yelled into the house as she entered.

"Mommy!" Lianne ran to into the hall and hugged her leg, eliciting a large smile from Lenora who picked her up.

"Hi angel! Did you and daddy have fun today?"

"Uh-huh! We went to a movie!"

"Oh, did you?" Lenora grinned as Reno entered the hall. "Was it good?"

Reno removed his glasses and beat his head against the wall as an answer to the question, while Lianne nodded. "It was great!"

Lenora chuckled. "I'm glad." She put her daughter down. "Why don't you give me and daddy a minute to talk, then you can tell me all about it?"

"Okay!"

Lenora smiled as she ran off. Reno stepped up and kissed her. "If she wants to see that movie again, you're going."

Lenora laughed. "Don't even start. Would you like to compare the number of movies we've each taken her to?"

Reno huffed. "So not fair. Fine, since you're cheating, let's change the subject. How was lunch?"

Lenora smiled widely. "It was great. We talked a lot and plan to do it more. She's willing to be open."

"Oh, so you won't go crazy?" he grinned.

"No, I won't go crazy." Lenora gave a wry smile. "I'm surprised you're teasing me considering I'm talking about a close friendship with your boss that includes sharing all sorts of things."

"Well, I…" Reno blinked. "I, uh… Okay, you're bluffing, right?" Lenora just smiled over her shoulder as she walked away. "Honey? You're bluffing, right? Say you're bluffing! Get back here!"

~ ~ ~ ~ ~

"So this mystery man just contacted you out of nowhere and gave you information about Kintashi."

"Yep. Not suspicious at all, right?" Sano grinned.

It was early evening and Katsumi was already getting a bit tired again. Truth be told she was looking forward to getting back to Ayane and didn't really want to deal with anything, but Sano had said that this was important and now that he'd told her everything about this "John Briggs", she agreed completely. "And he wants to meet me in return for the information?"

"Yeah. I told him you probably wouldn't, but he said you'd want to. Said he had 'some information about your condition', whatever that means." Katsumi suddenly jerked in surprise and Sano blinked. "Wait, is there a condition?"

"No," she answered evenly. "It just confuses me. The wording surprised me is all, like he assumes there's something wrong with me. I suppose I'll meet this man."

"Right… Well, he knows you're back and said to meet him tonight, so we can go now if you're sure."

"I'm too curious not to go," Katsumi answered, heading for the car.

They arrived right on time and Sano led her into the basement level. She watched him open the secret side tunnel. "This Briggs is a little paranoid, isn't he?"

"Tell me about it. Fake name, secret location for meetings, he even gives information on pieces of paper he leaves in a concealed cubby before you get there. Never see him on this side of the glass, either." They entered the room and Sano looked through the glass into the dark room beyond. "Mr. Briggs? I'm hoping you're in there, 'cause this is your big chance to meet Captain Sama."

The light on the other side flicked on, revealing Briggs. The man seemed a little odd for a second before he smiled and spoke in a soft voice. "Katsumi…"

Katsumi's eyes widened and she took a step back, bringing a curious look from Sano. For a few seconds all she did was stare, no words leaving her lips. Then, in an instant, her face contorted in a rage Sano had never seen before and she drew her gun, firing several shots at the man. Sano jumped back with a yell. "What the hell, Katsumi?!" His eyes shot from her to the man behind the glass and he immediately drew his own pistol, aiming at the man on the other side as his eyes narrowed. He had no clue who it was, but obviously Katsumi recognized him – and wanted him dead.

The thick glass stopped the bullets and the man sighed, taking a sad look at Katsumi before shaking his head and walking through a door behind him.

Sano lowered his gun and watched as she ran at the glass and slammed her fist into it repeatedly until it finally shattered, at which point she jumped through before the glass had even fallen and ran through the door after Briggs. Sano jumped through after her, chasing her through the tunnel to help her catch whoever the man was. "What the hell is going on?!"

The tunnel came to some stairs that went up and up and up. Katsumi took them at a dead sprint, leaving Sano behind. He pushed himself to keep him, arms and legs pumping, leaping up them when he could. At the top Katsumi bust out of a door and onto the roof and Sano came out seconds behind to see a helicopter flying away. Katsumi stood on the edge of the roof firing and yelling at it. "GET BACK HERE YOU FUCKING COWARD! GET BACK HERE!" Her pistol ran out of shots and still she focused angrily at the chopper that was too far away now, roaring in rage. "COME BACK AND FACE ME, FATHER!"

Chapter 10: Habitus

Kurasano stood in shocked silence, something he felt he'd been doing far too often lately. "F… Father?" Katsumi just glared at the distant speck that was the helicopter, knowing it was impossible to catch. "John Briggs is your… father?"

"Not John Briggs," Katsumi corrected. "Joseph Elwood."

The venom she poured into the name sent a chill down Sano's spine. "I thought your father was…"

"Whatever you thought obviously doesn't matter, because all you know about him now is that he's here," Katsumi spat out. She whirled around and headed for the door back down. "I need… I need to get out of here."

"I'll come with you."

"No, Sano, you won't."

"Katsumi, it's obvious you shouldn't-"

"SANO!" She spun on him. "Now is NOT the time to fucking push me! Leave me the fuck alone! Go back to your home, go to headquarters, I don't care where the fuck you go as long as it's not near me!"

"Look," Sano shook his head, "I'm your friend." He narrowed his eyes as his own anger came forward. "Stop fucking pushing me away! I'm not going away, I'm following you and your arguments aren't going to stop me."

Katsumi's fingers curled and tightened into fists as she glared at him. "You don't know me at all, do you? Sano, I'm telling you one more time, leave me alone or I'm putting you down and leaving anyway."

Sano cracked his neck, his eyes never leaving hers as he started walking towards her. "You're gonna have to try to put me down, then." He stopped right in front of her, staring into her eyes and wondering if she'd actually do it. For a minute she looked conflicted; her hands started to loosen.

But Sano had forgotten to take into account what had just transpired. Katsumi's unexplained rage at her father's appearance was still boiling over and pushing right now was, as she had said, not the right move. She slammed her fist into his stomach and he stumbled back a few steps, grimacing as he straightened back up. "It'd take more than that."

He brought his hand up and blocked the punch she threw at his face. Her other fist came low again and he slapped it down, grabbing her arm and pulling her past him. As he did, though, she spun left and slammed her elbow into his face, knocking him back. Fortunately he had the presence of mind to jump back, avoiding the kick she followed up with. Sano jumped back in and threw his own punch but she ducked under it, coming up outside and bringing her knee up into his stomach hard enough to lift him off the ground, knocking all breath out of him. Her palm slammed into his chin right after, sending him back and to the ground.

Sano wasn't done just after that, though. He kicked up and came back at her, ducking the punch she met him with and scoring his own on her stomach, wincing himself as he heard the pained gasp and realized he'd just hit the spot she'd recently been shot in. The fist that hit the side of his face prevented any apology, however, and he was forced to duck another strike in order to get back into an even position. After that their strikes connected less, blocks and counter-attacks meeting in a flurry of speed.

They'd done this many times before, training and practicing against each other to get better. Sano was a little worried this time, however. He knew Katsumi would never seriously hurt him, even in a situation like this, but… that only meant she wouldn't *intentionally* hurt him. In her anger, he could tell from the hits he received that she was using more and more of her strength every second, forgetting her control. If it continued this way Sano could end up with a broken neck or splattered head in a total accident. His fears proved well-founded several seconds later when Katsumi, in a move of pure speed, seemed to simply appear beside him outside his defenses.

Her fist slammed into her stomach and, as he doubled over, her foot kicked out his own, sending him face-first to the ground.

Sano would forever after this moment be grateful for their sparring practice because Katsumi's foot continued the arc and came down in a vicious axe kick. A flash of memory triggered Sano's reflexes and he threw himself to the side, watching Katsumi's heel meet the cement in an impact that shattered it and sent cracks out in every direction for several feet. There was a virtual crater where his head had been less than a second earlier and a bit of light shone from where she'd broken through to the floor below.

It went deadly silent after that; neither of them moved to continue the fight. Sano looked up to see Katsumi's eyes wide, her gaze fixed on the spot her foot was in – the spot where Sano's corpse would be had he not reacted as quickly as he had. The expression of horror was clear on her face and all traces of anger were gone. "I-I'm… I'm sorry… I didn't…"

"I know," Sano said as he pushed himself up and dusted off his suit. "I knew I should've backed off." Katsumi looked scared so he moved to put a hand on her arm. "It's fine, Katsumi."

She shook her head, looking at him fearfully. "I almost…"

"Yeah, well, I'm the dumbass who thought it'd be good to fight you angry." He smiled at her, knowing she needed to see it. "Look, forget that."

Katsumi looked away, her voice a lot softer than it was before. "Sano, I… I really need to be alone right now, okay?"

"You always do that."

"Well it's how I deal with things. And this…" She looked back at him, her eyes pleading with him to let her go. "I can't talk about this right now. I'll… I might talk later, but not now."

Sano tilted his head. "You'll forgive me for not wanting you to just run off again after last week."

Katsumi smiled sadly. "I'm not going to run off. I just really can't be around other people at this moment." She looked down at the cracks beneath her feet. "It's just making it worse, and I'll do something I can't take back."

"I understand," Sano sighed, folding his arms. "Go."

"Thank you." Katsumi met his gaze for another few moments before walking into the building.

Sano shook his head, looking up into the night sky with a thousand thoughts in his mind.

~ ~ ~ ~ ~

Sano was lying on his bed looking at the ceiling when his phone rang. Seeing as it was two in the morning he didn't expect many calls so he picked it up quickly, especially once he saw the name. "Katsumi?"

"Sano…" It sounded like she'd been crying which, frankly, didn't surprise him after the way she'd reacted tonight, especially after all the events of the past two weeks.

"Everything alright?"

"I just… Well I… I don't know where you are, but you could come over now… if you wanted to. I know you wanted to before."

Sano smiled at the weak 'cover' she used as he headed for the door. "I'm just down the hall. I'll be there in a sec."

"Well you complained before about not being able to-"

"Yeah, I appreciate you doing this for me," Sano chuckled, hanging up and opening the door after knocking. He noticed Katsumi on the couch staring down at an older pistol in her hands and moved to join her, pointing at the weapon as he sat beside her. "What're you doing with that?"

"You know how people always have one thing from their parents that means something? That they keep forever?"

"Yeah. Your father gave you that?"

Katsumi shook her head. "I took it. It's the first weapon I ever tried to kill him with."

"Ah…" Sano looked at it. "You know, I don't think that's the same kinda thing other people keep."

"I think you're right."

"Why'd you keep it for that meaning?"

"Because I failed to kill him with it. I usually take it out a few times a year to clean it and remind myself."

"You're planning to kill him with it eventually, then."

"When I get a chance," Katsumi nodded.

"That's a morbid reminder, Katsumi."

"Maybe so."

"You know…" Sano scratched his head. "I had no idea who he was…"

She smiled at him. "I know."

"Why do you hate him so much?"

"That's…" Katsumi looked down. "I'm not quite sure how to answer… it's nothing I've ever talked about."

"Okay, so how about this: you're good at clinical facts, right? Just state a few facts about what he's done. Or about him. Whatever you're comfortable saying."

"Might be easier… Okay. He… killed my mother indirectly."

"He what?!" Sano looked at her in shock. "How? What do you mean indirectly?"

"Joseph Elwood is a criminal. He's always been a criminal." Katsumi narrowed her eyes. "Even though my mother didn't know that. He had some… twisted form of family loyalty. It was like he cared and didn't care at the same time."

"I'm not sure I understand."

Katsumi sighed. "He wanted my sister, Ayane, and I to be 'great', but his definition of great is as twisted as he is. He wanted us to be the 'next generation of criminal'. Skilled killers tearing cities apart by ripping out the upper ranks. He said our family could take over; he had a plan for it. He even trained us both for it for years, but mother eventually found out. She told him to leave. That he'd never see us again."

"Did he kill her?"

"No," Katsumi shook her head. "He didn't need to… He had a way of twisting people's minds. He twisted her and she came after us. He was going to take us all somewhere no one could find us and complete what he was going to do."

"So what happened?"

"I was fifteen by then; Ayane was twelve. We could think for ourselves and take care of ourselves, all we had to do was get out… But he wouldn't let us. I stole one of his guns with the intent of forcing him back and… he didn't like that. He ordered our mother to kill one of us as an example."

"That's insane… What did you even do?"

Katsumi looked away. "What do you think I did, Sano…? Either I died and my sister was taken by him, or she died. So when mother – what was left of her – came after us, I killed her."

"Jesus Christ." Sano shook his head. "I can't imagine a situation like that. I guess you did the only thing you could."

Katsumi closed her eyes. "That's what I hope." She sighed and sat back, laying her head on his shoulder. "You always wonder if there was another option you missed."

"Yeah, that's how you drive yourself crazy. You have to just accept what you did was the right thing. What happened to your sister?"

"She's alive," Katsumi answered softly. "I visit her all the time. She's the only thing that keeps me sane."

"I never even knew you had a sister."

"I never mention her," Katsumi replied in a harder tone. "And you won't either. You're the only person I've told and I expect you'll keep that trust." She sighed. "I won't have my job endangering her. She never wanted this kind of life and I won't force it on her."

"I can understand that. She's lucky to have you."

Katsumi smiled softly, pulling her legs up onto the couch beside her and leaving her eyes closed. It was late; she was tired. "Maybe you'll meet her sometime. But not yet. I need to go see her tomorrow… Tell her about this in person." She sighed. "I'm not looking forward to that."

"Do you think he knows where she is?"

"I don't know… I may have to move her if he does."

"Move her?"

"It's a long story…" Katsumi grimaced as a headache came on. She opened her eyes and lifted her head from Sano's shoulder, putting her fingers to her forehead. "You should go."

"Huh? I thought you wanted me to come-"

"Yes, of course. But it's late and I'm still catching up on sleep."

"Oh, right! Stupid me." Sano stood up and moved towards the door. "Lemme know if you need anything." He smiled at her.

Katsumi summoned up her willpower and forced herself to stand and walk straight, returning his smile. "Thank you. For now, just… keep this to yourself."

"Of course. Night, Katsumi."

"Goodnight, Sano." Katsumi closed the door after him and leaned back against it, sliding down it to sit on the floor.

I've probably spent almost as many nights on the floor as in the bed, she thought as she looked longingly at the bed that grew harder to see in her swimming vision. After a moment she made herself grip the door handle and pulled herself up painfully, using the wall to help her stumble to the bed. She fell on it gratefully, curling up in the sheets as pain wracked her, thinking of Ayane as she blacked out.

~ ~ ~ ~ ~

Date: April 5, 2068
Time: 5:00 AM
Location: South Ashfield Hospital, 3rd
Floor, Room 302

Ayane sat up, blinking groggily. It was early morning, judging by the dim light streaming in through her windows. She looked at the door as another knock came and it began to open. She smiled, assuming Katsumi was here for another of her way-too-early morning visits. Her smile faded as Joseph Elwood appeared in the open doorway, a man she hadn't seen in over a decade. Suddenly she was fully awake.

Elwood took a step into the room. "Ayane... You've grown into a beautiful young woman. Your mother would be proud..." That was as far as he got. Ayane reached beneath her pillow as soon as she was over her shock, withdrawing a pistol and firing. Elwood moved with unnatural speed and dodged out of the doorway, speaking from out of view in the hallway. "I'm saddened that my daughters would react so harshly to our reunion. Perhaps another time..."

Ayane threw away her sheets and dropped out of her bed, running to the door and stepping out of it, aiming down the hallway. Unfortunately no sign of Joseph Elwood remained; all she saw was a few terrified nurses. Ayane cursed and slammed her fist into the door frame, cracking it and sending a few pieces of thin metal and plaster flying. She leaned against the doorway, dozens of emotions flooding through her, charging and draining her at the same time. *Katsumi...* The way Elwood had said 'my daughters' made Ayane think he'd paid her a visit as well, and she hoped it wasn't worse than that.

Ayane got a few unfocused thoughts in response from her sister at first, the sort of thing she recognized as her sister coming out of an attack from her illness. *Where are you, Katsumi? Are you alright?*

I'm... My apartment. Fine, I'm fine. I need to... come there today. You can see for yourself.

I think I just saw for myself, Ayane answered as her glare focused down the empty hallway. *I saw him.*

There?! He showed up there?! Now Katsumi was awake, that much was clear. *He went there?!* And there was the expected rage and panic.

Yes, and before you ask I'm fine, except that my shot missed. I'm on my way.

Don't rush yourself.

Katsumi was there in a short time, pacing Ayane's room, caught between seething and worrying. "I can't believe he was here. After all the trouble of hiding you..."

"It's fine, he didn't do anything."

"This time." Katsumi stopped to face Ayane. "What if he came when you were asleep?"

"He did. He knocked."

"I mean if he didn't. But he did ask to meet me, as well, instead of just coming to me."

"It doesn't make any sense, unless..." Ayane frowned. "You don't think he's trying to get us to join him, do you?"

Katsumi looked at her incredulously. "Join him?! Is he insane enough to think it's possible?!"

"Maybe he is." Ayane looked off to the side. "He mentioned mother..."

"As if he has any right to," Katsumi growled. "Did he..."

"No," Ayane answered the unfinished question. "He didn't try to blame you for it like last time, and I wouldn't take that if he did."

"I know you wouldn't, I just..." Katsumi sighed. "Hearing it makes it harder anyway."

"Then forget it. Let's focus on now: what are we going to do about this?"

"He's impossible to find, we'll have to wait for his next move. I'm not leaving you here, that's for sure."

"What are you going to do, lock me in a guarded vault?"

"No…" Katsumi folded her arms. "I'm going to do the opposite. I think it's time my team met you."

Ayane blinked. "I… didn't expect that. Why?"

"It will give you more people to call on for one. And two…" Katsumi sighed. "As much as I hate to admit it, we can't hide from the one person I least want to find us… So there's really no reason to hide from the people on our side. Besides, we're trying to build a life here and we're on the right track to do so, it's not fair to move again."

Ayane smiled. "I'm glad you're thinking that way. To be honest I didn't know what you would want."

"I *want* to kill him, I *want* us to be cured and I *want* all of this to stop so we can just live. Unfortunately we can't get all of that at once so we might as well try to be happy in our current situation."

Ayane stood and stretched. "In that case, I need to go shopping!" She smiled at Katsumi's smirk. "Come on, we both know that if we can't kill him, forgetting him is the best option. We've been miserable because of him enough; at least now he's within possible reach. Besides, if I'm going to meet people I'll need more clothing than patient attire."

Katsumi sighed. "You're very right. Okay then, we'll do that today and meet people tomorrow, if you're feeling up to it."

"Oh, I will be. And then later this week you can meet my friends!"

"I don't see how that's necessary…"

Ayane gave Katsumi her best 'kicked puppy' look. "You… You don't want to meet my friends?"

Katsumi's eyes widened and she held up her hands. "I didn't say that! I'd love to!"

Ayane beamed. "Great! I'll let them know!"

Katsumi groaned, closing her eyes. *This is promising to be a fun week.*

~ ~ ~ ~ ~

"I'mcomingI'mcomingI'mcomingI'mcoming!" Lenora skidded around the corner, picking her ringing phone up off the bar. "Hello?"

"Hi, Lenora. I hope I'm not interrupting anything."

"Katsumi!" Lenora smiled, taking a seat. "No, nothing important. How are you?"

"That's… a complicated answer. My father is in town."

Lenora blinked. "Your father's alive? I didn't know you had any family."

"It's not a good thing," Katsumi followed up quickly.

"It isn't? But-"

"I might talk about that later, but it's not a favorite subject. Listen, this call isn't about that, it's about my other surviving family member, the one I actually care about: my sister."

Lenora brightened. "You have a sister?"

"Yes, and I- hey!"

There was the sound of shuffling and two voices, leaving Lenora confused. "Katsumi?"

After a moment a different voice came over the phone. "Hello! I'm – Katsumi, lemme go! *I* wanna talk on the phone!" There was a sigh and a 'fine', followed by a laugh. "Thank you! Where was I? You're Lenora, right? The only woman that Katsumi knows because she's all tough and macho."

Lenora smiled. "That would be me. I assume you're the sister?"

"*The* sister? I like it! Makes me sound important. In case you want my name at some point it's Ayane. Anyway, Katsumi's finally giving in and letting me meet people, so we're going to see if we can get everyone together tonight."

"Oh, that sounds perfect! We have no plans."

"Great! If the others agree we'll send details. See you tonight!"

The phone cut off and Lenora looked at it, unable to suppress a smile. Apparently Katsumi wasn't as alone as she seemed.

~ ~ ~ ~ ~

Date: April 5, 2068

The conversation was about the obvious topic as Reno, Lenora, Kurasano, Rufus and Samuel sat at the table, waiting on Katsumi and her sister. It'd been revealed that Law knew her but he wasn't answering any questions, leaving the others to speculate. They sat and guessed about the person they were going to meet and why they didn't even know she existed before now, though Law did caution them that questions along that line should be avoided.

Eventually they entered; Katsumi wearing a casual black shirt, pants and jacket, while Ayane was more colorful in a blue tank top and skirt that matched her hair. Their clothing was only the first difference as the group soon learned. Ayane waved cheerily, meeting Law as he stood up and hugging him. "Hi Big L! It's nice to see you actually out with people."

"I could say the same for your sister," Law chuckled, catching Katsumi's smirk. "Besides, I'm always up for seein' you blue-hair."

"That's because I'm special." Ayane turned to the rest of the group, holding up a hand. "Shhh! Lemme guess!" Katsumi's smirk widened as she folded her arms and watched. Ayane pointed at Lenora, smiling. "Lenora obviously. You're easy because you're the only woman."

Lenora smiled. "Because Katsumi is tough and macho?" Reno snorted and Katsumi just rolled her eyes.

"Yes! And that must mean you are Reno."

"Glasses give it away?"

"That and the fact that you laughed at my sister's expense," Ayane grinned and received one in return. She pointed at Rufus next. "You're obvious. Sunglasses, white suit, appropriate posture and fancier drink? You're very distinct, Mr. Ivanov."

Rufus smiled, taking a sip of his drink. "Being bland was never my thing. It's a pleasure, Ms. Samakura."

"For me as well. And… Sano." Ayane smiled at him. "I think we know each other a little already, even though we've never met."

Sano returned the smile. "I've heard a bit, yeah. It's great to actually meet you, though."

Ayane looked around. "Aww, M didn't come? I guess he didn't have to, but I'm gonna have a talk with him later!"

"You know M?"

"Of course!" Ayane smiled. "He's the one that set up the whole thing, including paying for my… expenses."

"If we're done with the introductions," Katsumi interrupted, "then I think we should get started with the drinks. Lord knows the more she talks the more I'm going to need."

Ayane grinned. "Better believe it."

As the minutes went by things seemed to get easier and more fun. Ayane was talking with the others and laughing as, while Katsumi was gone to get a drink at the bar, she was being told a story of Katsumi's tough personality. "I don't get any of that, myself."

Reno snorted. "Everyone gets some of that."

"She's different with me."

"Uh-huh."

"No, really. I'm an exception to everything." Ayane smiled. "Katsumi's been wrapped around my finger since we were little, and those were *her* words first, I've just started using them because it's funny."

Sano raised an eyebrow. "That's a little hard to believe."

"Oh, yeah?" Ayane looked over her shoulder, seeing Katsumi on her way back. She looked back to the others. "You want proof?" As Katsumi returned to the table Ayane looked at her. "Sumi, I'm thirsty."

"Oh, I'll be right back then. One second."

Ayane beamed as the others simply blinked. Once Katsumi started returning, Ayane pouted. "I wanted a yellow drink…"

"Oh!" Katsumi laughed and rubbed her head. "My mistake – be right back guys!"

Reno watched her walking back towards the bar, shaking his head. "This is glorious."

Ayane smiled at him. "Your problem is you've only seen one or two sides of my sister. She's a lot more than that."

"I'm just amazed someone is an exception to her usual attitude."

"Hey, it's not just me. I just bring out other parts of her personality. Katsumi is a lot more than anyone thinks." Ayane stopped with a gasp, her eyes widening as a new song started playing in the bar. She spun around to see Katsumi with her own eyes widened, almost back to the table. "Sumi!"

Katsumi began shaking her head. "Now, Aya, I don't…"

Ayane jumped up and grabbed the drink from Katsumi's hand, setting it on the table. "Sumi, it's 'Golden Sky'! Come on, we have to!"

Katsumi sighed, looking up at the ceiling before a smile broke out. "Okay, let's do it."

Ayane grinned, grabbing her hand and pulling her to an open spot on the floor. What followed, as the high-energy dance song kicked in, left four people at the table staring in both shock and amazement. The sisters began side by side, laughing as they mirrored each other's movements with kicks and sidesteps before they spun into new positions, clapping and moving to the song.

Law grinned over his drink, looking between the choreographed dance and the people at the table. "You know they won a competition with that when they were kids."

Reno looked from Katsumi twirling Ayane to Law's grin, shaking his head in bewilderment. "I have a hard time believing Katsumi was a kid!"

Ayane was saying something as they danced and Katsumi's grin was one the others had never seen, a look of someone who, at the moment, was living with nothing but good memories.

Lenora smiled as she watched. "Katsumi looks happy, doesn't she? I'd hoped she'd be able to be that happy one day, I didn't think she had it now."

Law set his drink down, his mood more somber now. "It probably isn't my place to talk about this, but I care about both of them. Ayane lives in the hospital." The others turned to look at him, paying attention to his words as they took glances back at the other two. "No one knows what she has and they can't fix it, so they," he pointed at the two sisters, "just have to hope."

Lenora saddened. "That's terrible…" Reno shook his head and Sano just looked angry at the things he couldn't fix.

"I've been hopin', too," Law continued. "You've seen just a little tonight, but lemme tell you this: if Ayane doesn't make it, neither will Katsumi. Everything she does revolves around that girl, and all her plans include her. She doesn't bother plannin' for the darker possibility."

"I guess there's nothing we can do?" Rufus questioned.

Law shook his head. "Not really."

"We can be there," Sano shrugged. "If either of them needs help we can do it. Especially considering this new stuff with their father that we're gonna be told about."

The rest nodded and Rufus looked over at Katsumi and Ayane. "We should act like nothing's wrong, too. I'm sure they both know very well just how much is wrong, they don't need us reminding them."

"Yeah," Reno agreed, "and we all know how much Katsumi hates things like pitying looks or condolences anyway. I think we're smart enough by now to avoid things like that."

Lenora smiled. "So we just support them by being friends."

"A team," Sano added. "We're a team in everything, and now Ayane's part of that team as well."

They looked over as the song finished and Ayane jumped on Katsumi's back, bringing laughter from the older woman. The sisters weren't thinking about it at that moment, but they had five people who were determined to make sure they stayed that happy.

They came back over and Ayane sat down beside Sano, smiling at him as her sister took a seat beside Lenora. "So, Sano. I've heard a lot about you."

Sano set his drink down and raised an eyebrow. "Not all bad, I hope."

"Nope, not all. I hear you're my sister's best friend, though, so I feel I should warn you about a few things."

"Things I don't already know?"

"Oh, it'll be different now. Number one? I know I say it a lot, but don't call her Sumi. Only I can do that."

"Right, I won't use your name for her."

"That's good. Neither of us will like it if you do. Next thing? Now that you know about me, prepare to hear about me a lot."

Sano blinked. "Hear about you a lot?"

Ayane nodded. "Our favorite subjects are each other. You can ask Law how much he's had his ear talked off about me. Oh, and if you become my friend too, you'll hear a lot about Katsumi. Really a lot. Like, really a whole lot."

"Huh…" Sano smiled. "I can deal with that. Can't hurt to learn more about you two."

"It could." Ayane grinned. "Okay, third thing? I've heard about your mannerisms. When I'm living with Sumi, we're going to move, but whether we have or not at the time, no barging in without asking!"

Sano laughed, leaning back in his chair. "Not a problem. You know I nearly got killed last time I did that anyway, so I don't think I will again."

Ayane nodded. "Smart man. Keep your head in one piece. Why'd you nearly get killed that time? Was she showering or something?"

"No, she looked like she'd just been sick, and you know how she is when she's like that."

"Oh…" Ayane's smile faltered for a moment but she replaced it almost instantly. "Yes, I think I remember that. All the spring storms can really wreak havoc with immune systems."

Sano looked at her. "Speaking of… You talk about living with her. Are you leaving the hospital?"

Ayane sighed. "I don't know yet. I'm feeling a little better recently, but that doesn't really mean anything, and besides Sumi is a bit… protective."

"I know." Sano thought back to the few details he'd been told about their past. "And I can see why."

"Oh, so can I. And I really appreciate her protectiveness; besides, it goes both ways."

"What about you, how do you feel? I know you said you like to talk about your sister a lot, but I've known her for six years and have only just met you."

"Me? Well I'm a lot less tough than Sumi. Attitude-wise, I mean. I don't act as tough. I'm generally nicer and much more open to meeting people, which I actually like doing."

"You two do seem very different."

"Different and similar at the same time." Ayane smiled. "My point is that I don't like the hospital because it's very lonely. I'd like to leave it, but unfortunately simply wanting something can't cure you. That's the only reason none of you have met me."

"Katsumi didn't want her enemies to be able to learn you exist."

"Right. If I wasn't sick that wouldn't be a problem."

Sano raised an eyebrow. "She wouldn't be trying to protect you if you were healthy?"

"No, she would, just… not the same way. I'm very capable, but my skills don't mean much whenever I'm weak and can't even walk straight."

"Ah, I get it. Well now we can all help both of you. And we can visit."

"More visitors? I *love* more visitors!"

A few feet away Katsumi sat sipping her drink and watching her sister talk to Kurasano. She couldn't hear what they were saying, but Ayane looked happy, so Katsumi was happy. It must have been visible because Lenora looked at her and smiled knowingly. "You really care about her, don't you?"

"Mmm." Katsumi set her drink down, glancing at Lenora. "More than anything. We're a pair; neither of us would work without the other."

"I'm glad you have something so important. I know how much you must worry, though."

Katsumi sighed. "I just… I try not to think about certain things, but it's hard. Seeing someone you love in a hospital bed, being uncertain if they'll continue to be there, it's one of the worst things there is. And I rarely see Ayane outside her bed. I know she hates it, I know she wants to go places and do things; she's always been an extremely active person. I still hope this will end and we'll be able to do all the things we keep planning for."

"Well both of you certainly deserve it. I'm a nurse, I've seen many people stuck in hospital beds and it's always a terrible burden. I know the feeling of helplessness that comes from being unable to do something; I think everyone here is feeling that tonight. At the very least you're lucky to have so many people feeling that way."

Katsumi smiled softly. "Yes, I know. Believe me, I know I'm lucky. There's just one major fear keeping me from being happy and I can't be truly happy until it's gone."

"All of us will support you both until then. This is a good group of people, and they're determined."

"I did hand-pick them."

"Except for me."

Katsumi smiled. "You're one of the reasons I picked Reno."

Lenora blinked. "I am? Why?"

Katsumi looked back to her sister as Ayane laughed, giving a soft smile. "Family is strength."

~ ~ ~ ~ ~

It was just after midnight and Katsumi and Ayane were walking down the dark street without a care, laughing with each other as they shared opinions on the people they'd just left and their reactions throughout the night. They were in a joyous mood, and it seemed like nothing could ruin it. Of course, that's exactly the time when something tends to happen.

The cloaked figure raced out of the alley as they passed, moving immediately for Ayane after identifying her as the weaker one. He slammed a fist into her stomach, carrying the punch several feet until he ran her into the wall. Lifting his head to see the woman he'd just pinned to the wall he revealed himself to be a vampire; a recently made one, Katsumi was able to judge, not usually a big threat. She had her gun out in an instant but he held a knife to Ayane's throat, grinning at Katsumi. "Ah-ah-ahh, one more move and I'll cut this one's neck."

Katsumi raised an eyebrow. "*Really.* I don't see it working that way."

The vampire frowned, about to speak when an iron grip on his wrist cut him off. Ayane pulled his hand from her neck, giving him a look. "You have *terrible* judgment." She slammed her forehead into his, swept his foot out from behind and stepped to her left, yanking his arm around to slam him into the wall where he crumpled with a moan of agony. "This has to be a training mission, right?"

"Seems like it." Katsumi looked over her shoulder at the corner of the wall. "The Sire is close."

A vampire Sire was an older vampire with much greater power and the ability to turn others into vampires if they were willing. They usually took newly created vampires out on 'training missions' to teach them how to use their newfound abilities, select prey, and feed. Katsumi had tangled with more than one, and she knew he was going to be a bit trickier than his new apprentice. She tossed her pistol to Ayane, who understood she'd be better using that given her physical condition, leaving the brute force to Katsumi.

The night street was eerily abandoned, as if everyone knew to stay away from it. It grew even more silent as the seconds passed, that calm before its sudden, violent interruption. It came unseen, an invisible strike from the side that hit Katsumi's face and sent her reeling. Ayane immediately fired to her side and there was a quick rush of air as the vampire dodged. Katsumi threw her fist out and connected with his side, causing the vampire to reveal himself as he caught his footing. His fists came out in a blur and Katsumi went into a backpedal, defending herself from his rapid strikes.

Ayane leapt up to catch a window ledge of the building beside them, pulling herself up onto the narrow perch and firing down over Katsumi's head, achieving a hit in the vampire's shoulder. The man, pale, weary and animalistic, growled and drew the blood from his wound, flinging it into Katsumi's eyes. She responded by lunging forward and shoulder-rushing him, bringing them both to the ground. Ayane fired every time the vampire tried to wriggle out from under her sister, leaving him in a situation where he couldn't utilize his superhuman speed.

That turned out badly for him as Katsumi slammed her fists down repeatedly. He managed to evade a couple, leaving small cracks in the street from their impact, but eventually the brutal rain subdued him and left him unconscious. Katsumi took a breath and stepped back, lifting him up and throwing him beside the other one.

"Suddenly, vampires! Thousands of them!" Ayane dropped down and handed the pistol back. "I think you've been gone too long, Katsumi, chasing terrorists and such things. Dark creatures might start to feel like they can operate here again."

Katsumi nodded, giving her a smile. "I guess I'll have to change that, then. Looks like I'm going back to work."

~ ~ ~ ~ ~

A young woman with brown hair and gentle eyes stood with a sad look on her face as she looked through a store window at a variety of weapons on display. "Do I... really have to?"

"There is... no choice."

She shuddered a little at the harsh whisper that came from behind her, something she'd never get used to. She looked around but no one else was on the street at this time of night. She then looked back over her shoulder. "Why?"

Cold blue eyes – seeming to be made of pure energy – materialized in the air, glaring at her. There were no pupils, no iris, just a burning blue that emanated pure hostility and danger. "You have asked enough questions!"

"Okay!" The girl sighed, taking a calming breath as she looked back to the store window.

"Okay..."

The sound of breaking glass, an alarm, hurried footsteps, and a few seconds later the girl was clutching a strange old knife in her hands, breathing rapidly with her back against a wall. The floating eyes appeared before her again, as did the harsh whisper. "Don't panic! You will need a greater will for what I ask of you!"

"I'm sorry! I've never committed a crime before!"

"You will perform more than this."

"I'm a florist, not a criminal!" She glared at the image.

It seemed to bristle at that, blue flames lighting up around it as its voice seemed to roar inside her head. "YOU WILL BE WHAT I DESIRE YOU TO BE!"

"Aah!" The girl dropped the knife and clapped her hands to her ears uselessly, falling to her knees and trying to shake the voice from her head. "Stop!"

"Get up. Collect the weapon and leave here now!"

She picked up the knife again, unsure whether she felt more helpless or more afraid. She pushed herself to her feet and ran off as the sound of approaching sirens neared.

Chapter 11: Exodus

The car screeched around the corner, its tires squealing as it nearly spun out of control. It slipped into an alleyway, slamming through a pile of boxes and sending things flying. Behind the car a figure sprinted around the corner, his movements not only as fast as the car- he was gaining.

The driver, his jaw clenched in concentration, spun the wheel rapidly to execute another mad turn as the passenger banged on the seat with his free hand, gesturing behind them with a handgun at the pursuer he watched through the rear window. "Faster! Faster! Speed up, he's gaining!" He leaned out and fired the last three shots he had, but the man's saber somehow deflected them all.

The driver chanced a glance at the rearview mirror, which spurred him on to stomp down on the gas pedal again. "I'm going as fast as this piece of shit will go! What do you want me to do?!"

"Well do something! He's not stopping!" The passenger watched with fear as the man continued to gain on them, moving like no human he'd ever seen before. He *looked* human, that's what made it so unnatural; he was an older man with mostly neat hair in a low ponytail and a short-haired beard, both more grey than brown. He had glasses and wore a nice brown trench coat and tan slacks. He didn't look like he'd be able to jog for more than a minute, let alone move like a blur and keep up with their car. "What *is* he?!"

The driver, who, like the passenger, was a member of a pretty big criminal organization, had no more answers than his companion. All he knew is that he'd seen the man easily cut through a garage door with the saber he was carrying, and he had no desire to see what would happen if the guy caught him. "It doesn't matter what he is... All that matters," he muttered as he weaved around a chain link fence, "is that," he grunted as the car bounced off a building, "we lose him!"

The passenger looked forward after sensing a desperate tone in his partner's voice, only to see a train yard looming ahead of them, filled with numerous train cars strewn about the unused tracks. Worse yet, the car seemed to be heading for a gap between two train cars, beyond which there was only one train track before another unmoving steel train car. Finally, and without a doubt the worst part of this situation, is that the track his partner seemed to be aiming for was in use; a train could be heard coming from their left, getting closer by the second.

"Are you insane?!" the passenger yelled, gripping his seat tightly. "That'll kill us quicker than he will!"

"Trust me... I see it..." The driver sped up, as the man behind them was only a few meters away by now. The passenger started screaming at this point, and for good reason.

What happened next proved the driver was something special, as he slammed on the brakes and spun the car ninety degrees to the left; it slid perfectly between the two parked train cars with little room to spare, hitting the opposite car broadside but not injuring either. The situation only seemed worse as they both saw the blinding light and heard the blaring horn of the oncoming train, and the driver hit the gas again, wheels spinning as the car took off towards the speeding train.

The obscenities streaming from the passenger were impressive before he started screaming in fear, and the driver joined in screaming in anger and defiance. Both of them saw the man in their mirrors; he'd followed them through onto the track and was still after them, but that was what the driver had planned.

In an event that had both passengers of the car convinced that God was truly forgiving for past sins, their car reached the end of the parked train cars and swerved to the side less than a second before the train that would have turned them into scrap metal roared by. And better yet, the man- or whatever he was- was too far behind to do the same, and there was no space to dodge, leaving no choice but to get crushed.

Surging with adrenaline and victory, both passengers cheered loudly, slamming their hands on the dashboard as the driver hit the brakes.

"WHOOOOOOOO!"

"HELL YES!"

"Did you see that?! That was amazing! You were fucking incredible!"

The driver laughed, grinning at his rearview mirror as he watched the train speed by. "We got some sorta god watching us, man! There's no way we could've..."

He trailed off as his eyes widened, and both paled as they looked behind them. In the air above the speeding train their pursuer could be seen, somehow having leapt the locomotive. He sailed through the air far higher than any normal human could hope, landing on the roof of their car and creating a dent.

Both men could do nothing but stare as the saber stabbed in through the roof, piercing the driver's chest. The driver grunted in disbelief, grabbing at the blade before it twisted, jerking him into death. That shook his partner out of his shock and he scrambled for the handle, flinging open the door and stumbling out, sprinting away as fast as he could.

Joseph Elwood looked calmly after him, withdrawing his saber and standing slowly, whipping the blood free from the blade. The survivor jumped for a ladder on a train car, climbing up it as quickly as he could in his panic. Once he reached the top of the car, he turned back to look.

It was unfortunate. He was able to see Joseph sprint, barely more than a blur, from the car, across the tracks, and straight up the side of the train car in under two seconds; the man was only able to widen his eyes a bit as he blade came up at him, spraying blood into the night air.

Joseph sheathed the saber in its scabbard on his hip as he reached the trunk of the car, opening it up and spotting a black box. He ignored the money and other things in the trunk, not even bothering to close it as he started walking away. He withdrew his phone, making a call as he headed towards the entrance to the train tunnel, hearing another train coming. "I've got it," he said into the phone in an even voice as he tucked the black box under an arm.

"Excellent!" the other voice replied, and Joseph could hear the grin on Sigma's face. "Bring it immediately and we can get started on phase two."

"I'm on my way." Joseph ended the call as the next train sped out of the tunnel. He leapt up into the air, landing on the third car as it flew past. He straightened on top of it, having no problems maintaining balance despite the speed and the heavy winds that whipped his hair and coat around. He calmly began pressing keys on his phone, paying no attention to his surroundings as the train rushed into the night with its unknown passenger.

~ ~ ~ ~ ~

Date: April 6, 2068
Time: 7:38 PM
Location: SIN Tokyo HQ

1 Unread Message.
Text Message: She's getting worse. We both know it.

"Miss Samakura." Katsumi started, looking up to see M smiling at her. "Something important?"

"No," Katsumi replied as she shut her phone, smiling at him. "So, do you have the details?"

"Of course, I didn't call you here to waste your time. Get your team to the Briefing Room."

"Understood, Director." Katsumi used her cyber link to tell everyone to head to the room as she went herself.

Ten minutes later the full team was seated in the room and M walked in, dropping a file on the desk at the front of the room. "Missing persons."

Reno raised his hand. "Uh, 'what are the pictures on milk cartons representing?'"

"Your knowledge of last-century television being impressive as it is, Mr. Hillford, I don't think that reference is anything but anachronistic."

Reno shrugged. "*You* got it."

"*I* am a genius," M smiled. "Is there another comment you'd like to make, or shall we move on?"

Reno hung his head. "Sorry, teacher."

"Put him in detention!" Sano shouted as he leaned around from the seat behind him.

"Behaving like children does not make this a classroom," Katsumi interrupted. "Now settle down until recess," she added with a smirk.

The two chuckled, as did M while he turned on the screen on the wall on their side of the room. "I would have no problem handing out more homework if you'd like." He stepped to the side and a picture appeared on the screen beside him.

It was a picture of a smiling woman with shoulder-length brown hair and gentle blue eyes; she was pretty, and obviously didn't look like a threat, meaning she was probably the missing person M had referred to. Kurasano leaned forward to look at the picture. "Whoa, she's pretty. Please tell me she's not a horrible demon."

"Unlikely," M replied, "as demons don't have the kind of family she does. No, Mr. Lionel, this is our 'victim'."

Katsumi narrowed her eyes. "Victim of what?"

"We're not sure at this point, but certainly some sort of spirit. Security cameras at a local store caught this footage last night." The screen switched to video showing the woman outside the window. She looked scared and seemed to be talking to someone outside the camera's range; she eventually broke a window, grabbed a knife and ran. "She's a florist, and has no history of violence or criminal activity," M added.

"Someone was making her do it? She's talking to someone off-camera."

"And not just anyone, Miss Samakura." The video switched to a feed of a nearby traffic camera that showed her standing outside the store; more importantly, it showed that no one was standing anywhere around her.

"Invisible companion can certainly mean ghost," Rufus noted.

"Or dementia," Katsumi pragmatically cautioned.

"She has no history of mental illnesses, except one note." M smiled thinly, pushing up his opaque glasses. "She's made multiple claims over the course of her life about 'odd noises' and spectral visitors, dismissed as paranoid ghost stories. In addition, the knife she stole is an ancient sacrificial dagger – though the store owner had no clue as to its true origin and value."

The others looked at each other and Katsumi nodded. "Now it makes more sense."

"I thought it would. Now, as for the 'missing' part... Her shop has been closed for a week, and she's not contacted her friends or family in the same amount of time, which is very unusual in her case. Her apartment, however, remains locked, and we believe she's inside."

"Doing what?"

"That's for you to find out."

"Age?"

"She's twenty-eight."

"And single?" After M's nod, Katsumi smiled at Kurasano, who blinked in response.

"What, me?"

"You're our usual inside man anyway. Besides, if you go in alone, it will be less suspicious."

"Alright, I got it." Sano looked back to the picture. "So what's her name?"

~ ~ ~ ~ ~

"Hitomi Saizen," the young woman answered with a tired smile at the man. Honestly, she wouldn't have opened the door for anyone she knew, but this was a stranger and he seemed friendly enough.

"Fitting," the man smiled. "That name means 'beautiful virtue'."

"So what does your name mean?"

The man rubbed his head. "Kurasano? I dunno, I think my dad just thought it sounded cool."

Hitomi's smile grew a bit. "Your mother let your father name you?"

"Well she wanted to name me Richard, after him, but he thought Japanese names like hers – Matsumi – sounded better. My dad was kinda funny that way." Sano grinned. "Anyway, I was actually hoping I could come in and talk to you about something important." He pulled out an Aegis badge.

The surprise on her face was obvious, she knew that, but she couldn't help it. She looked over her shoulder, but he wasn't there at the moment, so… "Yes, of course," she smiled, "as long as it's quick."

"I won't take up much of your time." Sano stepped through the door as she held it open for him, his brown eyes scanning the apartment and taking in every detail. It was dark, with all of the curtains pulled closed and most of the lights off. The place was messy, but Sano had seen enough messed-up rooms in his experience to tell the difference between the types. This wasn't the type of messy that Katsumi's place was, with trash and clothing scattered about showing that the person didn't care about the appearance or organization of their home.

No, this was more the "messy" that you'd see after a place was broken into, with things rifled through and thrown everywhere. To her credit, though, the girl tried to pass it off as the former, despite it not fitting her profile.

"I'm sorry the place is such a mess," the young woman said with a sheepish smile as she removed some things from the couch for him to sit, and turned on a lamp. She took a seat in a chair beside the couch and ran a hand through her hair. "I've just had a bit of a rough week, and you know how things can slip when you're busy."

"Of course, we've all been there," Sano reassured her with a smile. "You won't get judgment from me; my best friend's apartment is so bad that maids want to compete to clean it for the bragging rights."

Hitomi smiled gratefully as she folded her hands in her lap. "I don't think I could live like that; usually I keep things pretty neat and clean, if not orderly."

"Extenuating circumstances, I'm sure." Sano noted that she seemed very tired, though he knew she hadn't been busy at her job seeing as it had been closed for a week.

"Yes, but I'd rather not discuss that. How about we move onto your business?"

"Right; well, I'm sorry to come in the evening. Half past eight is not the time I'd prefer to bother people, but this is a special case that had to be taken care of quickly."

Hitomi frowned. "I'm sorry?"

Sano sat back, wishing he had Katsumi's ability to seem so totally in control and knowledgeable. "There was a break-in at a store very early this morning; the security camera caught some interesting footage."

Hitomi paled, seeming to shrink a bit. "Oh no… Oh no, I thought I… Look, I have an explanation…"

Sano raised an eyebrow, showing a bit of curiosity without revealing any other emotion or knowledge; in reality, he was simply mimicking Katsumi and hoping it worked, which it seemed to. "Do you?" he said in what he believed to be his best impression of his boss. This obviously wasn't lost on the others as he could hear Reno's snickering in his ear, which made him have to fight to prevent a smirk.

"Yes, but it's… You're going to think I'm crazy…"

"Crazy is better than criminal. Continue, please; I am truly interested to hear your story."

Sano, if you don't stop doing that crappy impression of me, I'm going to hurt you.

Captain Sama, how dare you! It is a fabulous impression.

Fine. Here's my impression of you: I'm Sano! I don't know anything! Even though I'm thirty-three I'm still a child without even a grasp on the concept of maturity!

Okay, see, that was a crappy impression.

I also don't know what a good impression is! And I'm stupid!

Now you're just being hurtful, boss. And I'm not stupid! I'm really good at math!

What's a math? Two plus two is five! I'm gonna go play in the street!

I'm done talking to you!

"Um… Mr. Lionel?"

Sano blinked, looking up. "Huh?"

Hitomi looked confused. "You sort of blanked out for a second there…"

"Hahaha, nothing to be alarmed about, only thinking about something!" Sano laughed, waving it off.

"Oh… Okay."

"Please, go on with your story."

"Right… Well, you see… There's this, um… Person…"

"A person."

"Yes, a person… He threatened me to make me steal that knife, and wanted me to do worse…"

"So why didn't you call the police?"

"Well, I figured they'd think I'm crazy…"

"None of this sounds crazy so far. Where is this 'person' right now?"

"Well he might be coming back soon, but…" Hitomi looked at Sano. "You shouldn't be here when he gets here."

"Oh, I plan to be. It's not a problem."

"You can't! You won't be able to hurt him, he's… I mean, he's…" Hitomi swallowed. If she was hauled in to a psych ward, at least she wouldn't be used by the thing anymore. "He's a… ghost."

Sano opened his phone, doing something on the screen. "I know."

Hitomi blinked. "You…" She blinked again. "You… You know?"

"Yep. It's kinda why I'm here. Tell me something, can you tell me which of these he looks more like?" He held the phone out to her, which showed three pictures; one of a white spirit in a humanoid form, one of what seemed to be a vortex of static, and one that was a blue cloud of flame and burning coal eyes just like the one that had recently terrorized her. She had, though, seen all three examples before.

"These… These look like real pictures…"

"Yeah, they are." Sano leaned forward to look at the phone as well. "I mean, it might not be one of these, but we're betting it's one of these, so what do you say?"

Hitomi pointed to the one on the far right. "It's… That one…"

Sano blinked. "It's that one? You're sure? Like, sure sure?"

Hitomi nodded. "Y-yes… Why?"

"Oh… Shit. Um… That's not a ghost."

Hitomi blinked in confusion. "It's not? But it's…"

"That's not a ghost." He stood up, suddenly a lot more alert. "That's a demon."

"A demon?! From the stories?!"

"The stories came after the demons, not the other way around." Sano lifted a hand to his ear. "Guys, we got a problem. It's a Shade."

"THAT… WOULD BE CORRECT."

Sano grimaced at the voice behind him, turning around in time to see the wave that blew him off his feet and into the wall. Hitomi let out a cry and ran towards him but a claw of blue flame materialized, grabbing her wrist. "YOU ARE NOT RELEASED FROM MY SERVICE."

Kurasano drew his pistol as he stood. "How's this for a release form?" He fired several times and the demon let out a shriek, allowing Hitomi to run from it to Sano, curious as she was that the thing had actually been hurt by the shots. It was only hurt, though, and its eyes burned with rage as its flames grew higher.

Suddenly the door was kicked in and Katsumi stepped through. "Sano, that line was terrible."

As she lifted her pistol Rufus stepped in beside her, lifting his as well. "Honestly, you need to work on your one-liners. Amateur at best."

"Fuck you. How's that one?"

"Better."

"MORTALS HAVE NO PLACE INTRUDING UPON MY PROPERTY," the demon bellowed as its light filled the room.

Katsumi grimaced as she and Rufus began to fire. "Sano, get the girl to the car, now!"

Sano fired a few more shots as he pushed Hitomi in front of him. "Gonna have to trust us; get outside!"

It wasn't difficult to trust people who were in the process of saving you from a demon, so Hitomi ran as she was told, getting out of the apartment as the bellowing roars and sounds of gunshots followed. Sano pointed to a large black car and she got in the back seat, followed closely by Sano.

In the front seat Reno looked back at them, as he already had the car running and ready to go. "What's going on in there?! It sounds like a legion of tigers with machine guns!"

"Start driving; we don't have the gear to take this thing on."

"On it."

"But what about the others?!" Hitomi interrupted, looking frantically out the back window. She was answered by two thuds on the top of the car as it peeled out, zooming onto the road.

The demon appeared in the parking lot below, following them with a vengeance. Katsumi leaned her head down to one of the windows, yelling above the sounds. "Keep driving, Reno! I've got Law moving to intercept at the bridge!"

She went back up and Hitomi could hear both her and the other man firing from the roof, somehow holding on as the car swerved with deadly speed around every obstacle. She really had little idea what was going on; first of all, every one of these people seemed to be able to see the ghost… demon… as well as she could, even though nobody else had before.

Secondly, even though she was terrified, they all seemed to know what they were doing, which at least made her feel better. She'd been totally lost before, with no idea what to do, but suddenly she was surrounded by people who not only believed her, but seemed to have the will and ability to help her. "Relieved" didn't cut it.

Up ahead of the car, on a bridge it was currently speeding towards the tunnel of, Law sat perched on the edge with an absolutely massive weapon that looked more like a rocket launcher than anything. He had it aimed at a certain spot and was just waiting for the car to pass through it. "Come on…" A second before it did, he pulled the trigger, and the weapon gave a high-pitched whine as it charged up before firing a thick white beam that struck the Shade head on. "Bet that hurt."

It caused no physical damage to the surroundings, but the demon gave an unearthly scream and vanished from sight. The car finally slowed down to a normal speed as two doors opened and Katsumi climbed into the front, Rufus into the back beside Hitomi. The girl was watching behind them, looking from the empty street to the people with her. "You… killed it?"

"No," Rufus answered, smoothing his wind-ruffled hair back. "It was banished, but it can't be killed on this plane. All we did was delay it for a bit."

"Oh…" Hitomi looked between the other passengers. "I just… Who are you people?"

"We… are vengeance," Reno said in a super-serious tone. "We are the night."

"You are Batman?" Hitomi said with a smirk.

Reno grinned. "I like this girl."

"Seriously," Katsumi said as she turned in her seat to meet the other woman's gaze, "The answer to that is top secret. Don't worry, we're going to answer it for you," she continued with a smile, "but you'll have to keep it quiet. You're also going to need to stay with us, for a short time."

"You think it will come back," Hitomi stated.

"It will," Sano nodded, drawing her attention to him. "If you're with us it can't do anything about it, though. And then we'll get a chance to do something about him."

Hitomi sighed, putting a hand to her forehead. "This is all so… strange. Sudden. Fast."

"That's us," Sano smirked.

"I'm Fast," Reno added. "Rufus is Sudden." He gestured to the seat behind his in which Sano sat. "He's Strange."

Hitomi looked at Katsumi. "So what's she?"

"Someone I try not to call names," Reno muttered, earning a smirk from Katsumi.

Minutes later they were back at HQ, driving the car into a large garage. The team dispersed, as not all were needed now; Katsumi and Kurasano led Hitomi into a comfortable room where M met them with a smile. "Ah, Miss Saizen, I'm glad you could visit."

"Um… Yes, well, I really only had two choices, and the first was probably dying."

M chuckled. "Of course. Either way, you are in safe company now. I am M."

Hitomi blinked. "Just M?"

He gave a knowing smile. "Just M. I am the Director of this division." He pointed to Sano, who had taken a seat in a chair as he let the adrenaline wear off. "That is Kurasano Lionel, First Lieutenant of the division and second-in-command here."

Sano waved and gave a grin. "She knows my name already. Just Sano is fine."

Hitomi smiled. "Yes, the cool-sounding name," she said, eliciting a laugh from him.

"If you say so," M interjected, earning a glare from Sano, to which he of course responded with a smile. M then pointed to Katsumi, who was leaning against a counter with her legs crossed as she lit a cigarette. "And the woman to your right is Katsumi Samakura, Captain and leader of the team."

Hitomi had already gathered that the woman was the leader thanks to the banter in the car. She smiled politely and gave an uneasy wave. "Pleased, um, Captain."

Katsumi gave a friendly smile. "I appreciate the respect, but you can call me Katsumi. There's no point in adding stress to your situation."

Hitomi smiled more easily then, nodding. "Thank you. I'm not very good with strict, rigid rules."

Sano snickered. "Neither is Katsumi."

The older woman reacted with an amused smile, replacing the cigarette in her lips. "Maybe."

"Miss Saizen," M interrupted, drawing the younger woman's attention back to him. "We're Aegis Corp, as you no doubt already know. We happen to be the SIN Division."

Hitomi tilted her head. "I've never heard of that one. But then, I'm not very well-versed on your corporation's divisions."

"You wouldn't know it even if you were," Katsumi replied as she let out a breath of smoke, fixing the woman with a more serious gaze. "SIN stands for 'Supernatural Invasion Null'. Basically, we're the response to paranormal-based threats."

"Like… Ghosts and demons."

"And vampires, and other supernatural entities."

"I…" Hitomi blinked. "I didn't know those existed."

"You knew," M replied with a smile. "But you passed off ghosts, vampires and evil spirits like urban legends and myths."

"And demons have a natural defense," Katsumi added. "The thinking ones have selective invisibility, meaning only those they want to see them can see them. And the unthinking ones, the monsters that do things like randomly attack cities, humans will forget any details about them soon after they're out of sight. Considering they don't appear on any civilian-available manner of recording, this means everyone forgets whatever they saw and enables us to pass off their attacks as a more mundane event in smaller situations, or a terrorist attack in larger ones."

"But if humans forget about them, how does your team fight them?"

Katsumi tapped her head. "They're all immune to that, thanks to a special cybernetic memory chip. I am for different reasons."

Hitomi took a seat, trying to understand it all. "So all sorts of things exist that everyone thinks are just stories? Why don't you just tell the public about it so everyone is warned?"

"People, as a general whole, are very unreliable," M explained. "The world's governments have always believed- and rightly so- that certain things should be kept from the public."

She frowned. "You believe society would fall apart into anarchy?"

"That is unlikely," M admitted. "Society would likely adapt. However, that adaptation is not desired. People like to forget all the potential threats to their lives; if we told them of all these things against which they have no defense, fear would rule society." M folded his hands behind his back. "History shows us many examples of this occurring; the World Wars, the Cold War, oppressive regimes, ancient empires; society would once more return to a state in which strength of arms is the most valuable trait."

"Oh," Hitomi said lamely, realization dawning on her. "You mean life would focus on defense and brute survival, like early civilizations."

"Exactly. That isn't necessary; these threats are far rarer than more common, more mundane dangers. But humans fear the unknown, and that fear would drive them into an archaic state that would halt progress and reset the clock on human achievement; we would be back to the days of stockpiling destructive weapons and forming closed-off cities. Humanity's progress towards one unified whole would halt."

"I can see why it's a secret, then. But why tell me?"

Katsumi spoke up to answer that one: "You're directly threatened now. You deserve to know the situation you're in. It's our policy to explain things to someone who is specifically endangered by a paranormal threat."

"Well, I'm grateful for that, but what happens when this is over and your business with me is done?"

Katsumi shrugged. "That's up to you. You can tell people if you like, but they won't believe it."

"In your case, however," M added in, "our business with you may continue."

Hitomi looked at him, uneasy about the statement. "What does that mean...?"

"It means, Miss Saizen, that we have strong reasons to believe you may be a Silent."

Katsumi and Sano both sat up straighter, and the older woman gave M an incredulous look. "You think she's a Silent?"

"Almost positive, Captain. Her history fits."

"Excuse me," Hitomi interrupted as she looked between them, "but what's a 'Silent'?"

"A demi-human," Katsumi answered as she looked at her with more compassionate eyes. "It means you have the ability to speak with the Spirits of the Dead, as well as control their energy. It also means, unfortunately, that spirits are drawn to you, and not always good ones."

Hitomi sat back in her chair, a little pale now. "So I'm... So what does this mean?"

Katsumi was looking at the floor, but then she glanced at the other two. M nodded, giving Hitomi a smile. "I'll be around if you have any questions or needs. If you give me a list of everything you need from your apartment, I shall have it brought here for the time you stay with us."

Sano stood up. "I'll be around, too, if you need anything."

Hitomi just nodded, watching the others leave until Katsumi took a seat in front of her. The older woman looked a lot more serious now, which made her nervous.

"I'm a Silent," Katsumi started, getting Hitomi's full attention. "So is my sister. We're sort of... artificial ones, but it works the same way."

Hitomi blinked in confusion. "Artificial? I don't understand..."

Katsumi looked off to the side. "It doesn't matter. You don't need to know that part." Katsumi looked back at her. "This is a difficult thing to be. I know you've had something of a history with spirits and ghosts; this is the reason. You haven't imagined things, you've experienced things, and it's time you knew." Katsumi ran a hand through her hair. "I'm not going to lie... It's kind of a curse."

Hitomi folded her arms, likely seeking some sort of security. "What's so bad about it...?"

"You've already learned some of it," Katsumi answered. "Ghosts and spirits… they'll seek you out. You're one of the rare few that can truly hear and understand them, and they're desperate. This can be frightening; sometimes they're angry, even violent. Some might even blame you, simply because you're the only one they've found that can hear their condemnation. This is why you need to learn control."

"So that I can control them…?"

"You can only control their energy, not their will. However, you can use this to weaken the violent ones so they can't hurt you, or even to shut them all out when you need the silence. That's important to keep you sane. Though it's… harder to do when you're weak," Katsumi said softly, remembering the times the memories of spirits assaulted her mind during attacks from her sickness.

Hitomi nodded. "What about things like what happened this week?"

"Demonic spirits like to use humans as tools. A Silent is the most powerful tool one could gain. With more control you'll be able to stop, drain or shut them out, as well. Depending on the relative power."

"That would be nice… He said he had all kinds of plans for me."

"I'd love to know what those were," Katsumi stated with a slightly worried look. "We'll have to find that out; he'll be using another human as a tool soon."

"He had me steal a knife… Maybe he wants someone killed?" the florist offered.

"He could kill a human himself…" Katsumi frowned. "We think… He wanted a sacrifice. The knife was a sacrificial tool from an old, extinct cult."

"You think he wanted me to sacrifice someone to gain him something?"

"Sounds like the best bet," the purple-haired woman sighed. "Well you don't have to worry about that. For now, we'll just make sure you're comfortable and safe."

Hitomi smiled a little. "Thank you… Really, thank you all for helping me."

"It's our job," Katsumi said with a smile as she offered her a hand up. She pulled the younger woman out of her chair. "I'll talk with you more on all this Silent stuff, and teach you what you need to know. Let's worry about that later, though."

"That would probably be best… Today has been… very full of new information."

"It can be overwhelming," Katsumi said in agreement. She stepped outside the room, looking across the hall. "Sano."

"Sir," the man said as he exited the next room.

"Show Hitomi the room she'll be staying in, make sure she's comfortable."

"Not a problem," Sano said with a wink at Hitomi, which she responded to with a smile.

Katsumi held out her hand and Sano tossed her a phone, which she handed to Hitomi. "This contains all of our numbers, and it's as secure a connection as you can get outside of a cyber link. Call me if you need anything, whether it's help, a talk, or getting something you forgot in your car. And if you can't get me, try one of the others."

Hitomi smiled gratefully as she took the phone. "That's really generous of you. I wish I could thank you enough."

Katsumi smiled sadly. "I've been in similar situations. I just want to make sure your time here feels more safe and comfortable than confining."

"You're doing a very good job… What about friends and family?"

"You can contact them whenever you like, but don't mention the real situation. We're also known as counter-terrorists, so a good cover is to tell them you witnessed a crime and we're keeping you safe here until the criminal is caught. It's true enough."

Hitomi smiled and nodded. "That's good. I guess the only thing left is my shop…"

"It's being tended to," Sano smiled. "You had the foresight to call in a temp to keep it in good shape for your return."

"You people really did think of everything."

"Well, we're awesome."

"And it's our job," Katsumi smirked. "Either way, I'm just glad we're helping a pleasant person this time."

Hitomi looked between the two. "The last person wasn't pleasant?"

Sano scowled. "Hell no. The guy kept complaining about being 'held hostage' and how he'd 'sue us all to hell' and that we were 'worthless imbeciles who couldn't even do our jobs right'. He even tried to punch me."

"Wow. He sounds very… colorful."

"If you wanna put it that politely, sure." Sano folded his arms. "I was just upset that 'Shining Knight Katsumi' wouldn't let me feed him to a demon."

"Sano," Katsumi sighed. "I told you, even a demon doesn't deserve that stomach-ache."

"I'd risk it."

"I'd feed him to the demon."

"See? Hitomi knows I'm right!"

"A florist with a mean streak," Katsumi chuckled. "I like it. You should fit in here well. I'll leave you with Sano now; I need to meet up with Law and see if he's got any trace of this demon."

"Thank you again, Katsumi," Hitomi said with a friendly smile.

Katsumi returned the expression as she walked off. "Don't mention it. Don't hesitate to call."

Hitomi watched her turn the corner before she looked at Sano. "Your leader is a lot nicer than I first expected."

Sano snickered. "You got a way different first impression than most get. In fact, that was a lot nicer than her fourteenth impression. Or thirty-seventh."

"She's not usually nice?"

"Well, she's… Katsumi's very determined," Sano clarified. "She likes getting business done. A lot of times she can be abrasive and direct, even rude, especially 'cause she's pretty closed off. But I just mean she's usually not nice to people; at the same time, she's really kind. Even if you were a total asshole she'd still be doing what she could to help." He rubbed his chin. "Except give you her personal number. That she did because she likes you. Which puts you in a group of less than ten people. Congratulations!"

Hitomi smiled. "Thank you. I really do feel honored, actually. I really appreciate everything all of you are doing. This day has been very… intense, but you've made it a lot better."

"Honestly, dealing with all of this stuff every week, we know how it can get to you, especially when it's new. And besides that, none of us have perfect pasts, so we want to make hardships easier." Sano nodded down the hall. "Let's get to your room and get you set up for the night; it's getting late, and you've gotta be tired."

"I am, actually, now that you mention it. It's been very draining."

"Well, rest will help that." He led her to a comfortable, clean room that was obviously meant for just this purpose, set up with a large bed, a lamp, a desk with a computer, and a TV screen on the wall, as well as two comfortable chairs.

"Wow, this is nicer than most hotels," Hitomi said as she entered the room, inspecting it.

"Might as well be comfortable if you're stuck here," Sano said as he leaned against the door.

Hitomi turned around, clasping her hands behind her back. "So, um… Would you like to stay and talk?"

Sano raised an eyebrow. "Aren't you tired?"

"Yes, but…" She bit her lip, looking to the side. "Well it's just, I've been sealed up in my apartment for a week with no one to talk to, and after this week and today, I'd really like a normal conversation without all the talk of evisceration and blood rituals."

Sano sighed as he stepped into the room. "Aw, man, those are my favorite topics! Fine, I guess we can talk about something boring."

Hitomi laughed. "You know, boring would be perfect after the day I've had."

"Oh, well in that case I should go get someone else, I'm way too interesting to fill that need."

"Oh, but you've been doing so well at it so far!"

"Hey, hurtful things will not ingratiate you to me."

Hitomi flipped her shoulder-length brown hair in a haughty manner. "Who says I want to be ingratiating? I don't need to grovel to those below me."

"Ha," Sano grinned as he dropped into one of the chairs. "The only thing below you is your feet. And you've gotta look up to even see mine."

"Only I get to be mean." Hitomi held up the black phone with a wide smile. "If you act mean, I'll call your boss and complain and she'll teach you a lesson."

"Agh, another cheater. Women don't play fair."

"I always play by the rules. I just don't tell my competition the rules I'm going to play by."

"So you cheat by deciding that what you're doing isn't cheating."

Hitomi laughed, sitting on the bed. "It's only cheating if they can prove it's cheating."

Sano sat back, crossing a leg over the other as he smirked. "Katsumi was right. You might fit in here a little too well."

Hitomi smiled. "I might as well take advantage of the situation. Friends make everything better, right?"

~ ~ ~ ~ ~

Date: April 6, 2068
Time: 11:46 PM
Location: South Ashfield Hospital, 3rd
Floor, Room 302

"Katsumi!" Law sidestepped quickly as Ayane, beaming happily, leapt past him to hug her sister when she entered.

Katsumi caught her with a smile, hugging her back. "Aya… You seem to be doing well tonight."

Ayane nodded as she pulled Katsumi to sit on the bed with her. "I was just telling Big L that I feel good. He said he felt better because he got to use the Spirit Ray."

Law grinned. "Dead-on shot. Jus' too bad he didn' stick around."

"Yes, that's actually why I came," Katsumi stated as she sat beside Ayane, who gave her a betrayed look.

"You didn't come to see me?" She switched to a very sad look; Law simply smirked, knowing what was coming.

Katsumi looked at her sister. "Well, of course, I just also have business." Her eyes widened as Ayane sniffed a bit. Law looked at the wall to avoid laughing. "No, wait, stop crying! You know I hate that!"

Ayane rubbed a hand over her eyes. "It's okay, focus on your important stuff…"

"That's not fair! You're more important than anything!"

The younger Samakura smiled happily. "I know!"

Katsumi blinked and then growled. "Ayane…"

Ayane grinned at her. "You're too eas- ack!" She fell back as her pillow hit her, followed by her older sister who pinned her down.

"Apologize!"

"No!"

Katsumi gave a wicked grin as she lifted the pillow again. "Apologize or suffer." Ayane simply stuck out her tongue, so Katsumi pulled back her arm only to blink and give her own exclamation of surprise as Law grabbed her wrist and lifted her off the bed into the air.

Ayane sat up and clapped. "Teamwork!"

Katsumi shot the big man a glare as she hung in the air suspended by her wrist in his hand. "You betray me?"

Law gave a shrug. "Sorry, boss. Blue-hair's the sick one."

Ayane nodded. "Yeah, I'm sick! How dare you attack a sick little girl!"

"You're gonna be sick and *injured* when I get down from here!"

Law chuckled, setting her back on the bed. "C'mon, kids, play nice."

Katsumi couldn't hide her smile as she leaned back on her hands. Sometimes you really did need to just play. "Alright. Ayane, you're forgiven."

"Yay!"

"Law, you are of course fired."

Law chuckled again. "Saw that comin'."

Katsumi moved to the head of the bed so she could lean against the wall, where Ayane took the opportunity to lay her head on her older sister's shoulder, bringing out another smile. "Since you're loyal to Aya, however, you're re-hired."

"Truly you're a forgiving boss."

"Well, to tell the truth, seven-foot demolitions experts are hard to replace."

"I don't recall seein' a lot of 'em."

"It's a problem." Katsumi sighed, resting her arm around Ayane and getting more comfortable. "Back to that business, any trace on that Shade? I'm worried about its next moves."

Law shook his head. "Unfortunately, the thing vanished. I got its signature, though, and sent it to M, so if it has a lot of activity we should get something."

"Good."

"What about that girl you saved?" Ayane asked out of curiosity.

"She's safe at HQ now," Katsumi answered. "Strange part is, M thinks she's a Silent."

The other two started at that and Ayane tilted her head a bit to see her sister's face. "A Silent? Like, a real one, not like us? We haven't seen one of those in… six years?"

Katsumi let out a breath. "Yeah. Hopefully this won't end the same way."

Law leaned against the wall. "That explains why that demon was so interested in her."

"Was she able to tell you what he wanted?"

"Not specifically," Katsumi said with a frown. "She did think he wanted someone sacrificed, though. To what end I don't know, but it does mean we should pay careful attention to any murders in the local area."

"Do you think we could do anything about this, Sumi?"

"I'd rather not risk you out there with your health the way it is, Aya."

Ayane looked up a bit, frowning. *You're not much better,* she spoke over their cyber link.

Let's not have this discussion again. Please. Besides… "What you and I can do is help Hitomi learn about what she is and how to control it."

"Oh! Of course! You're right; the two of us can be great for her to talk to."

"She needs it." Katsumi looked over her sister's head. "Law, you'll be on the response team for when this Shade makes its move. So is Rufus."

"Me providing back-up and escape prevention, Rufus going in with you?"

"That'll be the basic plan. If we manage to corner it you'll come in as well, otherwise we'll try to push it your way. Reno will be transport."

"What'll Sano be doing? If I can ask."

"I'm putting him on protection detail for Hitomi. He's perfect for it; they seem to get along, he's smart, and he'll fit in best if she wants to go somewhere."

"Got it. I'm gonna head back to HQ and get out the fun toys, then," he grinned. He waved as he left the door. "Keep getting' better, Blue-hair."

"Escaping this place is a good motivator!" Ayane called after him, receiving a laugh in return.

Katsumi looked down at her sister. "It's past midnight, by the way. You won't ever get out of here if you don't sleep."

Ayane sighed. "Fine, I'll go to sleep." She pulled Katsumi down, getting comfortable with her head on her chest.

Katsumi smirked. "On me? I can't get up if you do that." In response, Ayane just pretended to be asleep already, leaving nothing for her older sister to do but turn off the light with a smile. "Fair enough. Goodnight, little sister."

Chapter 12: Flare

Date: April 7, 2068
Time: 7:15 AM
Location: South Ashfield Hospital, 3rd
Floor, Room 302

"Aww, they're so cute!"

"They probably won't like waking up to your face inches away, Yuri."

Yuri gave Mikoto a look. "I'm sure they'll appreciate my appreciation!" She was currently hovering over the two Samakura sisters, the younger of which was curled up against her older sister, whose arms were around her. Both were asleep, of course, which was why the three visitors were whispering.

Kyo leaned against the wall with a smirk. "Maybe you should poke them awake."

Before the more sensible Mikoto could caution against that, Yuri was already poking Katsumi, which, of course, was a bad idea, as she found out when the pistol appeared in her face as Katsumi suddenly jerked awake. Yuri let out a squeak and dove behind the bed, and Kyo burst out laughing as Mikoto let out a sigh.

Fortunately these sounds woke Ayane, who blinked wearily as she lifted her head. "Sumi, you're trying to shoot my friends."

Katsumi clicked the safety back on and slid the pistol back under their pillow with a yawn. "Mmm, sorry."

Ayane smiled as Yuri peeked over the edge of the bed. "You know how I said never to startle me awake? That goes double for my sister."

"No kidding," the pink-haired girl said as she stood up, "That's dangerous!"

Mikoto looked at the two sisters. "I'm very sorry for disturbing you, we didn't know."

Katsumi attempted to sit up, but Ayane apparently refused to move, so she just smirked and laid her head back down. "It's fine, but knocking would be more appropriate in the future."

"That's what I said," she nodded, brushing a brown curl from her eye, "but Yuri thought you looked 'cute' as you were."

Ayane smiled as she returned her head to its position. "Aww, Sumi, we're cute!"

"You are. I'm not."

"But you were in that situation!" Yuri sat on Ayane's side of the bed. "I've seen you on the news before. You're her sister, right?"

Mikoto rolled her eyes at the stupidly obvious question, but Katsumi just gave an amused smirk. "Yes, I'm her sister."

Ayane looked up at Katsumi. "You did say you were going to meet my friends."

"That I did."

"Regret that decision?"

"Almost immediately."

Ayane giggled. "Too bad. Guys?"

"Oh, right!" Yuri smiled and waved happily. "Yuri Amanake!"

"I figured," Katsumi chuckled. "What do you do?"

The pink-haired girl blinked. "Lots of things. Or do you mean for a living? I'm a journalist!"

"Interesting. You must have a curious mind. You're the youngest of this group, right?"

"Yep. I'm twenty-four. Ten years younger than you."

Katsumi raised an eyebrow. "You know my exact age?"

Yuri smiled. "Well it's hard not to remember all sorts of details, with how often we hear about you from Ayane."

Kyo raised a hand from his spot against the wall, brushing aside his black bangs. "Moving along to spare Ayane the embarrassment, even though it's funny… I'm Kyo Takagawa. I'm a researcher and inventor in cybernetics focusing on prosthetics and enhancements. Twenty-eight years old, if you're curious."

"Cybernetics?" Katsumi looked interested. "That's a very advanced field."

"Kyo's the creative one," Ayane explained. "He's even worked on some things you'd be familiar with."

"Consider me impressed," Katsumi smiled, before looking to the final visitor. "And Mikoto Suigi. It's good to see you again."

The young woman smiled, nodding. "The pleasure is mine as last time, Miss Katsumi."

Yuri looked at her older friend. "You already met her?"

"Of course," the brown-haired woman answered. "I've known Ayane for eight years. I met them before she was in here, when they lived together."

Katsumi nodded. "Hopefully we'll be back to that soon. How is your practice, Miko?"

Mikoto smiled. "It's doing very well, thank you for asking. It turns out a thirty-year-old lawyer is considered more trustworthy than one in her twenties."

"Perception is a strange thing," Katsumi chuckled.

"So how about you?" Yuri tilted her head. "What can you tell us about yourself? That's what we're interested in, since we always hear about you but never got to meet you."

Katsumi smiled. "Well, what can I say that my sister hasn't bragged about before…?"

Ayane blushed. "If you keep teasing me, Sumi, I'm gonna start telling all the bad things."

Katsumi chuckled. "Alright. What can I say that you three don't know already, though? You know my name, my age and my job."

"Well…" Yuri thought for a moment. "What about your relationship, since we've heard it from Ayane's side? Pay her back for it!"

Mikoto smiled. "Yes, let's make it even. *You* talk about *her* some."

Ayane grinned. "That's perfect! You embarrassed *me*, now *you* do it."

Katsumi gave a soft smile. "Talking about you never embarrasses me," she replied before looking to the others. "You probably already know all about how incredible my sister is, being her friends. If you'd like to know the difference, it's that she's part of your lives, but she's all of mine."

Kyo tilted his head. "Nothing's as important?"

"Not even close." Katsumi looked down, seeing her sister's smile as her hand ran down her pale blue hair. "Everything I do is focused around this girl, and I don't have a problem saying it."

"Wow," Yuri breathed, ever the dreamer. "That's so sweet!"

"Your relationship is very special," Mikoto added with a smile. "Knowing something about your lives, I'm glad you have each other."

Ayane looked at Katsumi. "I'm pretty sure neither of us could survive without the other."

Katsumi met her sister's eyes and nodded. "I can only hope we'll never have to test that."

Everyone fell silent then, their thoughts focusing on Katsumi's dangerous job and Ayane's sickness. All of them were hoping things would be okay. Mikoto spoke up for the others, as she often did, with a polite smile. "I know you don't get to visit as often as you'd like, so we'll leave you two to enjoy today and visit Ayane tomorrow."

The sisters smiled at them and Katsumi nodded. "I appreciate it. Thank you. And thank you for visiting my sister more than I can."

Yuri smiled. "She's our friend…we want to keep her happy."

"You know how much I appreciate that. Don't hesitate to visit her when she's back with me, either."

"Just remember to knock then," Ayane grinned.

Kyo smirked. "No worries, I think we all prefer not getting shot."

They laughed and the three said their goodbyes, exiting the room with a final wave from Yuri.

Katsumi sighed, sitting against the wall. "Your friends are admirable."

Ayane sat up, stretching. "Well, we both know how to pick good friends."

"I was wondering what to do with today, since I'm just waiting for that demon to make a move." Katsumi looked at her younger sister. "What do you say we take advantage of your friends' suggestion and spend the day together?"

Ayane smiled, her eyes shining. "Really? You mean it?"

Katsumi patted her hand. "Yes. I don't get to see enough of you; I'd rather not waste this opportunity for more. Once a week is just… not enough."

"You already know I agree… I miss you."

Her older sister smiled. "Well, let's try to change things, then. I'll visit more, and if you keep getting better, we'll move up our plans."

Ayane matched her smile. "Then we could move, and then we'd see each other every day."

"Yes… It'd be perfect." Katsumi grabbed her hand, getting out of bed. "No reason to put off joy, though. Let's get started on our day."

Ayane laughed as she was pulled up, grinning. "We should have more days."

"I promise, we're going to have as many as we can get."

~ ~ ~ ~ ~

"Alright, got it boss. Sounds great." Sano leaned against the wall. "Have fun. Thanks."

Hitomi tilted her head as Sano shut his phone. "That was Katsumi?"

"Yep." He smiled. "She's spending the day with her sister, taking advantage of a day with nothing to do."

"That sounds nice."

"They need it." Sano pushed off the wall. "That leaves me free, too. Anywhere you wanted to go?"

"Well, actually, if I could get my things from my apartment, that would be great."

Sano chuckled. "Shooting low, huh?"

"We could go anywhere after that, of course."

"Sounds like a plan," Sano said as he pointed at her. "Start thinkin'."

Several minutes later they pulled up to the apartment, and Sano looked at the car next to them as they got out. "Looks like we're not alone here; that car belongs to Rufus."

"That actually makes me feel a bit better," Hitomi said as they walked up the stairs.

As they approached the door, which was already open, they could hear a woman's voice. "…had to bring that up, of course. I could have slapped him for doing so, I mean, these are important clients."

"You'd think someone with his experience would know what he's doing by now and wouldn't stumble over himself and ruin it for you," Rufus replied as he stood up from the kitchen's bar. He spotted the two as they entered, smiling calmly. "Ah, Sano and Miss Saizen. I assume you're here to pick up some things."

The woman turned around as they entered, seeming to size them up a bit. She was very pretty but had a professional aura about her as well as a noble bearing; she wore a black business suit and skirt, and her blonde hair was long and neat, a darker blonde that matched her fierce blue eyes. She looked like she could be quite hard when she wanted to, but at the moment she smiled in a friendly manner. "Sano? The Kurasano from your team, Rufus?"

"That would be him," Rufus acknowledged as he tucked his hands into his white coat's pockets.

Sano raised an eyebrow. "Who's the pretty lady who knows about me, Rufus?"

"Winter Leon," the woman said with a smile that showed respect as she extended her hand. "I'm his girlfriend."

Sano shook her hand with a smile of his own. "Oh, that's- what?!" He pointed at Rufus. "You're in a relationship?!"

Rufus smiled in amusement. "There are many things you don't know about me, Sano."

Hitomi sidestepped around the befuddled Sano, extending a friendly hand and smile to the woman. "Pleased to meet you. I'm Hitomi Saizen."

"Oh, yes, you're this apartment's owner! You have a very nice place; I can tell you're organized."

"She likes that," Rufus explained. "Efficiency is important."

"Well thank you," Hitomi replied with a grateful smile.

"Hey, are we just gonna skip past the crazy?" Sano looked between the three. "How did Rufus get a girlfriend when I don't have one?" Winter looked amused at the statement, while Hitomi looked interested in it.

Rufus ran a hand over his light blond hair. "Perhaps, Mr. Lionel, it's because I'm an adult."

"I can beat you back to childhood if you'd like."

Hitomi put a hand on Sano's shoulder. "Um, as funny as your banter is, why don't we move on? Why are you here, Mr....?"

"Ivanov," Rufus smiled, "but Rufus is fine. Captain Samakura requested that I place a sensor in here in case the culprit returns."

"Oh?" Hitomi looked interested. "What kind of sensor can detect a-"

"Criminal?" Sano laughed loudly as he cut her off, rubbing his head. "Lots of kinds, Hitomi! It's really boring tech stuff."

Hitomi looked confused, but Rufus was nodding. "Needless to say, Miss Saizen, we shall catch the man- or men- if he or they return, and they often do return."

"I'm very sorry for what happened," Winter offered. "I've had experiences with burglars before, I know how it can shatter that feeling of safety a home is meant to provide. Rufus only needed to stop by here, actually..."

"Yes," Rufus pushed up his shades, "we were only stopping by on our way to the restaurant."

"Rufus doesn't get many free days," Winter explained, "so we were going to take advantage of his boss' suddenly-gifted day off. Maybe you'd like to join us for lunch?" She looked back at Rufus as she asked, seeing him nod his agreement.

"Oh, that's very kind of you," Hitomi said with a smile, looking to Sano. "Wanna go?"

"Sure, why not?" Sano shrugged. "Maybe I can figure out what Winter sees in Blondie."

Winter smirked. "You're exactly like he described."

Sano scratched his head. "Wish I knew if that was a compliment or an insult."

Hitomi pointed to the bedroom. "Just let me gather up the things I came for and we'll meet you out front?"

"Of course, take your time."

As the two of them walked out Sano pulled Hitomi aside, looking at the door as he spoke quietly. "Normal people don't know these things exist, remember? Don't say anything about demons or ghosts; for everyone outside of us, it was a burglary."

"Oh," Hitomi replied. "I thought his girlfriend would know about it."

"Girlfriends can come and go," Sano answered. "If you marry someone you can tell them. Immediate family can be told if they're considered trustworthy, like Reno's wife, Katsumi's sister and Rufus' brother. But to everyone else, we're counter-terrorists and security agents."

"I get it." Hitomi gave a sheepish smile. "Sorry."

"No worries, you're new. You'll get the hang of it."

"I'm not sure how comfortable I want to get with constant lying."

Sano shrugged. "Katsumi and Rufus say it's an important life skill."

"That's a little depressing."

Sano smirked, though it was a dry expression. "Their lives are depressing, so that doesn't surprise me."

~ ~ ~ ~ ~

Law stopped outside the Dovetail Bar, looking over the place. It was a true old-fashioned establishment, built using a lot of wood unlike most buildings these days. Law appreciated the simplicity of the whole thing, from its construction to its design. He walked through the door to the inside, which wasn't much different; wooden tables and chairs, and a long bar in the corner lined with stools.

Screens were placed at various points in the bar, showing the news or sports or local programs. Since it was the middle of the day the place was relatively empty, with only a few people here for lunch or break. This was Law's favorite time to come, a time when he could avoid the crowds and just have a conversation with-

"Lawrence!"

Law smirked as he headed towards the bar. The woman behind it was a dark-skinned bartender with "ex-military" written all over her. She wore a faded green tank top, tan pants and a darker green bandana that only kind of kept her hair out of her face. Though her name was Jaina Cardin, nobody that knew her called her that. "That boss of yours actually let you off your leash for a day?"

"She's off on her own t'day, enjoyin' it like I am," He said as he took a seat on a worn stool.

Jaina put on a disbelieving look. "Does she know *how* to enjoy things?"

"Now, Card, I ain't here to argue about Katsumi. Jus' let it slide."

"Fine. But what you see in that woman I'll never know."

Law chuckled. "I know, you tell me every time I come."

She picked up a glass, filling it with a drink and pushing it towards him. "I'm just dreading a day when you actually tell her how you feel. Imagine the two of you getting married, and I'm forced to be there smiling and acting like it's all good."

"What makes you think I'd be invitin' you t'my wedding?"

"You would. You would, because you wouldn't want to risk what I'd do if you didn't."

"Fair 'nough. Either way, don't be expectin' it t'come anyway."

"I'm not. She's a bitch."

Law gave her a look. "Already gave you a warnin', Card. Don't make it three."

She raised her hands. "Alright, alright. No more insults. So what's she doing that she's 'enjoying'?"

Sam heard the inflection she put on the last word, but he let it slide. "Spending th' day with 'er sister."

"She has a sister? Since when?"

"Since always, or at least since she was three," Law chuckled. "I've known 'er for ten years; knew Katsumi for four before she told me about 'er."

"Why'd it take so long? She an embarrassment?"

"You don't know her, so I'll let that go." Law took a drink. "She's a good one. Even you'd like her."

"I'll give her the benefit of the doubt," Jaina agreed with a nod.

"Good. An' thanks. She's not like Katsumi anyways. She's all hyper an' cheery an' outgoin'."

"And she's related to the-" she cut herself off at Law's look, "uh, to Katsumi? Why couldn't you have a thing for *her*?"

Law chuckled deeply. "She ain't my type. Plus I pity the person that looks at 'er wrong; her sister'll rip 'em to pieces before the day's over."

"Protects her, huh?" Jaina sighed. "Well, that's one thing I like about your boss, then." She held up a finger. "One."

Law grinned, passing back the empty glass for a refill. "Generous of you."

~ ~ ~ ~ ~

In a skyscraper miles away there was a large room with hardly any light. The windows all had blinds pulled shut, blocking the view of the outside world and making the room seem even more removed from the rest of the world than it already was. The only active light was a single hanging lamp of a smooth design that seemed to provide just enough illumination to see the oval-shaped table in the center of the room, and little else.

Eight people sat around this table, their faces half-shrouded in the darkness left by the single light. The shadowy nature of this room served a purpose, mainly to distance them from the world and personal attachments as a whole. The Aegis Corporation believed that the best decisions were made with as little human emotion as possible. For good or for ill, the people that sat around the table, the Aegis Board of Directors, were the best at forgetting human emotion.

There were usually nine people seated around this table during important meetings, and it showed that the members noticed; the company's Chairman, Hackett (otherwise known as H) stood, looking over the others at the table. Each wore a fine suit, most of a different style. Several were smoking, causing an ethereal curtain to hang about the table that gave the room an even more shadowy appearance.

Hackett himself was something of a large man, broad-shouldered and tall. His salt-and-pepper hair made it difficult to guess his age (57), and his face had the weathered sort of look of a hardened businessman. He looked at the others, who were all, like he, known by a single letter: R, L, A, V, K, N, and J. The eighth Director, M, was not present.

"What's the point of this meeting, H?" K asked, leaning back in his chair with already-apparent boredom. Outside of the company he was otherwise known as Kell Bison, Director of Civil Protection. He was younger than Hackett at 36, and he looked it, wearing a brown suit in a casual manner that matched his shoulder-length brown hair. He didn't seem to care for his appearance much, and the general opinion of him among the other members was rather low.

"And where is M?" J asked as she looked to the empty chair, drawing full attention to it. Julia Noir; her reputation for ruthless business practices had enabled her to reach the position of Director of Trade at the age of 36, and she'd held it for eight years so far. The stern blonde woman was rarely ever seen to smile and almost always seemed agitated, as she was now. Her chest-length hair was kept straight and tidy at all times, matching her personality.

"Obviously," L said as he topped up his glass of wine, "he's not here because he's the subject of the meeting." Hackett looked at L, studying him for a bit longer than the others. Lucius Malik, Director of Special Protection, was someone Hackett didn't trust, and it was entirely because he felt L was too smart for his own good. The man was 42 and had black hair that he kept short apart from the bangs, which hung around his eyes in a manner that just made him look even less like a person one should turn his back on.

"In a way," Hackett answered. "More accurately, his division is the subject of this meeting."

Victoria Gray, known as V, made a distasteful sound, looking at H. "If his division is the subject of the meeting, shouldn't he be here to speak on it?" Hackett met her gaze; she only had one good eye, while the other was covered with a patch (she wanted no part of Cyberization, believing it was better to rely on natural talent), and yet still the dark-haired woman's stare was difficult to hold. Her waist-length hair held wide, wavy curls that gave her an elegant look, but the 38-year-old's sharp features still gave her the competent appearance that her position as Director of Military Action demanded. She was known to have a closer relationship to M than the others, so her defense of him against this perceived slight was not unexpected; especially since, out of the people in this room, she had the most morals.

A, otherwise known as Adrian Barstow, leaned forward, the new angle causing the light to cast even less-appealing shadows across his craggy face. "What are you trying to play here, H?" He grimaced, doing his 83-year-old face no favors. He was a man that looked to have led a hard life and crawled out of it on his hands and knees, but still, as the Director of Defense, he was respected for his reliability, if not his intellect.

"We should hear the Chairman out before we condemn him," admonished a deep, metallic voice. This belonged to Nathaniel Greir, N, the Director of Cybernetics. A mistake in a lab several years back had left N without a lower jaw and most of his chest; twenty years earlier it would have been fatal, but now the man wore what looked like a black metal filtration mask over the lower half of his face. It was necessary without lungs, and though technology had advanced to the point of creating fully synthetic bodies, he was one of the unlucky ones allergic to the synthetic materials. Still, Hackett thought the 46-year-old cyborg probably liked the intimidation factor it provided along with his chest-length shock of white hair that rested across his black suit.

The final director, R, sat to Hackett's left, his fingers steepled before him as he patiently waited for the others to calm down. Revan Kain was the Director of Weapons Research, and he was by far the youngest of the group at 30 years of age, which was one of the factors that made most of the Board dislike him. However, it was inarguable that R was brilliant; a genius, even. He was also calm and controlled at all times, emotionally and physically. His hair was long, black and silky, kept in perfect order like his expensive black suit, but the feature most noticeable about his appearance was his eyes; they were brown, so dark as to be almost black, and held a look that was as unreadable as it was intimidating. He looked at N with a polite smile. "Thank you for being a voice of reason, N. It is appreciated."

Hackett nodded, pushing away his impatience. "First of all, I can assure you, A, that I am 'playing at' nothing. Our Director of SIN has been doing his job better than we'd hoped, and his division is outperforming expectations."

"Then why is he not here?" Victoria replied with a bit of irritation; she never liked deception or dishonesty if it could be avoided. Every company had its white sheep, H supposed.

"M has other business to attend to today," Revan assured her. "And we would have put off the meeting, but we are having it at his request."

"He was meant to call in minutes ago," Hackett continued, annoyed. "But it seems his own meeting is not enough reason to be prompt."

"What's wrong with being fashionably late?" Everyone turned to the view screen to see M's face grinning at them, or at least, as much of his face wasn't hidden by his hat and glasses.

"How nice of you to join us," Hackett nearly grunted in irritation.

"Wish I could ditch meetings and just call in from home," Kell muttered, but he was ignored by the others.

"What is this meeting about, M?" Julia virtually demanded as she turned to the screen. "You aren't wasting our time, I hope."

To her annoyance he merely smiled in response as he always did, a trait Hackett hated more every day. "My dear J, feel free to leave if you'd like. I had simply thought my fellow Directors- and Chairmen Hackett, of course- would like to hear of some of my findings, especially considering they relate to both the Silents and the Ancient Ones."

That statement got the attention of everyone in the room. Even Lucius, who was usually quietly watching, sat forward in interest. "You've discovered new information about Silents and Ancient Ones?"

"Information?" M grinned. "I've discovered two existing examples."

"This is… quite an important event if it is true, M," stated Revan with trepidation.

"The Silent is natural?" Nathaniel spoke up, his eyes narrowed in disbelief. "Not artificial like your Captain?"

"That is correct. She had no knowledge of her state or abilities. She's with us now and Captain Samakura is willing to train her. However, I would advise the Board against our previous course of action of getting a Silent out into the field too quickly."

"Yes, I agree with M," Victoria said with a nod. "That was unfortunate, and we should try to avoid such a disaster this time. She must be handled with care; we cannot forget her own health and mental state."

"Agreed," Hackett stated. "We will put this fully in your hands, M, and trust you to handle it appropriately."

"I appreciate your trust, and will not let you down. But now we should move on, because I know you are all more interested in our second find."

"Wouldn't we have heard of an Ancient One's actions already, were it active on this plane?"

Adrian asked, looking to the others.

"Were it in a physical form, yes," M answered him with a knowing smile. "However, this one is currently in Shade form for the moment. I heavily recommend taking advantage of this and attempting to destroy it now."

"No," Revan replied with finality. "We will track it if we can, but capture is preferable to elimination."

"This is a very dangerous creature we are dealing with," Victoria said as she shot Revan a glare. "If it is allowed to take physical form, the damage and death toll could be catastrophic."

"If we wait and watch," Lucius countered smoothly, "then perhaps it will lead us to an even bigger threat. We all know the plans these things have are never small."

"I agree with this assessment," Nathaniel added. "I say we wait for a bigger opportunity."

"The only window of opportunity may be closing now," M argued, for once without a smile. "This is a foolish course of action. If we wait-"

"Enough," Hackett cut him off. "We will put it to a vote. All in favor of quick disposal?"

M, Adrian, Victoria and Kell stated, "Aye."

"All in favor of a wait-and-see approach?"

Revan, Lucius, Nathaniel, and Julia stated, "Aye."

"Aye," Hackett added, looking at M. "It's decided. You will inform your Captain to track the Ancient One, but make no direct attacks until it is absolutely necessary. We want as much information as we can get."

M's smile had returned; though it was false, most of them couldn't tell. "Very well. That concludes my business, then. Ladies, Gentlemen." The screen cut out as the call was ended.

As the board members began to leave, Revan looked at Hackett. "Do you think he will follow orders?"

"I don't know if even *he's* decided whether he will or not," Hackett replied gruffly. "We will keep an eye on him, however. The time may be coming when we have to do something about him."

As Hackett spoke he didn't notice the eye that was currently on him; the single eye that watched him with growing distrust. Victoria left without saying a word, but contacting M was the first thing the general planned to do once she was out of the building.

~ ~ ~ ~ ~

"You know what I like about days like this?"

Katsumi let the restaurant doors close behind them as they exited into the cool air, watching her sister walk in that sort of dreamy way she often did when happy, hands clasped behind her and feet meandering rather than walking in a straight line. "You don't have to stay in a hospital bed?"

Ayane smiled. "Well, yes, that too." She was looking up at the overcast sky; it seemed they would be getting rain soon. "But when the weather's like this, everything just feels so new. I smell the coming rain and not the city, and hear the cool wind instead of cars."

"Only you could think of old-as-the-earth weather as newer than modern technology."

Ayane laughed, turning to her. "Come on, don't you feel it too?"

They passed Shinjuku Station, heading east as they walked. Katsumi looked up at the sky after they crossed a street, studying the clouds. "You know what this reminds me of?"

Ayane tilted her head in curiosity. "What?"

"Kobe." She gave a slight smile.

A similar smile, triggered by memory, spread across Ayane's face as she thought back. "Oh yeah…"

July 28th, 2049… It was a bad year for the Samakuras in general. Naomi was dead, Joseph was mad (in both definitions), and their two little girls… Well, they had vanished, using all the skills they'd been forced to learn for the better part of a decade.

Ayane was twelve at the time, and her older sister was fifteen. It was only a month and a half after their mother's death; they'd spent that time running, hiding, and running again. They moved around in erratic directions, leaving no trace and staying unpredictable. They had no choice, no alternative; if they were found by their father that would be it. Their freedom- their lives- would be gone forever.

On this day they found themselves in Kobe, a big city that felt like a small town. It was perfect; tons of people going about their daily lives - lots of families - who wouldn't notice two young girls, and where two young girls wouldn't be a rarity. Ayane remembered hating her lighter brown hair at the time (something she got from their father), thinking it'd make her easier to recognize.

Katsumi had such beautiful black hair like their mother, silky and easily styled. Her older sister told her she was being silly, though; she liked her hair, said it showed her uniqueness. A simple thing, really, but Ayane remembered taking such pleasure in the compliment.

The sky looked fairly intimidating that day, and their warning had only lasted an hour before the rain came down in droves, soaking the two girls to the bone. Ayane pulled her jacket close around her and looked up at the sky. "We should find some shelter... There are a lot of buildings around here..."

"No," Katsumi said, continuing to walk forward purposefully. "I'm tired of huddling in alleys."

Ayane didn't see what was so wrong with the option but she went quiet anyway, following her sister. They soon arrived at a hotel where Katsumi managed to pass herself off as older than she was, securing a room with a bit of the small amount of money they had left. "Katsumi," Ayane whispered worriedly after the woman had left them in their new room, "We don't have a lot of money, we should save it!"

Katsumi turned around, shutting the door. "No! Aya, this is our life now. We can't just keep running and hope something better comes along, we have to make it better ourselves."

Ayane pulled her jacket off before Katsumi came over with one of the room's towels, throwing it over her head and rubbing her hair. "Hey- Sumi! You're gonna mess it up!"

*Katsumi smiled in amusement as she dried her sister's hair.
"It's already messed up from the rain, it can't get any worse."
After she pulled back she laughed at the hair sticking out every
direction and the glare on Ayane's face. "Okay, so it can."*

*"Gimme that!" Ayane grabbed the towel and jumped,
managing to reach her older sister's head and throw the towel
over it.*

*"Wha- hey! I was being nice!" They ended up wrestling for
the towel until they were lying on the ground panting, looking at
each other and realizing their hair was even worse now. "Okay...
Truce?"*

*Ayane caught her breath, looking up at the ceiling. "Truce."
She looked back over and smiled. "If you say I win."*

*Katsumi returned the smile, getting up. "Okay, you win.
Again." She tossed the towel back into the bathroom before
moving over to the room's window, leaning against it and looking
out, listening to the pattering of the rain against the glass.*

*Ayane sat up, watching her older sister. "What are you
looking for?" she asked, wondering if Katsumi was watching for
tails or hunters or their father.*

"I'm not looking for anything."

"Then what are you doing?"

"I'm just looking."

*Ayane stood up and took a seat on the bed instead, continuing
to watch her. There was something... different now, about her
older sister, she could tell that. It had only seemed to happen
today, but she didn't know what to think about it. "Katsumi? Are
you... okay?"*

*"Of course I am," Katsumi said with the hint of a smile.
Unlike the smiles she'd learned to fake years earlier, this one
seemed subconscious, maybe even unnoticed by her. Still, she kept
looking out that window at the rain, at the city; watching, listening,
but idly now, not alertly. "This city is pretty," she said softly. "I
like it. I wonder how much else of the world I'll like."*

*Ayane sat on the edge of the bed, listening to her sister's
strangely content tone with wonder. She was more curious about
Katsumi's attitude now, rather than afraid. She seemed... happy.
"Katsumi?"*

"Hmm?"

"If you could go anywhere in the world right now, where would you go?"

Katsumi smiled, turning back from the window to look at her with genuine sincerity. "This is the only place I want to be."

They'd reached their destination now: Shinjuku Gyoen, a large park with wide lawns, beautiful trees and large ponds. The main reason they came was that it was Spring and the cherry blossoms there were amazing this time of year, drawing smiles from them both as they walked beneath the branches. "It took me a long time to figure out what happened that day," Ayane said as she caught one of the pink blossoms as it fell.

"Even I wasn't entirely sure," Katsumi admitted. "Suddenly my goals had just changed. I didn't just want to survive anymore; I wanted us to be happy."

"And after realizing that, you were happy," Ayane said with a smile, remembering the days following that one, days full of just as many hardships as before, but many more smiles. It hadn't all been running anymore; sneaking into movies, exploring parks, spending a day in a museum – she and Katsumi had started doing all sorts of things just for fun. "And I couldn't help but be happy too."

Ayane watched her sister sigh and give her a look full of so many emotions only she would understand it. "Every hour I'm thankful you got out of there with me. If only I'd escaped-"

"Shh," Ayane said as she laid her hand on her older sister's cheek, giving her a soft smile. "Thinking about that won't do you any good," she admonished quietly, knowing how that line of thought would affect Katsumi. "And it doesn't matter anyway. I'm here. We're both here, almost twenty years later."

Katsumi looked away. "I'm sorry… It's just…. Seeing him…"

"I know," Ayane said. Of course it brought everything back. How could it not? "He won't get me though; he didn't then and he won't now."

"He won't," Katsumi said in a much harder tone. She looked at Ayane with an intense gaze. "I won't let him."

Her look and tone would've scared most others but Ayane just smiled, taking her hand. "I trust you. I'm not afraid." Katsumi started to smile again until a different, pained look crossed her face, one that Ayane unfortunately recognized. "Katsumi?" Ayane watched her sister waver on her feet for a moment before she fell. "Katsumi!" Fortunately Ayane was fast, managing to catch her before she hit the ground.

"Oh, no," Ayane moaned as it started to rain, looking down at her sister. She sat on her knees, holding Katsumi's head in her lap and cradling her. "Don't worry, I'll get you out of here."

"No…" Katsumi opened her eyes, speaking quietly. "I'm awake. I'm here."

"Katsumi, you'll get soaked! And you're sick! I have to get you home, get you in bed!"

"Water is good. And… what does a bed have… that this spot doesn't?" She watched her lift her hand and felt her touch her cheek, smiling weakly. "This is the only place I want to be. Just… stay here with me. Please."

Ayane caught her hand as she lowered it, squeezing it. "Okay." She smiled softly; at least they were comfortable. "You're still tired of hiding, aren't you?"

"Yes… Tired of hiding in… beds, in hospital rooms…" Katsumi closed her eyes until a wave of pain had passed, but she remained conscious, opening them afterwards. "I just want it all to be over… the surviving."

"I know. So do I." Ayane knew they were both as worried, and as tired, as they tried to pretend they weren't. At the same time that *she* seemed to be getting a bit better, *Katsumi* seemed to be getting worse. Who knew if, come this time next year, Katsumi would be the one living in a hospital bed? If she lived at all, that was. All it would take was one attack of this sickness during a dangerous situation…

Ayane shook her head, throwing aside those worries. She threw aside her fear, too, and her anger for good measure. None of those things would help either of them right now, and they could deal with them later, together. For now, this was their day, and no matter what tried to ruin it they were going to enjoy it. "Keep that Kobe feeling, Sumi," Ayane said, smiling down at her older sister as she saw her open her lavender eyes again. "Let's be happy while we can, when we can."

"That's the spirit," Katsumi said with an understanding smile. "As long as we're both alive…"

"…we're both happy," Ayane finished. "So I won't let Father, or my sickness, or your sickness, or the fact that I'm currently being soaked by freezing rain because my sister's a stubborn mule, dampen my spirits."

Katsumi chuckled, closing her eyes. "Please tell me that pun wasn't intentional."

"Sorry, I never lie to you," Ayane said with a grin. "And if you think I'm going to forget you made me sit out here in the rain, you're all wet."

Katsumi laughed. "Oh God that was stupid… I'm sorry to throw cold water on your dreams, but your jokes are dead in the water."

Ayane laughed and shook her head. "Insult me, will you? Oh, you're in hot water now!"

Katsumi was laughing much harder than she knew she should be because the jokes really weren't funny, but she couldn't help it. "It doesn't… doesn't matter… You won't hurt me, because… blood is thicker than water!"

The two sisters virtually dissolved into laughter as they were drenched by the rain, receiving many odd looks from passers-by who were fleeing the park to find cover, wondering what was wrong with the two girls laughing hysterically over stupid water puns while they were drenched by freezing rain. Ayane and Katsumi didn't even notice, though; it didn't matter to them. For that moment, nothing did.

Chapter 13: Inheritance

It was a dreary day; days like this almost always were, as if the weather matched the emotions of those experiencing it. The wind was colder than it should have been this time of year, rustling the leaves of the trees beneath the overcast sky. A small group of people, only a dozen or so, gathered around a pale blue casket, placing flowers and saying goodbyes. Soon the casket would be taken to the crematorium.

Two girls stood a fair distance away, far enough that they couldn't make out the priest's chants. They'd missed the wake the day before, but they risked coming here on this day. It was unfair; they should've stood at the casket themselves. They should've been able to go with the casket to the crematorium and put their mother's bones to rest with their own hands.

It couldn't be risked, though. Their father was present; he knew this was a good opportunity to catch them. Katsumi watched him accept condolences from the other mourners with a sad smile, as if he hadn't been the cause of his own wife's death. Her fists clenched in rage, but thankfully Ayane's hand on her arm prevented her from making the mistake of going after him.

Hours later, long after night had fallen and the cold had more strongly embraced the world, Katsumi and Ayane stood at the family grave the ashes had been placed in. There was a new name engraved on the front of the monument: Naomi Samakura. Katsumi stared at it as Ayane laid their flowers before the grave. Both girls were crying, but Katsumi made no sounds. Her eyes burned with darker emotions, rage and hatred that seemed to twist their brown color into a darker black.

She trembled with barely contained emotion, fists clenched so hard her nails pierced the skin on her palms. At that moment she was torn between grief and hatred. Apologies to her mother died on her lips without making a sound, condemnations of her father did the same, and frustration and hopeless tore at her until a flicker of something worse crossed her eyes. A scream of anguish left her lips as she slammed a fist into the stone, bloodying her knuckles and causing a small crack.

A soft touch distracted her from the torrent of negative emotion. She felt Ayane's fingers brush hers and she opened her hand on reflex, letting go of the fist and feeling her sister's hand slip into hers. She gripped it tightly but refused to look at her, fearing the emotions she could barely control would target her innocent sister against her will. They stood like that for a long while, as long as they dared, before disappearing again.

That night Katsumi's dreams would be no surprise to anyone but her. She saw once more the face of her mother, twisted into an expression of hate she'd never worn in life. She was back in that moment, watching what was once their mother coming towards her and Ayane with a murderous intent that left no doubts about the change. She tried to fight her off, she did, but Joseph had done something worse to Naomi, something that had made her a thing beyond human.

In the end, Katsumi had no choice but to fire, tears falling as she pulled the trigger. The dream continued past that moment, and suddenly Katsumi was back at the grave. Fifteen years old, she watched the grave rip open and the ashes pour out, reforming into her mother as she'd looked throughout their life. But the smile was gone and the look of hatred was back, directed at Katsumi as she spat her words with a venom that was the opposite of her true personality. "You... murdered me... Your own mother!" she screamed in rage. "Everything I did for you and you threw it away!"

The strong Katsumi was gone in the face of this accusation. She was timid, unsure, stammering out words even she didn't believe. "I had no choice... I tried to-"

"LIAR!" Naomi's words echoed powerfully, nearly deafening Katsumi. The young girl tried to cover her ears but it did nothing. "You didn't even look for a way to help me, to fix me! I would have done anything for you, and you barely tried! So willing to give up *on me, to cast me aside, to rob the sister you claim to care about of her loving mother!"*

"That's not true!" Katsumi shook her head, glaring in response as some of her strength and conviction returned. "I did what I had to do to protect Ayane! There was nothing that could've been done... We would've died!"

"You gave up," Naomi stated with far more conviction than Katsumi had. "You turned on me just like your father."

"She's right," Ayane said as she stepped into the scene, looking at her older sister with the same hatred Katsumi's own eyes had been filled with earlier. "You're the one that killed her."

"Aya..."

"No!" Ayane shook her head. "You're as much an enemy as he is! You're the one that pulled the trigger!"

The nightmare, it seemed, had learned how to win. Katsumi's resistance shattered with Ayane's words and she dropped to her knees, arms hanging limply as emptiness filled her. "You're right..." Her words were weak as the negative emotions from earlier turned on herself like hungry wolves.

"Katsumi..." Suddenly Ayane held the gun she'd used, aiming it at her older sister. Katsumi didn't even try to move, no longer having the will to fight her own death. "Sumi!"

Katsumi jerked awake, sitting up with a gasp. Sweat covered her and made the sheets cling to her skin and her hair stick to her neck and face. Her eyes darted around in a search for the visions that had tormented her, but the room was quiet. Finally her eyes landed on Ayane and she noticed the girl was crying and staring at her in concern.

"I saw it..." Ayane said in a whisper. Katsumi realized her intense dream must have been shown over their link, like the most intense thoughts and emotions they had often were. Suddenly Katsumi hated herself even more for causing her sister such distress. "Stop it!" Ayane yelled, glaring at her now.

Katsumi looked away, knowing what she meant. "I can't," she muttered in a broken voice. "I keep... seeing it..."

"We'll always see it," Ayane replied, sounding far older than her twelve years of age should allow. "We share that. But what we don't share is blaming you for it!"

"How can you not?" Katsumi nearly growled, looking back at her angrily. "I pulled the trigger."

Ayane matched her glare with one of her own. "That was *not* our mother. That was something Father created. All of this is *his* fault, not yours. And I hate him as much as you do." She took her sister's face with both hands. "But don't you go down that road, Sumi, do you hear me? Hating him is good, and I have nothing against anger, but I *need* you. I don't want you to be obsessed with him, or even with mother. I want to keep my sister."

Katsumi swallowed and nodded, trying to let those emotions go. "I'll… I'll try." She sighed, pulling Ayane into a hug. "I'll never leave you alone, Aya. These feelings will never be as strong as the ones I have for you." She took a deep breath, determination replacing the hatred in her eyes. "I promise."

Ayane smiled then, returning the hug. "You better keep that promise. Father's the one that focuses only on hate; mother was never like that."

Katsumi pulled back to look at her, smiling softly. "You're a lot like her, you know. Just a little more selfish about me."

Ayane gave a happier smile. "I think I'm allowed to be a bit possessive of my sister."

~ ~ ~ ~ ~

Date: April 8, 2068
Time: 10:14 AM
Location: SIN HQ, Tokyo

Ayane yawned, looking around the room with tired – but happy – eyes. Katsumi sat in a chair in the corner of the room while Ayane sat sideways in her lap with her head on her older sister's shoulder, watching the others in the room (the whole team was there, including Hitomi) as she mainly stayed in her thoughts and out of the conversation.

She'd spent much of the night taking care of Katsumi, who had only gotten worse as the day went on. She'd managed to stay conscious until evening, but after that it she alternated between being awake and unconscious. Katsumi told Ayane to sleep, but honestly Ayane had appreciated being able to take care of Katsumi for once since she was still feeling fine.

Still, both of them were pretty tired today, and relatively quiet, but the others seemed to know enough not to ask about it. Instead they talked amongst themselves as Ayane and Katsumi simply enjoyed the company. Ayane yawned again, shifting to get a little more comfortable and drawing a smile from her older sister. "What are they talking about?" Ayane mumbled softly. "I tuned out."

Her sister looked over the group with a smirk. They were in the room Hitomi was staying in; Law was sitting in the chair not occupied by the sisters, Rufus was leaning against the wall near the door, Reno was sitting on the floor against the bed, and Sano and Hitomi sat on the bed with their backs against the wall. "They're debating the validity of several ghost-hunting shows," Katsumi replied in a soft tone.

"Sounds important," Ayane said with a smile.

Across the room, while Reno was extolling the virtues of a certain night vision camera to Rufus, Hitomi was watching the two sisters as she leaned towards Kurasano and said quietly, "They're really cute."

Sano smirked. "You should tell her that."

"Why?" Hitomi looked at him curiously. "Would she not appreciate it?"

Sano looked thoughtful. "Actually... I don't know. I mean, before three days ago, I never even knew Katsumi could be like that."

Hitomi frowned, looking even more confused now. "What do you mean? I thought you'd known her for years."

"Going on eight years now, yeah. But it's... complicated. Of all of us, only Law and M knew she had a sister. She was kept secret for safety reasons."

"Oh. And that changed?"

"Not really. I mean, it changed in that the person she was being protected from found her anyway, so Katsumi decided it'd be better if her allies knew about her now that her enemies did."

"That's terrible," Hitomi said as she watched Katsumi whisper something to Ayane, making the younger girl grin. "Is she in danger?"

"We're all in danger," Sano muttered morosely. "But at least we'll all help each other. Don't you worry about Ayane; not only will everyone in this room fight for her, but Katsumi's the best protector she could have."

"Well, they look happy, so I guess it doesn't bother them a lot."

Sano shrugged. "I dunno. When you live the way we all do, I think you just learn to take happiness when you can get it."

"Sano seems to know what he's talking about," Katsumi said softly with a smirk, still pretending she wasn't listening.

Ayane smiled. "Think we can just get him to explain things to all new people for us? He's good at it."

"He does like to talk," Rufus muttered, bringing Ayane's eyes to him. She noticed Reno had switched to talking to Law, so Rufus had begun paying attention to the sisters.

"Are you worried he'll say more than he should?" Ayane asked.

Rufus tilted his head. "Sano…? Nah. Not intentionally, anyway. Though you might wanna make sure he knows exactly what he shouldn't give away."

"Probably a good idea," Katsumi mumbled, looking over at him.

Ayane looked up at her sister. *What exactly does he know?*

Let's see… He knows we want to kill Father. He knows a two-sentence description of our childhoods, but no details. He knows what happened to Mother. Those are the things he knows that the others don't, none if which I want him telling anyone else.

Yeah… Ayane sighed, laying her head back down.

I'm sorry, Katsumi said as she stroked her sister's hair. *I didn't mean to ruin your mood.*

You didn't, Ayane replied as she smiled. *I'm pretty happy today. This is nice. I like being here, being part of this group.*

It's a good group.

Ayane closed her eyes, listening to the voices around her. Katsumi was right, it was a good group. It was hard to feel safer than she felt at this moment.

~ ~ ~ ~ ~

"They're being foolish," Victoria Gray, Director of Military Action, stated over her secure phone, staring out the window of the café she sat in. It was sad, she reflected, that she trusted this place more than her office or home.

"I agree with your assessment," M replied as he walked past Hitomi's room with a smile, hearing snippets of the conversation within. "But I do not feel as if they are being entirely honest."

"You think the other directors have ulterior motives?" Victoria frowned. She'd considered that, but hearing that M did as well made it seem far more valid, and *that* she did not like.

"I do, General. I think there's a bigger reason they want us to capture this Ancient One alive than simply 'more information'."

"You think…" The General shook her head. "You don't think they want to use him, do you?"

"I do. In fact, I believe they want to use him to restart Project Origin."

"Project - but that's…" She sighed, rubbing the patch over her missing eye as the spot ached.

"That's ridiculous. Surely they know the folly of such a-"

"Arrogance is a major flaw in those that hold powerful positions such as ours, V," M chuckled. "They likely believe that if they throw enough money at the problem it will work."

"Then they have to be stopped. Even if it did work, even if such a being could be controlled by humans, isn't that too much power for one group to hold? And I don't even want to think about Origin's reemergence…"

"Of course it is. And I don't think either of us believes our company would be responsible with such power."

"No." V looked back out the window, her eye narrowed. "H and R would jump at the chance to wield such power. I can see it in their eyes every time they speak of such things. And I don't even know what G would do with it."

"Do you even believe the Aegis President would be left with the authority to do anything? Or the ability?"

Victoria grimaced. "You see the same thing that I do in H and R, don't you?"

"Unfortunately. R is cunning, but H is less so, and his nerves about the future are obvious to the observant. We both know H doesn't plan on simply staying Chairman forever."

"And he's the one I'm less worried about."

"Yes… He may not even get the chance to claim G's position if they make their move."

"Backstabbing?" V felt uncomfortable at the very notion of it. "I have no problem believing that R is capable of such a thing. If H doesn't already realize that R is using him, he's a bigger fool than I thought."

"His self-importance may be blinding him to that fact. Still, I thank you for bringing their watchful eyes and ears to my attention."

"Have they started yet?"

"Oh, yes. One device in my home and one in my car already, as well as two 'friends' who like to admire me from afar. Oh, and a device in my office that I removed and informed them about."

Victoria smirked. "Told them you're worried about what enemy succeeded in putting it there?"

"Of course. And I have every right to be worried, don't you think?"

"Considering that your worst enemies may be within our own organization? Yes, I'm worried as well."

"At least I have you as an ally, my friend."

"You know how I disapprove of these kinds of methods. And beyond that, your division is important." She frowned. "I'm just worried they'll attempt to remove you. I can't imagine what kind of person they'd put in your place."

"Someone not half as brilliant, I imagine."

V smiled. "I don't think anyone even half as brilliant exists, M. So… Are you going to take my advice?"

"Take out the Ancient One as soon as possible and inform the board it was unavoidable? Of course I will. Well, I will do the informing," M said with a smile. "Captain Samakura will be doing the taking-out."

"It's in good hands both ways, then." Victoria tilted her head. "Tell the girls I miss having them in my division, will you?"

"I can tell them to give you a call, if you'd like."

She smiled. "Yes, do that. I would enjoy hearing from them; it's been several months at least."

"Of course. Thank you for the call, V. And do be careful; you may be a soldier, but you're surrounded by criminals up there."

"Tell me about it," she said with a sigh. "I'll watch my back if you watch yours."

"Done."

Victoria shut her phone, looking back out the window at the street outside. She hated the type of people she had to work with these days; M's warning was legitimate. She was playing a dangerous game working against the others, but protection of the people was still her duty and if she had to do it from the inside of a viper's nest, she wouldn't shy away.

~ ~ ~ ~ ~

As M shut the phone a screen in his office began flashing, warning of rising demonic activity in a nearby building. He smiled, looking at the screen. "Speak of the devil and he shall appear," he said quietly, tapping the screen before striding through the hall to Hitomi's room, standing at the doorway and catching the attention of everyone inside. "Our spectral friend has revealed himself. Get on it."

Katsumi caught the tracker he tossed at her, immediately growing serious. The whole team jumped up as Katsumi stood, moving to follow them when something caught her shirt, preventing her from leaving. She looked back to see her sister looking at her with pleading but determined eyes. "I'm going with you."

Katsumi looked surprised, at a loss for words for a moment as she was caught off-guard. Then she smiled, holding out her hand. Ayane matched her smile, taking it, and Katsumi gripped her hand tightly as she pulled her out the door after the others. In the equipment room Hitomi looked around the quickly moving people until she spotted Katsumi.

"Can I… I want to go."

Ayane looked to Katsumi, who gave the woman a hard look. "It's dangerous."

"I know. I don't have to be in the middle of it, but this…" Hitomi took a breath, taking on a determined look. "This thing used me."

Katsumi and Ayane both took on an understanding expression at her words and Katsumi nodded, even giving her a smile of approval. "Of course. Sano? Can you stay on protection detail?"

Sano nodded with a grin. "Can do, boss."

"Good. You two will stay in the car with Reno." She looked back at Hitomi. "If this thing runs from us I want people ready to go after it, and you can help them track it."

Ayane smiled. "Just use your senses. It'll come to you."

"If you say so," Hitomi replied with a nervous smile.

Katsumi caught a pistol that Law tossed her, handing it to Ayane who immediately checked and loaded it with the same practiced ease her older sister showed, surprising Hitomi since she'd been told the girl was a civilian. "Reno, obviously you're driving."

"Yo."

"Rufus, Law, you two will be going in with me and Aya. Law, you have the gear you need?"

The muscular giant gave a nearly feral grin as he straightened up, patting the huge case at his side. "Got th' present for our friend all wrapped up an' ready for delivery."

Ayane laughed at him. "Try to look more excited, Big L!"

Law gave a deep laugh. "Kid on Christmas morning?" he asked, assuming she thought he looked like that.

"More or less." Ayane bounced over, clasping her hands behind her back and tilting her head as she inspected the huge case he held. "Can I fire it this time?"

"After what happened last time?" Katsumi asked with a raised eyebrow.

Ayane looked back at her sister. "That was an accident! I've got the hang of it now!"

Law chuckled, patting Ayane's head. "Sorry, blue-hair. Maybe if you grow a couple more feet."

"Are you calling me short?" Ayane grinned darkly. "Do you wanna fight again?"

Reno popped his head around Law's large frame. "Please do. I don't think I can die content without seeing Law get his ass kicked by a pretty girl."

Ayane laughed, but then her eyes widened. "My sister's beaten him up! Are you saying my sister isn't pretty?"

Katsumi smirked as Reno stuttered. "Uh... I was... I'm gonna get the car started!"

They laughed as he ran off and Katsumi pointed after him. "Everyone grab your gear and get to the car. We leave in two minutes with or without you!"

~ ~ ~ ~ ~

The swirl of power in the room was growing. It was impressive with all the flashing lights and heavy wind, very theatrical, Sigma thought. Joseph watched it impassively, of course, but Sigma looked very entertained. Though his eyes couldn't be seen beneath his hood, his mouth was fixed in a grin that could be described in a variety of ways, not the least of which was "unnerving".

The Shade floated in the center of the room with blue flame lashing out from it, its glowing eyes filled with hunger. Before it lay several humans who were confused and terrified, but the binds on them were strong and inescapable. Between them and the demon sat the black box Joseph had retrieved the day before; it seemed to be draining something from the unfortunate captives and transferring it to the demon, who was growing in power.

They were in an office building that had been chosen due to the fact that the company was shut down for the day, meaning there were only a few people in the building. It happened to be the perfect amount of people; enough to perform this little ritual, but too few to cause them any problems. Apart from Joseph, Sigma, the demon and the captives, there were four other people in the room; soldiers. They wore black and red armored uniforms and carried advanced rifles. On the front of each uniform was a crimson emblem of two feathery wings spreading from a saber. They were Blood Angels, members of Joseph Elwood's terrorist organization. Only four were here because the other two men in the room didn't need protection; the four soldiers were only there to perform tasks that might be needed.

The group was situated in the security room for a reason that became readily apparent; a beeping noise came from one of the computers causing Sigma and Joseph to look over and inspect the screen. It showed two doors being forced open; at the north entrance Katsumi and Ayane could be seen entering, while the south entrance was being opened by Rufus and Law.

Sigma smiled, looking to his companion. "Would you take care of this little annoyance, Joseph? We only need to stall them."

Joseph looked to the four soldiers. "Get to the south entrance. Hold off the two intruders; kill them if you get the chance." As the four saluted and exited the room at a run, Joseph himself strode toward the exit. "I will take care of the other two."

Sigma grinned as his partner left, looking back to the camera that showed the two sisters. "I do love family reunions."

~ ~ ~ ~ ~

Rufus and Law entered the building through the back entrance into a garage of some sort. The room itself was large and filled with giant boxes and crates of various sizes. "We get the storage room," Rufus noted. "This entrance assignment seems rather biased."

"I'd rather not take the front entrance."

"I always preferred to take the front entrance." Rufus smiled. "I like to warn my enemies and still avoid their preparations despite the advantage."

On a walkway that was raised a couple feet from the floor, the door burst open and the soldiers ran out, opening fire. The two SIN members hit the ground, leaping apart and each taking cover behind crates. Law put his shoulder against the crate, drawing a large shotgun from the weapon harness on his back. "Looks like they got a warning anyway."

Rufus adjusted his shades as he crouched behind his cover. "It's always *those* desires that are granted. It seems God has a bias, too." He took the chance to look over the crate, ducking back down quickly as shots tore up the edge of it. "Blood Angels," he said, clearly surprised.

"You're kidding." Law grunted, sliding the first two shells into the chamber of his shotgun.

"Wish I knew what they were doing here. Does this demon have terrorist connections?"

"It doesn't bode well, does it?"

Law stood up, unloading fire rapidly and causing the Angels to scatter before he ducked back down. "Only winged one. I wonder if th' Captain's having these problems."

~ ~ ~ ~ ~

"Blood Angels?" Katsumi frowned as she held a hand to her ear, gripping her pistol tighter.

Ayane blinked and looked at her in confusion. "What? Here? Why?"

"They don't know," she answered. "We'll keep a lookout," she replied to Rufus, "but we've got nothing right now."

They'd entered into the building's lobby. It was a very nice area with a lot of marble; smooth floors, large columns. To either side there were two staircases that led up to an open second floor where they could see the elevators. In front of them was a curved receptionist's desk, behind which were several doors.

The two sisters gripped their weapons tightly as they moved forward, each one alert and ready. They both paused at the same time, looking at each other with disturbed expressions. "Do you feel that…?" Ayane asked quietly, to which Katsumi responded with a nod.

Joseph suddenly landed hard on the receptionist's desk right in front of them, his long coat fanning out around him as his impact scattered papers up into the air around them. Both girls were shocked but their reaction time was still only a few milliseconds and both took aim and pulled the triggers.

Joseph was, however, even faster; his saber flashed in a movement too quick to follow, so quick that the air from the slash was several seconds behind. The sound of the front halves of their pistols hitting the marble echoed around them and before they could react further the older man spun as his foot lashed out, knocking both girls across the lobby and into the glass at the front, which thankfully didn't break.

Katsumi yanked a second pistol from the back of her belt, the one she'd kept with her for so long for this exact purpose, and opened fire on their father. Joseph leapt upwards in a graceful back flip onto the upper balcony. His sword flashed twice and a piece of the metal railing was suddenly hanging free in the air for a second before his free hand caught it and flung it at Katsumi in a blur.

She dodged to the side but the bar hit her hand, breaking several bones in it and sending her pistol backwards through the glass behind her and out onto the street. Katsumi cried out at the pain in her hand and Ayane bared her teeth in anger, vaulting up the stairs onto the second floor and charging Joseph. Her hands and feet moved rapidly and expertly but her father barely even seemed to try as he dodged, simply leaning or taking a single step in one direction or another.

His expression had remained the same the entire time, calm and impassive, uninterested even. Despite this Katsumi knew he could kill her sister at any time with the saber hanging from his right hand so she ran for the stairs herself, willing her legs to get her there as fast as they could. Joseph didn't seem interested in killing, however. He finally caught his youngest daughter's wrist in his empty hand, shaking his head as if in disappointment as he flung her aside and into the elevator doors to his left. She hit them hard enough to dent the metal inwards, slumping to the ground with all the breath knocked out of her, her fists still clenching in anger.

"Ayane!" Joseph turned as his eldest daughter reached him in a rage, launching her unbroken left fist at him. He shifted to the side with little effort and his own hand curled into a fist, driving up into Katsumi's stomach with an impact that sounded like a gunshot. Katsumi's eyes went wide as all air left her lungs and she coughed up blood that spattered onto Joseph's arm.

"Katsumi!" Ayane yelled as she pushed herself up from the wall, steadying herself against it.

Katsumi seemed frozen at the moment, her face a mask of wide-eyed pain as she leaned against her father, unable to move or even breathe. Joseph placed a finger beneath her chin, pushing her back enough to look at her face. "I had thought perhaps you had improved since our last real meeting," he said in an even tone.

Katsumi finally managed to grit her teeth, though her body still refused to move. "You-" She was cut off with a pathetic, whimper-like cry as Joseph's hand slammed into her stomach again. This time the blow lifted her off her feet and into the air and sent her rolling and tumbling until she skidded to a stop, laying face-down.

Ayane watched with a dozen emotions as Katsumi slowly placed her unbroken hand on the floor, attempting to push herself up, shuddering with every movement. She managed to make it to her knees but her hand remained on the floor supporting her. Her broken hand was pressed against her stomach as her body shook unnaturally, her eyes once more frozen wide open in shock and agony. She coughed again and more blood fell to the floor beneath her, dripping from her lips.

Ayane ran to her and fell to her knees to slide to a stop beside her, setting her hand on her sister's shoulder. "Katsumi…" Her voice was torn between anger and fear as she laid her right hand on Katsumi's on the floor, reaching her left up to brush her sister's violet hair out of her face. "You'll be okay," she stated softly, trying to convince herself as much as her sister.

Joseph shook his head. "This… is pathetic." Ayane shot him a glare filled with hatred, while Katsumi was still shaking, unable to move enough to even look up. "This is supposed to be my legacy," he said in disbelief. His words were made even worse by the lack of emotion in them; if they were filled with anger, hate, even sadness, anything, it would've been better. But they were even and uninterested, showing not even the slightest bit of care for his daughters, not even the negative kind.

Ayane growled, starting to stand before she felt Katsumi's fingers weakly grip her own. She looked to her sister who was still unable to move, but she saw added fear in her lavender eyes now. She understood that her sister knew neither of them could take on their father, and she could see how scared she was of what would happen to Ayane if she tried. So instead she threw another glare at Joseph, remaining at Katsumi's side. "Your legacy is hatred, cruelty and the murder of your wife, nothing more."

Joseph slid his saber back into his belt. "Naomi died by Katsumi's hand, not mine."

"That's a lie!" Ayane yelled, her voice full of rage. She could feel her sister shaking beside her and saw the tears forming in her eyes and dropping to the floor that her gaze remained fixed on; tears of frustration, hatred and sorrow. Ayane understood all of it; after all the times she'd promised to kill this man, all the promises she'd made that she'd protect Aya from him, and their dreams that they'd be entirely free of him one day...

He shattered all of that in his usual cold manner. They couldn't kill him; they hadn't even been able to touch him. He could've killed either – or both – of them at any time; he simply hadn't because he, apparently, didn't think them worth the effort. It seemed they weren't even a big enough annoyance to be removed.

"Believe whatever you wish to believe," Joseph stated, obviously not caring what they wanted to think was the truth. He lifted his phone to his ear as it signaled and Sigma's voice crackled into life.

"I hate to cut the play short considering how much I'm enjoying all three of your performances, but it's done."

"Very well." Joseph shut his phone, taking another look down at his children. "If this is as strong as you can be, then I was wasting my time with you in the first place." He turned his back and walked away. "I suggest you simply stay out of the way."

As he disappeared from sight Katsumi began to fall but Ayane caught her, pulling her against herself and not caring as her own hair and clothing got Katsumi's blood on it. "It's okay," she whispered to her older sister.

Katsumi closed her eyes, her jaw clenching with a shudder of pain. Her breathing was extremely shallow and she found it impossible to actually speak out loud. *It's not fair... We worked-*

"I know," Ayane cut her off, looking at the exit Joseph had taken. "But this just means we haven't found the way to do it yet. We will." She watched Katsumi nod silently and tried to keep her own hands from making fists. She lifted Katsumi's shirt very gently, inhaling sharply as she saw her stomach; the skin was already dark and the bruising was spreading, purple and even black in some spots. "The internal bleeding is... worse than I thought," she said softly, her voice nearly breaking.

Ayane kept one arm on Katsumi's back and slid her other beneath her legs, lifting her up and making sure her head was resting on her shoulder as she steadied her feet. Katsumi gave a very slight smile. *I prefer being the one carrying...*

"And I prefer being carried," Ayane smiled as she carefully made her way down the stairs. Her back burned with pain thanks to the meeting with the elevator doors, but at least she could move; she'd get it checked as soon as her sister was examined. "I don't think that would work very well this time, though, Sumi." She heard a faint rasping that she was able to recognize as a chuckle; this wasn't the first time either of them had been hurt so badly, after all, which was the only reason Ayane was able to remain as calm as she was.

As she came into view of the car Hitomi gasped in shock and Sano and Reno leapt out of the car, running to her. "What the hell happened?!" Sano yelled.

Ayane sighed gratefully as he and Reno helped her lay Katsumi in the car's back seat. She gave Sano a hard look. "Father," she said in such a cold, hate-filled voice that suddenly everyone could see just how similar the two sisters were in many ways. She then climbed into the car and moved to sit under Katsumi, laying her older sister's head in her lap.

Hitomi worriedly looked over her seat, speaking quietly to Ayane about Katsumi's injuries. What she wanted most to ask about was the fact that Ayane had just said their father had done this, which she could barely believe; fortunately she managed to stay quiet on that, figuring it wouldn't help at this moment. Still, she filed it away for later.

Sano and Reno looked at each other, their own anger rising. "I'm going in," stated Sano, drawing his pistol.

"No!" Ayane yelled, looking at him worriedly. "He'll kill you. That gun won't do anything to him." Her eyes narrowed as she continued speaking through bared teeth, "We were just lucky he didn't kill us."

Sano growled, looking back at the building. Reno set his hand on Sano's shoulder. "She's right. He may have left his daughters alive, but I doubt he'd do the same for any of us."

Hitomi moved to the edge of the car, leaning out. "We should tell the others what happened. What if he runs into them?"

"Shit," Sano muttered as he clapped a hand to his ear.

~ ~ ~ ~ ~

Rufus and Law watched as the two Blood Angels they hadn't killed ran back through the door, shutting it behind them. "They're retreating?" Law said with a frown.

Rufus stood up, heading for the door. "Or they're done." He paused as he noticed he was being contacted, and who by. "Sano? Something wrong at the car?" he said as he looked behind them, ready to run back out to them if they were in trouble.

"Wrong on Katsumi's end," Sano replied, obviously angry. "She's seriously injured, barely conscious."

"Fuck!" Rufus cursed, looking at Law who was listening as well and seemed to be growing angrier by the second. "What happened? Is Ayane hurt too?"

They heard Sano ask, followed by his reply, "Yes, but not bad. She says it's only some bruising. She said they ran into their father in there."

Law growled, heading for the door the Angels had retreated through. "The fuck is he doing here?"

"That might explain the Blood Angels," Rufus said as he followed Law. "They must be working with him."

"Hold on…" The two heard the door open behind them and saw Sano enter. "Ayane's watching the others," he continued in person, catching up to them. "We're gonna check for this demon. But she made me promise we'd leave if we saw Elwood."

Law slammed his fist into the locked door, punching it straight off its hinges and watching it crash to the ground. "We'll try…"

Rufus finished reloading his pistol, chambering a round. "…But no promises."

"That's what I said," Sano agreed.

The three entered cautiously and then began moving quickly through the halls. Eventually they found the security room and Sano's hands dropped to his sides as they saw the obviously-lifeless human bodies. "Damn it… Too late."

"They're long gone," Rufus said as he typed a few things on the security console and let out an angry breath. "Wiped the camera records, too."

Law shook his head. "Guess we weren't meant to end things here."

Sano called in the body count and then looked to the others. "Let's hope we get another chance."

~ ~ ~ ~ ~

Ayane sat in the back of the large car with Katsumi's head in her lap, watching her breathe as she held on to her. It seemed that, lately, every day together ended with one of them in pain. Today couldn't be blamed on any accidental sickness, though; this was all the fault of the man they hated most.

She looked up as she felt the car shake, watching Sano, Rufus and Law climb back in. Reno started the car as Ayane leaned forward. "Did you find anything?"

"Just bodies," Rufus muttered, looking back over the seat. He removed his shades, ice blue eyes focusing on Katsumi. "Is she okay?" he asked with a hint of concern in his voice.

"No worse than we've been a million times," Ayane answered with a sad smile.

Rufus smirked at that, sliding his shades back on. "Survivors. I admire that more than anything."

Ayane gave him an appraising look that he met with his own gaze, seeing in him an understanding about certain things that most people would never be able to accept; Katsumi had told her about his past as an assassin and she saw it now, that will to do anything to survive, the will that had pushed him to do things normal people would never consider, just like it had pushed her and Katsumi. She gave him an appreciative smile – appreciative of both the sentiment and his skills – and he returned it. It was rare they met anyone that shared an understanding of those certain things.

She was brought out of her thoughts by Law, who tried to look less worried than he was as he asked, "Is it bad? An' what about you?"

"Internal bleeding," Ayane answered the first question, deciding to take a clinical approach rather than an emotional one in order to keep her emotions in check. "I'm not sure of the extent of her injuries; I only know that he caused a lot of damage to her core. Certainly some muscle tearing and… I'd say the lower two ribs, at least, are broken, though it's probably four…" Ayane looked down at her sister. "I've been listening to her breathing and her lungs seem to be working; she coughed up blood so I think one may have been punctured by a rib, but that isn't as serious an injury as it would have been when we were… fully human."

Law reached a large hand back and patted her shoulder. "It's alright, blue-hair. You can get upset."

Ayane took a deep breath, fixing him a strong gaze. "I get upset after the fact." She gave a weary smile. "Once she's stable, recovering and awake, then I'll get all emotional. But you keep control of the emotion before then, because that's when you need to make rational decisions and get things done."

Hitomi watched her, having been listening quietly up until that point. "That sounds like a very difficult way to live…"

Ayane's blue eyes shifted to her and she smiled again. "It's a difficult way to live, but the only way to survive. If we lost ourselves to emotion any time one of us was hurt, we would've been dead by now. Once you've been through enough, eventually you learn to keep control when it matters, and only let it go when you're already safe. If you break down crying in the middle of a fight, that's a weakness that might just get you killed. Then you won't get to cry about it later."

Rufus spoke up, drawing the attention of the others to him. "They're professionals," he said simply; to him it was a factual statement, a description worthy of respect. "You have to master your emotions as thoroughly as you master your body if you want to be the best." He looked back and met Ayane's eyes. "I didn't join this team because they do good or because they protect people. If I'm honest, I don't care about any of that. I would've joined if they were criminals, too."

Hitomi blinked. "You'd work for criminals?"

"I did," Rufus smiled in amusement at her before he looked back to Ayane as if making sure she knew he meant what he said. "I joined because of Katsumi. I haven't respected anyone in a long time as much as I respect her. She's not just a survivor, she's a fighter, determined to do what it takes to make it. I'll be on her side no matter what she chooses to do." He extended a hand over the seat. "And after the few days I've known you, I've discovered you to be the same kind of person. So I'm on your side, too."

Ayane smiled, accepting the hand with a firm grip. Again that understanding passed between them; the others in the car were idealists and optimists. Ayane, Katsumi and Rufus were pragmatists, though; realists. They knew that, sometimes, you had to put survival over morals if you wanted to live. Sometimes you needed to just do what it takes and damn the consequences.

"I appreciate your respect and loyalty to my sister," Ayane said softly. "We lived a long time without seeing much loyalty. Allies are important to have." She gave a wry smile as she tilted her head. "Especially allies who understand you'll shoot them in the back if you have to."

Rufus chuckled, and both of them enjoyed more the looks of confusion on the others who were trying to understand how that was funny; they never would, which was even more amusing to the two. They were looking for a joke, but Rufus and Ayane were laughing because they understood that dismal fact as the unavoidable truth, and they understood that the only way to live with such a truth was to laugh at it.

~ ~ ~ ~ ~

Hours after the car had arrived at the hospital Ayane stood beside the bed watching her sister open her eyes. Night had fallen by now; it'd taken the doctors hours to stabilize Katsumi's condition. Ayane had been correct in her assessment of her injuries. The doctors had been shocked at the damage done and asked if she'd been in some sort of a construction accident. Fortunately they'd been able to repair most of it, though they said moving would be hard for a few days.

Ayane smiled at her sister once she noticed her eyes focus. "I'm supposed to be the one in the hospital bed. It's not nice of you to change our positions without telling me."

Katsumi groaned, closing her eyes for a second. At first Ayane was worried, but when she opened them again she seemed much more awake and alert. "I'm older," she said in a raspy voice. "I get to make the decisions."

"That's not fair. I'll have you know-"

"Aya..." Katsumi said softly. Ayane met her gaze and wasn't surprised her sister had already figured out she was avoiding things. Katsumi held her arm out and she took the invitation to climb onto the bed, carefully curling up against her side. Just as she'd explained earlier she began to cry, taking comfort in the arm around her that rubbed her shoulder, and the whispered words.

She'd lost count of how many times they'd played through this sequence of events. Eventually the repetition itself became comforting in some twisted way, as if it promised that it would always happen and neither of them would actually die. But this time Ayane also found herself crying over their father and their failure. And this time Katsumi was the one promising her things would change and it would eventually be over.

Ayane looked up as she felt Katsumi's fingers wipe the tears from her cheeks. "You know the worst part? He told us to leave... He gave us the option to get out of the way and we... we can't take it."

Her sister shook her head, sighing. "No, we can't. As much as we want an ending, we both know the only way it can come."

Ayane nodded. "I just... I just wish we had a guarantee. I wish we knew when it would happen. It's been almost twenty years, now, since we started running. Will it be another twenty?"

Katsumi traced her fingers down her cheek and Ayane leaned into the hand, looking at her for some sort of certainty. She got it, because her older sister gave her a smile that seemed to ignore everything that said their hopes were impossible. "It won't be twenty. It won't even be two. If you've ever trusted me at all, Aya, then trust me on this: before this year is out, we'll be free of him. I promise you."

Ayane sighed, a smile spreading across her face at the words. She trusted them; truly, she did. Her doubts disappeared all at once because, in over thirty-one years of life, Katsumi had never once failed to deliver on a promise. Not once. She still had no idea how it would happen, but that didn't matter anymore now that she knew it would. She laid her head back down, saying softly, "Thank you, Sumi."

Katsumi let out a breath, giving her own smile as she threaded her fingers through Ayane's, holding her hand. She didn't know how they'd do it, either, but that was no longer the point. It didn't matter how, it didn't matter where, and it didn't matter what she'd have to do in order to make it happen. All that mattered was that, somehow, she was going to do it. For herself. For their mother.

And, most importantly, for Ayane.

Chapter 14: Restless

Date: April 9, 2068
Time: 12:17 PM
Location: Tokyo Metro's Marunouchi Line from
Shinjuku Station

To absolutely no one's surprise, Katsumi was out of the hospital already. Ayane had barely managed to convince her to sleep in, and that had only worked because she couldn't get out of bed without her help. Now, as the two rode the subway, Ayane was of course taking advantage of the captive audience and lecturing her about her health.

"It's just not smart. I don't know how you've survived so long, refusing to get healthy before moving on," she said with an exasperated sigh.

Katsumi smirked as she watched her sister cease her animated hand gestures and slump back in defeat. "Are you done?"

Ayane jerked forward again, pointing her finger in Katsumi's face. "Not even close! I'm not done with you until you learn how to take care of yourself."

Katsumi sighed, looking away. "I miss my normal crutches. At least they were quiet."

"Are you telling me to shut up?" Ayane narrowed her eyes. "Because I think you're telling me to shut up."

Katsumi didn't know what it was, but for some reason whenever Ayane got into full-blown mothering mode, she herself took the role of a petulant child. Psychologists likely had all sorts of words for it, but she only knew it as 'fun'. She looked back at her younger sister with wide eyes, overdoing the 'innocent' tone as she replied, "I would *never* secretly wish for you to stop talking, dear sister!"

That obviously wasn't bought for a second. Ayane folded her arms and gave her a stern-but-amused look, and Katsumi couldn't prevent a smile at how much she reminded her of their mother at that moment. "Do I have to turn this train around? Apparently you need more discipline."

Katsumi grinned. "How are you planning to discipline me?"

Ayane blinked, then frowned, then looked at the ceiling in thought. "I don't know yet." Her sister chuckled and she glared at her. "I'll think of something!"

"That's a terrifying threat."

Ayane huffed. "You're mean."

"Sorry. It's just hard to fear you."

Ayane frowned. "Well… maybe I'll let it go this once."

"Can't remember what you were mad about, can you?"

"It'll come to me!"

"Uh-huh." Katsumi leaned her head back with a smile.

They got off at their stop near the HQ and headed for the building. Though Katsumi could more or less walk on her own, Ayane insisted on supporting her, so she had her arms around one of Katsumi's as they walked, letting her lean into her when she had to.

The main problem was that, while Katsumi's limbs were more or less fine (with the exception of her damaged right hand), her core had been severely damaged. Though the damage had mostly been fixed she was still in a fair amount of pain and had trouble holding herself up, as her abdominal muscles seemed all but useless at the moment.

Katsumi soon found she'd overestimated her ability a bit and ended up with her arm around Ayane's shoulders. Fortunately her sister was too concerned to say "I told you so", but she figured she deserved it anyway so she brought it up herself. "Okay…" She grimaced a bit. "You were right. Maybe I should've stayed in bed a bit longer."

Ayane sighed, stopping to look her sister over. "I knew it was a bad idea." She laid her hand on Katsumi's stomach, lifting her shirt. "Well, you don't seem to be bleeding again," she said with relief before looking at her with worried eyes. "Do you want to go back?"

"We're already here," Katsumi said with a nod at the building. "Might as well go in. I don't plan on doing anything today, don't worry."

"Asking me not to worry is like-"

"Asking rain not to fall, I know." Katsumi smiled at her. "You're here in person, though, so I have nothing to worry about."

Ayane allowed herself to smile at that; yes, she was back to being at her side instead of on the sidelines. "C'mon, let's get inside where you can sit down."

Once inside the building they ran into Kurasano, who warily asked, "Hey guys, how're you doing? Are your injuries... er... better?"

Katsumi sighed, not out of exasperation, but acceptance. "Just fine, Sano," she said with a small smile. "Painful but healing."

It looked like his assumptions had been right; normally asking his boss about injuries was a bad move, but she seemed not to care – and was more honest – since she was with her sister at the moment. Sano had to wonder just how much of her mood was based around Ayane. "How about you?" he said with a look to the younger girl.

Ayane blinked. "Me? Oh, I'm fine," she smiled. "I got checked up just in case, but they said I didn't take any real damage. I was lucky I hit the elevator doors; the thinner metal bent during the impact. A solid wall would've caused more damage."

Katsumi nodded. "Combined with a knowledge of how to minimize impact damage, she escaped with some bruises and nothing else."

Despite passing it off as light, Sano noticed an undertone of failure in Katsumi's statement; judging by Ayane's look at her older sister, she caught it, too. He wisely decided it wasn't his business and moved onto another topic. "Oh! One of our clean-up crew found this; fortunately I recognized it," he said as he pulled a pistol from his bag.

Katsumi and Ayane both looked at it in recognition and Katsumi took it with a sad smile. "Thank you, Sano. It wasn't any use yesterday, but hopefully it will still fulfill its intended purpose at some point."

Sano ran a hand over his hair. "Um... Yeah, I'm just gonna skip past that awkward conversation."

"Good idea," Ayane said with a smile. "In fact, let's all do that."

Since he could tell neither of them wanted to go back to that subject he felt annoyed at himself, having moved from one bad subject to another. Best to quit while you're behind, he thought. "Alright, well I'm gonna get going. M has me looking into something we found at the scene; weird box thing, don't know what it does yet. Did learn it was stolen from some murdered Red Sun members during transport, though, so me an' Rufus are gonna see what they know."

Katsumi frowned. "First Blood Angels were involved with that incident yesterday, and now Red Sun? What's going on?"

Sano shrugged. "Beats me. Not often you see crime wars and demons intersecting this much."

"Not to mention Father has something to do with this," Ayane said quietly. "But what, I can't imagine. Do you think he's working with the Blood Angels, Sumi?"

Katsumi blinked. "Sano, did you learn how those Red Sun members died?"

"Uh… Yeah!" He nodded. "I remember 'cause it was kinda odd; they were cut up, like with a sword." He blinked as both girls in front of him gained hard looks that made him nervous. "Did I say something wrong?"

"He uses a saber," Ayane replied fiercely.

"In 2068? When everybody else is using crazy amounts of guns and exploding things?"

"He's… not human," Katsumi said as she shook her head. "If you're different… Or you have a high enough CP… A melee weapon like that becomes a lot more useful because you're so much faster and stronger." Katsumi looked at her sister, her expression changing to one of pride. "Aya is actually rather amazing with a sword."

Ayane looked embarrassed. "I wouldn't say *amazing*." She sighed. "I'm not as good as Father, unfortunately. I've tried beating him that way. Anyway, we were both taught to use swords from a young age; speed, utility, versatility, no ammunition, and great stealth value. Not to mention that when you can punch through concrete, swinging a blade actually has more force than most bullets."

"Wow. I didn't know all this." He looked at Katsumi. "Does this mean you have a sword, boss?"

Katsumi frowned as Ayane giggled at her. "I do… I never quite took to it like Aya did."

"Sumi doesn't really like swinging things," Ayane said with a smile. "She prefers hand-to-hand, you know. It's actually best if she doesn't use one because this one time-"

"ANYway," Katsumi cut her off, eliciting a laugh from her sister, "The point is that they're not my thing. And getting back to the original point, I'm almost certain Joseph killed those men and stole that box, considering we encountered him where the box was left."

"Alright," Sano nodded, accepting that assumption. "And what about the Blood Angels? Is he working for them?"

Ayane shook her head. "That doesn't sound right. Father never liked working for others."

"Several years ago their leader was killed," Katsumi stated. "We never learned the identity of the new leader."

Sano's eyes widened. "Wait… You think Joseph Elwood is leading the Blood Angels?"

Ayane bit her lip. "It does make all the facts fit."

"So your murderous, beyond-human, lunatic asshole of a father is heading one of the most powerful terrorist organizations in the world, and they're currently helping a possible Ancient One demon do who-knows-what."

"That seems to be the situation…" Katsumi grunted, leaning more heavily against Ayane who shot her a worried look. "We'll look into all of this, then. You and Rufus learn what you can from the Red Suns. Be careful. In the meantime we're going to talk to Hitomi."

"Sounds good. What are you going to tell her about yesterday?"

"The truth," Ayane said with a shrug.

Katsumi nodded her assent. "Now's not the time for secrets, and besides, she deserves to know what she might be in the middle of."

"That's good. She has seemed a little lost."

"We're here to fix that," Ayane assured him. "Now, if you don't mind, I need to get my sister to at least sit down somewhere."

"Oh, right. Take it easy you two," he said as he headed for the exit.

"Sure," Katsumi said to her sister after he left, "just treat me like an invalid."

"Pff, what are you going to do about it?"

"…Something."

"Uh-huh," Ayane replied with a truly disbelieving look.

"I'll do something!"

"I believe you."

"Really, I will!"

"I'm sure you will, Sumi. I'm sure you will." She grinned at her older sister's defeated sigh as they walked slowly through the hallway, Katsumi leaning on her more as they went. It was obvious she shouldn't have even left the hospital, but seeing as how she was *impossible*, Ayane had no idea how she could've kept her there. They made it to Hitomi's room and, out of a good bit of luck, the woman was returning to it right as they got there.

"Katsumi, Ayane!" she said in surprise, switching the bag of food she held into one hand so she could open the door. "What are you two doing here?" She looked at Katsumi in confusion. "Shouldn't you be in the hospital?"

Ayane shot her sister a glare as she adjusted the arm around her shoulders. "She *should*. Sumi is very stubborn."

"I hate hospitals," Katsumi said with a sigh. "And staying in bed."

"That isn't healthy! You could be doing yourself more harm!" Hitomi said with a disapproving look. Katsumi only grunted in response; it wasn't like she could argue considering that she was currently slumped against her sister and, if it wasn't for her strong hold, she wouldn't even be standing. Hitomi swung the door open wide. "Well, get in here, at least you can lie on my bed."

They walked in and Ayane helped Katsumi into a chair. "That's too much like being stuck in bed to her," she stated, worriedly watching Katsumi wince as she bent enough to sit down.

"Honestly, Sumi…"

"Okay, *enough*," Katsumi said with a tone of finality, her expression becoming more serious.

Ayane understood she'd gone a little too far; certainly she was allowed to say what she wanted to her sister, and to worry and chide her and tell her what she should be doing. Others weren't allowed into that, though, and Ayane realized she'd been a bit too open around Sano and Hitomi about her injuries. Katsumi *hated* people seeing or hearing about her being hurt; she shouldn't, but Ayane understood it like she did everything, so she should have remembered to keep it more private than she was doing. She sat close beside her in the chair, whispering into her ear rather than using the cyber link because it felt more sincere, "Sorry, Sumi. I guess I'm not used to talking to your friends yet."

Katsumi immediately smiled, her fingers affectionately brushing Ayane's hair from her face as she spoke softly, "It's alright. I'm sorry for sounding harsh, I just-"

"I know," Ayane cut her off with a smile, giving her a look that showed she truly understood. "I kind of got angry and forgot I was sharing a little much."

Katsumi chuckled. "I noticed. Trust me, next time I'll listen to you."

Ayane's eyes shone. "Promise?"

"Promise."

For her part, the polite Hitomi didn't listen in as the sisters whispered to each other, instead taking the chance to set out her food on her table and adjust the curtains to the now-noon light since she hadn't been in since morning. She smiled happily as she looked out of the window. It really was a nice room they had her set up in, more like a nice apartment, really. Once she decided to stay longer they'd moved her to this expanded room. Now she had things put the way she liked it.

The room they were in was now set up to be a living room, with comfortable seating and a TV. She also had a bedroom, a bathroom, and a small kitchen. It was far more than she'd expected. She and Sano had gone again to get more of her things that morning, so now she had the place the way she wanted.

Having finished their quiet exchange Ayane looked around the room, admiring the set-up. "You've really put some effort into this place, Hitomi. It seems very homey."

She smiled, looking at Ayane. "Thank you. They've been very generous, and honestly it was rather unexpected. When I first heard I'd have to stay here I thought it'd just be, you know, a bed in a room."

"You aren't the first person we've had to keep here for protection," Katsumi responded. "I'm glad you find it acceptable."

"It's more than acceptable." She turned away from the window then, smiling a little shyly. "Honestly, I've never been a person to have a lot of friends. I have people I know, but I spend a lot of time alone." She clasped her hands in front of her, walking over to take a seat at the table. "It's nice staying here surrounded by people. And you're all friendly."

"What about the danger aspect?"

"Honestly? I thought I'd be bothered by it more than I am. Instead it's… exciting." Hitomi gave a grin, looking back out the window. "I've always been interested in ghosts and spirits and creepy things. It started because of my experiences, but moved beyond that. I'm so happy now that I've been shown I wasn't crazy or anything. More than that, I'm interested. It's all so different and incredible."

Katsumi gave a slight smirk, tilting her head. "Want a job?"

Hitomi blinked, looking at her in surprise. "What?"

"A job." Katsumi's smirk widened into a grin. "You're a Silent. You have a very rare gift, one that could be put to incredible use here. You're already forming bonds with the team. You're interested in what we do, you have an admirable ability to adapt to new situations, and most importantly for me, it seems you *want* to be here."

"Do you…" Hitomi leaned forward, speaking in disbelief. "Do you really think I could?"

"Well I'm not going to send you into combat, but I don't send Reno into combat either. And given enough time your abilities would make that a moot point anyway. But if you're willing to put in the work and dedication it takes, then yes, I think you could."

Hitomi broke out into a huge grin. "This is… This is amazing! Are you… Do I really get to do this with this team? I mean, two weeks ago I was selling flowers, now I'm going to be dealing with ghosts, spirits and demons?"

"Katsumi has a unique way of choosing people," Ayane added, drawing the attention to her. "You're getting the offer because you're a Silent, obviously, otherwise you'd have nothing to add to the team. But she wouldn't offer it to you even though you are one without you being the person you are. It's that combination she wants."

Katsumi nodded. "Everyone on this team was hand-picked by myself and M. I had the final say, and while each person has a set of skills I wanted, the specific individuals were chosen based on factors like personality, morals and personal history."

"What about Rufus?" Hitomi asked quietly. "He said he was a terrorist…"

Katsumi raised an eyebrow. "He did? That's odd."

Ayane shook her head. "He said he'd worked with them. She assumes it's the same thing."

"Oh, I see," Katsumi nodded. "Yes, Rufus didn't have any particular preference when it came to employer. I actually met him when we were both on a job after the same person, he for another criminal organization and myself for a counter-terrorist unit."

"Why did you choose a criminal to add to your team?"

Katsumi looked at her sadly. "It's nice to think the way you do; to believe that right or wrong comes down to a simple choice, and anyone doing something you consider 'wrong' simply chose that path. The fact is that everyone's concept of these things is different. Rufus didn't wake up every morning and think to himself, 'I'm going to do some evil things today'. No, he woke up and said, 'today I'm going to do my job', just like I did, just like you did. He doesn't see his job here as any different than that one."

Hitomi shook her head. "That's such an odd way to think…"

"Maybe," Katsumi said with a shrug.

"You have to remember," Ayane spoke up, "that his past wasn't yours. Katsumi and I have done things I *know* you wouldn't approve of, and the thing is, most of them we don't regret. It's idealistic to think that you'll always have a 'correct' choice you can make, but thinking that way would've driven us insane in our lives."

"That's how Sano thinks," Katsumi added. "He's far more idealistic than we are. He often has problems with actions I take. You probably have the most in common with him, and that's fine. One of the reasons I picked him was because of that. I think our team needs someone like that, someone who will strive for the most just and righteous path, because if I don't have someone like that, I know how I'll act."

"How will you act?" Hitomi asked softly but curiously.

Katsumi's eyes grew a bit distant, but she answered. "I'm very… pragmatic. As well as judgmental, vengeful, violent, and harsh. I have a lot of what are considered 'personality flaws' by others but 'lessons learned' by myself, due to the life Ayane and I have led. If I believe someone will be a threat, I'll usually pursue a very final solution as the first option. Sano, though, can usually keep this from happening. He'll tell me about how people can change and who deserves a chance, and many times, I'll realize he's right and listen. I'm cynical so I rarely think of it myself."

Hitomi looked to Ayane. "What about you? Are you the same way?"

Ayane smiled. "Katsumi's very *direct*," she started, looking at her sister and receiving a smile. "She tends to be outwardly harsh and abrasive with others, even when she knows them. Whether or not she's friendly depends on her mood and the situation, but she's always caring, and I think that's important to remember." Ayane looked back to Hitomi. "The reason I'm saying this is that I tend to be a lot friendlier and more welcoming. I'm easier to meet, not to mention a lot less intimidating because I don't often do that 'grrr' glare."

Hitomi smiled as Katsumi laughed, making Ayane grin at her sister before looking back to the other girl and continuing, "I'm more light-hearted with everyone, while Sumi tends to only be that way with me. Because of this personality difference, people often tend to assume I'm different from Katsumi in terms of actions, morals, and what I'm willing to do. Right?"

Hitomi nodded a little. "I admit, I've thought that."

"Right." Ayane smiled, but this time it didn't reach her eyes and seemed dry. "Well, that's why they're always more surprised when I break someone's neck than they are when she does it. Here's the thing to remember: Katsumi and I? We're dead in agreement on how things should be done, and what's okay. We've had the same life, we've learned the same lessons, and we've never been apart for more than a week, not in over thirty years of life. We've both killed many people, we've both done things that we'll probably never tell you not because we're ashamed, but because, really, it would be impossible for you to understand."

Hitomi sighed. "I guess I can see the logic in what you're saying. I just grew up with that whole 'superhero' mindset; you know, thinking only the bad guys killed people and the good guys were shining knights without a stain on them. I know it's not realistic, I've always known that, but I suppose 'idealist' just describes me well."

"And that's okay," Katsumi said with a smile. "In truth, all we ask is that you try not to judge people like me, Ayane and Rufus at face value, because you don't really know what our lives have been like or why we've done anything we've done."

"I won't," Hitomi promised them. "I'd never do that. I don't care what you've done in your past; you saved me, and you're becoming my friends, and you want me to work with you. And more than that I care about you. As far as your past goes... I'm sad that you had to go through what was obviously too hard for me to understand. But the only feeling I have about the things you did to survive is that I'm glad you did it so you could be here today."

Both sisters smiled and Katsumi nodded gratefully. "Thank you. Few people are understanding enough to accept someone wholly that way."

"We appreciate it more than you know," Ayane added. "And now that that's over, we can get to what we came here for in the first place."

Hitomi blinked. "Oh, right! I didn't even think about a reason for your being here."

"We don't really need one," Katsumi assured her. "But it's even more important if you're joining. We need to teach you how to control your Silent abilities."

"It would be nice to even know what they are. I mean, starting with basic things, why is it called a 'Silent'?"

"It sounds like a bit of a misnomer at first," Ayane admitted. "Really, you'd think it should be called a 'Speaker' considering you can speak with spirits. But the name 'Silent' is very, very old. It was coined thousands of years ago. People thought that, since someone could speak with spirits, the spirits would be able to use them as a sort of vessel into our world."

"So they were forbidden from speaking normally," Katsumi continued. "In extreme cases they were forced to wear masks, had their tongues cut out, or had their lips sewn together. The whole point was to prevent them from speaking to anyone but spirits because they feared the spirits would escape through their speech."

"That's horrible," Hitomi said as she subconsciously traced a finger over her lips.

Katsumi shrugged. "People fear the unknown. Really it isn't that surprising; they had no reason to believe otherwise, and it isn't the only time ignorance caused such things to happen. Fortunately this is a better age since most people don't know we exist. Now we keep quiet about what we are, which means the name 'Silent' is still fitting. You can't tell anyone outside of this group what you are unless they're a spouse; it's simply too dangerous."

Hitomi nodded. "All of that makes sense. So what, specifically, is a Silent? What can I do?"

"Those are two different questions," Katsumi said with a smile. "I'll handle the first one?" At Ayane's nod she continued, "A Silent is basically a conduit between both planes. It's kind of like you have one foot in the Underworld, so you can see and interact with everything else that's in the same position."

"Okay… So, being in that position, what can I do?"

Ayane jumped to her feet. "My turn!" With a grin she lifted a hand, holding it before her as if she was holding a ball. The room instantly became colder as senses seemed to dull; the colors of the room washed out a bit and sound seemed like it was coming from further away, and even touch was strangely distant. Ayane closed her hand into a fist and she faded, her image now blurry and transparent.

Hitomi just watched without an idea of how to respond, not really knowing what was going on, until Ayane waved and stepped through a wall, at which point she jumped. "What… I mean… What?!"

Ayane stepped out through the wall beside her, swinging a fist at her with a wide grin. Hitomi flinched but the hand simply passed through her, leaving a cold feeling behind. She heard Ayane laugh as the girl backed away, returning to normal. The room also returned to normal as Ayane explained, "Basically, becoming a ghost is one of your abilities. If you weren't a Silent I'd have been invisible to you. You'll be invisible to most people. If you stay too long you'll make the room cold, though, and electronics will start going all crazy, so it's not perfect." She tilted her head. "Unless you *want* to create cold spots and mess with technology to scare people, then it's *really* useful."

Katsumi smirked. "Playing tricks isn't something a responsible Silent would do, though, I'm sure."

Ayane folded her arms. "If by 'responsible' you mean 'boring', then sure."

Hitomi leaned forward. "What else can you do?"

Ayane's smile returned, wider than before, and she lifted up her hand again. Blue flames appeared and licked over her hand, beginning to coalesce into an orb above her palm. "Aya… If you let that go you'll damage her room."

The flame disappeared and Ayane pouted at Katsumi. "It was only going to be a little…"

"What was that?" Hitomi questioned, glad it had stopped; it'd felt a little threatening.

Ayane looked back to her. "Have you heard the stories of spirits with blue lanterns? Or spirit lights? It's basically that. Spirit Fire is the actual name, and when concentrated, it can be pretty destructive. Great weapon in the right situations though."

Hitomi sat back. "Do you use it a lot?"

"Oh, no, not us," Ayane said as she shook her head. "We're…" She looked back at Katsumi and only continued after seeing her nod. "We're artificial Silents," she explained. "We weren't born with the abilities, so they're different. Similar enough to teach you, especially with our knowledge of the subject, but different. Your pure Silent abilities will be a lot stronger."

Hitomi frowned. "What do you mean you're 'artificial'?"

Katsumi sighed. "Our father had a lot of… ideas for us. Turning us into what we are was one of them. We don't know exactly what he did; I think only he could answer that. He's not human, either, so maybe we're something like him."

Ayane met Katsumi's eyes. "Too much like him and not enough like him at the same time," she stated sadly.

Hitomi looked between them. "If he's not human, what is he?"

"Something different," Katsumi said with obvious disgust. "More than human, or maybe less. He was human at one point, at least I think so. Whatever he is now, his view of humans is very low. He basically doesn't think of humans as sentient creatures – they're just trash to him, like insects."

"I don't know if I should ask about him," Hitomi said quietly, "but it's really… curious. When you two came out of that building and Ayane said your father did that to you, I was shocked. Is it…" She trailed off having noticed Ayane's hands were shaking slightly, curled into tight fists.

Katsumi noticed as well and reached up to catch one of her hands. Ayane opened it, clasping her sister's hand and letting out a breath as she looked back at Hitomi. "There isn't a worse subject for either of us, so asking about him is… discouraged. But you deserve to know something, just like everyone else here. What you have to know is that there is nothing we hate more in the world, no one we want to kill more."

Hitomi's voice was even softer as she spoke, as if she almost didn't want her words heard, but still she said, "I'm not naïve enough to think no child ever hated a parent, but your feelings seem like so much more."

Ayane's blue eyes were hard, while Katsumi seemed a bit more distant. For Ayane it was rather hard discussing her father as she stood beside her sister who was still suffering a lot of pain that had been inflicted by the man just a day before. It made the subject a lot more fresh and real. "He *used* us. He spent our childhoods turning us into weapons for his own uses. Then he killed our mother and forced us to run in fear for years, and now he…" She looked at the floor, aware that directing her glare at the other girl was making her uncomfortable.

"He thinks we're worthless," Katsumi finished for her, looking at Hitomi with a depression that tore into Ayane even more because it was put there by that man. "Normally I wouldn't give a damn what he thinks, but after all that he put us through in the name of making us 'useful', to hear him say it wasn't even worth it…"

"You feel like the pain was even more pointless," Hitomi quietly guessed, receiving a nod. "So what you went through is even more senseless. He might as well have left you alone."

"We're failures to him," Ayane said with emotion. "At least if-"

"You can't think like that," Hitomi cut her off. "You only failed his purpose. Despite what he did you escaped and made your own lives outside of his influence. If anything he's probably angry that the most promising thing he's ever done slipped through his hands and did better without him."

Katsumi smiled sadly. "We can pretend that's true."

Hitomi sighed. "Now I understand why the others wanted to kill him, too. If there's ever a way I can help…"

"You are," Ayane said, shifting to a smile as Katsumi pulled her back to her seat and whispered to her, repeating that she was fine and healing and reminding her of her promise the night before. Ayane closed her eyes, letting out a deep sigh as she let go of her anger for now. She laid her head on Katsumi's shoulder, opening her eyes to look at Hitomi again. "Just be our friend. We spent so long with just the two of us, it's really nice to have additional support."

Hitomi smiled at her. "I can do that. I'm a good friend, and you deserve the support. My life's been pretty easy," she said a little guiltily.

"That's good," Katsumi replied honestly.

"Well, it's just… I feel like it makes it harder for me to understand, help, or relate to people like you. People that have actually been through the intense things you have."

Ayane smiled. "You shouldn't be worrying about that with us, Hitomi. No one will ever relate to the two of us on more than one or two things; no one will ever really understand us. Sumi and I figured that out a long time ago."

Katsumi nodded. "And honestly that's for the best. Neither of us would be happier if you'd gone through anything like that. Personally I'm glad you haven't because you don't deserve it."

"Neither of *you* deserve it."

"*No one* deserves a bad childhood, because children are innocent. So I'm happy when I meet anyone who had a good one. And I enjoy seeing people who have had happy lives. I am beyond grateful to have a sister who understands everything, down to the tiniest detail, about me and my life," Katsumi said as her arm hugged Ayane, who gave her a smile. "But do you honestly think I wouldn't give anything to have spared her from it?"

Hitomi shook her head. "No, I guess you would. I see your point, I just assumed… Well, misery loves company, you know?"

"Sometimes. But seeing someone else miserable doesn't make you feel any better about it. Seeing someone happy does. For me, anyway. I've met a lot of people who tried not to talk about happy memories or good times with their parents around me because they thought I'd just be jealous and angry." Katsumi smirked. "If I'm honest, yes… Maybe I'm a little jealous sometimes. How can I not be? But hearing the stories of others' happiness is what makes me want to protect them."

Hitomi studied her. "You're good people. The rare kind."

Katsumi smiled. "It feels good to hear that. It's Ayane's fault."

Ayane looked at her. "Fault? I prefer the term 'achievement'."

"However you wanna say it." Katsumi looked from her to Hitomi. "Not everything was bad, you know. Our mother was amazing. I sometimes wonder how she would've felt had she known what he did, but I'm glad she didn't. And even after all of that I have a lot of good memories. If I'd lost Ayane as well…" Katsumi shook her head. "Then, I can guarantee, even if I did somehow survive, I wouldn't be this person. I'd be gone, really; no positive emotions or good feelings. No sense of justice or moral code. No happiness. Just a lot of hate and chaos."

Ayane hugged her, bringing back her older sister's smile. She met it with one of her own, speaking in a voice that suggested she was thinking back on fond memories. "We had a lot of happiness. It wasn't just survival." She looked at Hitomi. "I know it sounds bad sometimes because we can get kind of negative, but honestly I wouldn't trade my memories with Sumi for anything. We played in snow, we took trips, we celebrated holidays. And it's hard not to feel good when I think about how we still do all of those things, and we always will."

Hitomi sighed. "I'm glad you had each other for all of that. I'm glad you still do. And I'm glad I got to meet both of you." She smiled, shaking her head. "I don't care what your father says. You're both so worthwhile, so… worth knowing. I feel blessed just to be able to know you."

Katsumi smiled. "And you said you'd have a hard time helping."

Ayane nodded. "I know, it's like she doesn't know how much words like that mean to us."

"I'm glad they mean something," Hitomi said with a soft laugh. "I doubt I can do anything to help you fight, at least not yet. But I swear I'll do everything I can to help you keep your reasons for fighting."

~ ~ ~ ~ ~

Victoria moved to her computer as it announced someone was contacting her. She smiled as she saw the name, taking a seat and pressing a button under her desk that activated a device M had made for her, one that switched all surveillance and bugs to a loop, giving her privacy. She then tapped the screen on the wall, which showed the two women she'd been hoping to hear from. "Hello, girls," she said with a fond smile.

Katsumi and Ayane were standing and both snapped off a salute. "General," they said in unison. "We were told you hoped to hear from us," Katsumi added.

Victoria grinned. "I appreciate the formalities, but none of us are in uniform. And take a seat, weren't you injured?"

Katsumi looked a bit sheepish as she and Ayane both sat on her couch. "Unfortunately. It's rather minor though-"

Ayane snorted. "Relatively, but still something to be in bed over." The blue-haired girl grinned and looked at Victoria. "Oh, General," she said in a sing-song voice, "Could you order my sister to get bed rest?"

The dark-haired woman leaned forward, steepling her fingers. "Captain Samakura, are you ignoring your health again?"

The older sister sighed. "Not ignoring, General Gray, just… I'm just busy, that's all."

"You'd be a lot less busy in the grave."

"…I get your point," Katsumi said, "But you know how much I hate that."

"You aren't as effective injured. You should take that into account." Victoria leaned back, her expression growing serious. "I heard what happened. I can't believe he's still causing me trouble."

Ayane sighed. "It's just our luck he's mixed up in all of this. He's made everything more complicated, again."

Victoria's expression grew dark. "I've always tried to be a professional, but if I was ever able to get my hands on that man, I'd take my time making him die."

Katsumi smirked. "It's not like you to harbor personal vendettas, General."

"I have a few weaknesses," she replied with a smile. "Do you need any help down there?"

"Keep an ear open," Katsumi stated firmly.

"Understood. So how are the others? How is Lawrence?"

"Tall," Ayane answered. "Really, very tall, and big."

Victoria grinned. "That's exactly what I was asking about, Ayane, thank you."

The girl beamed. "Not a problem!"

"I suppose that means nothing has changed since he was under my command with you two."

"Not a lot," Katsumi said, and then smirked. "Well, he's a lot quicker about following my orders these days."

Victoria chuckled. "Of course. I remember the complaints I got when I sent you to Central America; 'a twenty-year-old officer, are you insane?!'" She smiled at Ayane. "It didn't get any better when her seventeen-year-old sister showed up at the same time as the new medic."

Ayane grinned. "I wasn't trying to help *you*."

"That much was obvious. My word, the arguments I got from you two when I tried to split you up…"

Katsumi smirked and folded her arms. "Well you should've known better."

"I know now, believe me. M was wiser than I was, he didn't even try."

"It was part of the deal," Katsumi reminded her. "Though… I do miss being under your command," she admitted.

"Both of us do," Ayane added with a nod.

Victoria smiled softly. "And I miss having you. You'd think seven years would be long enough, but sometimes you just don't want to let someone go."

"If it helps, ma'am, we're still under you in all but title," Katsumi said. "We'd follow any order you gave without hesitation."

"I value that, but my only order is to contact me more. Maybe even visit."

Ayane tilted her head with a smile. "We can do that. Both of those. Maybe we should visit after this demon thing is over?"

"I would love that," she replied with a smile. "Keep yourselves safe so it may come to pass. I don't like the dangerous situation you're in; it feels wrong."

"As does yours," Katsumi responded. "M said he's suspicious about what's going on up there."

"As he should be," Victoria sighed. "I don't know what they're planning but I don't trust it." She held up a hand. "Don't worry, I'm being careful. I know how to play the politics, even if I hate it."

"It's always better when it's a straight fight, isn't it, General?"

Victoria smiled. "At least it's easier that way. Unfortunately, I don't think that's the way things are going... Whatever is happening, it's happening in the shadows. We can only hope it comes to light and doesn't simply stab us in the back."

~ ~ ~ ~ ~

Date: April 10, 2068
Time: 1:32 AM
Location: Culsor Apartment Building,
Apartment 6711

Tonight was not a good night for Katsumi. Oh, it started perfectly – Ayane was in bed at home, still feeling well enough to not go back to the hospital. The talk with Victoria continued for two hours with the three reminiscing about good times. She was even feeling better, able to stand and walk around on her own. However, she slept fitfully despite Ayane's presence, disjointed dreams overtaking her consciousness.

She awoke an hour and a half past midnight with cold sweat and clammy hands. The nightmares were odd as she couldn't quite make sense of them. She glanced at Ayane and sighed, thankful that at least she hadn't woken her up. She carefully slipped out of the bed and got up, making her way into the bathroom. She ran the sink quietly, splashing water on her face to wake herself up a bit. A flicker of movement caught her attention from the corner of her eye; something she saw in the mirror. There was nothing there, though; a trick on her eyes by her mind, paranoia caused by her nightmares.

Still, Katsumi hadn't lived as long as she did by waving anything off as paranoia. She grew more alert and cautious, examining the mirror and turning to examine the bathroom behind her. She always checked these things out even if it was most likely nothing, especially with her sister in the house. A sudden noise of pots or pans clanking together in the kitchen – just a small one – jerked her attention in that direction. She exited the bathroom but found Ayane still asleep. She considered waking her in case there was someone in the place, but if it was just her imagination then waking her would only cause her to worry. She picked her pistol up off the nightstand; it was always kept loaded and with a round chambered when she slept.

She crept slowly into the kitchen area, which was small and only separated from the living room / bedroom by one wall. Katsumi's place really only had three rooms, so there wasn't a place for anyone to hide. Nothing was in the kitchen, but a couple of the lower cabinets were open, as if someone had been looking for something. The hair on the back of her neck stood on end as she felt the air grow cooler. Her grip on her pistol tightened as her eyes darted around the small kitchen. The most likely explanation was paranormal; strange dreams, spotting things in the corner of the eye, a sense of paranoia, odd physical occurrences and cold air were all signs of a spiritual presence, which could be as deadly as a living intruder.

Something brushed her calf; a light, faint touch, followed by a strong grip on her leg. She spun around and aimed the pistol down. Her lavender eyes locked onto brown ones and the pistol dropped, bouncing impotently on the tiled floor.

"Do you know what I'm going to do, Miss Samakura?"
"Don't..."
"I'm going to give a little show."
Katsumi dropped to her knees, staring into the eyes of the young boy who died in the Square, the final victim of Jerne Kintashi. Why his ghost had chosen to seek her out she didn't know; he simply stared at her. "Why?" she asked softly. "Why are you here?"

The young boy just continued to watch her. How old was he? She guessed he was five or six at most; she wondered how much he knew about her. Enough to come here, but why? Katsumi could feel herself shaking as the nightmares reorganized themselves in her mind, finally making sense. Her guilt was released in full force as she reached out slowly, laying a hand on the boy's head. "I was... late," she said quietly. "It took me too long. I'm trying... Really trying to do better, but I can't... bring you back," she finished as she looked away.

The boy stepped forward and she felt him press against her, felt his small arms hug her. Her eyes widened and she looked down at him, slowly bringing her own arms up to embrace him as the tears finally escaped her eyes. "I'm sorry," she whispered.

He stepped back after a few moments and beamed at her. He hopped backwards as if playing a game of tag, laughing and waving before he started running and disappeared. "Katsumi?" Ayane said softly as she stepped around the corner, spotting her older sister on her knees with tears running down her cheeks. She carefully knelt beside her, brushing her hair from her face. "What happened?"

Katsumi looked at her, smiling despite the tears. "It looks like... forgiveness is possible, after all."

Chapter 15: Showtime

Date: April 13, 2068
Time: 9:15 PM
Location: SIN HQ, Tokyo, Japan

Things were going well. Katsumi was actually smiling as she took on a backlog of paperwork for once. The city was quiet, with no serious troubles anywhere. Her injuries had healed fairly quickly once she'd listened to Ayane and rested for a couple days. They'd been doing some work with Hitomi, mostly getting her used to what she was and the extra sense she'd never known she had; she was progressing rapidly. And finally (and most importantly to Katsumi), Ayane was spending her last night at the hospital. Tomorrow Katsumi would be going to purchase their new home. If she relapsed, they would deal with it then, but for now everything was looking good.

Which was exactly the time for things to start going wrong. It started as simply as anything could: a single text to Katsumi's phone. She flipped it open to examine it, expecting something from her sister.

Good evening, Captain. I thought we'd have a little fun tonight; a game. Who doesn't like games? So here are the rules for tonight's game: I've learned about two attacks that are just about to happen, a personal one at the South Ashfield Hospital (oh my, isn't that an important location?) and a much bigger one starting at the Garrus Limited Building. That second one is going to kill quite a few innocent people, but the first attack will kill one not-so-innocent person. I wonder how you'll handle this? Let the game begin! - Σ

Katsumi was already up and running out into the light rain that was just beginning as she held her phone to her ear, calling M as she sent the message to him. "Get the entire team mobilized, and get them to Garrus Limited! I'm on my way to the hospital!" She grit her teeth, yelling over the link to her sister. *Ayane, WAKE UP, NOW. Someone's coming after you!*

~ ~ ~ ~ ~

WAKE UP, NOW. Someone's coming after you!

Ayane sat up, blinking awake. *Huh...?* The door to her room opened quietly and a masked soldier wearing Blood Angel colors stepped in, raising a rifle. Ayane rolled off the bed as he opened fire and shredded the sheets and pillow. She hit the floor on her knees and narrowed her eyes, shooting her hand under the mattress and withdrawing the katana hidden there, the one that had been a gift from Katsumi years ago. She gripped the blue sheath tightly, standing to her feet after the firing stopped, her eyes a hard glare as she unsheathed the blade.

The soldier blinked in surprise, taking a moment to stare. *Is... that a sword?*, he thought. He was going to question the worth of such a weapon in this age, but questioning anything became something of a problem as his head split horizontally just below his eyes despite his full-cover helmet. Blood sprayed outwards as the top half of his skull hit the floor, followed by his convulsing body.

His ally saw the blood and pressed against the wall for cover, firing at the doorway to catch the girl when she came out, but she didn't. Instead severe pain shot through his side when the sword was driven through the wall beside him, piercing his hip. He cried out in agony and the girl took the chance to step around the doorway. She used her sheath to knock the rifle from his hands before she grabbed his head, pulling him painfully off of the blade. The last thing he saw was his head being shoved back towards the blade that still jutted from the wall.

Ayane stepped back into her room, yanking her katana from the wall. *I'm alright, Sumi, thanks to your warning,* she said over the link as she flicked the blood from her blade before sliding it back into its sheath. She then took the pistol from under her pillow before stepping back out. She looked back and forth down the hallway, deciding on a direction before four more soldiers appeared at the end of the hallway. She ran two steps and flipped over the desk in front of her room as they opened fire. She sadly noticed the nurse that worked outside of her room lay dead behind the desk; she'd always been kind, and had always allowed Katsumi in outside of normal visiting hours – she'd been a friend. Her sadness fed her rage as she grabbed the rolling chair, shoving it across the hallway. The soldiers opened fire at the movement and Ayane sprinted around the corner, returning fire with her pistol. They were too slow to adjust and two of them went down to bullets before their aim tracked her.

She spun to the side away from the bullets, ran two steps up the wall and flipped to the other wall, gaining distance the whole time before she launched herself off the wall towards them, drawing her sword in the air. As she spun past the remaining two soldiers her blade took the head from one. She landed and turned, dodging a burst of fire from the last one and removing his hand with her katana before she flipped it around and drove it up under his chin and through his head. She yanked it free, letting his body drop as she took off down the stairs. Another soldier was coming up the stairs and opened fire but she flipped over the rail, firing down into him as she went, then landed behind him and continued running as he fell.

~ ~ ~ ~ ~

There was a very large number of soldiers outside of the hospital, dozens even. Katsumi noticed this as the SIN car she'd taken screamed around the last corner, tires squealing as she kept her foot on the gas and barreled towards the building. It wasn't a stealthy approach and they all unloaded their weapons on the car, but it was pretty well enforced. Katsumi threw herself down and lay across the seats as gunfire shattered her windshield and windows, tearing apart the tops of the seats and making dozens of dents in the hood. Rainwater sprayed into the car from the newly-opened windows but she kept her foot on the gas and her hand on the wheel, steering the car for the glass doors to the lobby. Soldiers dived out of the way as the dark grey car blew past them, leaving the smell of burning rubber behind as it smashed through the glass doors and sent yet more glass and shrapnel everywhere.

Katsumi opened the door and dropped out of the car behind it as the soldiers inside the lobby began firing on the car. She couldn't handle all the soldiers outside, though, and they were coming, so she didn't have time to hang around and pick off the ones in here with her pistol. She grabbed the car door's handle, slamming her foot into the door. The metal joining it to the car bent and groaned. She then slid back, growling as she threw her shoulder into the door and broke it off. She kept a grip on it, rushing forward as bullets pinged off the metal and the floor around her. She turned it vertical and fired around it, taking out two soldiers. She reached one and slammed him in the head with the car door, sending him to the ground. She then flung the door at another soldier, dropping him as well.

She took off down one of the hallways, ignoring the shooting behind her. *I'm here, Ayane. Making my way to you as fast as I can.* The elevator wasn't going to work so she headed for the stairs. Four soldiers stood guard at the bottom and Katsumi shot two of them, but her pistol clicked on the third one, empty. Katsumi growled and flung it at the third one instead, dazing him as it hit his helmet. She went into a slide as the fourth soldier fired at her. She kicked his legs out and spun as she rose, catching his neck and driving his head up into the wall. She then spun to the recovering third soldier, grabbing his gun and jerking it to the side as he fired, then driving her elbow into his neck. As he backed off unable to breath, she flipped the gun in his grip, holding down the trigger and unloading its magazine into his chest.

As the soldier slipped to the ground Katsumi grabbed the other's rifle and sprinted up the stairs. The next two soldiers were simply gunned down, but the magazine ran dry at the third. As he fired she leapt from the stairs onto the railing, then flipped upwards, landing her feet on his shoulders. As he staggered backwards under the weight she slipped one leg under his chin and the other behind his head, falling back until her hands touched down so she could use the momentum to flip him back over her head, snapping his neck as he hit the floor. She grabbed his gun next and continued running, knowing she had no time to waste as she could hear many, many soldiers coming behind her.

~ ~ ~ ~ ~

Reno brought the chopper to a stop above the entrance to the Garrus Limited building, lowering it enough for Kurasano, Law and Rufus to drop out. Hitomi had remained at the SIN HQ, as they knew she wasn't ready for something like this and would just be in danger. Sano really had no idea what to expect as he led Rufus and Law into the building. They were expecting soldiers, but the building was strangely empty. M informed them that sensors indicated something bad going on deeper inside the building, though, so they kept going. This building was in the middle of a densely populated area; if anything big happened here a lot of people would die, so they found themselves running.

It was in the building's auditorium meant for big conferences and speeches that they found what they were looking for. The Shade they'd been after was something different now, almost humanoid in shape. It was composed of blue fire and energy, constantly flickering like a TV channel getting bad reception. It was huge, some twenty feet in height, standing on two thick legs with reverse-bent knees. Its arms were held slightly away from its body in an aggressive pose. Its head was angular, with two large horns jutting out from either side bent straight back and up. Two pits of cold fury in narrow shapes were its eyes, directing a burning hatred at the three men.

"That is… not good," Law stated as he raised the large weapon in his hands.

"Our men will be here in a few minutes," Rufus said. "If we can just hold it off-"

A booming laugh interrupted them and the demon, despite being faceless at the moment, seemed to smile. "You will be dead before then," it said in a voice that was a deep rumbling and a high-pitched scream at the same time, unearthly in every respect. "You are the final obstacles between myself and physical manifestation. You will suffer and bow before Belphegor, the Lord of Opening!" A loud whine filled the air as the specter spread his arms and two massive shadowy wings spread out behind him.

Rufus adjusted his sunglasses, looking at the shade of the being before them. "It's true, then… an Ancient One, one of the two hundred angels that followed Lucifer in his rebellion against God."

"Don't really care what he is," Law said, readying his weapon.

"Law's right, it doesn't matter," Sano said. "We have to kill him regardless."

Belphegor didn't bother paying attention to their words as a portal opened up on either side of him. Inhuman howls tore at their ears and abominations began to pour through the portals. The eyes of all three men went wide as they watched. They looked at each other, and then all three raised their weapons and voices at the same time, opening fire on the demons. This was a bad, bad situation, and the chance of survival dropped with every creature that stepped into their world. Sano could only hope their Captain was doing better, and could get here soon.

~ ~ ~ ~ ~

Katsumi ducked beneath the barrel of a rifle, slamming her fist into the soldier's stomach. She slipped behind him and lifted his arm, pulling the trigger on his weapon and shooting two of his allies. She curled her arm around his neck and snapped it before shoving him away and racing ahead. Blood sprayed out of a doorway ahead of her and her heart lightened as Ayane slid out of it. Blood coated the girl's hair and clothing, but none of it seemed to be hers.

Katsumi reached her and caught her in a hug, feeling relief as well as Ayane returning it. They shared a smile before Katsumi looked over her shoulder. "There's too many of them. We have to get to the roof and go from there."

Ayane nodded. "The stairs up are mostly clear. We should be able to make good time. Should we do something to stall them, though?"

"Good idea," Katsumi said as she looked around. They decided to move two desks into the stairwell, wedging one atop the other to block the doorway. It wouldn't take more than a minute for the soldiers to clear it, but that was a minute without bullets at their heels. Knowing time was short the two sisters took off once more, racing up one flight of stairs after another side by side, panting for breath but making no stops. Both grew hopeful as the door to the roof finally came into view minutes later. Together they threw themselves into it, breaking through onto the roof.

Then they stopped.

Joseph stood in the rain with saber in hand and a lack of emotion on his face, graying brown hair soaked enough to show he'd been waiting for them. He used a single finger to wipe water from his glasses as if a bit bored. Ayane had her katana but they had no other weapons, no firearms. Both were tired, having just fought and sprinted their way up through the building with no breaks. Neither of them hesitated before charging the man with matched looks of determination and rage. Their steps fell into a rhythm, their muscles working in unison. Two steps before reaching him they shot apart and launched themselves at him from either side.

~ ~ ~ ~ ~

At the SIN HQ, Hitomi paced back and forth in her room. She had been in the command center with M, but listening to the screams and sounds of violence over the radio had gotten to her. She hated that she couldn't yet help any of them. She knew Katsumi and Ayane were in trouble, and she knew that Sano, Rufus and Law were all in trouble, too. Even Reno was in danger as he flew recon for the others, having to dodge demon attacks that could bring him down in a fiery crash.

And here Hitomi sat, unable to help, unable to do anything but wait. It was frustrating and it drove her crazy, but what could she do? She hoped and prayed that they would all make it back alive. She was broken out of her thoughts as M appeared in her doorway. "Miss Saizen, you seem upset."

Hitomi jumped at his sudden appearance and didn't bother hiding her emotion. "Of course I am! I'm just sitting here while they're all out trying not to die, fighting to keep the city alive! Why wouldn't I be upset?!"

M tilted his head. "I understand the feelings. That is actually why I'm here; they need your help. Would you like to come with me?"

She blinked. "What? Really? Are you... I mean, what can I do?"

"First Lieutenant Lionel asked for you himself. All of us must play our part, and it is time to play yours," he said with a sly smile.

"Of course! I mean, yes! I'll go!" Hitomi grinned, excited to be able to do something. She was supposed to be part of the team, wasn't she? It was dangerous out there, but if they were all risking the danger, she wouldn't shy away. "Lead the way!"

He nodded, folding his arms behind his back as he led her down the hallway and out of the building. Beneath the advanced disguise, Sigma smiled.

~ ~ ~ ~ ~

"This is seriously not what I planned for," Sano said as he fired his assault rifle at the oncoming hordes of demonic abominations. He, Rufus, Law, and the dozen or so remaining soldiers had all taken up positions near the entrance to the building, trying to contain the demon attack. It wasn't working. Sano cursed and leapt backwards as a massive, twisted claw tore through the stone beside him. They had been overrun quickly and were outnumbered by at least three to one already.

They just weren't able to cut them down quickly enough, and in here they were being slaughtered. He called for a retreat and all the survivors moved out into the streets. The sounds of gunfire, eerie howls and screams filled the air. Law brought his empty hand up, clasping it around a demon's head. The seven-foot man slammed it into a wall, crushing its head with a satisfied grin. Another demon lunged at him and he swung his large gun like a club, smacking it out of the air. He set a foot on its back and unloaded into its body, spraying blood and limbs in all directions.

Rufus ducked, dodged and flipped around claws and teeth that sought to tear at him. He held a submachine gun in each hand, spraying their special imbued bullets into everything around. A particularly large demon attempted to grab him and he hopped up onto its arm, then onto its back, sticking one barrel against the back of its head and pulling the trigger, splattering whatever it had for brains onto the floor.

Sano, meanwhile, had taken a shotgun from one of the soldiers. He was less acrobatic than Rufus but he managed to evade their strikes all the same. An odd creature with three arms – one coming from its chest – managed to grab him and he jerked himself upwards, kicking up and striking its disturbingly human-like head under the chin. Setting his feet on its chest he shoved the shotgun under its chin and blasted its head away, freeing himself from the arms.

The fact that ordinary demons were once humans that had been sent to Hell made it difficult, sometimes, to kill them like that, especially when they still retained a face. Fortunately, the pure mutated horror of their twisted forms made it easier, almost a reflex even.

The battle spilled out across the streets and demons began going after civilians, as well, breaking into nearby buildings and running down cars. The screams coming from these unfortunate victims were the hardest to hear, but honestly there was nothing to be done. M informed him he was working on something to help, but Sano had no idea what that could be.

This was a nightmare. Hundreds of demons unleashed, soldiers dropping by the minute, innocents being slaughtered by each abomination they let past, and to top it off, they hadn't heard from Katsumi at all. Whatever she was doing, the three SIN members hoped that neither she nor Ayane had been a casualty of this hellish night.

~ ~ ~ ~ ~

Joseph brought his saber up to deflect Ayane's katana and slapped Katsumi's hand away at the same time. His eyes followed neither of them as he spun, slicing at his older daughter while his empty left hand curled into a fist and struck at his younger one. Katsumi ducked the blade and connected with a punch to his side; Ayane leaned to the side and curled her arm around her father's, tossing her blade behind his back as his right arm swung his saber rapidly at Katsumi.

She caught her younger sister's blade as it passed, whirling to block the strike that would have cut into her shoulder. Katsumi went into a defensive form to deflect his attacks as Ayane tightened her grip on his other arm, keeping him hindered and waiting. After several seconds of sparring with Katsumi he slid back, getting a footing and flinging Ayane at her sister. Both had anticipated this, however, and Katsumi threw the katana a few feet into the air, bracing her own feet and lifting her hands. Ayane turned in the air, aiming her feet for Katsumi. Her feet hit Katsumi's hands and she caught her blade as it fell, shoving with her legs at the same time as Katsumi did with her arms. She flew back at Joseph and he turned to deflect her attack as she passed.

Katsumi slammed into him and took his legs out from under him as he was distracted but he spun rapidly and set his free hand on the ground, shooting both legs out to catch her around the waist. He yanked her from the ground and spun again, slamming her into the ground and stabbing down with his saber, managing to pierce her thigh and elicit a hiss of pain. As he stood he pulled his blade from her leg and kicked her, sending her bouncing across the roof. That angered Ayane beyond reason and she came at him with a vengeance, her blade darting in from every direction.

Joseph backed up as he fended off her attacks, still showing no emotion. He dodged a stab and grabbed her wrist, flinging her past him as Katsumi somehow came back already, throwing a punch at his face. He ducked it and slammed his own into her stomach, just as he had days before. The shock and pain it caused Katsumi was obvious, but he didn't trust it to put her down again so as she fell past him he slammed his elbow into her back. The impact made her hit the roof so hard her body bounced off, flying a few more feet before landing again. Katsumi couldn't breathe at all, couldn't move; all she could do was struggle to achieve both, her fingers trying to grip the wet stone.

Joseph turned back to intercept the thrusting blade of his younger daughter, who appeared to be enraged at his treatment of her older sister. Her blade was fast and skilled, even managing to cut a few bits out of his longcoat and draw blood on his hand. She was getting better with each passing second which forced him to make a move. In a blur he was beside her, setting his hand over hers like a gentle father might in an ordinary family. He jerked his hand and broke her thumb, causing the sword to fall from Ayane's hand as she gave a cry of pain.

He used her wrist to yank her body towards him as he drove a knee up into her stomach, lifting her bodily from the ground. She flew a few feet to land on her back, coughing. Joseph wasn't finished, though; still eerily lacking any emotion he walked over, setting a heel on her hand. He slowly pressed down, breaking her fingers one by one as she screamed.

Katsumi shuddered, tears mixing with the rainwater on her face as she struggled to stand. Her body refused her demands, ignoring her emotions. She watched as Joseph calmly moved his foot to Ayane's chest, putting pressure down to crack her ribs one after another. Her screams were piercing, full of agony and fear. Joseph was clearly torturing her for some unknown reason and Katsumi felt it clawing inside her, her emotions a roiling storm of terror and hatred.

Hate, fear, Ayane was going to die, Ayane's screams pounded at her ears like the waves of an ocean, tormenting her soul along with her. She couldn't take it, not the torture, not the pain, and not the loss of her sister at that monster's hands. *Ayane's going to die… Ayane is… going to die… Ayane is… not… not going to die… She's not going to die… SHE'S NOT!*

Katsumi lost it.

The eruption of violet flame drew a small look of surprise from Joseph. Katsumi rose to her feet as an inky blackness flowed over her, turning her hair and eyes black. She exploded from the spot and her fist connected with his cheek before he could react. The impact knocked him off Ayane and spun him around but his saber flashed out as he spun. Katsumi ducked, losing an inch of violet hair, but came up with a flurry of blows.

Joseph's saber went spinning away off of the roof. He found his footing as his eldest daughter came after him and they traded blows, but Katsumi didn't stop this time. The emotion in her eyes was the perfect opposite of his blank ones. His fist lashed out and connected with her chin, hers responded and hit his chest. He gave her the same punch to the stomach that had dropped her before but she kept coming, working her hands and feet in a frenzy to force him back.

His strikes grew harder as time passed, jarring her frame with each impact. She wouldn't last long even like this, but at the last second she saw it; his hand shot out to grip her throat. She avoided it with the narrowest of margins by bending her knee as she jerked to the side, and came up with an uppercut that sent him back a few steps; that was all she needed. He was on the very edge of the 80-story building's roof and off-balance, and thanks to the rain-slicked stone, he couldn't recover. As he fell, the tiniest flicker of irritation flashed in his eyes.

The response was a victory. Katsumi's hair returned to violet and her eyes to lavender, and almost immediately she felt the effects of the fight that she'd been ignoring. It didn't matter to her, though, as she wasted no time in moving to Ayane's side. The younger Samakura was in bad shape, bleeding from numerous wounds. Katsumi knelt beside her, leaning over to shield her face from the rain. "Ayane…? Ayane?!"

Ayane forced her eyes open, feeling the tears landing on her face that weren't hers. *I'm here… Don't want to try to talk out loud, though. Everything… hurts.*

"I know," Katsumi said softly. "I'm sorry. I tried…" She squeezed her eyes shut. "Couldn't protect you, again. I keep failing, but I…" She looked at the door into the building. "Father's not dead, only stalled… He might be coming back up as we speak, and at the very least, all of those soldiers will…" She looked down at Ayane, unwilling to move her but unable to leave her here.

Ayane closed her eyes again. She couldn't just tell Katsumi to leave on her own; she wouldn't do it and it would just hurt her to ask. She tried to think of ideas but she was so tired, and pain was making it hard to think of anything else.

They both looked over as sounds came from behind the door. Katsumi stood slowly, placing herself between Ayane and the door as it burst open and soldiers spilled out, over twenty of them, far too many of them to do anything about it. She sat on her knees, looking back to Ayane as she took her hand. "No ideas either, huh…?" she said with a small smile.

Ayane returned it weakly. *Nope. At least… neither of us will be without the other.*

That's the most important part, Katsumi responded, facing the soldiers. Before they could speak further the soldiers all raised their weapons, and a hail of gunfire filled the air.

But those were two different events. Not one soldier was able to fire as thousands of rounds tore through their ranks, sending them to the ground. Katsumi's eyes widened in surprise and she looked up to see three military helicopters dropping from the sky. One of them landed on the roof near them and Victoria Gray stepped out from it, walking quickly towards the sisters.

Katsumi couldn't help but smile and couldn't summon the will to stand and salute. "General…"

The dark-haired woman knelt beside her, looking between her and Ayane. "This is…" She leaned down and laid a hand on Ayane's forehead. "I'm late… Ayane, are you…"

Ayane smiled weakly and Katsumi shook her head. "She's… alive, but bad… I need to get her help, now."

Victoria nodded, standing up as two soldiers brought an emergency stretcher from the helicopter and ran over. They held it as Katsumi and Victoria gently moved Ayane onto it. Katsumi looked at her old commanding officer. "I can't… We can't find someone to help here, can we? There are probably still soldiers in the building."

Victoria nodded. "You're right. I'll put her in my chopper to be taken to the nearest safe hospital." She set a hand on Katsumi. "What about you? You look injured, as well," she said with a frown.

"Compared to Aya, I'm fine," Katsumi stated solidly. "I… I want to go with Aya, but I'm needed elsewhere."

"Yes, I sent most of my forces to your team. I will leave one chopper here to await the others coming, they'll clean hostiles out and secure survivors. You and I can take the remaining chopper to meet with your team in the battle zone."

Katsumi nodded. She leaned down to Ayane, clasping one of her hands in both of her own. *Aya… I'm going to try to take care of this situation. There's a large-scale attack going on and I… have to run it. I want to go with you, though…*

Ayane smiled. *I know you do. I want to go with you. Don't worry, though, I'll be fine. You can see me afterwards, right?*

Katsumi caught the meaning in her last statement. She nodded, brushing Ayane's hair from her face. *I will see you, I promise. Keep talking to me while you can, okay? I'll let you know what I'm doing.*

Thank you. Take… Take my sword. Hopefully it will bring you back to me.

I will – and nothing will keep me from coming back. Katsumi squeezed her hand a final time before moving back and taking hold of the sword on the ground. She picked up the sheath as well and stood, sliding the blade into its place and looking at Victoria. "I'm ready, General."

"We'll waste no more time, then." They both watched the two soldiers carefully take Ayane to the chopper as another one came down towards the roof. "This is your mission, Captain," Victoria said as she looked at Katsumi seriously. "You're in charge. Can you give me orders?"

Katsumi gave her a hard look. "My sister was just nearly killed again. She's on her way to a hospital that can hopefully stop her pain, but it's going to last awhile." Her hand tightened around her sister's sword. "There is nothing in this world or the next that can stop me from getting back to her as quickly as I can, and I'm going to kill everything that tries."

The General nodded as they began walking towards the landing helicopter. "That's what I expected to hear. Don't let either of us down, Captain."

~ ~ ~ ~ ~

"They're through the third line!"

"North side, north side!"

"On the roof!"

Kurasano sprinted ahead, vaulting over a destroyed car. The numbers they were facing were insane; hundreds of the demons were out now, swarming over the hopelessly outnumbered defenders. Rufus was torn up, his normally-immaculate white clothing tinted red in numerous areas. Law's arms were shredded; fortunately they were synthetic and far stronger than ordinary limbs, but the pain was just as real. Sano himself was covered in bruises and a few slashes, but worse, ignoring a broken arm. He'd made his jacket into a makeshift sling for the limb; fighting without it was his main problem.

No one would know what the death count would be until this was over. Bodies lay visible in the streets, destroyed cars poured smoke and items from nearby buildings littered the roads having been thrown through the shattered windows. Sano remembered facing dangerous riots as a cop and this brought back those memories, but it was much worse than any of those. Above them, in the air, Reno flew rapid courses rescuing any civilians he could while using the chopper's weapons to take out dozens of the creatures. It wasn't enough, though; none of it was enough. This was only stalling and, eventually, they'd all be dead. In the meantime these things just kept coming.

"Whooooo!" Reno's cheer startled the three on the ground, who had no idea why he would be enjoying this. Even Law had stopped enjoying the fighting some time ago; only Rufus seemed to be having fun with the challenge, and Sano was worried his survival instincts would kick in soon and cause him to abandon the situation. The reason behind their ally's jovial shout became apparent in seconds, though, when three military helicopters came screaming into the area, strafing hordes of demons with surgical precision. Heavy-caliber mounted guns did most of the damage; missiles would cause too much collateral damage to the surrounding buildings.

The remaining SIN soldiers and Alpha-Unit members all felt an enormous amount of relief, especially when the choppers hovered over the ground they were holding and three dozen soldiers jumped out to join the battle. One of them reported to Kurasano, who immediately informed him of the situation. They formed their teams together and began to move back towards the building. The hordes of demons seemed to understand the new threat and began converging on the group, but the combination of soldiers and attack choppers mowed them down before they could reach them.

The ground began shaking and the SIN Unit called for everyone to separate and the choppers to back off. The soldiers all split into smaller groups and scattered, and the helicopters gained height. It was fortunate they were willing to listen and follow orders without question as the ground began to lift up before exploding upwards. Giant, worm-like things broke free, releasing guttural screeches. The creatures were grey and covered in red, back-swept blades; each had a strange metal-looking head plate that covered what could be called the top half of the head. They would slither up onto the ground and over the streets, eviscerating those they caught with the blades on their bodies or simply crushing them. They would then burrow back beneath the street only to come up in another spot.

The SIN soldiers led the military soldiers, telling them how to combat the creatures. They scattered to avoid being wiped out in large numbers, firing into the tail-ends of the worms, where the brains were kept. There seemed to be four worms in total and soon three of them were down; the helicopters continued to be the main threat, focusing fire on one worm at a time. As the final worm fell the front of the Garrus Limited building exploded. The soldiers watched as a towering behemoth stomped out onto the street, certainly something from a nightmare.

It had a humanoid body, but the knees were reversed. The head was jutted forward as it had a freakishly elongated jaw that went all the way to its waist. The thing's skin was black with a ridge of red fur from the top of the head down the center of the back. Its huge jaw was filled with four-story teeth and the thing itself was about ten stories tall, which unfortunately allowed it to swipe a helicopter out of the air with a clawed hand before all three could get away. It turned red-burning eyes on the soldiers on the ground and raised an ear-splitting roar that preceded yet more of the first demons racing out of the building with howls and yips.

Sano cursed, unsure how they were going to bring this thing down. It opened its massive jaws and a horrible sound emitted from its mouth, like the grating of metal being torn apart. Dozens of soldiers clapped hands over their ears and screamed. The rest, oddly, seemed unaffected, but that was little comfort when their teammates began leaking blood from their ears, eyes, nose and mouth before falling to the ground, unmoving. The creature ceased the noise and began sucking in a breath, preparing to do it again. The helicopters focused fire on the beast but it wasn't bothered; it was yet another situation that seemed hopeless until another party was added to the battle.

A single helicopter roared into the area at top-speed, heading for the beast. It flew above it, holding position over the creature as a figure appeared in the open side before dropping from the helicopter. "Well there's a suicidal lunatic," Rufus said as he cleaned debris from his shades.

Sano blinked, squinting at the person before his eyes widened and he pointed, looking towards Rufus and Law. "Hey, I recognize that suicidal lunatic!"

Katsumi spun in mid-air and flipped at the last moment, landing with a heavy impact on the back of the creature's neck. She immediately latched onto the fur there as it jerked around in an attempt to shake her off. She held something in her teeth as she held on with both hands, grimacing with effort. When it began reaching back to swipe at her she took off sprinting up its neck. A massive, clawed hand came sweeping towards her and she leapt up and twisted herself between two of its fingers before landing in a continued run. When she finally made it to the end of the creature's extended neck, at the base of its head, she drew Ayane's katana from her back, kneeling and stabbing the blade into the tough flesh.

The SIN Captain forced the blade as deep as it could go before yanking it from side to side. The creature shook wildly in rage and she was nearly thrown off, but managed to keep her hold. She pulled the katana from the creature and spun it once to fling the blood off before sliding it into its sheath, freeing up her hand to remove the item from her mouth. Jamming the large pack of explosives into the newly created hole, Katsumi used the sheath to stuff it as deeply as she could before she was thrown free, having no grip. As she fell she whipped the katana free and jammed it into the creature's side, cutting a line into it and slowing her descent. This only enraged it further and she lifted her feet, bracing against the creature's side before shoving off into a back flip to avoid the swatting claw.

Katsumi stabbed Ayane's blade into the thing's arm to slow her descent again but it flung its arm out rapidly, sending her flying at a building. Fortunately she hit a window, shattering it flying into the room, only stopping when she hit a wall inside the place. She forced herself to her feet, stumbling towards the window and watching as the creature rose up before her, sucking in a breath. The helicopter she'd ridden in on hovered a few dozen meters away and fired into the creature's head, drawing its attention. It turned towards the new threat, readying its attack before Victoria appeared in the open side. She lifted a detonator and smiled, giving a wave as she pressed the button.

Katsumi, twelve stories up now, stepped out of the window, falling rapidly as the explosion took out the floor she'd been on. It also severed the creature's neck entirely, sending its head falling after her. Katsumi kicked off the building as she fell, distancing herself from it. She reached up and allowed herself a small smile as a helicopter caught up to her exactly where she needed it, allowing her to catch one of the landing skids. It flew her away from the falling body and she pulled herself up, climbing into the helicopter. "We've gotta stop meeting this way, boss," Reno said as he headed for the main force.

"Believe me, I prefer climbing in when the chopper's on the ground like everyone else," Katsumi said as she wearily sat against the back of the co-pilot seat, taking advantage of the very short rest.

Reno chanced a glance back at her and whistled softly as he took in her bruised and bloodied appearance. "You don't look so good, boss. You sure you should still be fighting? And is your sister okay?"

"She's…" Katsumi looked out the side at the ruined street as they flew over the fight. "She's alive. She's not good. They're putting her to sleep soon to work on her injuries."

"That bad…?" Reno said as quietly as he could while still being heard.

"It was *him* again," Katsumi said venomously. "As if it's any surprise. Everything can be traced back to him, *everything*. All of *this*, even."

"We need to take him out," Reno muttered.

"*I* need to take him out," Katsumi corrected. "And I will." She leaned out the side. "Let me down here, Reno."

"If you say so, Boss."

Sano met her as she dropped from the chopper, jogging over to her position. "Man, am I glad to see you…" he said, trailing off as he took in his battered and torn boss. He shook his head, deciding it didn't matter; they were *all* injured right now. They would just have to deal with it.

Katsumi laid her hand on Sano's shoulder, catching his eyes. "I'm glad you were in charge here, Sano. You've done an excellent job of containing this."

Sano grimaced. "I don't know about that. The damage-"

"Is confined to three streets," she finished for him. "With this size of attack, that's honestly incredible."

"Well… Thanks."

Katsumi nodded, putting a hand over her ear as Victoria's voice came over her comm. "The worst of the attack seems to be over, Captain. The number of creatures leaving the Garrus Limited building is dwindling."

"Good. General, I want to make a push into that building. I want to end this now."

"I'll meet you at what's left of the main entrance, then. We can split the forces, one team for outer containment and three more to get inside through the entrances."

"Perfect. I'll put one of my team with each of yours." Upon receiving confirmation, Katsumi switched to her Unit's cyber link. *Reno, join the other helicopters in containment sweeps. Look for survivors. Law, head to the building's east entrance, you'll be leading the team there. Rufus, you're leading the team at the western entrance. Sano, you'll organize the containment team we're leaving outside; make sure they catch anything that gets past us. I'll be going in with the main team at the southern entrance.*

You got it!

Understood, Boss.

Not a problem.

I'll do what I can.

Katsumi started heading towards the southern entrance with Sano, who questioned her, "You're not leaving me outside just because of my arm, are you?"

She looked at him as if he was crazy. "Why would I give you a break just because you have a little injury? You're defense because you're the best at organizing defense out of all of us, myself included. Your stand tonight proves it."

"Oh," he said lamely. He grinned and she just shook her head, outpacing him with her stride.

Victoria met them at the entrance and Sano split off to coordinate the containment team. The general looked at the violet-haired captain. "Everyone is ready for whatever we find inside."

"They're not ready," Katsumi replied, meeting her gaze. "But let's hope they can get that way."

"Are any of us ready for an Ancient One?"

"If he's even still in there, no." Katsumi looked at the building. "But I don't think he is. He never came out when everyone was distracted, and I think that's what all of this was: a distraction."

Victoria gave a concerned frown. "If that's true, then what were we being distracted from?"

Katsumi sighed, shaking her head. "I don't know." She lifted her pistol, ejecting the magazine and sliding in a new one. "Let's get in there and find out."

Chapter 16: Tender

There was nothing inside.

Katsumi stood in the middle of the demolished auditorium, looking around as soldiers combed the rest of the building. There was no sign of Belphegor, only a few lesser demons that they cleared out with no trouble. Already the soldiers were beginning to forget what they'd been fighting; "biological weapons" Victoria told them, creatures created by a terrorist cell. The cell she named didn't even exist; it was simply invented by Aegis as an excuse for supernatural attacks too large to cover up with the usual methods. V herself, of course, had the same chip all the other Aegis Board members and SIN soldiers did, so she, along with Katsumi's team and the soldiers from the SIN division, understood exactly what had happened.

Victoria came up beside Katsumi. "I've got my men keeping civilians out of the area, but they're curious. And the press is already here."

The Captain grimaced. "They're like hyenas; never late to a corpse."

"Indeed. Listen, I'm going to organize them and M already has clean-up on their way... You should get to Ayane."

Katsumi looked at her. "Just... leave?"

"There's nothing here," Victoria said with a shrug. "Whatever the next step of this is, it's not happening tonight. Belphegor won't have the energy to do this again for a week at least."

Katsumi sighed, rubbing her eyes with the heel of her hand. "The on-and-off nature of this job drives me insane sometimes."

"Maybe it does, but no one could do it better. Even Aegis is realizing that... Major."

Katsumi lowered her hand, blinking. "What...? Major? A promotion?"

Victoria smiled. "It's long overdue, but just look at what you've done over the past few months alone, and tonight in particular. You're not just the best at your job, Major Samakura –

you're the best chance this world has against things like this." She held up a hand to stop Katsumi's protest. "Don't argue, please. Your new rank will give you more authority and freedom, which I know you will use well. It will help you protect."

Katsumi sighed. "I guess I'll accept that, then. As long as no one throws me a party."

The general chuckled. "Is anyone foolish enough to try that again?"

"I wouldn't be surprised." Katsumi looked at her. "Thank you, General. For everything."

Victoria smiled fondly. "I've done nothing you haven't earned, whether promotion, aid or friendship. Now go," she said with a wave of her hand, "I'd rather not suffer Ayane's anger for keeping you."

"Don't worry about that," Katsumi said as she walked away. "I can still feel her anger right now, and it's not directed at you."

~ ~ ~ ~ ~

Broken thumb. Four broken fingers on left hand, two fractured in two places. Five broken ribs. Punctured lung (two places). Torn wrist ligament. Dislocated shoulder. Torn abdominal muscle. Internal bleeding in multiple locations; immediate surgery needed to prevent fatal damage.

Katsumi sat on a bench in the darkened hallway, her forehead on her left hand supported by the elbow on her knee. Her right arm rested on her other leg with a clipboard loosely hanging from her fingers. She'd read it multiple times and the words on it hadn't changed once. Ayane's injuries had been worse under the surface according to the doctors, leading to her nearly drowning in her own blood on the way to the hospital, and then nearly dying once there from blood loss. Katsumi had been assured she was safe now, that she would live, but it was too close.

She was glad that the members of her team were busy and unable to come as she ignored the tears on her cheeks, focusing her will on reigning in her emotions. The technique wasn't working like it often did, though, not now; Katsumi could deal with near-misses, but not when it came to her sister. She couldn't even summon the anger to throw or break the clipboard, or punch the wall, or scream. All she could do was sit there and wait. When the doctors finally told her she could go in she stood slowly, barely remembering to hand them the clipboard as she more or less drifted into the room.

Ayane was out; unconscious, asleep, or somewhere in between. Katsumi couldn't prevent herself from checking her pulse just to be sure. She dropped into the chair beside her, looking around the dark room lit only by the light from a street lamp outside filtering in through the blinds. Katsumi hated hospital rooms, she really did; there was such an air of weakness in this room, a feeling of encroaching death and sickness. She almost felt as if she was deteriorating just by being there, muscles and mind atrophying from lack of use.

Looking at Ayane was even worse. Her little sister was only three years younger, but she looked so small in a hospital bed. Katsumi reached out and gently brushed her pale blue hair, giving a shuddering sigh. She had an oxygen mask and an IV which just made the picture look worse. The anger still didn't come this time, only fear. Fear, as she looked at her unconscious little sister who had been beaten nearly to death. Their plans to just move on, to start living together again tomorrow, to forget their past… they seemed so distant now, and pointless.

She watched light move across the wall as a car passed and found herself thinking of doing things she'd never accepted before. Maybe she couldn't beat Joseph. Maybe she couldn't protect Ayane from him. If he was really done with them, maybe they should just take the opportunity and leave, go somewhere else, forget everything.

Katsumi put her head in her hands and let out a shaky breath. She didn't want to kill their father any less, but it wasn't worth the risk of losing the most important part of her life. Was she giving up? 'Since when does Katsumi give up?' she imagined Sano or Law saying. *Katsumi gives up when her sister might die if she doesn't,* she answered herself. Her anger tried to rise up, tried to yell at her, but she just shrugged at it in response. In her mind she saw her pride, rage, hate, justice, and will to fight confronting her, telling her to keep fighting, keep going. And in reply Katsumi sighed and turned away, embracing resignation and fear instead.

What was worse was that she couldn't even summon the will to care about losing or the fact that she was running away.

She felt a hand on her knee and she let her own fall to cover it, gently encasing the bandaged fingers with her own. She lifted her head enough to meet the gaze of blue eyes. "I'm done," she said softly with a hoarse voice. "I can't go any further."

Ayane studied her carefully. *So you want to give up and run away?*

Katsumi lowered her head again, staring at the floor. *I'm sorry, I can't take more of this. You barely made it. If we keep going, you might not. That's the one chance I can't take. I refuse to.*

Ayane sighed, remaining silent for a few moments of thought. *You did make a promise.*

I've done a lot of foolish things. Maybe we can kill him, Aya, but what will that mean if you die in the process? What if I die and leave you alone?

That won't happen-

"We're not invincible!" Katsumi said loudly. "You can't just *assume* we'll survive. We have to *work* at it, we've *always* had to work at it, and attacking him isn't doing anything but getting us hurt worse every time."

Katsumi... I know you're worried. I know how you feel; you're just scared.

"Of course I'm scared," she said in a quieter tone. "During any of our fights he could have killed us, and he's getting harsher every time. The only reason we're alive is that he hasn't just decided to end it yet; the second he does, we're dead. He's just let us live so far, we both know that." Katsumi shook her head. "We're already sick, Aya. And we've already struggled to survive for so long, why get ourselves killed?"

Because we won't be free otherwise. What if he changes his mind and comes after us later? I don't believe he'll just let us go. I don't think we have a choice.

"So we're just… stuck. No escape."

It's okay, Sumi. You'll protect me.

"I can't. You're in here because-"

You're wrong, again. You fought him off which is why I'm alive. I won't have you hating yourself, not when it's all his fault. I love you and I hate seeing you like this, it's worse than the injuries.

Katsumi sighed, running her thumb over the bandaged fingers. "I'm sorry." She reached over and threaded her fingers through Ayane's hair. "I love you, too. I'm just terrified of losing you, and I don't know if I can stop it from happening."

Things beyond your control are frightening. But don't forget about me, Katsumi; I'll keep myself alive. I wouldn't do that to you.

They were both silent for a long moment, thinking over their options, of which there were few. Katsumi absent-mindedly stroked the hand in hers as she thought, looking at Ayane. "I did get promoted... I'm a Major now... I guess I shouldn't leave that."

Ayane blinked. *What? You mean they actually gave the most important and successful asset in the company some recognition? Finally!*

Katsumi smiled dryly. "I guess they're doing *something* right."

~ ~ ~ ~ ~

Kurasano entered the SIN HQ weary but alive. His arm was in a thin wrapped cast that would help the break heal and he had a few other injuries, but they were minor. Law and Rufus had gotten away with relatively minor injuries as well, for which he was thankful. He'd tried calling Katsumi to ask about Ayane's injuries, but both her phone and cyber link went unanswered. That probably wasn't a good sign, so he tried not to think about it. Inside he found M in his usual spot inside the command center. "Mr. Lionel, you did very well tonight," the enigmatic man said without turning as Sano entered.

Sano rubbed the back of his head. "Thanks. Don't know if I believe that, but I'll accept it. Is Hitomi still up?"

M adjusted his glasses. "I've no idea. She was in here earlier, but she left. She isn't used to the violence yet."

"*I'm* not used to the violence yet," Sano said with a shake of his head. "Tonight was... hell."

M turned his attention to Sano. "Large-scale attacks can be bothersome, I understand. The transition was easier for the others, who all had military experience. Widespread death and carnage can take some time to get used to." He smiled. "And then, of course, you begin feeling bad for getting used to such a thing."

Sano sighed. "Sounds great. Glad to know I have so much to look forward to."

M chuckled as he accessed the computer. He tilted his head, looking at the screen. "That's odd… Apparently Miss Saizen left several hours ago."

Sano frowned. "Where would she go? She didn't appear at the scene, and several hours is too long for a walk."

"We shall find out," M said as he directed the computer to display the security footage at the time. Both he and Sano went quiet as they watched him and Hitomi walk down the hallway and out of the building. M pursed his lips, tapping the brim of his hat before he looked at Sano. "I don't have to tell you that isn't me, I hope."

"I was hoping you'd say it was." Sano grimaced, testing out his arm. "What the hell is going on here? Who is that?"

"There's no way to tell." M removed his hat, running a hand through white hair. He actually looked disappointed in himself; annoyed.

Sano held up his phone and shook his head. "Katsumi's still not answering." He looked at M. "What're we gonna do about this?"

"We are going to get a search going." He looked at Sano. "But not you personally. You and the others are going to rest so you are ready to go if it's necessary."

"Alright, boss, good call. I'm just going to sleep in one of the rooms here, then."

"Very well. I will inform the others."

Sano nodded as he left the room, his anger growing with every step. This stupid night just wouldn't quit.

~ ~ ~ ~ ~

Rufus snapped his phone shut, looking at Law. "Okay, what the hell? No, seriously, what the hell? What is going on tonight?"

Law shrugged as he lit a cigarette. "Somethin' big, that's all I know. Three events: attack on Ayane, attack at Garrus Limited, abduction of Hitomi."

"We don't know it's an abduction yet. For all we know someone's trying to recruit her; Silents are big news."

"Neither is good." Law breathed out a puff of smoke. "It's all coordinated too well, y'know?"

Rufus folded his arms, leaning back against a building. The two of them were near the scene of the battle, neither trusting the situation enough to leave yet. They'd helped with the clean-up at first and were now in a nearby alley discussing the events outside the hearing of the soldiers, medical personnel and security officers swarming the site. "It's more than a little suspicious," Rufus said as he watched people clearing the rubble. Reconstruction would take a while here with the damage several buildings had taken. "There has to be some sort of inside information being leaked or stolen."

"That's what I'm thinking."

Rufus noticed Law checking his phone again. "Still no word from her?"

Law shook his head. "It's a little worryin', but t'be honest, she probably ain't in the best state o' mind right now."

"We'll see her tomorrow, I'm sure. She needs to know about this whole situation."

"I ain't gonna be the one to tell 'er."

~ ~ ~ ~ ~

Date: April 14, 2068
Time: 11:29 AM
Location: SIN HQ, Tokyo, Japan

Katsumi arrived at headquarters, but nobody wanted to speak to her. There was almost an aura about her, one that warned everyone to stay the hell away. Her hands were kept in fists as she simply slammed the door out of her way and stalked through the hall to her office, shutting the door hard enough for the sound to echo. Reno peeked out of his own office just enough to look down the hall. "I guess she heard about Hitomi…"

The other three entered the hall, having heard the sound quite easily. Law folded his arms, shaking his head. "It's not jus' that, it's Ayane, too."

"And her father," Sano added.

"Not to mention the other attack last night," Rufus continued.

"So…" Reno stepped out. "What you're saying is, don't go near her at all, and we really shouldn't even be talking about her right outside her office like this?"

The door opened and Reno literally *dove*, headfirst, back into his office. Katsumi stepped out and put a hand on a hip, glaring at the others. "What are you doing out here? Don't you have work to do?"

Law shrugged. "Nothin' to do but wait right now."

Katsumi folded her arms. "Oh, really? Have you lost all initiative? Don't you three want to get things done and over with? Oh, I'm sorry…" She moved a foot forward and shoved Reno's door open, sending him sprawling from where he'd been listening behind it. "You four?"

Reno stuck his head out again. "I wasn't hiding, I was… checking the door."

"I don't really care. What you *weren't* doing is *helping*."

Sano moved forward. "You're kinda being a little harsh, Captain."

"Major," she corrected as her lavender eyes focused on him instead.

Sano raised an eyebrow. "Major? Really? You got promoted?"

"Why do you sound so surprised about that?"

"I just… I…"

"We aren't used to you being shown the acknowledgment you deserve," Rufus offered.

"Yeah," Sano nodded, "that."

"I'm sure," Katsumi muttered. "The point is you're all getting on my nerves and nothing is getting done."

Hey, Law, Sano said over their cyber link. *Could you pick her up and carry her somewhere for a chat?*

I can only do that when she doesn't mind it. As it is now she'd break my nose. Or my neck.

Great.

"And now you're just staring," Katsumi sighed. "What a *great* response." She turned away, going back into her office. "Get back to work," she said as her door slammed shut behind her.

Reno stood up and scratched his head. "Well… Just like old times, huh?"

"It's worse than old times," Sano said. "She was just shut off and cold then."

"Right, and now she's *angry* and shut off and cold."

Rufus shrugged. "Can't blame her. Perhaps we should get to work."

"On what? There's nothing we can do."

"Find somethin' then," Law replied.

Reno turned back into his office. "Actually, I have an idea…"

~ ~ ~ ~ ~

"My husband is a coward," Lenora Hillford said as she selected Katsumi's number in her phone. Of course, she knew Reno hoped she'd have a better chance at helping with things, but she still found it funny how frightened he was.

"What."

Then again, Lenora thought as she winced at the tone in the voice that answered the call, *maybe he wasn't exaggerating.* "Hi, Katsumi," she said in her friendliest tone. "It's been awhile since I've heard from you."

She heard Katsumi sigh. "Lenora, this really isn't the best time."

"Is tonight a good time? Early evening?" Lenora bit her lip. "I was hoping we could have all of you over. Or just you, if you don't want to deal with the others."

"I… Would it take long?"

Lenora smiled. "No longer than an hour or so. Just a short thing, you know? I'd just like to see you."

"…Alright. But have the others come by after I leave, I don't feel like dealing with them tonight. And only an hour, I have to get to the hospital afterwards."

"Yes, of course." Lenora softened her voice. "How is Ayane, by the way…? I've been worried…"

"I'm…" Katsumi seemed to catch herself, and after that she seemed far more tired than angry. "We're both grateful for your concern. To be honest, I'm worried, too…"

"Are her injuries getting worse?" Lenora said with a hint of panic.

"No, she's recovering… for now. It was… close," Katsumi said in a shaky voice. "She's okay… for now. Who knows how long that will last."

Lenora frowned. "I'm sorry. Look… Lianne wants to stay at a friend's house, I can send Reno out with the others and it can just be us tonight. We can talk."

"I would appreciate that, actually… Though I can't promise I'll be the best company."

"Nonsense. It's settled, then. Can you be here at six? I'll just get something light and casual for us to eat."

"That's perfect. I'll see you then. And… thank you."

Lenora smiled. "Thank you for accepting." She hung up the phone and sighed with relief, grateful that she'd succeeded as she texted Reno the plans.

~ ~ ~ ~ ~

Reno grinned at the text. His wife never failed, ever, at anything. It was really quite remarkable. He was in the middle of replying when his door slowly opened and Katsumi stepped in. "You called her, didn't you?"

He froze mid-text, blinking nervously. "Uh… I mean… Well, it's kind of… Haha, you see, what I mean is-"

"Thank you," she said, interrupting him.

He blinked again. "I… Um… You're welcome." Katsumi nodded and left, and he grinned, hopping up on his desk to do his 'celebration dance'. "Who's the man? I'm the man! Who's the man? I'm the man!"

"That's quite the spectacle," Rufus said from the doorway, surprising Reno and causing him to fall off the desk, tumble over his chair and bring it *and* a shelf down with him, along with everything that had been *on and in* the shelf.

"Ow," Reno said from under the pile of items. "I hate you."

"I know," Rufus said as he left. "I just like earning it."

~ ~ ~ ~ ~

Katsumi arrived exactly on time that night, as she always did. Unlike last time, this time she simply wore a white t-shirt and black jeans and jacket. She felt a lot more comfortable in general than the last time she'd been here as she walked up the porch steps and knocked on the door. The warm whites and yellows of the house were a bit more to her liking this time; they still exuded a strong feeling of family, but this time she let it reinforce the fact that there were good, loving families in the world, and this was one of them. Maybe even she and Ayane could live in a place like this someday, worry-free. Lenora opened it and smiled kindly. "Your timing is impressive," she said as she stepped out of the way. "I'm glad you came."

"I almost didn't," Katsumi admitted as she stepped inside. "I really want to be alone… But I thought this would be a good idea."

"I hope so. I want to help, you know that," Lenora said, shutting the door. "I just made a pizza. I hope that's okay."

Katsumi smiled. "That's perfect. I don't want a fancy meal or anything like that tonight."

They just ate in the den, keeping everything simple. They had the TV on but neither of them was really watching it. The volume was kept low and it was really just there as a minor distraction. Katsumi needed those kinds of minor distractions sometimes to make emotions seem more distant than they really were. "I know you're scared for Reno because of his job," she was saying, keeping her eyes on the television. The screen was showing some kind of old black-and-white movie she didn't know the plot to; Lenora apparently liked the "classics" channels.

"Every day," the brown-haired woman said with a look at Katsumi.

"So you probably understand at least somewhat," the major continued. "I react to fear with anger myself."

Lenora nodded. "I heard you've been a little... um... short?"

"Is *that* what they're saying?" Katsumi mumbled with a smirk. "Anyway, I've... It's been a long time." She looked at Lenora. "When Aya and I first started running, my first thought every morning was 'we didn't die last night' and my last thought every evening was 'we didn't die today'. Every day had that chance; every day we walked the edge of a knife, praying we didn't fall. He could've found us at any point, and he did several times. It was always a slim escape, a near-death experience. For the first few months we didn't even try to think about the future. Looking back, I can see we didn't think we'd have one."

Lenora turned and pulled her legs up onto the couch beside her, focusing her attention on Katsumi. "But that changed?"

Katsumi nodded. "I got tired of nothing but fighting, running and hiding. It was unfair that all we did was survive, so I wanted to make it fair myself; Aya deserved a better life, she didn't deserve having hers ruined just because of our father. One day I just... woke up, I guess," she shrugged. "I decided we'd make our *own* happiness if no one was going to give it to us. After that things were better, happier. We started our own traditions, found ways to buy or make gifts for each other, called each move to a new location a 'vacation'. Some of those days worry didn't factor in, but it was always in the back of our minds. We'd relax, but stay alert. We'd smile and laugh, but glance at any passers-by cautiously. We'd have dinner in a nice restaurant, but sit in the back out of view of the windows. We didn't let caution rule our lives, but it definitely guided them."

"It sounds like that would get really stressful and tiresome."

"You'd think so, but humans can get used to anything. It was sort of like..." Katsumi looked at the ceiling thoughtfully. "Have you ever gone through a long, extremely busy work day, focusing on getting everything done, and only once you get off work, get home and see your bed do you realize how tired you are?"

Lenora smiled. "I'm a nurse, of course I have."

Katsumi nodded. "That basically happened to us. We did a lot of different things; eventually we joined the army, thinking Father wouldn't follow us to a battlefield, and he didn't. As we worked our way up the ranks we realized our Father had finally given up the decade-long chase, and that's when everything hit us. We had to re-learn how to live like normal people, and neither of us have it down yet. That's why we do things like pull a gun on people jumping out for a surprise birthday party, and reactively attack people who wake us up suddenly. We aren't used to normal life and I don't think we ever will be."

"I can see how such a long, intense period of your lives could have such a strong effect. You seem to be doing a pretty good job of it, though."

Katsumi sighed. "That's the problem." She rubbed her face tiredly. "I lost some of that armor I'd built up during that time. We expected danger, death and injury every single day. Not a year went by without both of us nearly dying. We got used to it. We hated it, but we expected it."

Lenora's expression changed to understanding. "So when this happened to Ayane, you weren't prepared for it."

Katsumi nodded. "It scared me a lot more because of that. And it was..." she laid her head back. "It's stupid of me, but I'd begun thinking things were almost over. I let myself start thinking of what to do after. Aya and I were even supposed to go looking at a new place to buy and move into today."

Lenora looked sad as she laid a hand on her arm. "That's not stupid. You need something to look forward to or there's no reason to fight. Reno talks about how seeing me and Lianne at the end of the day is what forces him to do everything right and with as much effort as he can. You can't face someone like your father unless you remind yourself of the freedom and happiness that will come after you win."

"You're right, but the problem is it just adds more hopes for him to dash." She looked at the brunette. "I don't think I can beat him, Lenora... Every time I try one of us just comes closer to dying. Eventually he's going to get tired of it and kill us, and I can't do anything but watch it happen. It's unfair, but in the end, what can you do when it's *reality* that's wrong?"

"I... don't have an answer for you. I can tell you that you'll win, but in the end I can't know that. And we both know that the hero doesn't always win in reality. All I can say is... None of us have ever met anyone stronger than you. I admire you, my husband admires you, and we know the others on your team do. The hero doesn't always win, but somehow *you* always find a way to. So I guess you'll just have to learn to trust yourself as much as your sister and the rest of us do."

"Easier said than done," Katsumi stated. She meant to say more, but a sudden headache was... *Damn. Damn it. Not now. Give me an hour, please.* Unfortunately it was intensifying quickly, but her practice kept it from showing on her face. "I should probably talk to her about it again... I should be over there soon anyway." Katsumi stood, looking at her. "Thanks for having me."

Lenora smiled. "Of course. I enjoy your company." She led her to the door, opening it. "Tell Ayane I'm thinking of her for me, okay?"

Katsumi gave a small smile as she stepped out of the door. "Thanks." As soon as the door closed she made for the porch steps and headed across the grass. Stress, intense emotion and injury had a way of making her sickness worse, and she'd had a heavy dose of all three over the last twenty-four hours. It seemed to be getting even worse because never before had it hit her this hard this fast. As soon as her feet hit the grass the world was already swimming, her car a confusing blur in her vision. She'd never be able to drive in this state. She pulled out her phone to call a taxi but it slipped from her weakening fingers to the grass below, and she couldn't distinguish it from any other dark spot in the grass.

The pain seemed to double itself every second, distracting her further. She reached out and felt the cool metal of the hood of her car as she reached it. She tried to brace her arm on it and follow around to the door but her arm buckled under the weight. She collapsed against the hood and slipped to the pavement in front of her car, knowing that she'd never make it now. *Aya... Going to be late... Sick... Can't move...*

Is it bad? Where are you?

Katsumi closed her eyes, glad, at least, to hear her sister's voice. *At my car... don't know how long I'll... be...*

At your car where?! Katsumi? Damn it!

Too late. Sensation fled from Katsumi as the familiar darkness consumed her mind.

Reno laughed as he stood up from the table, grabbing his coat, phone and keys. "I never claimed I could do that, just that I could jump it."

"Uh-huh," Law said, unconvinced, as he downed the last of his drink. "You leaving so soon? Willing to risk the wrath?"

Reno grinned, holding up his phone to show the time. "No worries. It's after eight, the boss left my house an hour ago, unless plans changed."

Sano raised an eyebrow. "Willing to bet on it?"

"If he calls and asks if she's gone yet, that will be a new level of cowardly, even for him," Rufus said as he sipped from his glass.

"I'm not that much of a wimp!" Reno said defensively as he pulled on his coat.

"That means he knows his wife will protect him," Law clarified.

"Damn right. And speaking of, it's a night without the kiddo, no way I won't take advantage of that," Reno said as he wiggled his eyebrows, causing Law to laugh.

"Ugh, too much information, man," Sano said with a shake of his head. He waved his hand. "Go, get out of here. Have fun."

"You bet I will." Reno left the restaurant and got on the road, trying not to speed, but failing as usual. His music blaring, his windows down, his long brown hair blowing, and his shades on even though it was night, Reno could have almost as much fun in a car as he could in a jet or helicopter. He made every turn perfectly and made no mistakes regardless of speed; it was his gift, really. He did, however, slow down as he entered his neighborhood, since an area with kids always made him drive like an old lady. As he approached his house his headlights fell on a sleek black car parked on the street outside it. His eyebrows rose in surprise as he drove around it and into the garage. "Huh, I guess she did stay late."

He turned off the car and climbed out, whistling a tune as he headed for the front door. He opened it with a grin, stepping inside. "Yo, the man of the house is home! No insults in response to that statement, please!"

Lenora met him in the hallway, smiling as she kissed him. "Did you have fun?"

"Yeah, it was fine. I thought I might have a bit more fun here, though," he grinned.

Lenora slipped her arms around his neck. "Really now? How so?"

"I'll be glad to show you right after Katsumi leaves."

Lenora smiled. "You're in luck, then; she left over an hour ago."

"Huh?" Reno frowned. "Then why's her car outside? Did she drink a lot?"

Lenora blinked. "Her car's outside? She didn't drink anything."

"Shit." Reno moved away and went back outside with Lenora following. "Gotta be an explanation-"

"There!"

Reno followed his wife's pointing and spotted the body in front of the car. "Shit... Shit, shit, shit," he repeated as they ran towards her. "You didn't hear any gunshots or sounds?"

"No, nothing!" They reached Katsumi and turned her over, noting that she was unconscious. Lenora checked her over but shook her head. "No blood, no new wounds. Reno, call an ambulance. Do you know what hospital Ayane is in?"

"I don't, but Law does. I'll call him after this," he said as he pulled out his phone, dialing the emergency number. "What's wrong with her? I mean, she's alive, but..."

"Pulse is weak, breathing labored... She seems to be in pain..." Lenora lifted one of Katsumi's eyelids. "She appears to be dreaming, which is unusual... This isn't a seizure or heart attack... I'm not sure what this is..."

Reno paced back and forth with his phone to his ear. "Well then this makes no- yeah, hi! I need an ambulance sent to my location now, someone here is hurt or sick and we don't know what with, but she's unconscious." Lenora looked up at him as he spoke rapidly, continuing his pacing. "Yeah. Yes, I know her, she's a family friend. Yeah, I have it. Right, okay thanks." He hung up and looked at Lenora. "Fifteen minutes. Should we get her inside?"

Lenora nodded. "If we can. I don't see any injuries so we might as well make her comfortable."

~ ~ ~ ~ ~

August 14th, 2051

Two girls, seventeen and fourteen years of age, had broken into a complex held by the criminal organization known as the Blue Shield. That was the information they had, anyway; whether or not the individuals currently searching the warehouse believed it was up for debate. The warehouse was poorly lit, but that had more to do with the two having taken out half the lights than it did poor planning. Crates and boxes of various sizes filled the building, leaving only thin aisles between them for the soldiers to move through. The girls weren't in any of those.

Katsumi knelt atop a wide crate, nestled in the shadows between two taller ones. She watched two soldiers move past beneath her and looked across the aisle. Ayane was atop a stack of three crates, too high to be in any line of sight. Four soldiers had set up searchlights in the building, one on each side; they swept the bright floodlights across the piles of crates, meaning the two couldn't trust some shadows to hide them. Each soldier had a headlight and special rifles that rapidly fired needles. They couldn't fire standard ammunition, as this warehouse was full of munitions and the whole thing would be caught up in an explosion. In total there were nineteen soldiers; fourteen exploring the room and four operating the lights. The last one was this unit's leader, organizing the whole thing. He was their target.

Katsumi nodded to the side and received a nod from Ayane in return. Katsumi dropped into the aisle behind the two soldiers that had passed them. She moved silently, approaching the one in back. No matter how quietly she did this, the one in front would hear something and look back, but that would be fine. Katsumi moved quickly; her left hand whipped around and hit the soldier in the throat as her right caught the hand holding his gun, one of her fingers slipping behind the trigger so it couldn't be pulled. Her left arm instantly curled around his throat, choking him out now that he couldn't make a sound.

The soldier in front turned at the small noise and his eyes widened as he brought his gun up, but Ayane landed beside him and caught his gun, twisting it to break his finger. Of course he yelled in pain, but that was preferred at this point; Ayane quickly spun his weapon and shot him with it, and Katsumi let the other now-unconscious soldier slip to the ground before picking up his weapon and killing him with it. Then the two were back up in the crates, racing as far as they could before slipping in between two crates as searchlights swept across their position towards the source of the sound. As soon as the lights were past they began moving to the side, taking up hiding places.

The soldiers that found the bodies seemed angry. Four of them climbed the crates, and they could hear others being ordered to watch the aisles around the area. From below them, between two crates she'd pushed apart to make just enough room, Katsumi watched as they unfortunately moved towards the spot her sister was hiding in. That wouldn't work; she waited until the fourth soldier was passing her, then grabbed his ankle and yanked his leg down into the crevice she was in, breaking or twisting something judging by the sound he made. The other three turned and she leapt up on top, wrapping an arm around the soldier's neck and turning his body to intercept the fire from the front two soldiers as she shot the third. The front two dropped from Ayane's fire in the next few seconds, then the two sisters were up and moving again before the searchlights landed on the new bodies.

Six down. Katsumi paused to shoot one of the searchlight operators, followed by shooting out the light. They then ran towards another side of the warehouse, hopping from crate to crate before finding a new hiding spot. Seven down, eleven to go before the target was clear. Three soldiers ran beneath them and Katsumi loudly landed behind them. They spun around to see her, but two of them went down as Ayane shot them from the other side. The last one spun in confusion to find the new attacker and Katsumi easily gunned him down before disappearing back into the supplies. Ten down. Two soldiers moved carefully across the crates as they looked in each crevice with increasing caution.

It didn't help, even though both sisters' weapons were empty. As one of them looked into a dark spot Katsumi appeared in it and smashed the butt of her gun into his knee. As he fell forward with a cry she jammed the gun into the spot and caught his head, yanking it down so his neck landed on the edge of the gun, crushing his windpipe. She ducked back down as the other soldier began firing in her direction, hitting his ally more than anything. Ayane came up behind him, bashing the back of one leg. As he went down on a knee she kicked his gun from his hands and brought her own up against his neck from behind, pulling it tightly until he went limp. Twelve down. They grabbed the new weapons and moved; had to keep moving.

The three remaining soldiers exploring the room were extremely nervous now, jumping at every shadow. It didn't help when Ayane's fire took out another searchlight and operator. Thirteen down. Even the unit's leader looked scared, as well as angry. He yelled at them that he wouldn't be beaten by two little girls. He was on the edge, though, and he would flee the second the last man went down; that couldn't happen, they needed his information. The two sisters split up, each moving towards a different wall. Ayane fired to make the three exploring soldiers follow her. They took out the remaining two searchlights at the same time; fifteen down. The leader was shaking now, calling for the three soldiers to return to his side. Cowards were so easy to predict.

Katsumi landed in front of him, startling him so much he wasn't even able to get his gun up before she hit him. As he stumbled back she ripped the gun from his hands, then moved behind him and put it to his head as the remaining three soldiers came out. They immediately raised their guns but he waved his hands wildly, shouting, "No, no! I'm right in the way, fools!" They paused but didn't lower their weapons, unsure how to proceed from this side of things. Ayane helped them out by shooting one from behind. The other two spun and as Ayane shot one, Katsumi turned the gun and shot the other one. The leader tried to use this to escape but she kicked out his legs, sending him to his back.

They set up a chair, using the same heavy-duty tape that secured most of the room's crates to secure him to the chair. He looked between them, disbelieving that girls of that age had killed his whole unit and captured him. "What do you want?"

Katsumi stood in front of him and folded her arms. "Eli Vans was here yesterday," she said, using their father's current alias.

"We want to know what he's doing and what he's planning," Ayane added as she moved to his side.

The man laughed. "You... You're kidding, right? I tell you, he'll kill me."

"If you don't, we'll do much worse," Katsumi said without hesitation.

"Sorry, but he's a little more intimidating than you. I'm not saying a word."

Katsumi shrugged, not at all bothered by the refusal. It was only temporary anyway; it always was. "Fine." She began walking around, looking over the tables lining the side of the warehouse.

"...What are you doing?" the man asked in confusion.

"She's looking for something to use," Ayane answered simply.

"Ah." Katsumi picked up a sheet of sandpaper. "This'll work." She walked towards the man. "Last chance. Sure you won't talk?"

"Being able to kill doesn't mean you're able to torture. I'm sure. Good bluff, though."

"Alright," Katsumi nodded, looking to Ayane. "Hold his eye open."

~ ~ ~ ~ ~

Lenora paced the hallway nervously. Waiting for information on Katsumi in a hospital hallway was too familiar a feeling; Reno looked nervous, too, while Sano looked bothered by something at the same time. Law and Rufus had declined to come, saying they were sure she'd be fine and they preferred to do what she'd want. Maybe that was the best option, but Lenora couldn't see herself doing that. This time, however, they only had to wait a few minutes, not hours. They were actually surprised when the doctor came out so quickly.

He looked at Sano. "I'm glad you were able to get me the information of her usual doctor. There's nothing new to report, I'm afraid; this is simply her pre-existing condition. It's quite known, even expected by this point, he said."

All of them were caught off-guard by this announcement, understandably. Lenora shook her head. "Pre-existing condition? This isn't something new?"

The doctor smiled. "No, it's no new threat."

"How long has she had this condition?" Sano spoke up.

"Are you family?" Sano shook his head and the doctor gave an apologetic smile. "Then I'm sorry, I can't tell you anything more."

Reno looked between the other two. "You think she has what Ayane has?"

Lenora shook her head. "Probably not. Ayane's is slow, extended, and weakening; she doesn't collapse suddenly."

"I wonder if this is related to when I found her sick that one time," Sano said more to himself than anyone. "She reacted really harshly to any questions about it."

"We'd have to ask her ourselves," Reno stated. "And I don't know about you, but if she's hid it for however long, that doesn't seem like a good idea."

Lenora looked away, toward the room she knew Katsumi was in. Why couldn't anything ever go the way they planned?

Chapter 17: Omega

Katsumi came to with a throbbing headache and heavy fatigue. She felt like she had to fight her way to the waking world against the weakness pulling her back. The shock helped; she forced herself up upon realizing she didn't recognize her surroundings, and then her mood darkened even further once she understood she was in a hospital room. A nurse glanced in, noting her movement. "Oh, good, you're awake. You have visitors, I'll go get them," she said with a smile, leaving before Katsumi could say anything.

She realized she was still dressed from the night before, thankful for such a blessing as she stumbled out of the bed and slipped into her shoes just as Sano, Reno and Lenora entered. They all looked rested, so at least she knew they'd gone home, but she was still annoyed that they'd come back, and at the situation in general. It was unfair that her secrets kept getting revealed. Lenora stepped around the other two. "Katsumi, you really shouldn't be up yet-"

"*Really?*" Katsumi turned around, raking her glare across all three and making them shift uncomfortably. Good. They deserved to be as uncomfortable as they were making her feel right now. She had no idea how many times she'd told them not to come when she was sick or injured, that it just made her feel worse. They didn't listen, though; they didn't seem to accept that she was different from them. They'd rather make themselves feel better by checking on her than listening to her wishes. She was tired of it. She folded her arms, keeping her glare on them. "Perhaps you'd like to tell me all about my sickness? Maybe you'd like to tell me exactly what I can and can't do, how I can deal with it?"

Reno stepped forward. "Come on Boss, that isn't fair."

"Shut up." Katsumi shook her head. "I'm tired of this. At first I felt bad, you know, you guys were only trying to help, only trying to make me feel better, even though I told you it didn't work. It just makes it worse. But you needed some time to understand that, I knew that. But now? Look, if you can't just drop things like this, then you can't be in more than a business relationship with me." She sighed, rubbing her temples. "Thanks for caring, thanks for bringing me here, thanks for making me important enough to worry about. I appreciate it. But please... *Please* just let it go, and try *listening* for once." She grabbed her phone and turned around as they looked down sheepishly, grabbing her jacket and pulling it on. "I can't deal with this right now anyway. What floor are we on?"

Lenora blinked. "Um... Third?"

"Good." Katsumi pulled open the window, slipping through and dropping out. She heard the other woman gasp and could feel her watching a few seconds later as she landed on the pavement with both feet, standing and continuing to walk without breaking stride. *Let's see if you've learned this time... Leave me alone... Leave it.* She kept her team cyber link open and looked at her phone as she walked. Several minutes passed without any attempt at contact from them and she sighed in relief, sliding the phone into a pocket. She really didn't want to deal with the whole 'why didn't you tell us you were sick' thing. It was enough having Ayane worry about it, she didn't need her entire team doubting her abilities and treating her like a sick little girl. Her illness may be new to *them*, but *she'd* had it for years, and they needed to realize that.

Katsumi took a roundabout path, heading back into the hospital through a side entrance. She stepped into an elevator, hitting the button for the fifth floor. She was sure they knew she was going to her sister's room, but she didn't think they'd be stupid enough to try to meet her there. She got out of the elevator and headed towards the room, thankful the hospital was so quiet at this hour. She smiled when she saw Law sitting on the bench outside Ayane's room; she didn't know if he was waiting for her or Ayane to wake up, but she knew he was one of the only people in the world she wanted to see right now. The dark-skinned giant looked up when she approached, giving a nod. "She's asleep," he whispered.

"She better be," Katsumi replied in a quiet voice. "C'mon, there's a coffee room down the hall."

"Perfect." Law followed her down the hall and into the room, thankful he could speak normally here. "Heard about the incident. They bother you about it?"

Katsumi sighed, grabbing a cup and filling it with straight, black coffee, adding nothing before beginning to sip it, hoping it would wake her up more. "Of course they did. Not thirty seconds after I wake up, they're crowding into the room acting like I'm dying."

Law chuckled, beginning to make his own coffee. "Well, give 'em a break, you surprised 'em last night."

"It wasn't my idea. I tried to leave before I collapsed, I just wasn't fast enough." Katsumi leaned against the wall, crossing her legs as she blew on her coffee. "I might apologize later, but I'm just really tired of them not listening. I've been put in a hospital so much recently, shouldn't they be used to it by now? I am."

Law shrugged, looking at her. "Shouldn't you be used to Ayane getting hurt by now?"

Katsumi frowned. "That's different. She's my sister."

"You're their friend."

"If I died they'd be sad. If Aya died I'd break."

"Fair enough, an' I get your point, but they're not as hard as we are." Law leaned against the counter, looking a little funny with the tiny cup in front of his large frame.

"I just want them to be like you," Katsumi said as she looked over at him. "You and Rufus understand. You don't look at me with that concerned pity."

"No, we like our bones where they are," he said with a chuckle, drawing a smile from Katsumi.

"I've known you longer than they have. Besides, they feel a bit betrayed now; their friend didn't trust them enough to tell them about a sickness she was dealing with."

"It's not a matter of trust. It's *my* business, not *theirs*. I don't have to tell them *anything*."

"*You* know that, an' *I* know that, but *they* don't know that."

Katsumi sighed, rubbing her cheek. "Fine, I'll try to clarify it later. I probably overreacted a bit…"

"Why, what'd you do?"

"Jumped out the window." He laughed and she smirked at him. "It was the quickest exit! And I wanted to make a statement. I've just been so stressed and emotional lately, I lose control so quickly. Sometimes I even *know* I'm losing control *while* it's happening, but I can't seem to stop myself."

Law cracked his neck. "Sounds like a problem. Maybe it's somethin' you should think about a bit more, talk to Ayane about."

"You think so?" Katsumi looked down at the cup in her hands. "I just… I guess it could be more than stress… But you know, I've always been a difficult person to be friends with."

"Oh, I know," he said, receiving a dry look from her. "You still somehow got a bunch of 'em. I hope they at least appreciate how hard you're tryin'."

"*Thank* you," Katsumi said with a sigh. "Do you know how much effort it takes for me just to visit someone? Or to smile when asked a question instead of shutting off completely? A lifetime of behavior is hard to undo."

"I think they understand that. I try to explain a bit to them."

"Oh, so you talk about me behind my back, do you?"

"All the time," he said, grinning as he pulled out a cigarette and lit it. "But it's all good things. Mostly."

"Uh-huh." Katsumi walked past him, yanking the cigarette from his hand as he brought it to his mouth, sticking it between her own lips. He gave her an amused look before pulling out another. Katsumi let out a breath of smoke as she stood at the doorway, looking down the hall. "I appreciate you running interference." She turned around, leaning against the doorway as she studied him. "Do you know me better only because you're my oldest friend?"

Law thought about that as he took a draw from his new cigarette, looking at the ceiling. "Maybe. Although it could be 'cause we're more alike, too. After all, Rufus understands most of it, an' you haven't known him all that long."

"True." Katsumi rolled the cig between her fingers. "They'll never fully understand me, but they can at least accept what they don't understand."

"It's not that hard when y'get down to it," Law said as he looked at the floor. "What you do is, look at the situation: would you give a normal person a 'get well' card for whatever's goin' on? If so, leave Katsumi the hell alone. Simple."

Katsumi chuckled softly, leaning her head against the wall. "Surely I'm more complicated than that."

"*You* aren't that simple; *dealing with you* is."

"I guess so. I don't get angry at you nearly as often."

"Maybe you should just have your sister give 'em some lessons."

Katsumi grinned. "Dealing With Katsumi 101?"

Law shrugged. "Couldn't hurt." She looked down the hall again and he chuckled. "Why don't you go in there?"

Katsumi looked back into the room, tapping her cigarette over the trash can. "She needs her sleep."

"She needs her sister."

"Think so?" He nodded and she looked down the hall again. "Well, if you say so. Make sure you come in if you're still here a few minutes after she wakes up," she said before putting the cigarette out on the rim of the trashcan, dropping it in and heading down the hall.

Law chuckled. "That took a lot of convincing."

Katsumi slipped into the dark room, closing the door quietly behind her. Ayane looked a lot better; she had more color, and no longer had an oxygen mask. Katsumi took a seat, not wanting to wake her, but also wanting to wake her. She settled for watching her, leaning back in her chair with a smile. Despite what their father had done to her, she was still beautiful even though it hadn't all healed yet; Katsumi made a mental note to tell her that once she woke up.

Unfortunately her visit didn't last for very long before Law opened the door, gesturing to her. With a concerned glance she left the room, pulling the door shut and studying Law's serious face. "What is it?"

"Sorry, boss, there's something important goin' on at HQ. Director wants us over there; we might have found Hitomi."

Katsumi narrowed her eyes. "Let's go." She glanced back at Ayane's room before leading Law out of the hospital. Half an hour later Katsumi stood in M's office surrounded by her team, watching a recorded video M had received shortly before.

Sigma was on the screen in his black, electronically-lined cloak and hood, the bottom of his face visible but hard to read. Katsumi was finding it difficult to see the person from her dream (which seemed like ages ago) in real life, but there he stood. "I've located your missing teammate. This is my third warning to you, Major Samakura. You only get three." Shoot the heart, the text about the two attacks, and this – that did add up to three warnings, but the text had made it seem like he was partly responsible for the attacks it had warned about. But then, this man did like to play games, so it still made sense – he was just a sociopath. "She is here," Sigma continued, and an image of an old abandoned house along with a GPS location appeared around him. "Another important note, Major - my surveillance was able to determine that your father often visits there."

Katsumi tensed up, forcing herself to remain still as the rest of her team glanced at her. Sigma continued speaking, lifting a hand and causing numbers to scroll over the screen. "However, I was able to hack into his computers and communications and discover that he is never there between six PM and six AM. Apparently the house is cursed and the door can only be opened between those hours, so he leaves it shortly after six in the evening and returns shortly before six in the morning. He leaves no guards because it would attract attention, and because he does not believe he needs them. Your father is quite arrogant, is he not?" Sigma finally offered a slight smile. "I suggest you go when he is not present, then perhaps set a trap for him afterwards. But I would certainly go tonight," he said as the image switched to an interior camera showing a restrained Hitomi. "She might not be left alive for much longer."

The message ended and M turned to Katsumi. "This could very well be a trap, obviously."

"Right…" Katsumi sighed. "But we have no choice. We're going."

"Are you taking his advice?"

"It's worked out for me before… Besides, he said the door won't even open before six. We'll send someone to verify that it won't open, and if it doesn't, we'll get there around seven to be sure my father isn't in the area."

"So what's with this whole set-up?" Sano said with a shake of his head. "What's going on?"

"I don't know nearly as much as I'd like to, but I would guess my father is planning on trying to use Hitomi to lure me and my sister into a trap at some point, or maybe bargain for our allegiance. This could be that very trap, even. But like I said, we have no choice."

Rufus spun a knife over his knuckles, staring at the screen that had frozen on the final image, one of Hitomi. "Being the good guys is such a disadvantage."

Katsumi glanced at him, smirking. "You're right about that. That's why we have to be the best." She turned around. "Clear your schedules, everyone; tonight's going to be busy one way or another."

~ ~ ~ ~ ~

"So some of our agents gathered info on the house we're going to," Reno said as he leaned back in his chair, staring up at the ceiling.

"Uh-huh?" Law asked distractedly from his office across the hall, looking over info on his computer.

"There's a lot of history to this house. A *lot*."

"Well, it's old."

"No, I mean *our* kind of history. It's not just cursed, it's haunted. Like, ridiculously haunted. Woman-in-white-prowls-the-halls-screaming-for-her-murdered-kids haunted."

"That *is* our field of expertise."

"Why are you calm?!" Reno sat up, looking through their open doorways at Law like he was insane. "It's a HAUNTED. HOUSE. This is like, the number one horror cliché! This is big!"

"We've done haunted houses before."

"Yeah, but this one is super creepy. Faces in windows and stuff."

Law stared across the hall at him. "You're afraid of faces? What about the psychotic superhuman serial killer that might be there?"

"Well, yeah, that's bad too, but seriously man…" Reno held his hands up to either side of his face, wiggling his fingers. "Faaaaaaceeeees!"

"You watch too many movies."

"Probably." Reno sat back, twirling a pen between his fingers before pointing it at Law. "But it's worse being in one."

"I'll hold your hand."

"Should I bring a blanket for us to cuddle under?"

"Only if you want me to strangle you with it."

Reno shook his head. "See? The creepy curse is already making you more violent."

"If threats of violence are caused by cursed homes, I never want to set foot in the one Katsumi grew up in."

Reno shuddered. "Dude, if her father's any indication of what her childhood was like, I wouldn't do that anyway."

~ ~ ~ ~ ~

So you're going in tonight?

Katsumi smiled at the incredulity in her sister's voice. *Not alone. I'll have Sano and Rufus with me.* She glanced out the window, squinting at the afternoon sun. Three hours until they left for the house. If this wasn't a trap, they'd be getting Hitomi back, and they might be able to learn some more about her father's plans. If it was a trap, this might be her chance to end things once and for all.

No, they're good, it's just…

You wish you were coming with me, Katsumi continued for her, going back to checking her weapons and equipment for the thirty-seventh time that afternoon. She wasn't good at waiting for things to start.

She heard her sister sigh over the cyber link. *Yes.*

I don't.

That's because you're selfish and self-sacrificing.

Katsumi chuckled. *You can't be both.*

Somehow, you are.

If our father is there... Katsumi sighed, closing our eyes. *I'll get out. The three of us can fight him long enough to get out, and Law will be there, too, just a call away.*

You promise?

I promise. I wouldn't say it to you if I didn't mean it.

I know... I'm sorry. Just... be careful, okay?

I'm... sometimes careful. I will be. I can't abandon you.

You better not. Now that I'm sure you'll be safe, though... How did the whole sickness-hitting-outside-of-Reno's-house go? Katsumi groaned and Ayane giggled – no, *snickered* at her. *That bad, huh?*

Yeah, laugh it up, Katsumi responded with a smirk. *I woke up and they all crowded into my room like mother hens.*

Again? They're kind of thick, aren't they?

Kind of.

What'd you do?

Window.

There was a pause. *...Did you jump out of one, or throw them out of one?*

Katsumi laughed, clapping a hand over her mouth as Sano gave her an odd look from across the room. She waved him away before shaking her head, grinning. *I jumped. I'll keep the other option in mind for next time, though.*

It wasn't a suggestion.

That doesn't mean it's not a good idea.

Throwing your friends out of multi-story windows is the very definition of a bad idea, Sumi.

They bring it on themselves!

They aren't used to lunatics.

I'm just a victim!

Poor you, your friends care.

I can't help that I'm... sniff... damaged...

Ayane's tone was dry. *That usually works better if you actually sniff instead of just saying "sniff".*

Damn.

Sorry, Sumi. You just don't have my talent for emotional manipulation.

I like that you're proud of that.

One should always be proud of their skills.

You've got issues.

Thank you, Mrs. Pot.

You're too smart these days. I miss eleven-year-old Ayane; she was so much easier to win conversations against.

So you're saying you can't outwit anyone smarter than an eleven-year-old?

Katsumi paused. *...Some twelve-year-olds are really smart, you know.*

Uh-huh.

Mhmm.

Right.

Yes.

Sure.

Correct.

Indeed.

Most assuredly.

Which one of us is supposed to be the mature one again?

I forget.

~ ~ ~ ~ ~

Date: April 16, 2068
Time: 6:57 PM
Location: Lexington House

"That... is creepy as hell," Reno muttered as he stared up at the huge old house. "That thing is ancient! Who keeps these around? Shouldn't they be torn down to prevent freaky ghost possession?"

Katsumi smiled as she stepped up beside him, sipping from a cup of coffee. "Most people don't know 'freaky ghost possession' exists, Reno, you know that. Besides, not every old house is haunted."

"No, just all the ones *we* visit."

Rufus appeared at Katsumi's other side, looking up at the place himself. "So what terrifying history does tonight's home have?"

"I'm glad you asked," she replied as she studied the front of the house. "Murder, of course."

"Obviously."

"But there's a twist. This murder was supposedly committed by the children."

Reno looked at her incredulously. "You're kidding. Are we actually going to be facing little child ghosts? Are we *really* going to be facing *creepy little children ghosts*?!"

Kurasano popped up on the other side of him. "It gets better," he grinned, "they were never found. And the lead investigator on the case went missing soon after as well, as did his replacement."

"Okay, that's cool, hey I'm gonna head back to HQ, but you guys lemme know how it went, alright? And make sure you tell me how you responded when they asked you to play with them forever and ever and ever."

Reno spun around to walk away but Katsumi's hand caught his shirt, hauling him back. "Not so fast."

"Aww, c'mon, boss, I'm just the pilot! I can't pilot anything inside a house!"

"That is indeed true, which is why you'll be outside."

Reno stared at her as if she had just turned into a ghost. "You want me to sit outside the creepy haunted house alone all night?"

"Not alone." Katsumi pointed with her thumb over her shoulder. "Sam will be here as well."

Law set a heavy hand on Reno's shoulder. "No worries. I can take any ghost that comes out."

"Oh, alright. But I better be getting paid a lot for this."

"Don't be a baby," Sano chuckled.

"Don't be a baby," Reno mimicked in a high-pitched voice before walking over to sit in the chair next to Law's. They had a small computer set-up with a couple computers, tracking and communication equipment. He edged up to a computer, helping to set it up. "Think we'll get a lot of interference from weird ghost-vibes?"

"Not sure," Law responded as he typed rapidly. "That last investigation wasn't a problem."

"Yeah, but each one's different." Reno glanced at the clock. "Time, boss."

"Right. You two keep track of us; Law, monitor human activity near and within the house. Reno, you're watching spiritual activity. Stay in communication and let us know any important readings as always." Katsumi gestured to Kurasano and Rufus. "Let's go." She reached for the door, watching it shimmer as she took hold of the handle and pulled it open. Gaping darkness greeted them and the three walked in without hesitation, disappearing from sight as the door shut behind them.

Immediately Reno and Law clapped their hands to their ears and tore off their headsets as intense static feedback nearly deafened them. Reno glared at his headset and held it away from him like a bad-smelling piece of garbage, still able to hear the static. "What the hell?!"

"Reno…" Law interrupted, pointing to one of the computers. "We've got a problem."

The screen was flashing a continual warning, showing three blinking dots just beyond the door with two words flashing above them: *CONNECTION LOST.*

~ ~ ~ ~ ~

The three SIN members stepped into the darkness, hearing the door shut behind them. Suddenly the darkness drained like watercolors being washed away, revealing that they were standing in the entrance hall to a very nice home; there was not a cobweb or speck of dust in sight, no signs of age or damage. An expensive chandelier hung from the ceiling supplying most of the light, but old electric lights lined the walls to provide additional lighting. Before them stretched two curved staircases that met at a balcony above. Below the balcony were two doors and an open hallway that stretched away, and to either side of them was an additional hall. More doors could be seen on the balcony above.

Kurasano whistled, walking ahead with his hands in his pockets and taking a look around. "This is a weird one."

"It seems like a past reflection," Katsumi said softly as she glanced down one of the hallways.

Rufus removed his shades, grey eyes examining the room. "Like a spirit echo, but for an entire building. I've never seen this before."

"Neither have we," Katsumi admitted. "We have no rules for this type of situation."

"So," Sano smirked, "making it up as we go?"

"It won't be the first time." Katsumi put a hand to her ear, speaking into her headset. "Law, Reno, we've got an unusual situation here." Nothing came back but silence. Katsumi frowned. "Communication is… blocked?" Something was eating away at the back of her mind, though. Something else was wrong, something worse… When she figured it out her expression must have revealed a lot, as the other two shared a glance and studied her warily.

"What's wrong, boss?" Sano asked carefully.

"I can't reach her." Katsumi immediately headed for the door, but the handle refused to turn and the door refused to open. Katsumi growled, slamming a fist into the door, which did nothing. "Damn it!"

"And… We're stuck," Sano stated. "Excellent…"

Rufus slipped his shades back on. "I guess we've got nine hours to figure this out and solve it."

"It looks like it," Katsumi sighed as she backed away from the door. "And if we don't, we might never get back out."

~ ~ ~ ~ ~

"This is wrong," Law stated as he stood up, grabbing his gun case and moving towards the house.

"What're you… You're going inside?" Reno stood up.

"We're useless out here if there's no contact. I'm going in to help them. You stay here in case it gets fixed, we'll need someone on the outside."

"You want me to sit out here alone all night?"

"If you want company…" Law looked back at him. "Call Ayane. If the cyber link between her and Katsumi is blocked like ours is, she could use some information. Besides, she's good company."

"I… sure." Reno sighed and shrugged. "Go in. I'll be out here."

As soon as Law went through the door it swung shut, and the computer flashed the same warning of a lost connection with him. Reno looked despondently at the screen before switching it over to video, contacting the video screen in Ayane's current room. It was answered so quickly that Ayane had to have been waiting for it, and she appeared in front of it sitting on her bed with a worried expression. "Reno? What's going on? I can't contact Katsumi."

"Yeah, we know." Reno spun the screen's camera to face the house. "They all went in there." He spun it back to himself and leaned back in the chair. "Communications won't go through. Law went in after them to help from the inside. I think everything else is fine, though; we just have no contact."

Ayane sighed, sitting back. "I knew something was going to go wrong. No one should have gone in at all. This is some sort of trap."

Reno shrugged. "Maybe so, but I've learned to trust Katsumi anyway. We've walked into traps knowingly before. She's got a knack for turning a trap back on those who set it up."

"I… You're right. I'm just a worrying person."

"Ha, don't worry about that, so is my Lenora."

Ayane smiled. "So I've heard. And now she worries about my sister, too, and I worry about you."

Reno chuckled. "Great, a crossfire of fear. Always good. You don't have to worry about me, though. I'm just sitting out here."

"They left you alone?"

"Yep. Alone." He looked up at the house. "Outside, at night, in front of a terrifying house of violent nightmares full of screaming hell-children."

Ayane laughed. "Sounds like fun."

"This is my life," he said dryly. "Mind keeping me company?"

Ayane smiled at him. "Of course not! I mean, it's either that or sit here bored, staring at the ceiling and worrying about Sumi."

"Good to know I'm a better option than that." He swung his chair around a bit, spinning from side to side. "I've been meaning to mention, 'Sumi' seems like a pretty cutesy nickname for the boss."

Ayane smiled, leaning back against the wall behind her. "When I was little I had trouble with hard consonants like the sharp 'k' sound, so I couldn't say 'Katsumi'. I just called her 'Sumi' and it just kind of... stuck."

"She seems to like it."

Ayane tilted her head, looking distant. "I think it reminds her of a much more innocent time. Katsumi and I are partners, but she's also always going to see me as her little sister. I want to reinforce that because it's important."

"You like that role?"

Ayane nodded. "We have a perfect relationship. It evolves, but it doesn't change." She smiled.

"And I'll keep calling her 'Sumi' because she'll always be my big sister."

"Siblings never really lose that feeling of relative age, I think."

"Do you have any siblings?"

Reno nodded. "Yep, two. I have an older sister named Sage and a younger sister named Luna."

Ayane blinked. "Sage, Reno and Luna?"

He grinned. "My parents are kind of into the whole 'hippie' type thing."

"That explains your hair and fashion sense."

"Don't it, though?" He spun around in his chair once, looking at the sky. "We plan to have another kid pretty soon. Lianne's five and she already really wants a sibling."

"Oh, you should!" Ayane leaned forward. "Especially with parents like you, it'd be perfect."

Reno looked back at her. "Remember it might not be a sister, might be a brother."

Ayane shrugged. "That's great, too! Law is basically a big brother to me."

"He definitely cares about you two enough."

Ayane smiled. "Sumi and I have been pretty lucky in this part of our lives. We have a lot of people who care about us; even if she doesn't show it, she appreciates it as much as I do."

"Not enough to keep her from jumping out windows, though."

Ayane grinned. "That has nothing to do with appreciation. That's just Katsumi."

~ ~ ~ ~ ~

As soon as Law stepped into the house the door slammed shut behind him. Pausing to try it he found it wouldn't open, which explained Sano's face when he sprinted into the entrance hall and appeared on a balcony above Law. "Is it open?! Oh, shit… You're stuck in here now, too?"

Law looked up at him. "Stuck, huh?"

"Yeah, the door won't open from in here."

"So, trap was right, then."

"Seems like it. That or the house is planning to eat us."

"I'm not fond of either situation."

Katsumi walked back into the entryway with Rufus, blinking at him. "Sam?"

"No use sittin' out there," Law said as he walked further in, setting his large weapon case on his shoulder. "Not when we can't communicate. Figured I might as well come in an' help."

Katsumi folded her arms, smiling at him. "I'm glad you did, we've a better chance with you here. Did you… talk to Aya and tell her what happened?"

"Reno's talkin' to her right now. They're keepin' each other company."

She gave a sigh. "That's a relief. I hope she doesn't worry too much. Anyway, we've been exploring this house; it doesn't seem nearly as old on the inside as it does on the outside. Or if it is, it's in incredible shape."

"The house out of time, huh?"

Rufus smirked. "Please don't give the house ideas; we don't need a Lovecraftian nightmare driving us all mad."

Law chuckled. "You don't wanna test yourself 'gainst an Outer God?"

"Not particularly."

Sano hopped down over the rail, walking over to the others. "Well whatever's going on in here is bad either way. This screams 'trap', but where's the part where two dozen guys with machine guns pop out?"

"Well," Katsumi said thoughtfully, looking around. "This might just be a paranormal event. The last time we-" she was cut off as the house began shaking. All of them moved to grab the handrail on the stairs as everything shook, causing the chandelier to swing wildly and making all of the lights flicker.

"Okay," Sano shouted over the rising sound, "Is this part of the trap or part of the paranormal stuff?!"

"We ain't goin' anywhere," Law replied to him, "So we'll have to wait an' see."

Cracks appeared across the floor and the walls of the house seemed to warp; everything around them seemed to be warping or twisting in some way. Suddenly, with a massive, grinding and tearing sound, the walls began rushing upwards past them. Faster and faster they went as if they were in a rapidly-dropping elevator. The feeling of being lifted up soon hit them and everything shook harder, warped further and moved faster until finally, the world shattered, and then everything stopped moving and fell silent. All of them stood slowly, looking around in shock and confusion.

They were in a twisted version of a skyscraper, surrounded by clean, shining metal and glass. The others looked at each other but Katsumi walked between them. Their eyes followed her as she moved to the windows, and then they all moved silently after her until they stood in a line looking through the glass. Outside was an odd wasteland of purple and red rock in unearthly formations. The rocky plain stretched forever into the distance, and the skies above were a maelstrom of terrifying storms filled with purple clouds and constantly arching lines of red lightning. The storm outside surrounded the skyscraper they were in as if it was in the eye of an otherworldly hurricane.

Katsumi carefully set a hand on the window and leaned forward to look down, counting the distance and judging them to be on the 6th floor. She pressed against the glass to look up, noticing that the skyscraper seemed to go ten times higher than their current height. She stepped away from the window and turned to the others, all of whom were looking to her for answers; she had none. She shook her head, looking back over her shoulder at the hellish landscape outside. Wherever they were, whatever this was… She had no idea. They were trapped on another plane or world, and suddenly the chances of getting out seemed much smaller. Her team looked to her for leadership and she walked past them as if she knew what she was doing, but when it came down to it…

She had no idea if any of them would make it out of this place.

Chapter 18: Fight

Katsumi led her team through what was basically a corrupted office building, using stairs to get to the 7th floor. An old elevator plate let them know that the building had 66 floors, but the elevators weren't working and she had no idea where to go anyway.

"Do you have any idea what this is?" Sano whispered to Rufus, who shook his head.

"I've never seen anything like this. We're in another place entirely, maybe even another plane."

"Why don't you tell them, Major?" The team whipped around to see a screen on the wall that had come to life and now showed Sigma's grinning face. "Well? Go ahead!" Katsumi remained silent as the others glanced at her, continuing to direct a wordless stare at Sigma. His grin seemed to widen. "You can't, can you? Because you have no idea. Now you've gotten your team into quite a situation."

"I'm not here to play games," Katsumi said harshly, fighting her rising anger.

"Yes, you are," he corrected, spinning away from the camera to be fully visible in the shot. "Whether you want to or not, that is what you're here to do! And I am Sigma, your game master for the evening. You see, what you funny little mortals have done now is stumbled into a Demon Tower."

Katsumi blinked. "A... Demon Tower?"

"Yes! It's quite an impressive bit of construction, don't you think? Let me tell you a bit about your situation." He sounded nearly giddy as he disappeared and the screen switched to a three-dimensional wireframe model of the skyscraper. The image zoomed in and the seventh floor began flashing. "This is your current location…" The image flew up dozens of floors to finally stop at the top, where the top floor flashed. "And this is the 66th floor… your destination!"

"What are we climbing this tower for?"

"Ah, yes, we have location and destination, well, here's your motivation!" The screen flipped back to Sigma, but this time he was standing to the side. In the background was the demon Belphegor, a towering and intimidating presence even through a screen. This wasn't the shade they had encountered before; this was the true demon, an Ancient One in his physical form. He held similarities to his shade, but where once had been smoke and color was now an ash-grey body with scorched and scarred hide; he had a thick grey beard, bent horns and long, sharp nails that looked able to rend stone. The twenty foot demon had massive wings stretched out behind him and hovered several feet above the ground, appearing as if he was waiting. Nearby they could see Hitomi chained to a wall, pressed against it to get as far away from the demon as she could. "She is unharmed… for now," Sigma continued, popping back into frame. "But should you take too long to get here, we'll be sacrificing her to our demonic friend, so don't tarry!" He let out a crazed laugh as he floated back from the camera, spinning a staff in his hand. "Let the game begin!"

The screen cut off and a roar filled the short silence that followed. The team looked over to see a horde of creatures moving through the twisted office building towards them. They looked like twisted humans with deadly limbs that shifted between massive hands, blades, spikes, and other dangerous shapes. Katsumi grimaced as they all readied their weapons, looking at her team.

"This isn't going to be easy."

"Easy isn't our job," Rufus said, loading a rifle.

Law cocked a shotgun. "If it was easy we'd have sent someone else to do it."

Sano spun both pistols in his hands, grinning. "Let's kick ass."

Katsumi couldn't help but smile at them, glad for the thousandth time that she had such an incredible team. She turned to face the oncoming demons and readied the pistol in her right hand, using her left to draw her katana from her back (which she'd brought at Ayane's insistence, and thank God for that). The team yelled back at the demons, took two steps forward, and broke into an all-out charge.

Katsumi leapt and slid over a desk, firing three times through a demon's head. She leaned back on the desk, going under a slicing blade-arm from another creature before coming up and hacking off the offending arm. The creature gave an eerie cry and brought its other arm around, shifting it into a heavy cudgel that it brought down on her. She leapt off the desk and over it, turning upside-down in the air as she went and firing into its head from behind before landing right behind Law.

The large man spun his shotgun around and bashed away one of the creatures before flipping the gun back around and blasting it away. He held out his left hand and Katsumi grabbed it, letting him fling her forward; she spun as she flew, her blade slicing through various limbs of the crowd she passed. Rufus slid underneath her as she went by, drawing two machine pistols and spinning in a circle to finish off the creatures she had wounded. He got to his feet and holstered the smaller weapons, kicking his rifle back up into his hand and firing at a creature directly in front of Sano.

Sano kicked the new corpse into an oncoming group of creatures, slowing them all down enough for him to gun them down. He pulled an explosive satchel charge from his belt and tossed it above a crowd of the creatures; Rufus followed its arc and shot it just as it was above them, causing an explosion that tore apart the closest ones and knocked down the ones further away. Law and Katsumi went for the fallen creatures, putting bullets in their heads, crushing them or cutting them off. Once the last one was finished, a large brute of a creature burst into the room and slammed a two-foot-wide fist into Katsumi. She went flying and Law caught her, sliding backwards and going down on one knee.

Rufus extended his rifle and powered it up, resting it on Law's shoulder for stability and firing at the oncoming behemoth, putting a large hole in the thing's chest and slowing it greatly, causing it to stumble. Sano came running at it from the side and Law released Katsumi, who took off running at it as well. Sano fired multiple times into the confused creature, running around it to cause it to spin around. Katsumi ran up its back, driving her blade into the base of its neck before leaping off and avoiding its wildly swiping arms. Rufus' next shot hit the beast in the back of the knee, bringing it down onto its back, which only drove the blade in deeper. Law reached it then, gripping the hilt of the blade and setting a foot on the demon's skull before using his impressive strength to yank the blade up and twist it around, cleaving the thing's neck.

As it jerked and died he ripped the blade free and tossed it to Katsumi, who caught and sheathed it in one smooth movement. She began walking as Sano joined her; Law picked up his large case and Rufus collapsed his rifle, and the two joined the others as they headed for the next set of stairs to continue on to floor 8.

~ ~ ~ ~ ~

Reno laughed. "I'm sorry, it's just hard to believe, you know?"

Ayane chuckled. "Why's it so hard to believe?"

"I'm just now getting used to the fact that apparently the boss has a softer side. To me she's always been, you know; 'I chew steel and spit out bullets, I'm tough!' I didn't even know there was more."

"Oh, there's lots more!" Ayane held up her moogle in front of the camera. "She got me this, you know. I didn't ask for it. She always gets me things like this, or flowers, or mushy cards."

Reno leaned forward and stared. "You're kidding. She picks out mushy cards?"

"Oh, no, she *hates* pre-made cards." Ayane grinned. "She writes them herself."

"She writes mushy cards." Reno removed his glasses. "Ayane... Have I told you I love you?"

"I'm the best thing to ever happen to you, huh?"

"You have no idea." He replaced the glasses. "You have to read me one of those cards. You *have* to."

"I could *never* do that to Katsumi! She only trusts *me* with that stuff." She smiled. "You'll just have to imagine."

"Aww, come on, I wouldn't tell her!" Ayane simply gave him a look. "Okay, I would, but I wouldn't tell her you told me!"

"No one else could have!"

"Well yeah, obviously she'd *know*, but I wouldn't *tell* her is the point I'm making."

"How does that help keep her from killing me?"

"Oh, am I supposed to be helping you? That might take more thought."

Ayane laughed, but her mood seemed to fall as a voice spoke off-screen. She then sighed and looked back at the screen. "Hold on, it's time for my medicine."

"Hey, I hear you'll soon be taking that at home, so it'll get better!"

She smiled. "You're right. Anyway, this should only take a few minutes. When I get back we can discuss how selfish you are."

"Or how you ruin my fun!" Ayane just grinned and his screen paused, leaving him in silence. He checked the other screens' readouts but determined he could still do nothing useful. He tried contacting the team inside again, but it still wasn't working. So, he just sat back and looked at the creepy house. "Could've joined any other team," he said to himself. "But no, I had to join the one where I sit outside of a haunted house alone. Great idea, Reno!" After a few minutes of quiet he heard a sound behind him and nearly fell out of his chair turning around, only to see an older man with light brown, slightly graying hair and beard and wearing a long trench coat, a few meters behind him. Reno sighed and sat back. "You nearly gave me a heart attack, man."

Joseph walked forward to stand beside the man he recognized from Sigma's files as Reno, looking up at the ancient house. "I apologize. What is going on?"

Reno adjusted his glasses and looked back at the house as well, unable to see the saber on Joseph's left hip or the way his fingers rested on it, ready to draw it. "You live around here? We've received a few reports about this place, but we've got people inside right now."

"Is Captain Samakura inside?"

"Oh, are you with us? You one of the Directors maybe? She's a Major now, you know; not Captain."

"Is she inside?"

Reno was a little put off by the man's cold attitude; he was definitely the type of person who could be on the Aegis board.

"Yeah, but I wouldn't go in there, we've been having some communication problems."

"You won't be going in there."

Reno was about to say something about how obvious it was that *he* wouldn't go in because *he* wasn't insane, but that moment happened to be the exact one Ayane chose to return. "Sorry it took so long! I tried to tell them I'm feeling better, but they-... Father!"

"Fa-" To his credit, Reno reacted with speed he should've been proud of, drawing his pistol and trying to stand. But Joseph was inhuman; his blade whipped up and hacked Reno through the computer equipment, sending him sailing as Ayane shouted his name. He bounced and skidded across the yard before hitting the side of the house and falling limp.

With another slash Joseph destroyed the rest of the blood-spattered equipment, then flicked his blade clean and sheathed it as he headed towards the house and stepped through the front door after his eldest daughter.

~ ~ ~ ~ ~

Date: ???
Time: ???
Location: Belphegor's Tower, 17th Floor

Katsumi grit her teeth and twisted her sword before yanking it out of a demon's skull and letting it fall; their tenth floor was finished, only forty-nine to go. Katsumi allowed herself to catch her breath as she looked around, making sure the rest of the team was alright. All of them were covered in blood; mostly demons' blood, some their own. They were beginning to look weathered, but constant fighting did that. Every floor seemed to have more enemies than the last and it was beginning to frustrate them. Eventually one of them might make a mistake, and Katsumi didn't look forward to losing someone in here. She called for a break and they all took a seat somewhere, drinking water or just staring at the ceiling. They didn't have any real supplies as none of them had expected to be trapped inside, so that was one more reason they had to finish this tonight. Katsumi finished cleaning her sword and checking her guns, deciding to not even bother with her hair or clothing and instead looking at the other members of her team.

Sano had his head in his hands but was tapping his foot at a quick pace; Katsumi noticed the headphone in one ear and realized he was listening to music to get himself ready for the next room. Whatever he had to do was fine with her; she was proud of the way he was handling this, especially with how close he had gotten to Hitomi prior to this incident. Despite that personal connection he was remaining a true professional and following every order, not letting his emotions get the better of him. Sano was more emotionally-involved in things than the rest of the team and that could make things hard for him, but it also gave him a determination and personal drive that Katsumi hoped he would never lose.

Law looked as cool as he always did. The giant of a man was cleaning one of the massive weapons he had brought, and Katsumi was happy he'd had the foresight to bring the case full of them and ammunition. In general she was glad that he had come after them himself, because she knew they would need him to get through this, and having her oldest and closest friend outside of her sister with her gave her a lot more confidence. He was a wall, a tank, that drove his way through their enemies and gave them a fighting chance. Katsumi had always considered Sano the moral anchor of the team, and Law the cornerstone that kept them strong.

Rufus was the specialist, the survivalist, the one she held most in common with when it came to ideals and practicality, and he looked it. He leaned against a desk after collecting the last of the knives he had thrown, replacing them in their spots around his body. She could see his mind working, calculating where he'd hit the demons and what spots seemed to do the most damage. He would get better at fighting these things with every floor they went through. Katsumi knew Rufus wasn't eternally loyal, he wasn't emotional, and he wasn't the most trustworthy, and that, ironically, was what made her trust him the most. She understood him, she knew what he would do in what situation, and in a situation like the one they were in right now, he was exactly the type of person she wanted with her.

After ten minutes passed Katsumi stood up and holstered her pistol, hoping to stick to her sword and conserve ammunition.

"That's enough, let's get going. You get another break in five levels." There were no groans as she headed for the stairs to the 18th floor, no complaints, no hesitation; her team stood and followed immediately. They were professionals and this was their job. It was Katsumi's job to keep them alive, and she did her best to ignore the self-doubt that whispered in her ear that she couldn't do it this time.

~ ~ ~ ~ ~

Date: ???
Time: ???
Location: Belphegor's Tower, 4th Floor

Joseph walked through the tower with purposeful steps and an emotionless expression. The demons within the tower were not ones that followed orders, and so they rushed him as surely as they did his daughter's team. As a demon leapt at his face he simply swatted it aside with a hand like an insect. A horde charged him and he stepped through them with invisible cuts of his sabre, leaving a rain of lifeless body parts behind him. Nothing was a challenge, nothing required effort; all of this was simply trash that failed to even slow his steps. He moved through the levels at a steady pace and never slowed until he reached the elevator on the 6th floor and pressed his hand to it, activating it. He stepped inside and began his ride to the top floor, glancing at a screen that showed him the location of his eldest daughter and her team.

When the doors finally opened he stepped out and took in the room as Sigma greeted him. "You've arrived with plenty of time to spare," the man said as he gestured to his command screens. "They've got quite a ways to go, although they're advancing more quickly than I'd expected."

"My daughters are not without some talent," Joseph responded as he looked at the screen. "Is it working?"

"Indeed," Sigma said with a grin, looking to a large mass of pulsing veins and flesh near Belphegor. "The energy they're expending fighting, and the blood they shed, is fueling it quite nicely. By the time they make it up here it should be completely ready for the ritual."

"Then we need only do this once," Joseph asserted. "That is good. We can dispose of them all once it's complete."

"Even your own daughter?" Sigma asked, more out of excitement than actual curiosity. He received only a cold look in return, which made him chuckle. "I didn't doubt you would do it. Humans are so interesting. What about the other one, will you kill her too?"

"If she gets in the way."

Sigma grinned and turned back to the screens. "This might become the greatest play I've ever directed."

~ ~ ~ ~ ~

Ayane arrived at the house faster than she had any right to expect, bringing the motorcycle she had stolen from the hospital's parking lot to a screeching halt. She hadn't even taken the time to change clothes and was still dressed in a simple white t-shirt and black shorts, meant to be slept in. However, her sword was in hand, sheathed but ready. The first thing she did after stumbling off of the bike was run as best as she could over to Reno, falling to her knees beside him. "Reno! Can you hear me?"

To her surprise he groaned and rolled onto his back. "Loud and clear. Really loud, in fact – can we not yell?"

"You're okay?" she asked incredulously.

"More or less," he answered. "I'm glad Aegis doesn't buy cheap models," He added, pointing to the two pieces of his gun lying beside him. While it was ruined, it had prevented Joseph's strike from being a fatal blow, leaving him with only a nasty gash across his chest. "It cost me a good weapon though, plus a nice shirt. Mostly it's my head that's killing me."

"You probably have a concussion," Ayane said, checking his head for blood and thankfully finding none. "Where is my father?"

"He went inside; he was asking if Katsumi was in there."

"Okay…" Ayane was silent for a few moments before looking at him. "You should stay out here and head to the hospital."

"Aren't *you* supposed to be in a hospital right now? Aren't you just recovering from some serious injuries?"

"My father is here," she said in response. "I'm not leaving while he goes after my sister. I'm going in after them."

"I'm coming with you."

Ayane paused as Reno held her stare, unwilling to back down; she smiled at his support. "Alright, but you better not die on me in there."

"You better not, either," he said as she helped him up. She immediately headed for the door but he caught her wrist, nodding towards their car. "I don't have a weapon. Let's stock up first, huh?"

As they stepped inside the house with two cases full of weapons and ammunition, plus more on Reno's person, an assault rifle in his hands and two pistols on a belt around her waist, Ayane was glad Reno had the foresight to suggest bringing supplies, especially once the door shut unflinchingly behind them and they realized the place they were in. "It looked like a house on the outside…" she said quietly as she took a few tentative steps further in.

"I'm a little torn," Reno said as he walked beside her. "On the one hand, it's not a haunted house with ghosts. On the other hand, it's some kind of fucked-up demonic office building with gore, blood and bodies everywhere."

"These bodies aren't decoration," Ayane said as she knelt beside one. "My father did this; his work is hard to mistake."

"At least he's clearing the way for us."

Their conversation was cut off as a screen on the wall flickered on, and the message that had played for the others played for them – Sigma had it on repeat in order to taunt Katsumi, but it worked now to inform the two of the situation. Ayane glared at the screen as it shut off. "It's just a game to him – I can't believe he's toying with Katsumi. They must be on their way to the top, but they're going to have him, Belphegor and Father to deal with. I still can't contact Katsumi in here and she has no idea Father is here now – we have to get to them before they get to the top. They're going to need our help."

"And we're going to give it," Reno said as he moved over to an elevator and tried the button. "Yeah, I didn't think it would work; I guess everyone's taking the stairs." He stepped back and looked at the numbers above the elevator. "Apparently there are sixty-six floors. Of *course* there are. I'm just surprised there aren't six-hundred-sixty-six floors."

"It's not supposed to be a kind of 'number of the beast' thing," Ayane explained as she walked the room, glancing at the stairs. "Besides, there's some debate as to whether that's six-six-six or six-one-six."

"So if the sixty-six floors isn't a number-of-the-beast-thing, what is it?"

"Gematria."

"I'm sorry, what?"

"It's a Hebrew system of assigning numerical value to a word or phrase. It's kind of like Arithmancy, if you've ever heard of that."

"So what does that have to do with this place having sixty-six floors?"

"Well… The numerical value of sixty is related to samekh," Ayane said as she looked up at the numbers above the elevator. "The letter 's'. But, more importantly, 'samekh' and 'mem' form the abbreviation for the Angel of Death, or Samael."

"So the six is 'Mem'?"

"No…" Ayane shook her head, frowning. "Numerical value of six is attributed to vav… or w."

"'Sw'? That doesn't mean anything."

"The only thing I can think of is that when vav is used at the beginning of Hebrew years, it means six thousand. But there are no years indicated by the floors of this building, unless it's just implied, in which case…" She trailed off, staring at the numbers.

"In which case what?" Reno asked curiously, peeking around at her face. "Ayane?"

"…In which case, this tower has stood for six thousand years, and was built either by or for Samael, the Angel of Death," she finished as she looked at him. "Belphegor may be here, but this is *not* Belphegor's tower."

"Is that good or bad? I mean, Samael didn't follow Lucifer, right? He's one of the good ones isn't he?"

"He wasn't – or isn't – either good or bad. Samael is the closest to the personification of death that exists; he's basically the grim reaper. That's not the point, though – this is not Belphegor's tower, so why is he here? He's using it for something specific…

What is the Prince of Sloth, Lord of Opening, doing in Samael's tower?"

Reno shook his head. "All of this is over my head; I just know he's a big monster. A big, bearded monster with really sharp claws and horns and a lot of power."

"Yes, but it's his plan I'm worried about." Ayane looked towards the stairs. "Whatever the case... We can't do anything until we meet up with Katsumi. That's our first priority. We have to get to her and warn her that Father is here."

"Then let's get started." Reno matched her stride as they headed for and up the stairs, wary of what was ahead but determined to catch up to their friends.

~ ~ ~ ~ ~

Date: ???
Time: ???
Location: Samael's Tower, 23rd Floor

"This is just a waste of our time."

Katsumi continued to ignore the voice, along with the face it was coming from.

"Katsumi, please!"

She wished it would shut up. She couldn't remember how she ended up in this room alone, or where her team was, or why she suddenly found it so difficult to move; all she knew was that she wanted it to shut up.

"Just think about it," the thing that looked just like Ayane said as it slid up beside her. "I may not have a lot of time left; you might not have a lot of time left. Why are we wasting our time apart like this? You should join Belphegor; he can actually help!" Katsumi looked away but the thing just moved closer. "If you turn on the others, all of this can end and we can spend the rest of time together. He can make us immortal! You care about me more than them, don't you?"

"I do..."

"Then why are you choosing them over me?" Ayane suddenly looked very sad as Katsumi looked back at her. "We could finally be happy. We could have the power to kill Father and then do whatever we want. No more running, no more hiding, no more fighting – for the first time in our lives we could have a normal life! Why are you throwing that away to fight for some company that doesn't care if you live or die?"

"I…" Katsumi looked down, unsure how to argue. Her mind felt foggy and sluggish; thoughts came slowly and slipped away like sand. She couldn't find a reason for what she was doing, or a reason that Ayane was wrong, and on top of that she felt so *tired* of everything. She often felt tired, and now it was worse than ever before. Didn't Ayane have a point? Wasn't *she* what she wanted? "I'm not throwing it away," she said weakly.

"I'm not blaming you," Ayane said, looking concerned for a moment. "It's not your fault. You've been fighting to protect me. But I don't need that anymore. What I need is to be with you. All you're doing now is hurting me."

"I didn't mean to," Katsumi said sadly as she looked at her. "I want to be better."

"Then do this for me," her sister said. "We have no loyalty to Aegis. They haven't done anything for us. They can't even help us – they *won't* help us. Belphegor will help us. Sigma helped you before, didn't he? He saved your life with his information. They can help us get rid of Father and be free of everything."

"But the others…"

"They don't mean as much as I do," Ayane said before looking hurt again. "Do they?"

"No," Katsumi answered with a shake of her head. "Just let me… It's so hard to think… What do I do?"

"Fight them," Ayane responded. "I know you don't want to, but we do what we have to in order to survive. If you don't, Father will win – he almost killed me last time. Next time, he will. Please, make this choice – I don't want to die…"

Katsumi stood slowly, unsteady on her feet as she turned towards the door behind her. "I won't let you die."

Forty-three floors above her Sigma clapped his hands, letting out a laugh as he watched the screen. "That was perfect!"

Beside him, Joseph had no reaction. Using his advice and the demon's power, Sigma had managed to direct and manipulate his daughter well. Joseph was somewhat impressed with his skill, but whether or not this would be useful to them had yet to be seen. He watched as Sigma switched the scene over to their new visitors – his younger daughter and the man from outside, who he was surprised to see alive. Sigma was planning something for them as well. It was unfortunate, Joseph thought, that Ayane had chosen to come, but if she was as foolish as her sister, she would share the same fate.

~ ~ ~ ~ ~

Kurasano shook his head as he stepped through the doorway, rubbing it as he moved aside for Law and Rufus to come through. "This floor is just weird. No enemies but we're all suddenly split up? Something's going on."

"We need to find Major Sama before anything else," Rufus said. "This 'Sigma' seems to be especially interested in her, so who knows if he has some sort of trap meant specifically for her."

"I already don't like this," Law added. "Wait…"

Sano turned with the others as Katsumi appeared in a doorway. "There you are! I guess we didn't have to worry," he said with a smile that disappeared as she drew her pistol. She aimed it directly at him and his first reaction was to immediately glance behind him, thinking she saw a demon. He heard a click and turned back to see her look at the empty pistol before tossing it aside and drawing her sword. In a flash she was within a few feet before he even realized something was wrong, but Law saved his life by shoving him out of the way.

The large man brought his arm up and blocked Katsumi's overhand strike; her sword dug a bit into his arm, sending a few sparks up. He looked into Katsumi's eyes over his arm for a few seconds and she seemed angry or annoyed until she suddenly withdrew her blade and aimed a horizontal slash at his stomach. He managed to catch the blade and lift her up, hurling her towards the wall. She spun in the air and landed her feet on the wall before launching herself off of it back at the others. Sano still stood in confusion, unable to make a move, but Rufus wasn't suffering the same problem.

The blond assassin stepped into her path and slid a knife into each hand, twirling each into a reverse grip until she met him. Their strikes came hard and fast, some even causing sparks as metal glanced off metal in a rapid progression. Rufus was faster but Katsumi was stronger, forcing him to deflect her blows rather than block them directly. Added to that, at the moment he was unwilling to go for a killing blow, while that seemed to be what she was doing. Eventually she gained the upper hand and whipped the blade around in a powerful horizontal strike, forcing him to back flip over it and out of the fight.

Sano came in to replace him, finally having realized a reaction was needed. Katsumi reacted to him with more speed than he'd hoped for, and Sano had the unpleasant realization that she had been holding back during their sparring matches. He focused everything into avoiding that sword, getting in a counterattack when he could and landing a few blows. Unfortunately, during a roundhouse kick she caught his leg and kicked out his supporting one, spinning and slamming him into the ground. She attempted to stab down into him but a thrown knife from Rufus knocked her blade off course, causing it to stab into the ground beside Sano instead.

Katsumi shot a glare at Rufus, but before she could withdraw her sword Law charged into her, carrying her away from the blade and into the wall. Sano stood up and yanked the sword free and Katsumi narrowed her eyes, glancing from Law to the approaching wall he was hoping to pin her against. She kneed him once in the stomach to free up a bit of room, then pushed to get more room before shooting her knee straight up into his chin. Taking advantage of the small opening she kicked off his chest and flipped onto the wall, then leapt over him and landed in a run towards Sano.

As she reached him he slashed horizontally with the sword but she slid under it and kicked his legs out, driving her elbow up into his solar plexus as he fell towards her. The blow knocked all the air from his lungs and she shoved him back, then knocked his hands up and sent the sword into the air. She leapt and placed a foot on his shoulder, vaulting up higher and catching the sword before coming down in a slash that Rufus was barely in time to block.

Katsumi glared at Rufus and flipped back through the air, landing a few feet away.

Rufus tossed a knife to Sano, who readied it as he caught his breath. Law moved behind Katsumi, leaving her surrounded. "What the hell is going on?!" Sano asked in confusion, looking to the others for answers.

"Yes; why are you doing this?" Rufus added, but out of curiosity.

Katsumi switched her gaze between them after glancing back at Law once. "It's our only option," she stated sadly. "If I don't do this, Aya will die. Belphegor will help us kill Father. He will give us the life we deserve."

~ ~ ~ ~ ~

```
Date: ???
Time: ???
Location: Samael's Tower, 18th Floor
```

Ayane whipped her sword around in a rapid motion, performing dozens of slashes within a few seconds and removing limbs from the demons surrounding her before removing heads. She flicked the blood from her blade and sheathed it in one motion, standing straight. "Demon trash," she said dismissively. "That's all that's left." She turned to see Reno staring at her.

"Aren't you supposed to be sick?"

Ayane smiled. "So is Katsumi."

"Oh yeah. You two do more when you're sick than I've ever done at my peak of health."

"We've certainly put in the work for it," she said as she looked around the room. "This would be harder if we weren't following Katsumi. They've killed almost everything."

"You actually sound a little disappointed."

"In a way," Ayane admitted. "I just like being able to do something for once. It used to be me and my sister doing everything, you know?"

"You miss working with her."

She nodded. "And I miss her in general. That probably sounds weird since we never go a week without seeing each other, and we can talk all the time, but…"

"It's not enough," Reno said with a smile. "You're talkin' to the right guy. I miss my wife and daughter as soon as I step out the door."

"Yes!" Ayane smiled. "I get that, too. As soon as Sumi leaves I miss her. And it doesn't feel fair, because even when she visits I can't fully enjoy it because I know she has to leave soon. Sometimes I miss her even when she's still there because of that." She sighed. "That's why I can't wait to live with her again. Hopefully she'll be able to take more time off in the future, too."

"I really hope this all works out," Reno added, "because I think we all need a little break."

~ ~ ~ ~ ~

"She's being influenced, right?" Sano looked at the others. "I mean, she has to be."

"I am curious to know," Rufus said as he lowered his hands and straightened up. "Is this an actual decision, or manipulation? The answer will determine my decision."

"You can't be saying that you'd join her if she turned on us."

"My loyalty is not with Aegis, or even with fellow humans; it is with Major Samakura. If this is the path she chooses, I will follow it as well. If she is being influenced, then I will kill whatever is influencing her because I refuse to follow something other than her."

Law smirked as he cracked his neck, fixing what Katsumi's knee had done to his jaw. "At least you're easy to predict, Rufus. Major, tell me – how did you come to this decision?"

Katsumi looked distracted for a moment before looking over her shoulder at him. "Aya talked to me," she answered, no longer angry. "She was… upset. What I've been doing has been hurting her. I can't do that anymore."

"Influence," Rufus said darkly. "It looks like I have someone to kill."

"I really am sorry," Katsumi said, looking at them sorrowfully. "If this is the best way to protect her, though, then this is what I'll do."

"It's not," Sano responded, drawing her attention. "The demon can't be trusted – it's working with your father."

"What?"

"They attacked in unison. He's probably helping it manipulate you."

"But Aya..."

"Where is she?" Law pointed out.

"I..." Katsumi lowered her sword and looked over her shoulder at him. "She stayed behind... It was safer..."

"Since when does she do that?" Law said with a shake of his head. "Does she ever leave you to face danger alone?"

"She..." Katsumi shook her head. "No, it made sense. She said... She was upset..." She looked down. "That... wasn't her?"

"It was a trick," Rufus asserted. "Most likely thanks to the demon or your father."

"That's not..." Katsumi tightened her grip on her sword. "I remember waking up... She was there... *It* was there," she said as realization dawned. "I *knew* it wasn't her, and then I forgot. Things grew... fuzzy..." She shook her head. "I can't... It's still hard to think, like I'm... walking through quicksand..."

"Keep going," Law said as he laid a hand on her shoulder. "They used your weakness against you."

"I thought it was my only option..." Katsumi suddenly looked very tired. "I'm slipping... Years ago, this wouldn't have worked on me. I don't know how much longer I can do this..."

"Hey, don't talk like that," Sano interjected. "Everyone has a weakness."

"I tried to kill you."

"Yeah, well, dying just happens to be my weakness," he said with a laugh, causing Katsumi to give a weak smile.

Rufus stepped forward as he slipped his knives back into their hiding spots. "So you don't want to side with the demon, then?"

"No," Katsumi said as she met his gaze. "It wouldn't help us."

He nodded understandingly. "Perhaps there will be a better opportunity later."

"You're kidding, right?" They both looked at Sano, who looked from one to the other. "The only reason you're not joining with the demon is because it wouldn't help you?"

"That's not the *only* reason," Katsumi replied. "It's just the biggest. I would ignore the other reasons if it was necessary."

"Well *I* feel safe."

"You have to understand-"

"Katsumi!"

Her eyes widened as she turned around and saw Ayane and Reno enter the room. "Aya!" Basically forgetting everything that had just happened, she was in front of Ayane in a second, pulling her into a tight hug that she returned in kind. "You aren't hurt, are you?"

"I'm fine," Ayane assured her, relieved that she had found her before their father had.

"What're you two doing here?" Law asked Reno as he walked over, glancing over him. "Nice scar."

Reno grinned at him. "Thanks. I think it makes me look tough."

"Scar?" Katsumi let go of Ayane and looked at him. "What happened to you?"

"Just a little encounter with your father outside," he answered.

Katsumi's eyes narrowed dangerously. "He tried to kill you?" she asked in a cold voice that made him nervous.

"Well, I mean, he failed…"

"And he's here," Ayane said, bringing Katsumi's attention back to her. "Reno said he entered after that."

"We haven't seen him," Rufus said, "So he's probably waiting up top with Sigma and the demon."

"I guess you were right about him helping, then," Katsumi said with a frown.

"Helping what?"

Katsumi looked at her sister, then averted her eyes. "They used something I thought was you to turn me against them, along with this strange mind-influencing magic."

"They used me against you?" Katsumi nodded and Ayane grew angry. "That's…" She couldn't even come up with words. Something like that could actually hurt their relationship; they had absolute trust, and it could damage it. Searching Katsumi's eyes she was relieved to see that hadn't happened, but it infuriated her that it could have.

"Why are you guys in here?" Sano asked out of curiosity.

"I wasn't going to leave Katsumi to face Father without me," Ayane said as if it was obvious.

"And I wasn't going to let her go in alone," Reno added. Katsumi gave him such a grateful look that he hoped he would always remember it. "Besides," he continued as he held up the cases they'd brought with them, "we brought gifts!"

Law grinned as he took one of the cases. "Just what I asked Santa for."

"You must've been a good boy this year!"

As Law set them down and opened them to begin reloading their weapons, Katsumi laid a hand on Reno's shoulder. "Thank you," she said quietly.

He knew she wasn't talking about the supplies. "You would have done the same," he responded. "Besides, I don't want her hurt any more than you do."

Katsumi smiled. "I know. I'm glad you're here, though – we can really use you."

"I don't see a lot of things to pilot or drive in here."

"You do a lot more than that. I'm glad the whole team is here to get one of our own back. Just don't get too injured or Lenora will kill me."

Reno grinned. "That's just like what I told Ayane."

"I guess we had all better make it out of here in one piece," she said as she turned to the others. "We all have people who would miss us."

"Then we're gonna need to go in hard," Law said as he lifted the large case he'd been carrying since the beginning and rested a long rifle on his shoulder. "Beat them down and tear them apart so we can be done with this shit."

"That's the kind of plan I like," Rufus said, readying a shotgun. "They have even less of a chance of winning now."

"That's right, the trump cards have been brought in," Reno said with a grin, hefting his assault rifle. "You guys are safe now."

Sano took in the sight of the newly-scarred Reno holding the huge gun and grinning. "Dude, tell me again why you always stay in the car?"

"Well it just wouldn't be fair to the monsters, y'know? You can't play the Ace all the time."

"Ahh, right. It's very generous of you to give the monsters a fighting chance."

"I thought so. I'm the magManimous kind of hero."

"That's 'magnanimous'."

"Right, that one."

Ayane smiled, looking at Katsumi. "We can end this now – together."

Katsumi nodded, returning the smile and looking around at the group before turning towards the stairs. "Forty-three more floors… Should've made it a hundred." She led them towards the next floor and one step closer to the final confrontation, swearing that tonight, things were going to end.

She was right, in a way – some things were certainly going to end, but what, exactly, she had no idea.

Chapter 19: Undone

Katsumi and her team entered the tower's fortieth floor wary and ready for anything. The fighting had been getting more difficult with every floor, and the floors that were a multiple of five seemed to be the worst; on twenty-five they had faced a horde of demons that had flooded in for a full twenty minutes without break, forcing them to kill quickly or be overrun. On thirty they had faced a giant demon with an armored hide that took explosives to get through. On thirty-five the floor had wild temperature swings from freezing to burning, distracting them during the fight with demons that seemingly weren't affected at all.

And on forty... On forty, they stood facing some sort of abomination that was waiting for them. It was very tall, mainly brown in color with rough, stony skin. On one swelled-up shoulder was a stretched face that grinned at them and gnashed sharp teeth; the arm connected to that shoulder was very long and thin, ending in a spear-like point. In the middle was the creature's head, long and thick like some sort of wolf or lizard, but not earthly enough to recognize. Its left arm was more natural but incredibly muscular and holding a large, heavy sword. Seeing as the creature reached the ceiling and its sword was nearly as tall as it was, blocking it was not going to be a possibility.

They were tired and each of them had minor injuries, but they were ready. Katsumi and Rufus took off and split apart, running to either side of the creature; Ayane, being the fastest out of all them, ran straight at it. It began moving instantly and lurched forward, swinging the massive blade, but that was far too slow to hit Ayane; she was keeping her eyes on the long, thin arm as she leapt onto the other one, and her instinct was rewarded as it lashed out at her. She twisted around the spear point and ran up and over the creature as Katsumi and Rufus hacked its legs to divide its attention. As soon as Ayane was out of the way, Law, Sano and Reno opened fire on the creature.

It let out a roar of pain and moved in earnest now, spinning with the large sword and lashing its thin arm out like a whip at times, and a spear at others. The three kept on the move, hacking at its legs as the others held fire on its torso, distracting it more than anything as gunfire was unlikely to pierce its skin. The stretched face on its shoulder spat out acid that narrowly missed Katsumi, splattering and beginning to melt through the floor. They added that to their list of things to avoid, but Law saw an opening; he raised his rifle and called to them to turn the thing towards him, which they did. Ayane caught his meaning and landed in front of the creature, waiting; the face opened to spit and Law fired a grenade at it. Ayane dodged the acid and the grenade went in perfectly. The three near it immediately dodged back as it exploded, ruining the shoulder and severing the whip-arm, although it also sent acid everywhere that they were lucky to dodge.

As the creature went berserk they went to work, hacking at it and easily dodging the heavy sword until the beast finally went down. The fight was basically without challenge, which gave them confidence as they pressed on to the forty-first floor. Each floor was conquered, adding to their overall fatigue but not individually impossible. The forty-fifth floor was harder, filled with *several* monsters just like the one from forty, but they were able to cause them to injure each other, thus escaping without injury themselves. The fiftieth floor, however, was different.

When they entered Floor 50, nothing was there. They walked carefully into the room but, still, nothing could be seen; there were no traps, no environmental hazards, and no giant beasts. It put them on edge, especially considering the dim lighting on the floor – unlike the others, this one seemed not only corrupted, but dilapidated. It seemed very old and as if it had been abandoned for a long time. It was exactly the type of place they would expect to find haunted during a normal job, and it even held the same uncomfortable, oppressive atmosphere. There was a heavy silence here along with a smell of rot that choked the air, making it more difficult to breathe. They progressed through the room looking in all directions, straining their eyes under the flickering lights.

The first thing that happened was Katsumi crying out. The others turned in time to see blood spray from a new gash on her shoulder, but before they could ask what had happened she had whipped her sword around and it clanged off something. She seemed to be fighting something and Ayane was at her side in a moment, stabbing into the air. Something gave a cry and Ayane felt it leave before she lifted her blade to spot black blood on it. "It's invisible…"

"There may be more than one," Katsumi stated. "Backs to the wall! Law, I want something covering this area and giving us at least a hint of where these things are."

As they moved to the wall, Law fired a smoke grenade into the center of the room. As it filled up, movement could be seen creating waves in the smoke. They began firing at the trails, bringing down two of the creatures before long. More seemed to be in the room though, and they wasted a lot of ammunition killing them. Most disturbingly, the things never appeared even after being killed, so they had no idea what they were or what they looked like. Eventually Katsumi called for them to move to the stairwell and they went quickly, setting up there instead and holding the stairs. The others covered Law as he opened a case and took out two demolition charges, tossing one into the room and planting another at the base of the stairs.

The team then moved up the stairs and detonated the explosives, killing whatever was near the one in the room and blocking the entrance to the stairs with rubble. In case they dug through, Law set an explosive mine on their side of the rubble. "Well done," Katsumi said with a nod. "Is anyone hurt?"

"Besides you, you mean?" Reno said as Ayane moved up to inspect her sister's shoulder.

"It's not too bad," Ayane said in relief. "Looks like a thick blade did it." Reno tossed Ayane a bandage and she went to work wrapping it.

"It felt pretty forceful," Katsumi responded, watching Ayane wrap it and getting way too many flashbacks of the action. Meeting Ayane's eyes, she saw she wasn't the only one, and they shared a look of understanding that made them both smile a bit as they once more realized they were working together again. After a moment Katsumi forced her gaze from her sister's and looked at the others. "I think they're supposed to stab. Whatever blades they're using are wide enough to cause a wound that would be impossible to stitch up outside of a hospital."

"Then it's a good thing they didn't get you with that," Ayane said seriously, tearing the bandage at the end and putting away the remainder. "I'd say we should be more careful, but honestly, we were as careful as possible, it's just impossible to be ready for invisible enemies."

The others nodded. Ayane had basically taken a "second-in-command" position during this mission; she had simply slipped into it, she and Katsumi easily falling into the partnership that had enabled them to survive endless hardships and dangers. The rest of the team recognized this partnership and deferred to it, preferring to trust their experience. As a team, it turned out that the six of them worked very well together. While the fighting was wearing them down, none of them needed to stop and none of them were terribly injured. It was going as well as could be expected – now all they had to do was survive the last sixteen floors.

~ ~ ~ ~ ~

Date: ???
Time: ???
Location: Samael's Tower, 66th Floor

Sigma chuckled, looking from the screens back to Belphegor. The demon was fully corporeal now, and fully empowered. All of the fighting the team had been doing, their emotional and physical energy spent, and the power Katsumi and Ayane had been putting out, had powered the demon to a level Sigma had only dared to hope for. "Our goal has been met," he said as he stood up from his chair, looking at Joseph. "If all goes well, we should have our hands on it soon."

"I admit, your plans have gone well." He looked over at the now-unconscious Hitomi. "Should we dispose of the girl now?"

"She should be useful during the fight," Sigma said with a wave of his hand. "I'm sure they will be distracted by her presence. Besides, it never hurts to have a failsafe."

"Very well. We should prepare now."

"As you say," Sigma responded with a nod. Louder, he said to Belphegor, "They're coming. Have your fun – they are no longer needed alive."

Belphegor, the Prince of Sloth, smiled darkly. "They shall be the first slain by my own hand in millennia. I shall enjoy rending them apart."

"Whatever," Sigma replied dismissively as he walked past the demon, following Joseph. "Just try not to bring the building down."

~ ~ ~ ~ ~

Date: ???
Time: ???
Location: Samael's Tower, 66th Floor

"So… We're here," Reno said as he looked at the gate in front of them. "I thought I'd be happier about that."

"What awaits us on the other side is not a celebration," Rufus stated. "Your hesitation is understandable."

"Nah, it's just the last obstacle b'tween us an' the celebration," Law said as he set down the case he had been carrying from the start, entering the code to open it.

"You really think it's going to be easy?" Ayane asked curiously, leaning over his shoulder to get a look at what he was doing.

"Let's not get cocky," Sano said. "I mean, yeah, we kick ass, but don't forget there's some kind of mega-demon on the other side of that door, plus a terrorist or whatever that Sigma guy is, plus the most evil man in the history of evil."

"That means it's our chance to tie up all of these loose ends at once," Katsumi said confidently. "We're ready. We couldn't be more ready. The only thing I want to ask is that none of you die."

Ayane smiled at her. "I'm not dying! I wouldn't miss getting to live with you again."

Katsumi shared the smile. "You better not. I swear I will pull your ghost back and make you pick out a place anyway."

Ayane grinned. "I'd haunt you anyway!"

"I'm not dying," Reno added. "Len would find a way to kill me again if I did."

"And me," Katsumi replied with a smirk, though it was half-hearted. "I swear if you make me tell that woman and girl that you... I will *never* forgive you."

"No way, I couldn't do that to a friend."

"I do not plan to die here," Rufus asserted.

"I didn't think you would. Always a survivor, right?" She smirked. "Think you would kill me?"

Rufus raised an eyebrow. "If I was dealt a good enough hand, but you're a Straight Flush so it would have to beat that," he responded, making her chuckle. "Royal Flush only. For now, however, you should know that if it looks like I will die, I will retreat."

"That *is* the wisest course of action," Katsumi said with a sly smile, "Although the others may not appreciate it."

"Yeah, thanks for the support," Sano said with a chuckle. "Don't expect me to die, either, Major. I'm not done here."

Katsumi looked at him. "You're right. I still have a lot of hope for you. You aren't even close to done."

"An' neither am I," Law said as he stood up and hefted the massive gun he had just removed from the case and expanded. He grinned as he set it on his shoulder. "B'sides, I got a friend who'll be mad if I die without doin' somethin'," he said, glancing at Katsumi and glad the shades hid his eyes. *Jaina said you gotta tell her*, he reminded himself. *Too bad I didn't know this would happen or I'd have done it earlier.*

Katsumi smiled at him. "What are you supposed to do, blow up a continent?"

Law chuckled. "Maybe I'll tell you after we're done 'ere."

"I'm holding you to that," Katsumi said with a wink. "Can't have my oldest friend keeping secrets."

"Yeah, you'd *never* do that."

"I'm the boss, I'm allowed to be a hypocrite because I say so," Katsumi laughed before looking over the rest of her team. She studied them all for a moment before her eyes hardened. "Let's end this now." She turned and slammed a hand into the massive gate, cracking it. She then shoved it open with both hands and stepped inside with the others at her heels.

Before them stood the demon Belphegor, Prince of Sloth, Lord of Opening, in his full physical form. His power filled the room; he nearly reached the ceiling despite its height; his roar echoed around the chamber and hurt their ears; his eyes were burning purple coals of rage and violence; his grin was that of one preparing to toy with his prey. And not a one of them stepped back as he stepped forward – they instead went forward to meet him.

The first movement was a joint one between Katsumi and Ayane, discussed before they'd arrived here – Katsumi charged the demon and he laughed and charged her, while Ayane darted around him and across the room in the blink of an eye. As the others opened fire, Katsumi raised her sword to block a giant fist that still brought her to her knees beneath its force. Meanwhile, behind him, Ayane's quick sword slashes severed the chains that held Hitomi. The woman looked at her gratefully, obviously weak, having been drained. "It's a trap," she told Ayane as she was helped to her feet. "They're waiting in the back."

"We figured as much," Ayane said as Law met them after circling around the demon, which was still focused on Katsumi.

"I got 'er," Law said to Ayane. "You go help yer sister." Ayane didn't need to be told twice and took off instantly, going to join Katsumi. Law grinned at Hitomi as he lifted her easily in his arms. "You've looked better, flower girl."

Hitomi smiled as he ran and moved her to a corner of the room near the entrance. "I knew you all would come for me."

"We don't leave people behind," another voice replied.

Hitomi craned her neck and smiled. "Sano! I'm glad you're okay."

Kurasano grinned and winked at her. "Same for you, Tomi. We were all worried about you after you disappeared." He grew more serious as Law set her down. "Did they hurt you?"

Hitomi leaned against the wall and shook her head. "Not really. They just drained some power. Most of the time they didn't even pay attention to me."

"Good." He smiled at her. "Now, this fight is gonna take awhile, but you're gonna be about as safe as you can possibly be."

"Why is that?"

Law slammed down a large tripod as Sano grinned. "That's why."

Law's grin was even bigger as he set the massive gun he had carried throughout the entire tower on top of it, locking it in. "Blue-hair has wanted to use this thing for years, but she only got to do it once."

Hitomi blinked at it, looking over the giant weapon. "Why only once?"

He rubbed his head. "We don't talk about that. Insurance reasons. Anyway, nothin's gettin' into this corner."

Sano nodded, tossing her a wave. "See you after we're done with this thing."

"Be careful!" she called after him as he charged back into the battle. For her own part, she focused past Law, on the massive demon. She couldn't join in, but she would certainly do what she could to weaken him – extending one arm, she began to draw power away. It was a very slow trickle without a large effect, as she was still untrained, but who knew – perhaps she could make a difference. She wasn't going to just sit out and let others fight for her; at the very least she could weaken their enemy.

Back in the battle, it was total chaos. The massive demon's limbs rent metal and his breath drained life and energy from those it hit, forcing them to move constantly. Katsumi and Ayane kept the demon occupied, using dodge-and-counter tactics designed mostly to annoy and draw attention. They seemed to be enjoying it, and it was obvious why – it had been years since they had been able to work together as a pair like this against a real challenge. Helping their attitude was the fact that this was just a demon, a target, and not someone they had a personal vendetta against. Belphegor had done nothing to them personally, not really, and he wasn't something they hated, allowing them to enjoy the fight. Katsumi ducked under his claw and hacked at the underside as

Ayane hopped on top of it, sprinting along it and slashing at his face as she passed.

In the meantime, Sano and Reno focused fire on the demon while Rufus took up a solid position further back with a heavy sniper rifle, going for damaging shots. Soon Law joined in as the thunderous sound of his heavy machine gun filled the air, sending round after round into the massive beast. Belphegor roared and turned towards Law, taking a step before Katsumi barred his way. Enraged, the demon brought a massive arm down at her, but she brought her own arms up in a cross and caught his strike. She staggered a bit under the powerful blow, but she was able to throw it off with a yell. She then lunged forward and drove her sword into his stomach, causing him to stagger back in pain.

As the demon attempted to grab Katsumi, Ayane dropped down and jammed her sword into his wrist, yanking the hand away. Law's shots hit a leg and brought him to one knee, and Ayane pinned his hand to the floor with her sword as Katsumi did with the other. Sano and Reno fired into his chest as Law focused fire on the same area, drawing a roar of rage from the beast – and Rufus' round flew straight between his teeth, driving up into his brain. As the demon wavered in a daze, Katsumi and Ayane removed their swords and raced up his arms, driving their blades into his neck. With a final twist they crossed each other and the demon's head was removed.

A second later its body detonated, flinging the sisters into opposite walls and knocking everyone else off their feet. Fire swirled in the center of the room, scorching the floor and ceiling for a few seconds before everything became calm. Sano checked on Ayane, helping her up as Reno pulled Katsumi to her feet. Katsumi coughed and brushed part of her charred clothing away, looking around. "Everyone alright?"

They all looked around at each other, seeing that none had any real injuries. Reno said what they were all thinking: "Uh… I don't wanna sell us short, but did that seem a lot easier than expected to anyone else?"

Most of them nodded and Katsumi shook her head, going to inspect the center of the room filled with ash. "I thought that fight would take a few hours… That barely took a few minutes."

"Is he really dead?" Ayane asked as she moved to stand next to her sister.

"I don't…" Katsumi frowned, suddenly bending down to sift through the ashes. "What is…" She pulled out a large ruby that held a shining golden light within. The others stepped closer and she held it up for the rest to see. "Does anyone know what this is…? Was he carrying it, or…?"

Reno shook his head. "Never seen anything like that before. Maybe it was part of him."

"We're going to need that." Everyone turned and leveled their weapons as Sigma smiled at them from the doorway with Joseph just past his shoulder. Katsumi recognized every detail from her dream; the black body armor with the glowing blue lines, the floor-length coat, and the hood that hid all but the shock of white hair and the irritating grin. "Although we both know you're going to make this difficult, don't we?"

Katsumi's pistol shifted between him and her father, who showed no emotion even in this situation. "What is it? What do you want it for?"

"The answers to those questions are beyond your comprehension," Sigma stated with firm conviction. He stepped into the room and walked around the edge as Joseph remained at the door. "Let's be honest here," he said as he spread his arms. "You aren't going to simply hand it over, and we aren't going to leave without it. So let's get this little party over with so we can spend our time on more important endeavors."

Sano glanced to his left, watching the sisters and knowing exactly what was about to happen. The hatred flowing from them was palpable, and he wasn't about to get in the way. "Boss," he said, drawing her attention for a second.

Katsumi looked at him and understood the message after a moment, turning her attention fully to her father as she tucked the stone she'd just picked up into her jacket. "Ayane," she said softly, meeting her sister's eyes. A second later they were both sprinting forward, their swords meeting their father's as he backed into the other room.

The team started running a few seconds later but Sigma appeared before them. "Let them have their family time," he said, smiling and beckoning with both hands. "Let's play."

~ ~ ~ ~ ~

Katsumi and Ayane were as one; their blades went high and low, weaving around each other like a choreographed dance. Joseph countered it all as they moved around the round room, all of them spinning and twisting in desperate attempts to get around blocks or parry dangerous slashes. Katsumi had the strength and Ayane had the speed, but Joseph had both, and he played them against one another, tripping one into the other or blocking the blade of one with the blade of the other.

It was a frustrating dance, but the sisters were determined; this was their chance to end it all, and they had let too many chances slip through their fingers before. Joseph kicked one away and they panicked to get back to the fight before he could do something to the other, and while their emotions helped their conviction, they also served as distractions. Joseph suffered no such issues; it only remained to be seen whether powerful emotion or cold logic would emerge the victor.

~ ~ ~ ~ ~

The fight, Sano thought, should have ended already; he hadn't expected a five-on-one fight to be so one-sided in the wrong direction. Bullets flew from all sides but Sigma was able to deflect them with some sort of force field, and he was too fast to target for long. They had to watch their shots as he kept moving between them, meaning concentrated fire would cause them to hit each other. Sigma would approach one of them and disarm them instantly, inflicting some seriously painful unarmed attacks and dropping them to the floor before moving on. He dodged retaliation and countered with even more pain.

As he appeared before Kurasano, he thrust a knifehand at his neck that could've crushed his windpipe. Sano managed to deflect it, striking out and attempting to grab Sigma as he knew that he was alone for these three seconds – his allies couldn't risk firing into a melee. Sigma ducked under his arm and gripped his wrist, turning around and coming up under his shoulder with enough force to dislocate it. Sano gasped in pain, briefly realizing yet again that Katsumi had gone *really* easy on him during sparring before Sigma spun him to the ground. As Sigma moved on to combat Law, Rufus came up beside Sano and helped him re-set his shoulder (an act that caused a brief scream followed by a stream of curses).

Sano was thankful that he'd remained conscious as he stood uneasily, shaking his head to clear it. "This isn't going well," he said, watching Law's massive strength fail because he simply couldn't catch Sigma. "We need a new plan."

"I've got an idea," Rufus responded, looking over at Sigma. "Think you can distract him for a minute?"

"Oh, yeah, yeah, no problem," Sano chuckled. "Want me to dare him to break every bone in my body, one at a time?"

"Sure, that would work."

"I kind of hate you."

Rufus smirked. "I know. I just like earning it."

~ ~ ~ ~ ~

Katsumi slid, kicking at his feet before spinning and slicing upwards. Joseph leapt over her, deflecting Ayane's attack as she met him halfway and pushing her back to the ground. He landed between them and spun; while they managed to block his blade, the force sent them both sliding backwards. Katsumi gave a growl and drove her sword into the floor, slowing to a stop. She then drew her pistol and fired it several times, but Joseph deflected the bullets with his own sword. One of the deflected rounds came frighteningly close to Ayane so Katsumi tossed aside the pistol, pulled her sword from the ground and charged.

When her blade met Joseph's, sparks flew from the meeting point of the metal. They both moved in a slow circle as the blades met again and again, the sound of the metal rising even over the gunshots and shouts a couple dozen meters away. Katsumi could see it; she could see how close she was, an opening that was coming soon. It happened within the next few seconds – Ayane suddenly appeared behind Joseph and his sword flicked over to knock away her strike, and there it was.

Katsumi drove her sword forward with all the power she could summon, feeling the edge of victory… but Joseph continued his slash around, reversing his grip on the sword instantly and stabbing back at her. Katsumi jerked backwards, hearing the whistle of the blade as it flew past. It was so fast that she didn't notice how close it had been until she felt the drops land on her face. She jumped backwards, lifting her hand to find the gash the blade had made through her cheek and eyebrow. A few millimeters deeper and it would have bisected her eye as well. Katsumi took a moment to breathe, knowing her reaction time had just spared her having the sword driven up through her jaw and into her brain. It was close.

For Ayane, it had been too close; her blade began moving so fast it distracted a few members of their team as they looked on in awe. Ayane proved that she was the better swordsman of the two as Joseph turned to focus on her, their blades meeting so rapidly that individual strikes could no longer be discerned by sound, instead joining into one loud ringing of steel. Ayane was not spinning, jumping, or sliding – she was simply striking at different angles and different speeds, forcing a constant reaction as she worked to find one gap in her father's defenses. Katsumi weighed whether or not she'd get in her way before deciding to rejoin the fight; her strength could possibly off-balance or slow their father enough for Ayane to get in a good hit, and then that would be it – they would eviscerate him.

For the first time, Joseph seemed on the defensive; he was backing up, trying to move the sisters to one side of him, but they were in synch now, keeping him between them. There was no way he would be able to keep this up – it was only a matter of time until it was over. He knew it, and his daughters knew it, and the realization drove all of them to fight harder. This time Ayane saw the opening coming; with all his spins he had to do to guard against them both, Katsumi could knock him off-balance just enough to keep him from spinning to meet Ayane's blade. Her sword would pierce his side, Katsumi would knock down his sword, and then they would have him. She told her older sister through their link, and then they moved.

Katsumi's sword drove down with such force that Joseph had to slide his foot back a few inches to keep his footing, and that was it – Ayane's sword screamed in at his back, and he was unable to spin in time; it cut through the air like a thunderbolt, creating a sharp sound like a diving eagle. Suddenly, everything seemed to slow down and all other sound seemed to vanish as one loud, metallic ring sounded like a bell. Their eyes widened as they saw the wakazashi – a short blade – in their father's once-empty hand, deflecting Ayane's strike harmlessly upwards. Their surprise was their undoing as Joseph knocked their blades away with his, spinning and delivering a kick to Ayane powerful enough to send her into the air and across the room. She hit the wall painfully, followed by the floor.

Katsumi barely managed to save her own life once more, deflecting the stab meant for her and backing away, but Joseph came after her now, his two blades pushing her to her very limits. She backpedaled a few feet before standing her ground, knowing she couldn't let him back her up to the wall. He was relentless and she had to summon up everything she had to stay alive, driving her body past its limits, feeling her muscles burning and straining. And somewhere, in the back of her mind, there was a realization of a fact that she didn't want to face.

Ayane saw it first – the stumble in Katsumi's step, the loss of balance. The others noticed it soon after, distracted from their fight; even Sigma turned as a dark grin took over his expression. Her sickness was hitting her at the worst time possible, as Ayane had feared would happen for so long. Katsumi tried; she shook her head in an attempt to clear it, gripped her sword tighter in pain… It didn't matter, though; Joseph saw it as clearly as any of them and deflected her angry, desperate strike with little trouble.

His blade went through her as if it met no resistance at all. The point erupted from her back like an explosion but hung there like some horrible fang, dripping blood. Katsumi's eyes went wide and the expression on her face was one of frozen shock, as if her mind was struggling to understand what was happening. Joseph kept the sword through her stomach and lifted her off the ground, calmly removing the stone from her jacket before tossing her aside like trash. Katsumi hit the ground and skidded a few feet before landing facedown. Her father flicked the blood from his blade before dropping the stone he'd taken into a pocket.

~ ~ ~ ~ ~

They all heard Ayane scream her sister's name, and as soon as their eyes found Katsumi's body, several of them did the same as well. Sano took off in a sprint towards her, while Rufus just backed into the shadows and vanished out of sight. Hitomi clapped her hands over her mouth in horror, Reno looked utterly defeated, and Law went into a rage, rushing to follow Sano. Before Sano could get to the doorway, though, Sigma appeared in his way, smiling. "Come now, you can't be willing to abandon our game for some dead girl."

Sano lashed out in anger, but of course Sigma was better; he countered each move without trouble, chuckling to himself as he did – he was certainly having fun. He caught Sano's wrist and yanked it behind his back, forcing the man to his knees. "It doesn't look like anger makes you any better."

Sano grunted, looking over his shoulder. "It doesn't have to."

Sigma tilted his head. "Hmm?" He didn't get to question him, however – in that moment Rufus appeared out of the shadows behind him, driving a knife directly into the side of his neck. Sigma gave a cry of surprise and spun around to throw Rufus away from him, who was thrown off by the shock that Sigma was still alive and able to move. Sano stood up and turned around as he drew his pistol, firing several shots directly into Sigma's back. The man gave a growl of both pain and rage, turning around to deal with Sano only to find that Sano had stepped aside to make way for Law. The giant man barreled into him like a freight train, his large hand catching his head and driving it straight into the ground with enough force to shatter the floor and send a web of cracks outwards from the point of impact.

A massive fist punching him further into the ground stunned him for a few more seconds, but once Sigma regained his bearings he realized that all of them had backed away. A grenade landed right beside him as he looked up to see Reno wave, and he tried to dodge away only to find that he couldn't move – Hitomi was using the last of her power to keep him there. A grin spread across his face and he began laughing, harder every second until the explosion blinded them all, tearing him apart.

~ ~ ~ ~ ~

Ayane barely even registered the explosion. All of her attention was focused on her sister and the pool of blood that was gradually expanding from her body. The entirety of her being wanted to be there, but she couldn't reach her. Joseph stood in her way, and no matter what direction she tried to take to get around him, he wouldn't let her. Joseph refused to either let her by or finish her off, seeming to prefer forcing her to watch her sister bleed out slowly. Tears coursed down her cheeks but her expression was one of rage as she threw herself at Joseph, her sword clashing off his every time.

Faster and faster she tried, every way she could, using every maneuver she had ever learned, but he calmly knocked her away each time, barely even moving from his position, preventing her from reaching her older sister. Finally, it was just too much, and Ayane… snapped. Her limits shattered as she reached her breaking point and the true depths of her power were unleashed. She slammed into Joseph and both of them were blasted back from the point of impact. Joseph looked surprised as she came at him harder and a white flame ignited in her eyes as all color drained from her hair, leaving it a blinding white. Blue flames erupted around her and her sword whistled through the air, nicking Joseph's cheek followed by his arm. Another tear appeared in his coat and, though he was still able to defend himself, he was forced to back off.

"Maybe not such a waste," he said quietly to himself as Ayane flew past him. His eyes travelled over to spot Sigma's remains but he showed no change of emotion, merely checking that the stone was still in his pocket.

Ayane slid to her knees beside Katsumi, her appearance returning to normal as she gently turned her over. She was surprised to find that Katsumi was still conscious as she opened her eyes.

Katsumi looked up at her, forcing a breath as she spoke in a quiet voice. "If I die," Katsumi started, making Aya lean down to hear her, "you have to forget about him."

Ayane shook her head. "You better not die, then, because we both know I won't do that."

"I figured as much. Just… thought I'd try asking."

"If you ever do again, I'll hit you myself."

Katsumi smiled a little, closing her eyes again. "Yes, sister…"

~ ~ ~ ~ ~

We're all dead, Sano thought as he slid backwards. They had attempted to stop Joseph, but they were so far out of their league that even trying to perform a single attack on him had an extremely high risk of death. At this point all of them had simply backed away, but he didn't seem willing to let any of them survive. Suddenly a massive chunk of the ceiling landed between Sano and Reno, sending up a cloud of dust that had them all coughing. "What the hell is going on?!" Sano asked, covering his mouth to filter out the dust.

"This tower's creator no longer exists," Joseph answered him, looking up at the cracks spreading through the walls and ceiling. "It has been weakening since his death, and is now beginning to fall apart."

Ayane appeared beside Sano, carrying Katsumi. "We have to get out of here, now."

"You aren't taking her," Joseph stated, readying his sword. "The two of you have been troublesome enough – either I'm taking you both with me to fix this disobedience issue, or she dies here."

Sano put a hand across Ayane. "Go!" Law came and took Katsumi from her arms, both of them looking back as they started to run back towards the elevator. Sano drew both of his pistols, spreading out his stance and beginning to fire on Joseph as he backed away, forcing the man to focus on deflecting the shots. Sano entered the hallway and, as soon as his pistols were empty, Reno stopped beside him, unloading his SMG in Joseph's direction and forcing him to dodge.

The team continued running as Rufus met them in the next room, tossing an explosive in to collapse the hallway. The elevator was in sight now as the rubble suddenly exploded outwards a few seconds later, diced by Joseph's sword. Sano, Rufus and Reno all opened fire on him as they moved towards the elevator. Law set Katsumi down gently inside, moving away as Ayane joined her. "I was gonna tell you somethin', but it might be better if I don't now," Law said as he looked outside. "Still, I never was one to listen to logic, an' I did make a promise…"

"I'm out!" Reno said, beginning to run as Sano and Rufus followed.

"What are you talking about…?" Katsumi asked, fighting her blurring vision and keeping a hand to her stomach to staunch the blood as best she could.

Law chuckled, stepping out of the elevator. "Always did wanna be a hero," he said as Reno ran past him into the elevator.

"Law…?"

Rufus moved past him and Law gripped Sano's shoulder, shoving him into the elevator as well. Law then turned to meet Joseph, who didn't slow – he was determined to make it to that elevator. Law heard Katsumi yell his name, but he knew she didn't have the strength to follow. Joseph flicked his sword up to dispatch him quickly, but Law blocked it with an arm, feeling it cleave through and bounce off the steel beneath his skin. He stepped forward and knocked Joseph back by throwing out his arm. As the elevator started to move, those inside were able to see the saber dart back in and pierce Law's heart, sliding out through his back.

"LAW!" Katsumi threw herself forward but all the others had a grip on her, restraining her as she fought against them. "SAMUEL! DAMN YOU!"

Law grinned as he reached up and grabbed the hilt of Joseph's sword and his arm, pulling it in further. With an iron grip like a machine, Law kept hold of Joseph and charged ahead, enjoying the look of surprise on the man's face. Samuel Lawrence didn't bother giving a final line or quip – he just let out a yell that rose in volume with every step despite his struggling heart until he, and Joseph with him, smashed through a window of the sixty-sixth floor and out into space, letting gravity do the rest.

As the elevator dropped below the floor, Katsumi dropped to her knees, the only sensation she could feel being Ayane's hand gripping hers tightly. Silence reigned in the elevator as each person sat in shock, listening to the sounds of the tower falling around them. What none of the others aside from Ayane noticed was that, seconds later, Katsumi's expression was suddenly overcome with a shocked and pained look. Her eyes darted up, looking outwards as she listened to something – and her look was almost as broken as Ayane had ever seen her. There was no time to ask about it, though; everything was falling apart, and now it seemed like it wasn't just the building.

~ ~ ~ ~ ~

Date: April 17, 2068
Time: 3:29 AM
Location: Lexington House

Flashing lights were nearly blinding Katsumi as she sat outside the rubble in the back of an ambulance. They had more or less stopped the bleeding for now, but she refused to go to the hospital until she knew. She was struggling to stay awake, keeping a hand to her stomach and forcing her breathing to remain even. Ayane sat beside her, hand still in hers – nearby stood Kurasano, Reno (who was on the phone with his likely worried wife), Hitomi, and Rufus. None of the team were willing to leave, either. Their clean-up team was currently scanning the area – they would have a lot of work to do to get rid of all the rubble that had suddenly appeared, of a tower that hadn't existed the day before. Thinking up excuses and explanations wasn't Katsumi's job, though; no, her job was just to lead people to their deaths.

The sisters sat apart from the others even though they were physically close, in their own world as visible tears ran down their cheeks. Despite all their experiences and hardships, losing their oldest friend was a new one for them, and they would have to deal with and acknowledge that on their own. At the moment they were putting it off, but it wouldn't be for long.

All of them looked up as one of the clean-up team approached, and Reno told Lenora to hold on. The man removed his helmet, meeting Katsumi's eyes. "I'm sorry. We… found Sergeant Lawrence."

Katsumi nodded slightly; it was the answer she had expected. "And…" Her voice broke and she cleared her throat, beginning again, "And Joseph Elwood? Did you find his body?"

The man shook his head. "No, ma'am."

She sighed and felt Ayane lean against her; of course it was too much to hope he was dead.

"What we did find was the terrorist you said you had killed, but…"

Katsumi rubbed her cheek, letting out another sigh. "But what?"'

The man shrugged. "It… wasn't real, ma'am. It was just a robotic body with no human parts at all."

Katsumi's head shot up. "It was *what*?"

~ ~ ~ ~ ~

Date: April 17, 2068
Time: 3:30 AM
Location: Unknown

Joseph entered the hideout and turned on a small lamp, removing his tattered coat and pulling the stone from its pocket. He set the stone in a place that had already been prepared for it before hanging up his coat and switching on a computer. The machine powered up and the screen flickered on; seconds later, Sigma's face appeared on it, and smiled.

Chapter 20: Shatter

It was raining – of course it was raining. The day was as dreary as could be, with a solid grey sky and no sign of sunlight. It was a military funeral, so soldiers were lined up nearby. Katsumi stood in her dress uniform with Ayane beside her. Looking to her side she could see the rest of her team, including their family if they had them; practically everyone Katsumi knew was there, from Lenora to Winter to Sano and Ayane's friends. Not everyone knew what Samuel Lawrence had died for, but they all at least knew of him. Even M seemed grim today, exhibiting none of his usual smile.

Katsumi looked ahead as the casket was moved into position; because of the fact that Law had been born in the United States they were giving him a Western burial. The casket was a tasteful black, but Katsumi's eyes saw it as pale blue. As she and Ayane watched others lay flowers upon the casket and say final words, instead they felt themselves watching the proceedings from a hidden and distant position, watching their father accept condolences.

Katsumi didn't hear anything the priest said; she barely moved as the casket was lowered into the ground; she didn't flinch when the rifles were fired twenty-one times. As people filed past she didn't even notice; as it grew later and the weather grew colder, less and less people remained, but she didn't leave. Finally there was only the team left. An hour passed, and Reno and Lenora had to leave due to their daughter; Sano and Ayane's friends had long since left, and Winter had business to attend to so Rufus left to drive her. Sano finally left to take Hitomi back to the HQ, and M was the last to leave. At the end, only Katsumi and Ayane remained standing there, staring at the grave as evening came upon them.

Katsumi walked up to the gravestone and brushed her finger over the name, watching it change to "Naomi" in her mind. Katsumi's hand trembled and she nearly fell; her scream of pure emotion startled Ayane as she slammed her fist into the stone, cracking it just above the name. Her anger boiled over so much that she felt physical pain from its intensity, and she had absolutely no control over it. Ayane knelt beside her and hugged her, but she didn't say anything. Neither of them had anything to say.

Katsumi had tried to be strong for a long time, but these days, crying wasn't something she could even pretend she didn't do.

~ ~ ~ ~ ~

"So it's settled, then."

"Yes."

"We can't let M know about it beforehand – are you sure of your choice?"

"Indeed. Rufus is the perfect selection – he is the least loyal and the most self-interested. There is a lot we can offer."

H stood up and turned away from the table, clasping his hands behind his back. "Then let's do it."

~ ~ ~ ~ ~

Rufus left the bedroom quietly, looking at the message on his phone once more as he entered his office and shut the door. He switched on his computer screen and instantly the view was taken up by L, the Aegis Director of Special Protection. Rufus snapped to attention and instantly wished that he had grabbed his shades – he never liked others being able to see his eyes, as he felt that eyes gave too much away. "Specialist Ivanov," the Director stated. "Aegis has an important mission for you, and if you accept it, the rewards will be quite satisfactory."

Rufus raised an eyebrow; he didn't hear anything he didn't like. "What is it that you want me to do?" *And why me*, he thought but didn't say out loud.

L steepled his fingers before him after brushing aside his black bangs, looking over his hands. "There is something that has suddenly become incredibly important for us to attain. While your team failed to acquire the demon, a new avenue has been discovered – and the key is within your reach. The target's name is Ayane Samakura."

Rufus went quiet, thinking it over. "You want me to *acquire* her."

"You will have the aid of a team," L said as he opened a file on his computer. "She has apparently checked in with Major Samakura at the hospital they've used previously."

"Major Samakura won't allow this," Rufus stated cautiously.

L gave him a direct look. "That is why we came to you. Do it without her knowledge if you can; no one else is to know about this so we need someone involved that knows her, which means a member of her team."

"What if she finds out and gets in the way?"

L gave a slight smile. "Specialist Ivanov, everyone is replaceable."

Rufus gave a nod, picking up a knife and spinning it between his fingers, his eyes watching the blade glint in the low light. "Understood, sir." He looked back up at L and smiled. "I *have* been looking for a challenge…"

"And now you have been provided one. Do well, and you could get whatever you wanted."

"I won't let you down." After the call cut off, Rufus turned off his computer and left the room, moving into the hall and slipping on his white coat.

"Rufus?" He turned to see Winter standing at the bedroom door. "Where are you going? It's the middle of the night."

He turned away and slid his shades on, opening the door. "I have something important to do." He stepped outside, looking back with a smile. "I don't know when I'll be back… I've been waiting for this for a long time, though, and I'm not coming back without a victory." With that, he pulled the door shut behind him and headed for the hospital.

~ ~ ~ ~ ~

"Okay, still a little sore," Katsumi admitted as Ayane helped her sit up with a laugh.

"Most people are after surgery. Then again, most people also sleep through the night."

Katsumi groaned. "I've been in bed enough as it is over the past few weeks."

Ayane grinned at her. "Maybe we can actually take a break now, huh?"

Katsumi sighed. "I wish we could, but... Despite everything we gave – and sacrificed – we still lost. Our father is still out there, and he has what he wanted. And Sigma may be out there in some form, too, whatever he is, or was. After all this time we still don't know anything, and we haven't accomplished anything."

Ayane sat on the bed beside her. "We defeated the demon – you protected the city, which is your job. Father has been a problem all our lives, that's nothing new. And whatever this Sigma is, we'll find out – you still have a great team, and all of them are with you. This isn't over yet, Sumi. Law didn't die so we could lose."

Katsumi rubbed at her face. "I know that... You're right, I know, you're right. It's just... It feels like... I just..."

"I miss him too," Ayane said sadly as Katsumi turned to face her.

"There was nothing I could do. I just keep thinking... If I'd been able to kill Father, or if I'd managed not to get injured and been able to help hold him off Law wouldn't have had to-"

"That's just going to drive you crazy," Ayane cut her off. "We knew him longer than anyone, Sumi – you know that's not what he was thinking when he did it."

"No..." Katsumi looked away sadly. "That's not what he was thinking..."

Ayane studied her for a moment, frowning at her sister's fallen demeanor. "Katsumi?"

Katsumi hesitated, biting her lip before looking back at her. "Ayane, I-"

"Katsumi." Katsumi looked at her sister, who was glancing over her shoulder; her tone and expression had both grown serious. "Roof of the building opposite – sniper."

Katsumi didn't visibly react, but she did stand and stretch, moving with Ayane out of the view of the window. "We need to get out of the room."

"I wouldn't do that." Both of them looked over as Rufus pushed open the door and entered the room. Six soldiers filed in past him, surrounding them.

"What's this about, Rufus?"

Rufus smiled at Katsumi. "The Board just wants your sister to come visit them, as they feel she could be an important asset," he stated casually. Katsumi and Ayane watched as the soldiers tightened their grips on their guns – this was no invitation, that much was obvious.

"I see…" Katsumi looked from the soldiers to Rufus. "So they asked you to bring her in."

She watched as a knife slid into each of Rufus' hands. "It's nothing personal – they dealt me a Full House."

Katsumi met his eyes through the shades. "Not even a Royal Flush, huh?"

Rufus shook his head, smiling. "Unfortunately…"

In the next instant, Rufus' knifes were buried in the necks of the two soldiers on either side of the sisters. Before the soldiers could even react, Rufus was driving a new knife into the throat of the soldier to his left, and Katsumi and Ayane had torn the knives from the other two soldiers' throats and killed two more. The last went down after Ayane kicked his gun, throwing off his aim and making his shots hit the ceiling; Katsumi grabbed the rifle of the soldier she'd just killed and pulled the trigger, gunning down the last one.

As soon as they were down Rufus looked at Katsumi. "They've got a car outside, a sniper on the building over there, and a spotter on a building to the northeast."

"We'll head out the south, then."

"Take a window, avoid the first alley – and head for the alley next to the bank two blocks south; enter the parking garage on the other side."

"Got it." Katsumi smiled at him. "Straight Flush beats Full House, huh?"

"You're just lucky this sounded more fun, boss," Rufus replied, making her chuckle. He drew his pistol and flipped it around, handing it to her. "You know what you're going to have to do – just try to find a balance between 'looks real' and 'fatal', if you can."

Katsumi sighed as she leveled the pistol. "I really am very sorry for this…"

She winced as she shot him in the side and he grunted, leaning back against the wall. "Not the first time…"

"That looks like it hurt…" Ayane said with a grimace.

"No, no… Feels fine…"

Katsumi stopped beside him, setting a hand on his shoulder. "Thank you," she whispered softly; he just nodded as they moved past him and out into the hall.

Rufus sighed, pushing himself off the wall and keeping an arm pressed against the wound as he made his way to the North exit, making sure he was visible as he stumbled out of the building. He knew the spotter would see him and call back-up; as soon as they arrived and the medic began inspecting Rufus' wound, he spoke to the commander. "They jumped us… I overheard them planning to head to the Major's apartment north of here." As the commander got his soldiers together, Rufus had to hide his smirk.

~ ~ ~ ~ ~

Katsumi and Ayane made their way around the soldiers, slipping by buildings and using their considerable experience at remaining hidden. Entering the alley Rufus had pointed them to, they found the parking garage just past it, and entered as he had said. Inside they discovered Sano and Reno waiting for them beside two cars, one of which was running. Katsumi recognized the sleek black vehicle as hers, and the two men smiled as they approached.

"Hey, you didn't die!" Sano said with a smile.

"Hey boss, you ever think about visiting a casino?" Reno offered. "I don't think the odds would be nearly as bad as all the ones you've beaten so far."

Katsumi smirked. "I don't exactly like facing bad odds, Reno."

"All your things are in there," Sano said with a nod towards the car. "Guns, swords, clothing, pictures, pretty much everything we could find in your apartment. Rufus is pointing them towards your apartment, so they'll think you just got there ahead of them."

Ayane looked surprised. "How did you set all this up?"

Sano shrugged. "It wasn't hard – Rufus called me right after he got his orders, and since I live like twenty feet from Katsumi's apartment I had all your stuff packed by the time Reno arrived with her car."

"Also, I already knew where all the tracking and ID transceivers were on the car, so I've removed them all, too," Reno added. "And then Sano changed the license plate because apparently you keep a spare one around your apartment?"

Katsumi shrugged. "It pays to be paranoid, doesn't it?"

"I guess so. Oh yeah, uh…" Reno rubbed his head. "I kinda told Lenora and she made me bring a bunch of food for you, too, so you shouldn't have to stop for a while."

Katsumi grinned. "You'll have to thank her for me. And thank you, too – I know the risks you're both taking for us."

Ayane nodded. "We aren't really used to people putting themselves on the line for us like this, so… thank you."

"Just be careful," Sano cautioned. "This is all worth it, but it won't be if you get caught anyway."

Katsumi smiled as she opened the door for Ayane. "Don't worry, we're pretty damn good at this." She shut the door after her sister was inside, pointing at Sano as she walked around the car. "You're their leader while I'm gone, Sano. Don't let any of them get hurt."

"I won't, boss – I promise."

Katsumi smiled at him a final time before getting in. Sano and Reno stood aside as the car backed out and then drove away, soon turning out of sight. Reno sighed and looked at his friend. "When did we all become crazy?"

Sano shrugged, giving a slight smile. "When we met each other."

~ ~ ~ ~ ~

"So we have two runners," Hackett said, barely concealing his anger.

"It appears that way," M responded, lacking his trademark smile as he reported to the board in the HQ control room. "At the moment we have no idea where they are, but I assure you, I have the entire team searching for the traitors." For once he actually seemed angry; betrayed, even.

H sighed and rubbed his face. "This is a disaster... Get those two back now, M. The future of the company may depend on it."

"Loyalty only goes so far," M stated harshly. "It ends with betrayal. They will be found." As the call cut off, M immediately smiled and turned to another screen where he had a different call open. "You know what I know, Major."

"Thank you for doing this for us, M," Katsumi responded over the call. "I know the position I'm putting all of you in..."

"Position?" M chuckled. "I'm looking forward to this."

"Well if I'd known that I'd have done all this sooner," Katsumi replied, sounding amused.

"I knew you were going to be trouble the moment I met you."

"That explains why you made me the leader. Alright, I'm running out of time – I'll contact you at the next opportunity."

"Do keep safe," M said before the call was disconnected. He then turned to the remaining four, who had been standing to the side listening to both exchanges – Sano, Reno, Rufus and Hitomi. M smiled at them, using two fingers to push up his reflective glasses. "Well, my friends, things are about to get interesting."

~ ~ ~ ~ ~

Outside of the boardroom at the Aegis Headquarters, one of the Directors moved down the hall away from the others, opening up a door none of them knew existed. Inside, the Director closed the door behind him and continued down a long corridor that appeared on no building plans. Eventually, the Director arrived at a hidden room and gave a sigh, sitting in a chair surrounded by computers and screens and lit only by the glow of the monitors. A switch was flipped on a monitor, a cable was plugged into a spot normally hidden on the Director's neck that a synthetic skin plate slid aside to reveal, and the SIGMA AI uploaded itself onto the network, establishing a connection with a hideout in Tokyo.

"So everything is in motion," Joseph said after the connection was made, his face appearing on the screen. "We have the Demon Soul, you've successfully convinced them that they need the sisters, and their team is split apart; are you certain everything will still go as planned?"

Sigma smiled. "No need to worry, it's all working out even if there are a few discrepancies from the original plan. I admit I didn't foresee it going exactly this way, but everything is still on schedule. I will have to put more effort into my next Active Shell, however; I didn't expect them to be able to destroy it."

"That will no longer be a problem; without my daughters, they are virtually harmless."

"We haven't come this far by being careless," Sigma cautioned. "Try not to forget this was simply the first step." Sigma grinned. "It's the next step that's going to cause all the chaos."

~ ~ ~ ~ ~

Outside of a gas station at the city's outskirts, Katsumi hung up the payphone she had used to call M. Their cell phones had been left back in the city, and using their cyber links wouldn't have allowed her to hear the conversation with the board. She didn't know quite what to think about Aegis' betrayal, but she didn't even consider that she could be making the wrong decision; especially when she turned around and smiled as she saw her sister leave the station's convenience store waving the candy she'd just bought.

They'd ditched their clothing, as well, and were now dressed in civilian clothing; Ayane wore a pink hoodie and blue jeans, while Katsumi had opted for a simple black long-sleeved shirt and black jeans. Comfort and durability were the main goals for clothing when on the run, because you never knew when you would get a chance to change. Katsumi walked back through the cool night air to the running car, getting back inside and shutting the door.

Ayane watched her from the passenger seat as Katsumi shifted the car into drive and pulled back onto the road. "I'm sorry we have to leave it all behind," she said softly, breaking the silence of the road and drawing Katsumi's eyes to her. "Our first real home, family, friends, your job, and everything else… I'm sorry it had to go this way."

Katsumi shook her head. "All of those things are nice, yes. I care about them, I enjoy them, I'll even miss them while we're gone. But there has always been one thing, *one*, that I've been able to count on for my entire life, and since I'm in the car with her right now, I don't care what else is going on."

Ayane smiled, leaning over to lay her head on her sister's shoulder. "So you aren't upset that you've ended up here?"

Katsumi looked out the window as rain began to fall upon it, taking in the road they were heading down. She then looked back at her sister, who was taking her hand. Katsumi squeezed it, giving a genuine smile. "This is the only place I want to be."

END OF FILE 1

###

About the Author:

Jake Taylor lives in Austin, Texas. A passionate collector of all things Final Fantasy, Marvel Comics and Star Wars, he writes both Fantasy Fiction and Science Fiction. His characters are his roommates (they unfortunately refuse to chip in for rent) and his writing is his life.

Discover other Titles by Jake Taylor
in the
Silence In Numbers Series
and
his Fantasy Fiction series, Victis Honor

Connect with Jake online:
twitter: http://twitter.com/@The7thShadow
Blog: http://www.theseventhshadow.com

www.ingramcontent.com/pod-product-compliance
Lightning Source LLC
Chambersburg PA
CBHW061303170626
46817CB00001B/34